The Woman *he* Loves

Also by Suzanne Higgins

The Power of a Woman

The
Woman
he Loves

Suzanne
HIGGINS

POOLBEG

This novel is entirely a work of fiction. The names, characters and incidents portrayed in it are the work of the author's imagination. Any resemblance to actual persons, living or dead, events or localities is entirely coincidental.

Published 2004
Poolbeg Press Ltd.
123 Grange Hill, Baldoyle,
Dublin 13, Ireland
Email: poolbeg@poolbeg.com

1 3 5 7 9 10 8 6 4 2

A catalogue record for this book is available from the British Library.

ISBN 1-84223-107-3

Typeset by Patricia Hope in Palatino 9.6/13
Printed by
Litografia Rosés S.A., Spain

www.poolbeg.com

About the Author

Suzanne Higgins was a DJ on 2FM, where she presented the highly acclaimed Great Giveaway Show. (Back then she was known as Suzanne Duffy!) She also presented several television programmes before "retiring" after the birth of her second child. She subsequently started to write.

Her debut novel, *The Power of a Woman*, was a national bestseller. *The Woman he Loves* is the sequel.

Suzanne is married and lives in south County Dublin with her husband and her three daughters. She is currently working on her third novel.

Acknowledgements

I did this once before so you'd think that writing the acknowledgements would be relatively easy second time around. Well, it actually gets more difficult! Back then I was deliciously ignorant of what went into the launching of a new novel and writer. Thus, I have to start by thanking the people who helped me to launch *The Power of a Woman* and doubtless will be as hardworking with *The Woman He Loves*.

Thanks to the Book People! They are all the incredibly nice folk I met the length and breadth of Ireland who actually sell the books. It was an absolute pleasure and I genuinely appreciate your support and encouragement. During the bookshop visits, I usually lunched and had tea (or even the occasional bottle of wine!) with local journalists and that was extremely pleasant too.

I was also delighted at how many people who read *The Power of a Woman* took the time to e-mail me. Many thanks for making the effort. I will reply eventually! Now, I want to thank *you* for buying *The Woman He Loves* – my second book. I hope you enjoy reading it as much as I enjoyed writing it. Please do e-mail me with your comments at www.suzannehiggins.com

I want to sincerely thank my three angels for giving me the space and time-out to write this story and of course I must thank my best friend and husband, Michael. I'm very lucky in that I have two families – the Duffys and the Higginses. Both are a terrific support and a great source of encouragement, which I will try not to take for granted. Thanks to: Helen, Fred, Peter, Dalila, Julia, Michael (jnr), Michael (Snr), Sinead and Sorley. Thanks also to Chris, Hunter, Kevin, Gillian and Brian – from the bottom of my heart. Nothing is as important as family.

Thanks to Poolbeg for continuing to mind me and help me along my merry way and special thanks to Paula Campbell for all the 'business lunches' and for making the writer/publisher thing such a pleasant experience! There's a terrific crew at Poolbeg and I love when we get the chance to meet up. You all make me feel so special! Thank you, Sarah (excellent shopping companion!), Bronagh, Conor, Georgina, Phil and Kieran and all the gang at head office. Thanks to Anne O Sullivan for terrific support and advice. In the Cork branch, thanks to Gaye Shortland who affords me no end of patience! Gaye, you're a fascinating person and a wonderful editor.

Big thanks to the best agent on the planet – Jonathan Lloyd at Curtis Brown for always making me feel more important than I really am! Thanks also to Lucy McNicholas who has just joined the Curtis Brown team.

Closer to home, thanks to Juliana, Pat, Esther and

Lydia for keeping my house running smoothly and to Ian O Grady, my GP who never laughed at me when I asked the most outlandish questions.

Likewise, thanks to Jenny, Jo, Sarah, Kathleen and Dr Paula Heaphy for their unending encouragement and support. Thanks to Berna, Judi and Helen and I also have to thank the Wednesday Club, Debbie, Suzanne and Ashling – the best club I've ever been a member of.

You're all brill!

For Mum & Dad
Thank you.

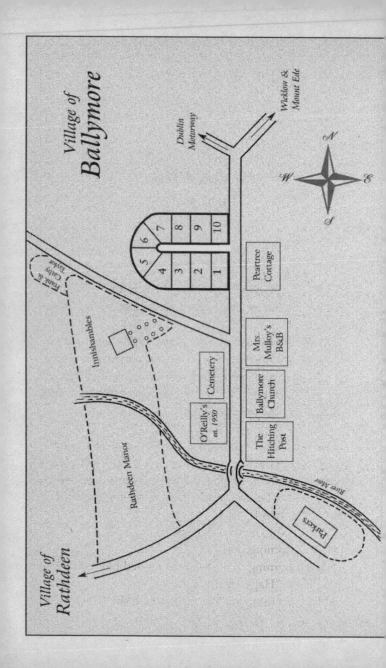

CHAPTER 1

"I think I'm going to die," Kelly whispered.

There was no response. She realised that she was alone in her misery.

"Why didn't somebody stop me?" she whined. Tentatively she opened her eyes. It was remarkably bright. The curtains were open. Had somebody already tried to wake her? Hardly likely, she thought. She probably forgot to close them the previous night.

"God, I was pissed! What a night!"

Her head began to throb even harder as she became accustomed to the brightness of the room. The sun wasn't streaming in as it usually did in the mornings, which meant it had to be after lunch. Food, however, was the last thing on her mind.

She turned to her bed partner.

"Good morning, Ted."

"Good morning, Kelly," she pretended her teddy was talking back. "Happy birthday!"

Kelly tried to stand. "Big mistake! Oh shit!" She made

a dash out of her room, down the hall and into the bathroom.

"Happy birthday!" Lauren called after her as she ran past. Lauren followed her sister into the bathroom. "Good morning, Sis! How are you this morning or need I ask?"

"Leave me alone," came a curt reply from the toilet basin.

"What? Too many Red Bulls? I did try to tell you but you weren't interested."

"I don't remember."

"No? You decided that because you were twenty-one years old, you should be able to handle twenty-one Red Bulls and vodka. I suppose we should be glad it wasn't your thirty-first!"

"You're kidding!" Kelly stopped retching for a moment.

"No, but don't worry. Good old Barney began to give you vodka-less Red Bulls. You didn't even notice the difference."

"Barney, oh shit!"

"Yeah. That was a particularly spectacular fight, Kelly, or should I say a particularly spectacular *barney*? Anyway, I think you owe him a big apology. He was only trying to mind you and you let him have it."

Kelly began to whimper.

Tiffany popped her head around the bathroom door. "I thought I heard voices. Good morning! Happy birthday, Kelly!

"What's good about it?" Kelly moaned as she sat with her head resting against the rim of the loo basin. The white porcelain cooled her hot pink cheeks. "I think I'm going to barf again."

"Good girl, get it all up," Lauren said, without much sympathy in her voice.

"Strictly speaking, it's not the morning at all. It's actually mid-afternoon," Tiffany continued, being her usual precise self. But seeing her eldest sister in such a wretched state, she changed tack. "Can I get you anything?"

"Another Red Bull?" Lauren offered with a chuckle.

"A little privacy!" Kelly yelled at her two sisters. "Just leave me alone!"

As the girls walked out and left their eldest sister in the bathroom, Kelly bade goodbye to the remains of what had been in her stomach. She collapsed onto the floor, relieved that it was over. Amazingly, she felt marginally better. It was then she realised that she was in fact, naked except for a tiny pair of white silk knickers. At first, Kelly didn't recognise them but then she remembered. Tiffany had given her a birthday present of knickers and an adorable matching camisole. She had no idea where *that* was now. Had she worn it to the party last night? She couldn't remember. If she did, it was to impress Barney.

"Oh God," she sighed as she thought about her boyfriend of three years. Barney Armstrong was her boss and her boyfriend, a dangerous combination. He ran Rathdeen Refuge where she worked. On the job, they got on terrifically well. They both loved animals and did their damnedest to find homes for all of the ones that came through the refuge. They were both heartbroken when animals had to be put to sleep. Recently, however, they seemed to be squabbling over the slightest thing. Last night was a biggy. Kelly thought back to the party. It was when she was with her old school buddies that things seemed to go badly with Barney. That entire gang were in

3

their early twenties and so were their boyfriends. They were all wild and partied hard. Barney, however, was thirty-six.

"*Thirty-six*! I mean, shit," Kelly argued aloud, "he could almost be my dad!" It didn't seem to bother her much when they were alone. It was only when she met up with her younger friends that she felt it. Reluctantly she dragged her mind back to their fight. She had been a real bitch. Doubtless it was the booze but deep down Kelly knew that that was no excuse.

"Ah, Barney, would you bloody well relax. What's the problem? It's only a joint," she had complained.

"Yeah, but I remember what happened the last time you had a joint, Kelly. You were as sick as a dog."

"Are you calling your girlfriend a dog, Barney?" she had asked through a lopsided vodka-soaked grin.

"OK, Kelly," he sighed patiently, "give me the joint. Who gave it to you anyway?"

"Francesca! She smokes them all the time and she has a ball."

"Francesca is a bad influence on you, Kelly Dalton. Give me the joint."

Francesca appeared beside Kelly in a flash. "Excuse me, Barney, I am *not* a bad influence on Kelly. You, on the other hand, are stealing her youth. You're no fun. Come on, Kelly!" Francesca grabbed her old schoolfriend's hand and began to drag her away to smoke the joint in peace.

"Yeah, leave me alone, you, you – geriatric!" Kelly stammered as she tried to find a suitable insult. Then she burst out laughing as her first drag on the joint took effect.

Remembering the event now, however, Kelly saw all too vividly the look of hurt in Barney's face. What was going on between them? Was this what happened when two people began to drift apart? Oh Jesus, is this what had happened between her mum and dad? Kelly's stomach began to churn once more.

Here we go again, she thought.

"Kelly's in a bad way," Tiffany commented to Lauren as they were clearing up the remainder of the previous night's mess.

"She asked for it," Lauren replied unsympathetically.

"Asked for what?" little Robin piped up.

"Never you mind!" Lauren scooped up her baby sister in her arms. Robin had become the little walking, talking toy doll of the Dalton household. With three elder sisters, she was spoiled rotten and loved to bits.

"Do you think she and Barney are breaking up?" Tiffany asked, her brow furrowed with worry.

"God knows," Lauren replied. "It's not our problem though, is it? You know, you worry too much. Leave them alone to sort it out."

"I know, I know. It's just that – he's like part of the family. I'd hate to see him get hurt."

"Oh yeah? Are you beginning to hold a torch for Barney, Tiffany? Not again?"

"No, not at all!" she protested vehemently. "Come on, you have to agree with me. He is like part of this family."

Lauren sighed. "Yeah, I guess you're right. But hey, you and Nicolas were once inseparable and me and Connor Cantwell and look what happened to those relationships! Love's cruel ways!"

"Now, they were totally different. Nick Junior was just plain weird. Gorgeous, yeah – but weird! Connor, on the other hand? You two should never have broken up. That was daft. In fact, you would still be together if you weren't both so thick."

"I'm not thick!"

"You know what I mean – stubborn."

"Oh, yeah, that's OK."

The girls looked at each other and laughed. Robin joined in, not knowing exactly why.

"Well, I couldn't exactly keep phoning him. I mean girls don't do that, do they?" Lauren tried to reason. "That's up to the guy."

"Yes, usually, but Connor specifically said that if you wanted to get back with him after his summer in the States, you were to phone him. I think he was just very insecure around you."

"Little old me?" Lauren put on her Southern Belle accent.

"Little old you!" Tiffany copied her. "So it's your fault you and he didn't get back together."

"You're forgetting. I did phone him that once and his brother said that he was out on a date."

Tiffany had no answer for that one. "Well, whatever the reason. There's plenty of fish in the sea!"

"That's easy for you to say, Tiffany Dalton, as you head off to one of the coolest ponds in Ireland – Trinity College! How cool is that? I'm still stuck in boring old Mount Eden!"

"The next two years will fly by. I promise, Lauren. Then you can do what you want."

"Not pure economics anyway. I'm not smart enough!"

"Yes, you are!"

"OK, well, I'm not interested enough."

"Now you're getting closer to the truth."

"To be honest, Tiffany, I've no idea what I want to do after school," Lauren sighed.

"Well, you could always go and work in Rathdeen Refuge, like your older sister."

"For the summer, yeah, but not for life. Not with Barney and Kelly at each other's throats!"

"I wonder if she's feeling any better?" said Tiffany.

Kelly was feeling a little better. She lay down on a warm patch of carpet in the bathroom. She had lived in Innishambles all her life and knew where all the hot-water pipes were, under the floorboards. There was a lovely warm section just next to the bath. When she was little and being bathed with her sisters by her mum, she always sat on that patch. It was like an old friend, it was so familiar.

"What a party," she sighed, almost contentedly.

When her mother had first suggested a birthday party for her twenty-first, Kelly balked at the idea.

"Are you nuts? Thanks but no thanks!" was her emphatic reply.

"But why not, darling? You're only twenty-one once."

"True, and I was only nineteen and twenty once. We didn't make a big deal of those."

Saskia, Kelly's mother, tried again. "Yes, pet, but this is special. You'll be twenty-one!" Then she dropped the bombshell, "And it may be your last birthday in Innishambles. I was thinking it might be time to change this big old rambling thing for something more modern."

"What?" all three girls chorused at their mother in unison.

7

"Well, now that the divorce is complete, Innishambles is mine – er, ours." She had corrected herself a little too slowly for Kelly's liking.

"Innishambles is *our* home, Mum. You can't seriously be thinking of parting with it!"

Saskia got defensive. "Do you have any idea how much it costs to run, Kelly?" Then she continued a little more confidently, "And can you imagine how much it's worth now? Girls, we could build a lovely home somewhere around here. How about one of those utterly modern ones in Ballymore Glen?" She was referring to the new development in Ballymore village, the same one they had all bitched about for the last two years. Her daughters looked at her incredulously, dumb with shock. Saskia persevered "We would still have plenty left over, maybe for somewhere in the sun!"

"In Puerto Banus, by any chance?" Kelly's tone was dripping with disgust.

"Well, it would be nice to have a place in the sun, wouldn't it?"

"Nice for you and Nicolas, you mean! You've spent every summer down there for the last three years."

Saskia blushed under her Spanish tan. "Well now, Kelly, I wouldn't call three weeks the entire summer. And we did ask you every time if you wanted to come. Tiffany, you came down with us a couple of years ago. You liked it, didn't you?"

Tiffany studied the floor, not trusting herself to speak. Fortunately nobody noticed.

"She only did it to please you! That's typical Tiffany stuff, you know that. The next year, wild horses wouldn't drag her back," Lauren answered for her sister.

"We want to stay here in Innishambles, our home," Kelly tried again.

Despite the warmth of the underfloor pipes, Kelly shivered as she remembered the conversation. She had no idea at the time that Saskia was in fact informing them of what was effectively a done deal. The estate agent had already been to the house and had put an estimate of five million euro on it and the land around it.

While they were shocked and delighted at the incredibly high price, the girls still didn't want to sell.

Each of them fought their mother bitterly in an effort to save Innishambles. The only one who didn't really care was little Robin. She was three years old and she had spent her summers in Puerto Banus with Saskia and her boyfriend, Nicolas Flattery, and so when she heard talk of possibly buying a home there she squealed with glee.

The three older girls however had enjoyed long, lazy summers in Innishambles. June and July in Ireland may not have been as warm as the south of Spain, but the summers were fun and free. All three worked in Rathdeen Refuge. Built by Nicolas Flattery when he first came to Ireland, the refuge was now very busy and always packed to capacity. There had been quite an amount of publicity done on the place when it opened. The fact that one of Hollywood's leading men was settling in Wicklow and opening a refuge for deserted dogs, cats and other animals was quite newsworthy. Kelly had worked there full-time since leaving school.

This summer was a little different, however. Tiffany had flown through her Leaving Cert and secured a place in Trinity College with ease. She was to study pure economics. Again Saskia used this as justification for selling Innishambles.

"If we sell this old place, there'll be enough money left over to buy a small apartment in Dublin for Tiffany and, who knows, maybe Lauren will be up there too in a couple of years."

The guilt of needing somewhere to live while at college quietened Tiffany's protests to some degree, but not Kelly's.

"The girls could commute. Daddy always did!"

Saskia's eyes flared in anger at the mere mention of his name. "Yes, well, we don't always do what Daddy did!"

Kelly shivered again. It was quite obvious that Saskia still hated her ex-husband, Richard Dalton. It was true, Kelly reasoned to herself, that he had been an absolute bastard to her but the girls were learning to forgive and forget. Why couldn't Saskia? If her mother and father were still together there would be no way they'd be selling their beloved Innishambles, she thought furiously. Now, however, Saskia was with Nicolas.

Everybody liked Nicolas Flattery. His laid-back personality charmed people. His tactile and loving manner worked as well on people as it did on the animals in the refuge. In starting up the refuge, he had given up acting and taken up writing. Now, however, three years on, to the best of Kelly's knowledge he had not produced anything worth printing. Perhaps that was the reason behind his slightly shorter temper and longer sulks.

Like it or not, it was now common knowledge that Innishambles was going to auction. The worst part was yet to come. The house would be on view soon, with strangers tramping through their home.

The idea made Kelly's stomach flip again.

Reflecting on her life in this hungover state was not necessarily the most prudent move, Kelly realised, as she sat up and lurched forward to the loo.

It looked like she was breaking up with her long-term boyfriend, who also happened to be her boss, which probably meant that she was going to lose her job into the bargain. The fact that she had lost her virginity to him didn't exactly improve the situation. And now she was losing her home too.

"For once in my life I can say, I really am *losing it*," she moaned.

Her stomach heaved, even though there was nothing left to bring up.

"Never again," she promised herself as she thought about the drinks she had knocked back so effortlessly the previous night. "Never again!"

CHAPTER 2

"Not again, please, God! Not again!"

Saskia Dalton was oblivious to her eldest daughter's predicament in another bathroom in the house. Not that it would have made much difference. She was so ill herself, she couldn't have moved if her life depended on it. She had been puking as badly as her daughter for what felt like most of the day, only there was one big difference. Saskia hadn't been drinking.

"I don't believe it. Nobody could be that unlucky," she cried to herself.

Saskia had enjoyed the party the previous night. It had been a late night but she had barely drunk anything. She was too nervous. It never occurred to her, when she told Kelly she could invite anybody she wanted to, that her daughter would invite her father, Richard. Even more amazing – Richard had accepted. Sas was terrified when Kelly told her that she had actually invited *Richard and friend*. Unfortunately, it was a done deal by the time

Saskia found out. It was only when she saw the letter of acceptance come into the house that she discovered what her eldest had done.

"Well, you're bringing Nicolas! Why shouldn't Dad be able to bring somebody along for moral support!"

In truth, Kelly prayed that he wouldn't but she was still furious with her mother for planning to sell Innishambles and this was her way of hurting her. Feeling every one of her forty-two years, Sas didn't relish coming face to face with one of her ex's sex kittens. To make matters worse, as it turned out Nicolas was still in the States so Saskia was going to have to face her ex and his little Barbie girlfriend on her own two feet.

But Richard had arrived with his mother Edwina! Saskia was much relieved. She could deal with that old battle-axe a lot easier than with some nubile young thing and, in fairness to Edwina, she did seem to be on her best behaviour. Mother and son maintained a low profile. They were friendly to anyone who talked to them but they did not seek out company, still less force themselves upon anyone. How Richard had changed, Saskia thought. The old Richard would have worked the room several times. He would have talked to everybody and flirted outrageously with his eldest daughter's friends. Edwina would have complained about anything and everything – but not tonight, amazingly. The most bizarre part of the night for Saskia, however, was *talking* with her ex-husband. She had been terrified of him coming. He hadn't been near Innishambles in over two years. In fact, he had only been in the house once since the night of their huge fight and bust-up. That was when he came to collect his clothes and a few personal belongings and even that he did when the girls and Saskia were out so as to cause as little trauma as possible. Twenty years gone up in smoke. Saskia and Richard agreed that there would be no fights over custody of the girls. They would obviously live with their mother in Innishambles and they could come to Richard any weekend that they wanted. He kept an open door policy. It took a few months, but surprisingly quickly the girls began to express an interest in seeing him. First Lauren, then Kelly and eventually Tiffany began to visit him on occasional weekends. Originally this upset Saskia – she thought her daughters were beginning to forgive him for his old sins – but slowly she began to accept their new separate lives. The girls would return full of happy stories of how they had spent their time with their father. Much to Saskia's relief, there was never mention of a new woman in his life – even if she had Nicolas in hers.

Robin was a different matter, however. She was too young to understand the concept of day visits to her father and Saskia did not encourage it. Richard had offered to take her once or twice recently, but in truth he wasn't good with babies. He had never changed a nappy in his life! Now that Robin was past the nappy stage, however, Saskia knew that it was just a matter of time. Robin was getting older and would want her father's love and attention soon.

Much to her relief though, all of Saskia's fears and worries about meeting Richard on the night of the party had been unfounded. She knew he was in Innishambles before she saw him. She heard her daughters calling to him over the latest Robbie Williams single.

"Daddy!" they yelled as he rang the doorbell and stood at the already open door, waiting to be admitted.

"I'm so glad you came!" Kelly threw her arms around him.

"Wild horses wouldn't keep me away!" he said, then added carefully, "Once I got the invitation . . ."

"Hi, Edwina," Lauren welcomed her grandmother just as Saskia arrived at the front door.

"Hello, Richard." Saskia attempted to smile but couldn't quite get it pasted on properly.

The girls disappeared into the drawing-room with their grandmother, leaving Richard and Saskia together. The house was beginning to get very full and so the hall was busy with other partygoers.

"We're putting the coats in here, if you like," Saskia continued a little shyly.

"In the study. Good idea. I have a little gift for Kelly too, nothing too extravagant, it's just . . ." he trailed off as they moved into the study. He turned to face her. "It's good to see you, Saskia. How are you?"

"I'm fine. You?" Saskia's voice sounded artificially high to herself. Damn, she thought, calm down, Sas – you're the one on home turf!

"OK. Working hard, nothing illegal, don't worry. Everything is above board!"

Saskia winced. "Look Richard, it's really none of my business."

"Oh God, Sas. I'm sorry. I didn't mean to make you uncomfortable. Look, thanks a million for letting me come to Kelly's twenty-first. It really is very kind of you. The house looks terrific."

"Nothing has changed."

"Isn't that what's so nice about Innishambles!"

Saskia wanted to get off the subject of the house.

Obviously the girls hadn't told him about the proposed house sale and she damn well wasn't going to.

Richard sensed her unease. He tried to move onto easier territory. "Where's Nicolas?" he asked casually as he took off his coat and handed it to her.

"Eh, he had to go to the States. He has to meet with his agent."

"How's the writing going?"

"Fine," Saskia lied. The truth was she had grave doubts about Nicolas's writing ability. "There should be a book deal very soon now."

"That's great. Well." He had run out of conversation and so had she. They looked at each other. Saskia couldn't believe it. For somebody she hadn't seen in two and a half years, she knew his face so well, every line, and every curve.

His strong jawline wasn't quite as defined as it had been but he still looked terrific. His hair wasn't as brown as it once was – it was a little more salt-and-peppery but funnily it seemed to suit him better and as always he had it well cut. His skin was still sallow. She knew his face like she knew the back of her own hand. It was his eyes that struck her most, however. They hadn't aged at all. They were still as dark as coal. Richard had friendly sparkling eyes, always looking for devilment. It was one of the things that had attracted her to him in the first place. Kelly, Lauren and now Robin had inherited his come-to-bed eyes! She smirked at the memory of when the girls were little and he used to give them piggyback rides to bed. *"Come to bed!"* he would chant in his Paddington Bear accent, making Saskia laugh because invariably he would try the same line on her later in the evening.

"Why are you smiling?" Richard asked Saskia.

She snapped out of the memory. "Oh, I was just –" She thought about lying to him and then thought better of it. "I was just remembering when we were younger and the children were babies."

"They were the best years of my life, Saskia."

She looked at him and saw the sincerity in his eyes and for a second she wondered if she had done the right thing in breaking up the family.

"Daddy, there you are!" Lauren came bounding into the study. "Gran needs you. She's all alone and not complaining. Something's definitely wrong with her!"

The tranquil intimacy of the study was smashed.

Richard laughed and called to Lauren as she rushed out again, "Tell Gran I'm on my way!" He turned to Saskia. "You look terrific," he smiled. "Your new life obviously suits you. I'm happy for you."

Saskia was left in the study, feeling surprisingly alone.

"Mum!" Lauren barged back into the study.

"Yes, pet."

"Is it OK if I introduce Robin to Dad?"

"Ohmigod no!" Saskia felt the panic rise in her stomach again. So far, Robin had shown little interest in knowing who her natural father was. Nicolas Flattery was the man in her life, the one who took her out for long walks, let her give sugar-cubes to the horses and read stories to her. Now Richard was suddenly back in her little daughter's life, in the same room as her!

Saskia looked at Lauren. "Introduce your dad as Richard. No more than that tonight."

"She has to know sooner or later –" Lauren objected but Saskia cut her off.

"Then let it be later! Not tonight. It's a crazy night and far too hectic to tell her the truth."

Lauren didn't look convinced.

Saskia's tone became more serious. "Lauren, do as I ask. Just introduce him as Richard. I'll talk to him about taking it to the next stage. That is, if he even wants to."

"Of course he will!" Lauren laughed. "He'll love her once he gets to know her!" She bounded back out of the study.

Saskia was left alone again. She looked around the room and saw Richard's old desk. It was hers now. Everything was hers now. She could sell it if she wanted to. Then her eyes fell on Richard's old leather reading chair. The antique lamp still stood over it, drenching the seat in a pyramid of light. She smiled. He always said it was the best seat in the world for a good read. Saskia thought that maybe she should give him back his precious armchair and lamp. It would be a nice thing to do. As she held Richard's coat in her hands she could smell his aftershave. It was still so familiar after all this time. Impulsively she hugged the coat tightly to her body but then she suddenly realised what she was doing.

"Cop on, girl," she snapped at herself and threw the coat onto the sofa.

She squared her shoulders and held her head high. Then she went back to the party revellers.

Sue Parker was by her side quickly.

"I didn't realise that your ex was coming!" she whispered urgently. Sas realised with horror that she should have warned her old friend that she would be coming face to face with her old enemy. Sas covered her mouth with her hand. "Ohmigod, Sue! I never even thought of it. I'm so sorry. Are you OK? Is Dave OK? He's not going to start a fight with Richard or anything, is he?"

The normally glamorous and sophisticated Sue Parker snorted with laughter. "God, no. Dave was a little –" she searched for the right word, "surprised to see Richard here but he says that if he is ballsy enough to be here then so are we."

Saskia looked at her neighbour in wonder. Richard had been positively brutal to her and Dave – he had taken advantage of an intoxicated Sue at a party and Sue's ensuing sense of guilt had almost destroyed her marriage. When Dave eventually discovered what had happened, he helped Saskia destroy Richard's business empire – his way of exacting revenge. Now, for the first time since then, all of them were in the same room. Well, they would hardly become best buddies but maybe life was moving on, Saskia thought philosophically.

When she entered the living-room, she saw Richard playing with Robin and Lauren. Edwina was sitting alone. She had aged considerably over the last three years. Saskia made the supreme effort of crossing the room to say hello.

Much to her amazement, Edwina was almost gracious. "This is a nice party, Saskia."

Coming from Edwina Dalton, this was praise indeed.

It amused Saskia enormously to see her ex-mother-in-law having to be so polite. It was quite obvious that Richard had given her strict instructions to 'be nice'. In the old days Edwina would not have bothered; perhaps she now realised that if she wanted to see her grandchildren, she was bloody well going to have to be more polite!

"I'm glad you're enjoying yourself," Saskia answered brightly.

The two women hadn't spoken since she and Richard split up. Back then the old wagon wouldn't give you the time of day unless there was something in it for her.

"This must be Robin. Hello, child." Edwina looked down at the little girl who had just run up to Saskia and begun to hang out of her mother's leg proprietorially.

"Hello." The little girl smiled shyly at her grandmother. Saskia saw Edwina's face pale with shock.

"Oh heavens, Robin –" Edwina stopped herself but Saskia already understood.

For once she actually felt sorry for Edwina. "Yes, it's a little eerie, the resemblance, isn't it?"

Both women admired Robin's open innocent face.

"She has her father's eyes, skin, hair and temperament," Saskia added honestly.

Edwina's colour returned. "I've never seen such a strong likeness between a father and a daughter."

"Who are you?" the little girl asked the old woman.

Now it was Saskia's turn to feel uncomfortable. She suddenly felt guilty for keeping Robin away from her grandmother as well as from Richard.

"Robin, pet, this is –" Saskia stalled, uncertain what to say. She didn't know how to introduce her ex-husband's mother but Edwina spoke up.

"I'm Edwina, Richard's Mummy, just like Saskia is your Mummy."

Saskia smiled gratefully at Edwina. Robin studied the older woman for a moment, but instantly lost interest when she saw the Parker children. They were near her age and much more interesting. She bolted off to play with them.

Edwina looked squarely at Saskia. "You're raising the girls well," she said.

Saskia was astounded. Her mother-in-law had never approved of the way she was raising her daughters. She had always maintained that Saskia was too soft on the girls. To hear a compliment on her parenting skills was just too much of a shock to Saskia.

"Thank you," was all she could muster. "Enjoy the party."

"Keep up the good work," Edwina muttered. It was quite obvious that she was uncomfortable praising her ex-daughter-in-law.

Why, then, was she doing it, Saskia wondered? "Yes, well, enjoy."

Saskia sat on the chair in her en suite this morning thinking it all over. It had really been a roaring success. Doubtless the house was in a terrible state downstairs, but the girls were very good about helping tidy these days and, with any luck, they would muck in today – if they had even managed to climb out of bed yet. She looked at her watch.

"Three-thirty! My God, where's Robin?" She grabbed her dressing-gown and ran downstairs.

Her youngest was the first to see Saskia sweep into the kitchen.

"Mummy," she squealed with delight.

Saskia lifted Robin into her arms and gave her a big cuddle.

21

"Good morning, Mum," Lauren smiled at her mother.

"Good afternoon, Mummy," Tiffany laughed, tapping her watch. "We thought you were going to sleep all day!"

"Hi, girls, I can't believe it's this late. Thank you so much for minding this little munchkin. It must have been very very late when we hit the hay last night."

"I last saw you around four am," Lauren told her mother.

"My God, look at this place! It's spotless. You've cleaned the lot, you angels," Saskia gushed.

"Well, you seemed to be tired and so we thought we'd muck in," said Tiffany.

"Yeah, but we did it all ourselves, Mum," Lauren was quick to point out despite a glare from her other sister. "Kelly didn't do a tap!"

"Where is Kelly?"

"She's barfing merrily upstairs!"

"Oh heavens, what's wrong with her?"

"Oh, don't worry," Tiffany smiled. "It's just alcohol poisoning!"

"Charming! I'd better go and check on her." Slowly Saskia ventured back upstairs, leaving Robin with her sisters. This was all she needed. As she walked up the stairs, however, she marvelled at how clean the hall and landing were. Lauren and Tiffany really had blitzed the entire house. How could have she have slept through it?

She knocked on the bathroom door.

"Are you all right, Kelly? How's my birthday girl?" She slipped her head around the door.

"Oh Mum, I'm not well!"

"Hardly surprising, pet. You wouldn't stop drinking

22

those bloody Red Bulls and vodka all night. I don't know how you kept going."

"It's more than that. I've drunk before. I think I had some bad food or something. I really feel bad."

"Come on, I'll tuck you back into bed. What a way to spend your twenty-first birthday! Dare I ask if you'd like anything to eat? Some cereal perhaps?"

"No," Kelly groaned as she climbed weakly back into bed. "I couldn't look at food."

"I know the feeling," Saskia mumbled under her breath.

"Are you sick too?" Kelly asked.

"Oh, just a little tummy upset. That's all. Now, how about putting on a nightie first of all, so you don't catch your death of cold? Then you can go back to sleep. You'll feel better later, I promise."

Saskia went to the chest of drawers to fish out an old nightdress and she helped Kelly into it.

"Thanks, Mum. You're brill."

"So are you! Sweet dreams." Saskia closed the curtains and left her eldest daughter in the quiet darkness.

She had been putting it off for long enough. She didn't really need a pregnancy test to confirm what she already knew but she had to do something to put herself out of her misery. Slowly she headed back to her own bedroom and en suite.

She had bought a pregnancy-test packet in Dublin the week before. Not exactly the thing you buy in O'Reilly's in Ballymore, she had laughed to herself. She had accidentally bought a double packet, such was her haste when making the purchase, terrified of being spotted by somebody she knew. The embarrassment of being pregnant again at forty-two really was too much. It was the same embarrassment that prevented her from actually using the pregnancy-test kit once she had bought it. To think she was pregnant was bad enough but to really know it was another matter altogether! Of course, maybe it was just her imagination, a phantom pregnancy. Then again, she was no fool, and God knows she had been through it enough times before to know the signs!

She opened the box and looked at the two sealed test-sticks. Which one will I use, she wondered. One will tell me if I'm pregnant and the other – hopefully – will never be used.

"Oh, just get on with it," she scolded herself.

Wilma, her little Yorkshire terrier, arrived just in time.

"Hi, Wilma. I'm widdling on a home pregnancy-test kit. Not something you see me doing every day."

Wilma didn't seem too perturbed.

"Now we wait," Saskia explained as she threw the unused test stick into her bathroom drawer.

"Three minutes. That seems like a very long time." She started to busy herself with tidying her bedroom and making her bed, which only involved smoothing out the light fluffy quilt. Then she pulled on a jumper and jeans and still it was not three minutes.

"Now what will we do, Wilma? Isn't it funny? Normally three minutes would fly by but because I'm watching the clock, it's taking an eternity!"

"Mummy, where are you?" came a familiar little cry.

"Robin, I'm in my room. I'll be down soon, pet," Saskia replied. But it was too late.

"Hello!" her youngest daughter announced as she landed in her mother's bedroom, delighted with herself for finding her mummy.

"What are you doing?"

"Just tidying," Saskia replied lightly as she put the pregnancy tester that she was using into her bedside locker, away from prying eyes.

"Please come and play with me," said Robin in her little-girl voice. "We'll take Dudley and Dexter for a walk. We can go to the river!"

Saskia was terrified of Robin's obsession with the river More. It ran along the boundary line of the Innishambles and Rathdeen Manor land. "You can only go down with an adult. You know that, don't you?"

"*Pleeeese!*" Robin responded indignantly.

"OK pet, let's go." She glanced at her bedside locker. "I suppose I can check on the result later. The outcome will hardly change!"

In truth, she was terrified of what the result might be and now dreaded seeing it for fear it was positive.

She shook the thought of another baby away as she re-entered the kitchen. There was no point in worrying about something that might not even be a reality, she reminded herself.

She forced herself to make a cheerful face as she looked at her elder daughters.

"Robin and I are going out for a walk – would either of you like to come with us?"

"You must be joking. We've had our exercise for the day," Lauren scoffed.

"Thanks, but no thanks, we're whacked," Tiffany added. "You guys have a nice walk. Do you want me to prepare anything for dinner while you're out?"

"Gosh, Tiff. You think of everything. I'm afraid we're not going to have much of a family celebration with Kelly for her twenty-first today. I doubt she'll surface at all. To be honest, I'm not too hungry either. Robin and you two, however, now that's a different matter, isn't it? How about pizzas from that new pizza place in Wicklow?"

The girls all cheered together. That was a definite winner. "I'll go and get them after my walk with Robin. OK?"

"Mum! Hello! I am eighteen. I'll go and get the pizzas. You go for your walk," Tiffany sniffed.

"OK, I keep forgetting that you're so grown up. My purse is in my handbag, which is in the kitchen, I think. Thank you, pet."

The weather was definitely getting worse. The clouds had thickened and the temperature had dropped considerably.

"The weather forecast said that it's going to deteriorate. They called it 'severe weather conditions'," Tiffany told her mother. "So wrap up warm."

Saskia made a feeble attempt at convincing Robin that maybe they should postpone their walk, but the child would not hear of it.

"You pwomised," she whined.

"Yes, yes, I did," Saskia conceded. "OK, let's get it over with! Dudley, Dexter, Woody, Wilma, do you want to come for a walk?" None of the dogs came to her call.

"It's called sixth sense, Mum. The dogs know there's a storm coming. They won't go out with you today."

"It's called common sense," Saskia grumbled. "Tiffany, I can't believe I'm saying this in August, but do you think you could light the fire while I'm out? We'll have our pizzas in front of it later. Thanks."

Within five minutes, wrapped up for winter as

opposed to summer, mother and daughter headed out into the forbidding weather.

"*Gone With the Wind* starts in a few minutes," said Lauren. "It's a brilliant movie – will we watch that?"

"As long as it's just Scarlett O'Hara who's gone with the wind. I hope Mum and Robin are going to be OK in that weather," Tiffany fretted. "It's just started to rain. Are they nuts going out in that?"

"Jesus, Tiff, you worry too much," Lauren scolded her sister. "Look, you get the fire going and I'll get some popcorn."

Presently she returned with a huge bowl of popcorn, which she placed on the table between the two large armchairs. Both girls snuggled down deeper into the chairs and began munching happily in front of a fresh crackling fire.

Kelly wasn't nearly as content. She lay in bed, feeling like death warmed up. Dudley and Dexter, Richard's dogs, had seen fit to keep her company.

"Hello, boys. Welcome." She patted her quilt, indicating to the dogs that they could jump up and sleep on the bed. "Did you see Dad last night?" Dudley's tail flapped on the bed at the mention of his old master's name. The two Labradors had been utterly lost after Richard moved out of the house. It was absolutely impossible for them to go with him to live in Dublin. They were far too big and so it was agreed that they would stay in Innishambles.

She played with the dogs, "Daddy," she said and the dogs began to get very excited. "Oh no, dogs! I'm too sick for this – sorry."

She lay there, feeling slightly comforted by their presence. Then it hit her.

"Forget *Daddy*, what about *Mummy*! Could it be?"

She suddenly sat bolt upright in the bed, forgetting about her aches and pains in an instant. She began to do some calculations in her head.

"No way," she whined. "Surely not!" The more she thought about it, the more it made sense. She and Barney had been using condoms when they were having sex but they had been getting a little careless and a couple of weeks ago the condom slipped right off and she got covered in *goo* – ugh, she winced at the memory.

"It would explain why I feel so awful and why my period is late," Kelly told Dudley. "Oh shit, this is not good."

"How are you feeling? What's not good?" Tiffany asked. Despite her best attempts, Tiff couldn't settle in front of the television so she had decided to check on her sister again.

Kelly burst out crying. "Oh, Tiffany, I wonder could I be pregnant?"

"What?"

"You heard me."

"Eh yes, I did. Eh, eh, can I get Lauren? This is a family crisis."

"Where's Mum? I don't want her to know."

"You're OK. She's gone out with Robin."

"In that weather!"

"Can I get Lauren? Please, she's brill in these situations!"

"Have you ever been in this situation before?" snapped Kelly. Then she softened. "Yeah, you can get her."

Lauren came running up after Tiffany had broken the news to her.

"Holy shit, Kellser! You can't be serious! Tell me you're joking."

"Would I joke about something like this?" Kelly snapped. "Look, I could be wrong, but my period is late and my tummy is bloated."

"Ah Kelly, your periods are all over the place anyway and you think your tummy is bloated after a glass of water!" Lauren answered. The three Dalton girls had slim figures, but Kelly was easily the skinniest.

"OK, well, I feel sick as a dog and," Kelly knew she was going to have to be honest with her sisters, "and – er – Barney and I have had a few – well, the condom slipped."

"Oh shit," Lauren softened. "Why didn't you just go on the pill?"

"I was thinking about it, but we haven't been getting on too well lately. Jesus, I was even thinking about breaking up!"

"Well, forget that for a start! OK, we have to find out once and for all if you're pregnant or not."

"Look what I've got." Tiffany re-appeared, looking triumphant, brandishing a pregnancy-test stick.

"Where the hell did you get that?" Lauren and Kelly asked in unison.

"Mum's room! She has all sorts of interesting things in her bathroom drawers."

"You were snooping through Mum's things?"

Tiffany looked suitably guilty.

"Do you go through my stuff when I'm not here?" asked Lauren accusingly.

"Hello, ladies! Crisis!" Kelly looked at both her sisters and pointed to herself as the crisis.

"Oh, well, try this, Kelly," said Tiffany, "and let's see if you're pregnant or not."

"Yeah, then we'll know if you're up the duff or off your rocker!" Lauren was trying to lighten the mood.

"Do you think Mum will notice that the tester is gone?" Kelly asked.

Tiffany winced but Lauren laughed. "Well, she's hardly going to come down to the kitchen and yell at us, 'Which one of you stole my pregnancy test kit!'"

Tiffany was the voice of reason. "Kelly, I'm sure it's been there for ages. Probably since she had Robin. You know she's always saying that her childbearing days are over. She'll never notice, don't worry."

"OK," Kelly hesitated, looking at the little packet. "I just pee on the stick, right?"

"Right," the other two sisters chorused. They all read *Cosmo*.

Reluctantly Kelly dragged herself out of bed. Dudley and Dexter sighed, disgruntled at having to move. They rolled over to let her out.

"Go on," Lauren encouraged her.

Kelly went back into the bathroom she had spent so much of that day puking in, and peed on the stick. When she came back out her two sisters were standing, waiting, holding their breath in anticipation.

"We have to wait a few minutes for a result," she explained.

"Ah, hell!" Lauren was fit to burst.

"Hi, girls, we're home! What appalling weather! We had to shorten our walk considerably – it really is awful

out there!" The familiar sound of their mother called to them from downstairs. "Where is everybody?"

They heard Robin come running up the stairs as fast as her little legs could carry her.

"Oh shit, Kelly, lose that thing," Lauren pointed at the pregnancy-stick in her older sister's hand. "Tiffany, you and me – *Gone With The Wind* now!"

"Hi, Mum!" Lauren called in as even a tone as she could muster. She went bounding down the stairs, two at a time, with Tiffany on her heels. "Come on in to the fire – we'll warm you up quickly."

Robin, however, followed Kelly into the bathroom in time to see her hastily throw the pregnancy-test stick into the bin.

"Come with me, pet!" Kelly took her little sister by the hand and brought her out of the bathroom. "I'm going to bed. Would you like to get into bed with me? I'll read you a story!" Robin watched her eldest sister climb back into bed with Dudley and Dexter.

"The bin is dirty," she told Kelly.

"Oh, yes, pet. The bin is very dirty. We don't go near that, sure we don't?"

"No," Robin agreed. She appeared to lose interest in the conversation. "Where's Mummy?" she asked.

"She's downstairs – do you want to go down to her?"

Robin didn't answer but ran out of Kelly's room calling for Saskia.

From the warmth of the drawing-room where a large welcoming fire was now roaring, Saskia heard her youngest daughter calling.

"I'd better see to her first," she sighed. "Her clothes might be a little damp."

31

She met Robin in the hall, at the foot of the stairs.

"This is for Kelly?" Robin exclaimed, brandishing the pregnancy-test stick.

"Oh no, Robin. That's mine!" Quickly she grabbed the stick and checked it. She sent up a silent prayer when she saw the negative result. *Thank you, God! Thank you!*

Robin began to cry. "Kelly! That's Kelly's!"

"No, pet. That is not Kelly's. That was Mummy's. Were you snooping in my bedside locker? You shouldn't have gone into my bedroom without me. Bold girl!" Saskia checked Robin's clothing as the child cried in frustration. "Well, you are actually dry enough. Why don't you go and play with your doll's house while I see how we're doing on the pizza front."

Saskia put the negative pregnancy-test stick in the kitchen bin, taking great care to push it down to the very bottom so it wouldn't be found by little hands, and then she went off to talk to Tiffany.

"I thought you were going to Wicklow for the pizzas, Tiff," Saskia teased her daughter.

Tiffany was sitting in her big armchair, in front of the fire, pretending to be engrossed in the film, while her mind churned over the idea of becoming an auntie. "Oh Mum, I'm sorry. I just got into this movie and the time just flew by."

"*Fiddle-de-dee!*" Saskia smiled as she watched Scarlett O'Hara pout in an outrageous hat. She was still on a high after the discovery that she was not pregnant. "I'll go. Keep an eye on Robin, will you? She should be fine. She's just wandered upstairs to play in her room but I'm much faster on my own."

"Sure, Mum." Tiffany watched her mother head out of the drawing-room. Both girls listened as the front door opened and then closed.

Lauren was the first to move. "OK, the coast is clear, back upstairs!" She was already halfway up the stairs. "Mum's gone," she said as she arrived back into Kelly's bedroom. "The few minutes are definitely up now. Where's the test?"

Kelly was out of bed in a shot and into the bathroom. In a flash she was back at the door.

"It's gone. The bloody thing is gone. I put it in the bin to hide it and it's gone!"

Tiffany had arrived. She was holding Robin in her arms.

"It can't just *go*, Kelly!" Lauren snapped.

They all went into the bathroom to stare at the empty bin.

"I put it in here and now it's gone," Kelly repeated tearfully.

"Mummy's stick," Robin piped up.

The three girls looked at their baby sister.

"What did you just say?" Lauren asked.

"Don't scare her," Tiffany interrupted.

"Did you take the stick that was in the bin, Robin?" Tiffany asked her little sister in an artificially good-humoured voice.

Robin nodded with a satisfied grin, happy to hear Tiffany's playful tone.

"And where is it now, honey?" Tiffany continued.

"Mummy," Robin answered conclusively.

"Does Mummy have it?" Kelly asked, trying to maintain the same happy voice.

Robin looked uncertain.

Lauren interrupted. "She couldn't have given it to Mum. She just went out for pizzas, for God's sake. Don't you think she would have said something if she found a used pregnancy-test stick in Robin's hand?"

Kelly and Tiffany had to agree.

"Where's the stick now?" Tiffany persevered, putting Robin down as if to encourage her to go and fetch it.

Robin looked around her and then ran into her mother's bedroom. The other three followed quick on her heels. Robin ran to Saskia's bedside locker and pulled it open.

"Here!" She handed the pregnancy-test stick to her older sister triumphantly.

Tiffany looked at the two little windows. Both had a pink line running through them. She looked at Kelly.

"It's positive, Kelly. You're pregnant."

"Ohmigod!" Kelly collapsed onto her mother's bed, clutching her stomach.

"Oh shit," said Lauren. "Look, don't panic just yet. At least we got to it before Mum did. We have time to think now. Let's get out of her room and have a think about this, and can we please dump that stick thingy somewhere she won't find it."

"What's there to think about? My life is over," Kelly wailed.

"Come on, let's get you back to bed." Tiffany took her older sister's hand. "Don't worry, it will work out OK in the end. We'll all stick together."

Kelly looked at Tiffany and burst out crying.

Lauren, Tiffany and even Robin helped putting Kelly

back to bed. Dudley and Dexter sensed that something was wrong and snuggled down on either side of her protectively.

"I guess it's just as well you didn't break up with Barney last night," sighed Lauren.

CHAPTER 3

Barney was in a thunderous mood the day after Kelly's party. Firstly his so-called girlfriend had been an absolute bitch to him. Secondly, thanks to online banking, on Sunday morning, he discovered that his paycheque from the Rathdeen Refuge had bounced and thirdly, and most importantly, huge *For Sale* signs had been erected on either side of the automatic gates at Ballymore Glen.

"Ballymore bloody Glen, who is going to believe that sort of name, Nina?" Barney asked his little mongrel. "I mean, Jesus Christ, it was a bloody field just two years ago."

Barney cast his mind back. It didn't feel like two years ago.

He and Kelly had been just heading out for a ride on her horse Mooner and Barney's old horse, Owl, when they spotted the innocent little sign. It was a planning application notice for a two-storey dwelling.

Barney had scowled. "We'll have to object, of course."

And he did, but it didn't do any good. They

subsequently discovered that the entire massive field of twenty-five acres had been subdivided into ten plots of two and a half acres each. Under the Wicklow County Council planning laws, the developer was entitled to build one dwelling per hectare. He was breaking no laws. The houses were not going to obstruct the views of any other Ballymore residents, nor were they going to affect their light. Barney tried to object on the grounds that there would be more traffic on the roads, but that was shot down too. There was nothing he could do.

"You should count yourself lucky," the man in the planning office said to Barney. "These are going to be big houses, expensive houses. The county council are looking for areas to develop a large housing estate, for social housing." Barney understood what the civil servant was saying but he still wasn't happy. He liked Ballymore the way it was. The only thing that he couldn't get a straight answer on was when the land had changed from agricultural to residential. Nor could he get the name behind the rezoning.

As property prices continued to soar in Ireland, the residents of Ballymore were surprised that the ten sites, now with full planning permission, were not put up for sale or auction. It soon became apparent why not. The developer had decided to build the houses himself and sell them as a *fait accompli*. The houses shot up at an alarming rate. The first thing the developer did was to lay a road down the centre of the site. There were five large sites marked out on either side of the road. Then the JCBs moved in. If the restoration job on Rathdeen Manor some years earlier had been a big job, this was ten times bigger. Within two years of being a huge green field, the land across the road from Barney's little cottage was now an exclusive development of ten mansions, each unique and behind big walls. The entrance to Ballymore Glen had a large set of private gates on it and so did every individual house along the private road inside.

"Imagine having to get through two sets of private gates to get to your house," Kelly laughed on one of the Sundays that she and Barney had sneaked up to have a look at the progress that was being made.

"Imagine, the developer is so rich he hasn't even put these things on the market yet!" said Barney, adding a little jealously, "Now that's serious money!"

Kelly didn't understand. "Why would he do that? Why didn't he sell straight away?"

"Wow, Kelly! The more he develops the sites the more money he makes. Property prices are still climbing so he's racking up a bigger profit every month that passes."

"Oh," she said a little vaguely.

Barney laughed at his adorable if slightly confused girlfriend.

"OK, now this is only guesswork but it could have been something like this. He would have paid about five hundred thousand euro for that land when he bought it. It would have shot up in value as soon as he got planning permission for his ten blessed houses. I would guess that each house site would have been worth about five hundred thousand then. So you see he has already increased the value of his portfolio by an order of magnitude."

"A what?" Kelly was now totally lost.

"It's worth ten times what he paid for it – add a zero on the back."

"OK."

"OK," Barney echoed. "Now he's laughing all the way to the bank. But this guy decides not to sell. He has made so much money, he decides, 'Well, why not develop the sites myself?'"

"How do you know that?" Kelly asked, still not following.

"Because he hasn't sold them yet," Barney said simply. "Now he has developed these ten amazing houses. God knows what he's going to sell them for. Would it be one and a half million each? If he does, that's fifteen million euro for him. Not bad considering he bought the field for only half a million."

"My God," Kelly gushed, "do you mean he has made fourteen and a half million euro profit on this development over the last two years?"

"Not quite. He did have to build these houses. But a five-thousand-square-foot house shouldn't cost him any more than a hundred-and-fifty euro per square foot – multiply that by ten houses. Subtract by twenty per cent discount for economies of scale –" Barney began to mutter figures to himself as he did a quick mental calculation. "At the very outside, I would guess that this guy didn't pay more than eight million, so yep, that leaves him with seven million euro profit minimum. Not bad!"

"And we still don't know who the developer is," Kelly sighed.

"We know the builders – Christ, we meet them often enough," said Barney. "We just don't know who the money is behind them."

Kelly liked to fantasise that it was a tall dark stranger, possibly with a broken heart and desperately looking for a soft, gentle woman to fill the aching lonely void in his life.

"I wonder who he is," she sighed.

"Maybe it's a woman," Barney said.

This particular thought brought him back to reality with a thud. Last night was meant to be a big celebration for Kelly. He was happy for her and particularly pleased that she had turned twenty-one at last. Like it or not, he had to admit that the age thing was causing a strain between them. He first took her to bed when she was nineteen. That had been an utter joy.

They had been dating for almost a year at that stage and he was getting pretty frustrated! But he couldn't in good conscience sleep with Kelly while she was still at school. He had let her finish her Mount Eden days as a virgin, despite her strong protests. The day she finished her Leaving Cert, however, Barney collected her from school and drove her straight back to Peartree Cottage. They had already discussed it. Kelly wanted it to be there. She loved Peartree Cottage and she loved Ballymore. She didn't want to go to some hotel that she didn't know very well. It would be a strange bed, in a room that meant nothing to her. She didn't want it to be in a place where doubtless loads of people had shagged before her. Peartree Cottage was special. It was Barney's home.

On that hot June afternoon, Kelly ran into the little house.

"Finished!" she laughed gleefully, ripping off her cotton jumper. In an unusual fit of generosity, the nuns had permitted them to give up their school uniforms when the school term finished. For the three weeks of her Leaving

Certificate exams, she was allowed to wear whatever she wanted. For Kelly this was her habitual jeans, a T-shirt or blouse and perhaps if the weather looked dodgy, a jumper.

"Finished for ever! I never have to set a foot inside that bloody school again!"

Barney followed her into the cottage with a very excited Nina running around his legs, yapping happily at all the excitement.

"Now I can do what I really want to do," Kelly continued as she threw her arms around Barney's neck. "I can come and work in Rathdeen Refuge full-time."

"Yes, you can, my love." Barney returned her embrace and gently kissed her on the lips.

"Barney," Kelly whispered softly as if reading his mind.

"Yes?"

"Can you take me to bed now? You always said that you'd have your way with me once I'd finished at Mount Eden. I'm not a student any more."

"No, you're not, and yes I can," he answered between kisses. He picked Kelly up as if he was a groom carrying his bride over the threshold. He brought her to his bedroom and put her down on his bed. "Stay here, don't move a muscle!" He smiled at her and ran back out of his bedroom.

She laughed at him. "Where would I go?

He quickly rushed back in with a bottle of champagne and two glasses.

"For you, my love," he beamed. "I want this to be a happy memory for you."

Kelly bit her bottom lip and her eyes glassed up. "Gosh, now you say it, it is a big step."

Barney froze and looked at her. "You're not getting second thoughts, are you?"

When she saw the look of sheer horror on his face, she cracked up laughing. "No, you eejit! Come on, open the champagne!"

He did as he was asked and filled the two glasses to the brim. Then he sat down beside her on his bed and smiled at her. "To us!" He raised his glass.

"To us," she echoed and clinked his champagne flute. Then she drained her glass.

He looked at her in amusement. "God, were you thirsty?"

She shook her mane of dark brown curls and smiled at him. "No, but I am a little nervous."

Barney thought his heart would burst with love for her. He put his glass down and took her face in his hands. He kissed her so softly on the lips that they were barely touching. Usually so uninhibited and adventurous, for once Kelly let him make all the moves. She kissed him back softly.

"God, Kelly, I love you so much!"

As Barney flashed back to the union now, he felt physical pain at the intimacy of his memories.

"I love you too, Barney," she had replied. Her beautiful dark eyes were wide with honesty.

Gently Barney rose from the bed and crossed the room to close the curtains. The sun was strong however and even with the curtains closed the room was still bright and warm.

"I'm sorry, Nina, but this is one time you're going to leave Kelly and me alone." Gently, he lifted his little mutt up and took her out of the room. Then he shut the door on her. Nina was not impressed but amazingly she didn't bark at the door. It was as if she knew that something special was going to happen between Barney and Kelly.

"Do you want another glass?" he asked her.

Kelly shook her head. She sat on the bed a little awkwardly and he came and sat beside her. Again he began to kiss her gently and she kissed him back. Gradually he began to undo the buttons of her blouse. Kelly stopped kissing him and watched his hands as he opened each button. Not exactly a roving Casanova himself, Barney could count his sexual conquests on one hand. All three of those had involved copious amounts of alcohol and absolute darkness. This openness and honesty terrified him. As he worked his way down her buttons, Kelly began to open his in a similar fashion. She started at the top and worked her way down slowly, then she took Barney's hands in hers and kissed them, gently leading his hands into her bra. He had undone her bra millions of times. Even though Kelly was still a virgin, they had had plenty of great romps together. He unclipped her bra easily and she stood up next to the bed to let her blouse and bra fall to the floor. Barney shook off his shirt and stood up with her. She made no effort to kiss him as she waited to be undressed by him. He unzipped her jeans and let them slither down her long, thin legs, then ever so gently he pulled her soft white cotton pants down. Kelly stepped out of them and stood before him, wearing only her ankle socks. He sat her on the bed and pulled off each sock separately, kissing her toes as he did so. The sight of her totally naked on his bed made him catch his breath. Her body was divine. Her skin was coffee-with-cream colour and her breasts tiny. Kelly regularly moaned about the fact that she had no breasts but Barney thought they were just perfect. She wasn't particularly curvy because she was so thin. Her limbs were long and willowy and Barney was filled with the urge to have those long legs wrapped around his body. He attempted to lie down beside her but she pushed him back onto the floor.

"You have to be naked if you want to make love," she explained simply as she began to undo his trousers. She undressed him the way he had undressed her. As he stood next to the bed, she gently pulled down his trousers and then his boxers. Next she took off each sock. He was considerably shyer than she was but he went along with it anyway. Then he came and lay down beside her.

Thinking back to it now, he still became aroused. That glorious feeling of skin next to skin. The anticipation of making love when you know it's going to happen and it's going to be wonderful. He wrapped his arms around her body and kissed her. He explored her mouth with his tongue, gently rubbing her body with his. He let his hands wander over her smooth cool skin, down her long back, around her soft small bottom. He knew that she was ready for him but he made her wait. He wanted her to pine for him, to need him urgently. He controlled his own desires although he nearly exploded the one time she tried to take him in her hands.

"No, no, don't do that," he laughed as they kissed.

"Why not?" She sounded confused. "I want you to enjoy yourself too, Barney."

"Oh, I am enjoying myself, believe me! If you do that though, it could all be over before we even begin!"

"Oh," Kelly giggled as she wrapped her arms back around his back.

Then she whispered, "Will you come inside me now?"

"Do you want me?"

"You know I do."

"I'm terrified I'll hurt you, Kelly."

"You could never hurt me, Barney. Just as I could never hurt you."

He winced at the memory now.

He moved on top of his girlfriend. Slowly he entered her beautiful, welcoming young body. He studied her face for any sign of discomfort as he did so but there was none. She arched her back to welcome him in and then, like wild ivy, she wound her long legs around his.

"This feels even better than I imagined it would," she groaned.

They moved together easily. Barney had romantic plans of spending the afternoon in bed together, slowly discovering each other's bodies and loving each other but it was quite obvious that Kelly had other plans. As her rhythm got faster, she began to groan.

"Oh, God, don't stop now, Barney! This is heaven!"

He moved with her, watching her face all the time. Kelly came quickly and urgently under his body. It was the most beautiful thing he had ever done. As her body began to relax, she opened her eyes. He was still looking at her.

"Were you watching me all the time?" she asked incredulously.

"Yep! You're gorgeous!"

"Barney!" she thumped him gently. "I didn't mean to close my eyes – it just kind of happened when things got a little hot and heavy."

"I didn't want to miss a moment of it. I wanted to remember it for all of my life."

"You're speaking like it's over," Kelly wriggled out from under him.

"You didn't come, did you?"

He shook his head. "Today was about you. All that mattered was your pleasure."

"What a load of rubbish," Kelly laughed as she rolled her boyfriend onto his back and mounted him. This time she confidently took his penis in her hand and slipped it inside her body.

"You want to go again?" Barney asked, somewhat surprised but equally delighted.

"This, my lover, is the advantage of having a young girlfriend. I could do this all day!" she laughed.

"Hey, you won't hear me complaining," he smiled as he began to move with her again.

"God, this is gorgeous! We must do this every day!" She smiled down at him.

"OK," he laughed.

She put her hands on his shoulders and moved up and down on him. "This is divine," she purred.

"Trust you to like being on top," he laughed. "It's not dissimilar to horse-riding."

"Howdy, cowboy," she laughed as she urged him into a canter.

"Well, you're certainly hot to trot!" he grinned.

"Yep," she smiled at him, "and game for a gallop!" She felt that familiar warmth in her groin. "Oh, I think I'm going to come again, Barney, please come with me! I want to feel it."

He watched her as she moved up and down. Just looking at her sitting on his dick was enough to make him come – she was delicious and all his. Being inside her was the nicest sensation he had ever felt. They came together in a glorious wave of love and sweat.

Kelly lay on top of him as the pleasure gently gave way to a contented feeling of satisfaction. Slowly their breathing returned to normal. Her head lay on his shoulder.

"Barney," she whispered.

"Yes, sweetheart," he stroked her hair.

"I love you."

"I love you too, Kelly."

As he thought back to that wonderful afternoon he shivered. What had happened? Obviously something bloody well had! He knew that he still loved her as passionately as ever. Had he changed so much that *she* didn't love *him* any more? Could it be that it was Kelly who had changed? Not in so far as he could see. She was still the young beautiful girl he had fallen in love with so long ago. Kelly had inherited her father's good looks. Unlike her father however, her hair was a mop of curls which had now grown down the full length of her back. She was tall and very thin; truth be told, she was marginally taller than Barney but he would never acknowledge it. He claimed that they were exactly the same height. Kelly had huge brown eyes, which sometimes reflected the insecurity she so often felt. Even Barney had to admit she wasn't the most academic of the Dalton girls, not that he would ever say that to her. She already believed that herself, however, and that was what made her so shy. She was constantly nervous of saying something daft (which she often did) but what she didn't realise was that if she did say something slightly silly, it only served to endear her even more to Barney. He wanted to mind her from the world and protect her from harm.

On a horse, however, Kelly was a different person. The shy little girl-next-door was replaced by a feisty hot-blooded woman. There was no horse or pony that Kelly wouldn't mount. She and Barney worked well together in the refuge. She never complained about having to muck out stables or kennels – in fact, it was clear she liked doing it. She did grumble a little at the cold weather but those were the joys of working outdoors in Ireland!

Kelly loved animals and spent as much of her free time as well as her working day with the dogs and donkeys that arrived daily from the Dublin suburbs. It was quite amazing how many she had found homes for. She had even managed to sell them. She put together a selection of photographs and a heartbreaking story about the plight of Ireland's stray dogs and, with her old headmistress's permission, placed the project in the foyer of Mount Eden's main entrance. The requests flew into the refuge. Everybody wanted a Rathdeen Refuge dog. It quickly became apparent that she would be able to charge these families for their newest acquisitions. She worked so hard at it that eventually it became the *done thing* to get a Rathdeen Refuge dog as opposed to a pedigree. Instead of paying three hundred euro for some overbred pooch, the Mount Eden mums were encouraged to put what they thought to be a 'reasonable amount' into an envelope. All monies raised would go towards the refuge. The irony was that these women were paying three and four hundred euro for dogs that were going to be put to sleep if they didn't get good homes.

As a knock-on effect of selling so many dogs to well-heeled homes, Kelly planned to set up another little business for herself running a pooch parlour and dog-sitting service for owners who wished to go on holidays.

Barney thought about his girlfriend. Academic she wasn't but smart she was. That pooch parlour business could make her a fortune. And it was common knowledge that kennelling dogs could cost a packet so she'd make money on that too. That was something else she had in common with her father. Kelly obviously had the Midas touch when it came to getting ideas for making money.

Barney respected her, he loved her and God knows he fancied her, so what was their problem? He knew that he had to face the truth whether he liked it or not. After three years together, it was obvious that Kelly was tired of him and wanted to live life a little. She had said as much at the party the night before. He collapsed into his favourite armchair. Damn it, the fact that he *had* a favourite armchair said it all! Nina jumped up on his lap.

"Oh, Nina. What choice do I have?"

Nina sighed and flopped her head down between her paws as if she shared his burden.

"If I really love her, I guess the right thing to do is to let her go."

CHAPTER 4

Sue Parker's Monday morning wake-up call was at five am. There was nothing new about that.

"*M-u-m-m-y*," was yelled down the hall at some considerable volume. Dave grunted in the bed beside her.

Sue jumped up in an instant. She knew that if she was fast enough, she could get to her little boy before he woke the rest of the house. DJ was always the first to rise every morning.

"Good morning, little one!" She smiled down at the apple of her eye despite the fact that she was exhausted and still half asleep.

"Milk," he scowled at her.

She lifted him out and tried to give him a hug but he was too strong for her and kicked to be put down on the floor.

"Down," he commanded and wriggled a little more.

"You know, just once it would be lovely if you would let me give you a big hug," she sighed, as she followed him out of the nursery and downstairs. The Parkers' kitchen was at the back of the house and sun poured into the room in the morning.

"Milk," DJ commanded again. He was standing beside the double doors of the huge General Electric fridge. Sue remembered when Dave came back with a brochure for the fridge. She laughed and asked who the heck would pay ten thousand euro for a fridge.

"I would," Dave answered. He was positively animated. "You should see it, Sue. It does everything except eat your breakfast for you!"

At the time, she thought he was getting a little carried away but now that they had it, she had to admit that it was lovely to have iced water available to drink, literally on tap. There was always ice made because the fridge did it for you. It was, in a word, huge, but that was good because there was plenty of room for baby bottles, she thought wearily as she retrieved DJ's bottle. He grabbed it with as much charm as a rabid Rottweiler and began to gulp.

Sue did a quick bottle count to ensure that she had enough formula milk made up for the morning at least. DJ would go ballistic if she ran out. Her friends thought she was mad to still have him on formula milk as opposed to cow's milk, but she argued that the manufacturers suggested that it was best to continue with formula until twenty-four months and, anyway, the one time she had tried him on natural milk he had gone wild and threw it onto the ground howling for 'his' milk.

"In a few months, you know, you'll be two years big, DJ!" She tried to stroke his little blond head. He shrugged her off and continued drinking.

"Would you like to go back to bed for a little while?"

she urged. "It's still the middle of the night." She glanced at the clock over the door to the utility room. Ten past five.

DJ stopped drinking for a moment. "Teletubbies?" he asked hopefully.

"It's far too early for Teletubbies." Sue smiled and tried to look shocked. DJ was not convinced however. He threw his bottle on the floor and ran up the step that separated the playroom from the kitchen. He pulled a video off the shelf and brought it back to her triumphantly.

"Ah, you want to watch the Teletubbies on video," she laughed resignedly.

"Yeah," he answered, gratified that at last she understood.

Sue knew that she was beaten. If she tried to get him back into bed now he would definitely have one of his famous tantrums.

"I still don't know why they call them the tantrum twos," she spoke to him as she switched on the television and clicked the video remote into life. "You've been having tantrums since you were born."

He pulled himself up onto the sofa and settled down. "Mummy, you here!" He looked up at her wide-eyed as he patted the seat beside him. Although his tone was hard and commanding, she saw the vulnerable and hopeful eyes.

"Well, I'm not going to get back to sleep now," she smiled, "and how can I turn down such a charming request? OK."

The two of them settled down to watch Tinky Winky, Dipsy, La la and Po play with their favourite things.

It was only half an hour later when Dave stuck his head around the door.

"Good morning, honey, have you been up long?"

"Daddy!" DJ was ecstatic to see his father and jumped down from the sofa to run straight into Dave's arms.

"Hi ya, big fella," Dave Parker responded with as much enthusiasm.

"No, we only surfaced around five," answered Sue. "Not too bad this morning."

"Are the other two still asleep?"

"Yes. My guess is Guy will be up soon and, of course, India will sleep on until I wake her."

"The Parker men know there's work to be done! Don't you, little man?" He turned DJ upside down and dangled him by the ankles.

The little boy crumpled with laughter. "Daddy, Daddy, stop stop!"

Dave gently righted his son and carried him over to the kitchen, where he fixed himself a protein shake.

"I've got a busy day today, honey. I'm in Birmingham all morning and then I fly straight to Belfast. Don't expect me home for tea."

Sue tried to hide her disappointment. "You're working very hard," she said, trying to sound normal.

"I know, but it will all be worth it," he promised as he downed the shake and kissed her on the forehead.

When, she wondered. We have all the money we could ever need. When will it all be worth it? When is it enough? But she kept her thoughts to herself.

Dave handed DJ back into Sue's arms and tried to explain to his son. "I have to go to the office now but I'll see you soon."

The child began to whine loudly.

"Now, David Joseph, you know Daddy has to work. Behave or I will be very cross." Sue called her son by his full name, instead of DJ, indicating that she was getting annoyed.

The boy didn't pick up on his mother's change in mood but her husband did. He knew it was hard running the house with three young children but he was working his ass off too.

"Lisa will be here soon," he smiled at his wife.

Sue nodded at his attempt to lift her spirits. Lisa was a super nanny and a huge help.

Sue and DJ walked with Dave to the front door of the house. There, he stopped and turned to Sue. "Hey, why don't you get on to the estate agents about Ballymore Glen? See how much they're guiding and maybe we'll go and have a snoop next weekend. What do you think?"

"I think that's a great idea."

It had been the talk of the village the day before when the big signs went up at the entrance of Ballymore Glen. Within hours everybody knew that the properties were now on the market. Ballymore's main source of information was Maureen O'Reilly who ran O'Reilly's newsagent's. Naturally enough, most people went into O'Reilly's on Sunday morning for the newspapers. She was beside herself with excitement to have this particular nugget of gossip for her Sunday patrons. She didn't know what "for sale by tender" actually meant, but Dave Parker explained that any interested parties would be given a guideline price and then they could put in a written offer indicating how much they were willing to pay above the guide.

"The highest offer will get the property," he explained simply.

"What's the guide?" Maureen had asked him greedily over the *Sunday Times*.

"You'll have to phone the estate agents tomorrow and ask them." He laughed at Maureen. "Are you thinking of moving?" he teased her.

Maureen blushed. "Maybe," she answered taking him far too seriously.

Lisa Keyes arrived as punctually as she did every other Monday.

"Good morning, everybody!" She had a smile in her voice and a spring in her step.

Sue was as relieved as ever to see her. She adored her children but they were a hell of a handful and by eight o'clock she was glad of the helping hand. She had, after all, been up since five with DJ and it was still only six am when Guy surfaced.

They exchanged pleasantries about the weekend. Lisa had had "a quiet weekend, as usual". She laughed it off lightly just the same as every other Monday but Sue secretly wondered why such a bright bubbly girl hadn't found a suitable companion yet. They talked about Kelly's twenty-first. Sue said it had been a wild night. She didn't mention Richard Dalton's surprise appearance. Nor did she mention how difficult Dave found it to stay in the house and remain civil to the man who had almost destroyed his marriage. Amazingly, now that Sue had seen him suffer for his 'sins', she didn't mind being in his company. In fact, she thought that she now actually felt a little sorry for the man she had once hated so much.

Sue continued, "The boys have had their breakfast, Lisa. Now I'm going to try to rise Lady Muck!"

This was the usual routine Monday through Friday. At twenty-two months DJ was very much an early riser. Guy was the ripe old age of three and a half now and it looked like he would always be a morning man. India, however, was six and she loved her bed. School was a shock to her system and India thought she had, at last, finished with early mornings when the summer holidays arrived. Sue, however, had other plans. She reckoned that her six-year-old would be bored at home all summer and so had booked her into summer camp for two weeks. India was furious when she discovered. With one week down and one week to go, the fact that it was meant to be fun didn't matter. She just didn't like early mornings.

Summer camp was in Wicklow. Thankfully the country roads were still very quiet and so Sue could wake her daughter as late as eight or even eight thirty in an emergency. She would get her dressed and fed and then drive her to camp. Despite the child's strongest protests, India was inevitably safely deposited at five to nine each morning.

As she drove her large bottle-green Mercedes back to Ballymore from Wicklow, she passed by Ballymore Glen. The first thing that struck her was the sheer size of the signs.

"Well, there's no missing that," she laughed aloud. She pulled up outside Barney's house, Peartree Cottage, to have a good look at the signs across the road.

"For Sale by Private Tender," she read. It was a well-known estate agent and the phone number was a Bray one. She knew about the guy who ran the Bray office. The girls in Rathdeen golf club had told her a few stories. He wouldn't let his left hand know what his right was doing. A knock on her car window shook her out of her daydream.

"Are you thinking of buying?" Barney laughed.

"Good morning, Barney! I'm sorry, I was miles away. No, no, we're very happy where we are. I wouldn't mind a peep though. Do you think they'll be fast to sell?"

"Well, judging by the passing traffic yesterday afternoon, I'd say they're going to be snapped up. Did you see the property supplement of the *Business Post* yesterday?"

"No. Why? Were they in it?"

"A full-page spread. It went on about the best of both worlds, how the new owners could enjoy the pleasures of country life while still being able to commute to Dublin."

"Sure we've known that for years, Barney."

"Yeah, but at least it was our secret."

"That's true."

"You haven't heard the best bit. There's a viewing fee."

"A what?"

"You have to pay just to see the bloody houses. How do you like that?"

"Well, I suppose it will cut out all the people who are just going in for a snoop."

"Snooty snoopers only need apply. Heh?" Barney laughed. "Only guess how much you have to pay for the privilege?"

"How much?" Sue was beginning to wonder if Dave would still want to see the houses.

"One hundred euro! Per person! A ton a head, just to

see the inside of Ballymore Glen. Do you think I could do tours of my little cottage for ten euro?"

"Barney, surely you got that wrong! Who the hell will pay that much to see inside a house?"

"Well, actually, you get a guided escort around all ten houses for that price and here's the real gem: you get it refunded if you buy one of the houses."

"Big bloody swing. What's the guide anyway?"

"Oh yeah, that's a bit rich too. They're going to market with a price tag of one point five to two million!"

"Two million? Two million euro each? For a house in Ballymore! You're joking! That's nuts. You must have got that wrong."

Barney shook his head. "And that's just the guide – they expect the ones with the optimum views to go for considerably more."

"I can't believe that."

"Believe it. If we have to have neighbours, at least we're going to have really rich ones."

"They won't be rich after they've forked out that kind of dosh."

"Yeah, well, I definitely won't be viewing the properties. Will you?"

"Dave wanted to see the houses, but after what you've just told me, I'm not so sure."

"If you do, you can tell us all about them. Now I really must dash – work beckons for us mere mortals!" Barney laughed lightly.

"Bye, Barney. I should be heading home myself. I'm taking Guy to mother-and-baby swimming today."

"God, you're great with those kids, Sue! You're always doing something with one or other of them." Barney marvelled at the woman who had once played golf six days a week.

Sue smiled as she started up her car. "They're young for such a short time. You have to enjoy them while you can."

Barney felt the weight return to the pit of his stomach as he remembered the conversation he was going to have this morning with his girlfriend, the woman he had once thought was going to be the mother of his children.

They bade each other goodbye and Barney set out for Rathdeen Manor. He decided to walk because the weather had thankfully returned to a pleasant late-summer temperature, unlike the day before. He had wanted to talk to Saskia about his bouncing cheque, but the weather had been so bad it had given him the excuse he needed to put it off.

This morning it had to be addressed, however, and sooner than he expected. As he walked through the village, the beep-beep of Saskia's Land-Rover shook him out of his daydreams.

She pulled up beside him.

"Hi, Barney, I thought it was you! I was just on my way up to the refuge to talk to you. Hop in, I'll give you a lift the rest of the way."

Bang goes my exercise for the day, he thought, mildly agitated as he climbed in.

"I think I know what you wanted to talk about," Barney replied darkly.

"You do?" Saskia was surprised.

"A small matter of a bouncing cheque. Does that mean that all the staff's cheques bloody well bounced? Saskia, I won't be able to contain them for much longer. What the heck is going on?"

Saskia locked her gaze onto the road. This was certainly not what she was coming up to talk about.

"Oh, hell, Barney, I had no idea. I'm sorry! I don't know how this could have happened. I'll get right onto it."

"When is Nicolas coming home?" Barney asked. "I know that it's not really your problem. It's just that Nicolas did leave you in charge in his absence. He can't seriously expect to run a business like this, can he?"

Saskia did her best to look positive. She wasn't going to tell Barney about the appalling fights she and Nicolas had been having. She had originally left all business dealings to him but it was rapidly becoming apparent that he was living off his capital. In fact, he was going through his lump sum of cash terrifyingly quickly. He had assumed that he would be a bestselling author by now. That hadn't happened.

"If you didn't know about the cheques, what was it you wanted to discuss?" Barney interrupted her thoughts.

"Ah yes, look, I'm sorry, Barney, but Kelly is really sick. I'm not sure what is wrong with her but she's not going to be in today."

"Well, that's bloody typical," Barney exploded. "That girl has had more sick days in the last month than I've had in my life. Are you going to get a doctor, Saskia?"

She was very surprised at his outburst. It was so unlike him.

"Kelly won't let me get one," she replied feebly.

"Well, tell her that she either sees a doctor today or she comes in this afternoon. I really am tired of this. Does she know her cheque bounced?"

"I don't think so, Barney. She has had a rather busy

weekend as you know. It's not every weekend that you turn twenty-one." Saskia got a little more defiant.

"Yes, and that might be the reason behind the ill health this morning. What do you think?"

"I think you might grant your girlfriend a little more slack, Barney Armstrong," Saskia snapped.

Barney glared at her. "I'm trying to run a business here. Personal issues don't come into it." They had arrived at the refuge. "If you could get Nicolas to sort out those cheques today, I might be able to keep the staff from walking out." He climbed out of the car but turned as he was about to close the door. "Tell Kelly that if she wants to continue working here, she'd better be in this afternoon or have a doctor's note tomorrow." He closed the door before she could argue.

Saskia tore up the gravel driveway of Innishambles. Dudley and Dexter barked as they heard her car. Tiffany had just wandered down for a leisurely breakfast. She was enjoying her last few weeks of freedom before she started college.

"Good morning, Mum," she smiled as she saw her mother enter the kitchen.

"Is it?" Saskia scowled at her daughter.

"Jeez, what's got into you?"

"Where's Robin?" Saskia asked automatically.

"After you left, I think I heard her wander in to Kelly."

"Really, Tiffany, is it too much to ask you to keep a slightly better eye on your baby sister?"

Saskia stormed up the stairs to Kelly's room. She walked in purposefully and threw back the curtains violently.

"That's the last time I'm doing your dirty work. You can do it for yourself in future, Kelly."

Kelly groaned from under the quilt where she was snuggled up with Robin and the two Yorkie terriers. The little dogs had always slept with somebody or other. Originally it had been with Richard and Saskia, and then when Richard moved out they were quite happy to take up more space in the bed. In due course, when Nicolas moved in, they were highly indignant, even aggressive towards him. Reluctantly Saskia began to shut her two little friends out of her bedroom. Forced to choose between Nicolas and the dogs, her boyfriend won. Woody and Wilma were horrified and howled and scratched at the door for weeks. Eventually they moved in with Kelly. Now that Nicolas was in the States, Saskia was alone again and quite willing to let them back into her bed. The dogs had not forgiven her, however. They stayed with Kelly.

"Mum, what's wrong?"

"Barney is what's wrong. He's not impressed with the amount of sick time you've been taking over the last few months and now that I think about it, you know, he has a point."

"Mum," Kelly groaned, "look, I really am sick. Leave Barney to me. I'll call him later."

"No, you won't. You'll see him later or you'll see Dr Harrington."

"Mmm!" Kelly giggled. All the girls fancied the rather delectable Dr Harrington. He had started in his father's practice three years earlier. Slowly he had taken over the entire practice and now that his father had retired, the business was entirely his and he was one of Wicklow's most eligible young men.

"I'm serious, Kelly. Which is it going to be, Barney or Dr Harrington?"

Kelly dragged herself into a sitting position, much to the chagrin of Robin, Woody and Wilma.

"OK, OK, chill out, Mum. I'll get up, even though I am as sick as a dog. I'll go to work."

Saskia softened when she saw how pale and weak Kelly looked.

"Look, pet, why don't I take you in to Dr Harrington? If you have some sort of bug, he'll get to the bottom of it very quickly. He's a terrific doctor."

Kelly pushed a smile onto her face, "Oh Mum, I'm fine really. It's just a small tummy bug or something. No need to bother the good doctor!" The last thing she wanted was him trying to discover the reason for her morning sickness. "Look, I'm getting up. I'll go to work." She dragged herself out of the bed and onto her bedroom floor.

"Good girl!" Saskia was gone.

As she came back downstairs, leaving her youngest and eldest daughters to themselves, Saskia calculated that it was about two am in LA. Perfect, she thought malevolently. Nicolas should be tucked up in bed sound asleep. She went into the study and closed the door, then dialled his number in LA. The phone rang and rang. She was just about to give up when a very jovial and slightly drunk Nicolas picked up the receiver.

"Hi," he answered cheerfully.

"Nicolas, is that you?"

"Who the hell else would it be, babe?"

"Nicolas, are you drunk?"

"Yeah!"

"What are you doing?" Saskia asked irritably.

"Well, let's see now," Nicolas laughed. "I'm drunk so I must be drinking!"

"Who are you drinking with?"

"My agent, Brad Steinway. You remember him."

"Oh, Nicolas, tell me you're celebrating! You've got a book deal!"

"Not quite, babe, we're actually commiserating. Brad has sent the book to all the big publishers out here and in fact to a few of the smaller ones too and guess what?"

"Oh Nicolas, you're drunk and making no sense. What's happened?"

"It's crap! Crap, crap, crap! Nobody wants my story." Nicolas began to laugh deliriously and Saskia could hear Brad Steinway laughing in the background, an equally inebriated laugh.

"Can you believe it? I've spent three years writing a book of crap. It isn't worth jack shit!"

Saskia tried to control her temper. "Look, Nicolas, I'm glad that you find it so amusing but the reason I'm phoning you is because all the cheques have bounced up in Rathdeen Refuge!"

Nicolas began to laugh even harder. "No kidding!"

"It's a little more serious than that, Nicolas."

"Oh, you're right there, babe. It's a lot more serious."

"What do you mean?"

"Well, they damn nearly bounced a few weeks ago. I didn't tell you because I didn't want to unnecessarily upset you. Anyway, that's all academic now. I can't keep it from you any more. The reason for all these bouncing cheques is because all my money is gone. Every last cent. I talked to the bank manager in Wicklow and he extended me a bank loan. That's what has been keeping the refuge going for the last few weeks. Now that's gone, we're really over!" Nicolas began to laugh again.

"Oh God!" Saskia fell back into a chair. "What's to become of the refuge?"

"For Chrissakes, Sas, what's to become of *us*? To hell with the refuge!"

She had never heard Nicolas talk like this.

* * *

Kelly didn't know what to expect. She knew that she was going to have to tell Barney the truth, she just wasn't sure how to go about it. She saddled up Mooner and rode down towards the river More. In the late summer sun the entire valley was buzzing. Bees and other insects worked feverishly on the tall grasses and wild poppies. The heavy rains of the day before had left the ground soft and moist. The air smelt warm and heavy with pollen. Kelly inhaled deeply. The effect on her was almost intoxicating. She loved Ballymore – its peaceful serenity and great natural beauty. Looking at the valley, drenched in light as it was now, Kelly vowed that she would never leave Wicklow, baby or no baby!

Mooner was enjoying the leisurely stroll too. They walked down to the river and the big old horse carefully picked his way across the stony river-bed. In crossing the river, they moved from Innishambles land to the Rathdeen Manor estate. Slowly they climbed the southern face of the valley. It seemed a lifetime ago when these were all green fields. Now the gardens were extensive and the swimming-pool at the back of the manor was a constant source of fun when the Irish weather got hot enough.

"Nicolas Flattery must be a very rich man, Mooner," Kelly sighed. "I wonder if Mum wants all of us to move in with him? There could be worse places to live." Then her mind inevitably went back to the baby. "Of course, he may not want me anywhere around his blessed house within a few months. Babies make a lot of noise." She winced at the memory of Robin's tantrums and histrionics when she was just a little younger. "And she's a good girl! Oh God, what's to become of me?"

Reluctantly Kelly arrived into the stables. She had heard stories of women giving up horse-riding because they were pregnant. Over my dead body, she thought mutinously as she entered the courtyard.

"At last, you decide to honour us with your presence, Miss Dalton!" Barney's voice was dripping with sarcasm.

"Look, Barney, we have to talk."

"Aha, the real reason for your tardiness surfaces."

"What?"

"You weren't really sick, were you?"

"Yes, I was. Well, it wasn't a bug or anything. It's well, we have to talk," she stuttered as she dismounted.

"Damn sure we have to! I know what the problem is, Kelly."

"You do?"

"Of course."

"How?"

"Hello, Kelly! I'd have to be a bit thick to have missed the signs."

"I didn't know," she whispered softly, looking at the ground guiltily. "I'm really sorry, Barney. I'm sure it's my fault. I'm so stupid sometimes."

Barney thought his heart would break but it was easier

66

to be tough. He knew Kelly didn't love him the way he adored her. If he pretended that he didn't love her either, it would make a break-up much less traumatic. He knew he was doing the right thing. He just had to let her go.

"Kelly, you're not stupid. These things happen," he continued trying to sound as cool and distant as possible. "Look, there's only one real easy solution."

"What are you saying, Barney?" Kelly's body began to shake uncontrollably as she read his body language. He was being so cold.

"Termination." Inwardly he winced as he used the word: it sounded like he was ending a business merger, not a relationship. Kelly's mouth opened in shock but she remained mute. He tried another tack. "Look, who are we kidding, Kelly? It's over between us, whatever it was it's well and truly over-dead-kaput! Let's not make this any messier than it already is."

She continued to stare at him incredulously as he went on. Never in her wildest dreams – or nightmares – did she imagine this to be his reaction.

"You want your freedom, so do I. It's obvious that you still have a lot to do with your life. This is the only solution. You're too young for this level of commitment."

Kelly thought she was going to pass out. She had never thought that Barney would want her to have an abortion. Her knees went weak. Barney saw her pale and thought that she might faint. He ran to hold her before she collapsed.

"Get away from me!" Her own voice sounded strange to her. She sounded like an old woman, or even a witch. "You animal! Get away from me!" She stumbled back to Mooner and grabbed his thick neck for support. Then she clambered back onto his back. "You murdering bastard! I never want to see you again!"

Murdering? Barney wondered what the hell she was talking about. Then he remembered the old mongrel somebody had dropped at their door the previous week. The animal had been in a traffic accident and it was half-dead when they got to it. Kelly and he had fought over the little dog. She had wanted to keep it at Innishambles until she found it a home and he wouldn't let her. Barney knew that it was unfair to keep the animal alive, such were its injuries. Against her will, Barney had put the dog to sleep.

"For God's sake, Kelly! Don't get so involved! It's not murder."

"Oh no? Then what would you call it?"

"It's kinder in the long run and you know it's painless."

"Jesus, I don't know any such thing! In fact, I don't believe we're having this conversation, you, you shit!" She was visibly trembling. "It just shows, you never really know someone. Do you?" She looked down at her now ex-boyfriend. "Barney, I never want to see you again. Never! I quit." She pulled Mooner's head up and galloped out of Rathdeen Manor.

As Barney watched her go the tears welled up in his eyes.

CHAPTER 5

When Sue Parker told her husband that there was a fee of one hundred euro per head just to see the houses of Ballymore Glen he was delighted.

"Well, the clever bastard," he laughed.

"Who? Why?"

"The guy behind this development, of course, Sue. Don't you see? He has just raised the stakes even further. Firstly he got himself a huge amount of publicity by pulling off this stunt and secondly he's just made himself an extra couple of grand for doing nothing and lastly he has managed to make Ballymore Glen even cooler and more exclusive while increasing its profile. The man is a genius."

"It could be a woman!" Sue laughed. "Do you still want to see them?"

"See them? Maybe we should move into the Glen!"

Sue had made the arrangements. Armed with her platinum American Express, she phoned the estate agents in Bray. She had expected to be fawned over a little considering she was going to pay two hundred euro just to look at a house or houses that she probably wasn't going to buy anyway. She was, however sadly disappointed. The telephonist told her that Patricia, the girl dealing with Ballymore Glen, was out on lunch and could Sue call back later? Sue suggested that Patricia might consider calling *her* back.

"She's very busy," the telephonist explained. "If you're really serious about seeing Ballymore Glen, I would suggest you call her back here this afternoon." The young girl's tone was unmistakably indifferent to gold or even platinum plastic.

"Of course I'm bloody serious," Sue snapped as she hung up, astonished at how little power two hundred euro held. "The country has gone mad," she sighed.

She was thinking the same today as she and Dave waited at the front gates of Ballymore Glen. It was explained to her when she eventually managed to track down the very busy Patricia that there would be a viewing day. All prospective purchasers would be collected at the front gates and taken on a tour of the ten houses. Dave was fed up that the viewing day was a Friday.

"Do none of these guys work?" he demanded as they waited. "This is ridiculous. Where's the estate agent?"

Dave and Sue had decided to drive so the other buyers wouldn't necessarily realise that they were actually snooping neighbours. It had been amusing when they had driven up to the locked gates.

"It looks like the Mercedes Appreciation Society's annual meeting," Dave had laughed. "Do you have to have a Merc to live here?"

Lined along the road were about ten Mercs. The cars looked like they were nuzzling up to each other – happily parked expensive bumper to expensive bumper.

"Oh no, there's a little old BMW," Sue had said, pointing to the last car in the line.

Just then a minibus arrived with ten very smartly turned-out young women. Patricia led the way. Each girl wore a navy skirt and blazer.

"They look like air hostesses," Dave mumbled as the giant gates of Ballymore Glen glided open smoothly.

"There are more viewers than there are tour guides," he grumbled irritably. "How is this going to work?"

Patricia checked off the names as she let her guests walk into the complex and then she addressed them.

"Good morning, ladies and gentlemen, you're all very welcome to Ballymore Glen, Ireland's most exclusive development."

"Now I know the difference between a housing estate and a development," Dave chuckled.

"What?" Sue asked.

"Oh, about a million euro!"

They were standing just inside the gates but Patricia kept glancing out onto the main road.

"Some of our guests haven't arrived yet. I'll wait here for them," she explained brightly. "Now, we have decided that the way to best facilitate you is if we place a guide at every front door. That way you can wander at your leisure from house to house. I would however strongly advise that you take the tour with the guide because every possible convenience and luxury has been poured into these amazing homes of distinction. I dare say that you'll miss some of the features if you try to walk around without the benefit of a guide." She smiled cheerfully, trying to ignore the small plane that was buzzing around above their heads. It seemed dangerously low.

"So what have we paid the two hundred bucks for?" Dave grumbled under his breath.

The plane circled even lower.

"It would make more sense if you do not all go to the first house together, but rather spread yourselves around a bit, if you know what I mean, so the guides can give each of you the personal attention that you deserve." Patricia was trying to talk over the noise of the little plane. It was now very reminiscent of a mosquito.

"That thing is going to land," a short man wearing dark sunglasses interrupted Patricia. Sue recognised his voice instantly.

"Dave," she whispered, "that guy wearing the sunglasses," she gestured with her eyes.

"What about him?" Dave whispered back.

"Isn't that Chris De Burgh?"

"My God, I think you're right!" He smiled conspiratorially at her.

Everybody was distracted as the little plane began to make its descent onto the private driveway that ran down the centre of Ballymore Glen. Even Patricia was struck dumb when she saw the plane boldly touch down on the furthest point of the driveway. It hit the brakes and gradually slowed as it taxied up to the little collection of prospective buyers.

The aircraft shuddered to a halt no more than thirty feet away from Patricia and her little group. They all watched in stunned silence, waiting for something more to happen. Eventually it did.

After some pushing and grunting the plane door was shoved sideways and a small set of steps unfolded.

"Ohmigod, it's Jerry Hall!" one of the women gushed.

"No, it's not," Sue commented under her breath. "Jerry Hall is over six foot. That woman isn't five foot eight." Although that was about the only difference. The woman was positively skeletal. She wore white tights and three-inch stiletto heels. They were bright red patent leather and she clutched the obligatory matching handbag. The hat was wider than the door of the plane so that necessitated holding in place too. With a figure any stick-insect would envy, she looked very unstable as she negotiated the tiny steps of the plane. Her dress was figure-hugging, white with huge red polka dots.

"She does really look like Jerry Hall," Sue whispered. "Look at all that blonde hair. Could that be natural?"

"She looks like a rash," Dave scoffed. "What's with the red and white polka dots?"

"*That*, Mr Bastion of the fashion world, is this year's Gucci. It's straight off the catwalks of Milan," Sue corrected her husband. "Thank heavens you only buy new sites for Parkers chain stores. Leave the fashion-buying to the professionals!" She gave him a gentle dig.

"Hi, everybody!" they were greeted in a broad Texan accent.

"It speaks," another in the group whispered. There was muffled laughter as the Texan Barbie began to teeter over towards them.

Next to emerge was a huge balding man who wore

a shirt three sizes too small for his bulk. He wore a thick gold wrist-chain and a matching chain around his neck.

"Hi, folks!" His Texan accent was broad and loud, not unlike himself. He waved from the top of the steps. Without the hindrance of high heels he managed to reach Patricia before his lady friend. He thrust his hand out towards her, as she was the one with the clipboard.

"Bob Bolton! Damn glad to meet you."

Patricia had not yet managed to regain her composure. "Heh," was all she managed.

"This here is my little wife, Cindy. Cindy Bolton."

"Sure is nice to meet you," Cindy chirped as she eventually reached the entourage.

"Mr Bolton, we were, we were expecting you," Patricia stuttered. "We just weren't expecting you to –" she trailed off.

"Fly?" Bob cut in. "I told you I was flying, didn't I?"

"Well, yes. Only I rather thought that you were going to fly from America to Dublin Airport and perhaps drive from there to here."

"Heck no – if that's what I was going to do, that's what I would have said, little lady!" He laughed at Patricia's stupidity. "OK," he clapped his hands together, "where do we start?"

Cindy giggled.

The guided tour went downhill from there. Patricia tried to explain to Bob Bolton that he couldn't just land a plane down anywhere he wanted to willy-nilly. The guides got far too excited and distracted in the presence of so much obvious wealth and glamour, especially since

there was even a rumour began circulating that some
rock stars were coming to view Ballymore Glen too.

Dave and Sue began to visit the various houses and
eventually they made it to house number three.

"Hi, Dave! Hi, Sue!" It was Lauren Dalton.

"Lauren, what in heaven's name are you doing here?"
Sue asked.

"Maureen O'Reilly told me that the estate agent's next
to Harold's office was looking for girls to show these
houses – so here I am!"

"Wow," Dave laughed. "Sure beats paying to see them!
What a rip-off!"

"Ah Dave, come on, a rich man like you," Lauren teased
gently. "And anyway, that's my wages you're talking about
there! Come on, I'll give you the guided tour of number
three and I can tell you who else has been looking."

"Now that information is a lot more interesting," Dave
winked at Lauren. "Who are we going to have as
neighbours?"

"Well, have you met Bob damn-glad-to-meet-you
Bolton yet?"

"He was a little difficult to miss," Sue sniffed.

"His bark is worse than his bite and I hope you get to
like him because he is definitely buying here. He more or
less said so."

"What's his story?" Dave asked.

"He'll tell you as soon as you meet him. He's just one
of those heart-on-his-sleeve types. Actually he's very nice.
To answer your question, Dave, he said that he is in the
telecommunications business and he wants to relocate

here because he thinks Ireland is the new Hong Kong!" Lauren continued in a Texan accent, "There's money to be made in this here li'll country."

The Parkers laughed at her attempt. "Well, he's right there," Dave agreed, "but why here?"

"He read about Ballymore Glen in the Sunday papers last week and he reckoned it was perfect for him and Cindy."

"Any kids?" Sue asked.

"Not unless you count Cindy one. She's his third wife."

"Jesus. Sue, I'll have to keep you under lock and key!"

"Thanks for your confidence in me!" Sue winked at her husband but, still, a chill went down her spine. Did he still not trust her? Richard Dalton was a long long time ago as far as she was concerned. She pushed those thoughts away.

"Did you get any idea as to how rich Mr Bolton might be, Lauren?" Dave continued.

"I have no idea, but he did tell Patricia that he wanted house number one. He also said that he would pay fifty per cent above his nearest rival."

Dave and Sue inhaled sharply.

"Well, we can knock that one off our shopping list," Sue laughed.

"Are you guys seriously thinking of buying in here?" Lauren asked, slightly surprised. "I assumed you were just having a look around."

"You never know." Dave looked around the reception hall. "They're very nice. Very bright."

"Can I show you around?"

"Please do."

"Well," Lauren began her pitch, "this is the main foyer,

as you can see. It's bright and spacious with plenty of storage space." She guided them to the cloakroom. "The security system is top of the range and linked straight through to Wicklow garda station. There are a variety of options on how you may wish to set your alarm."

Lauren showed the Parkers the cleverly concealed safe buried into the cement of the cloakroom floor. She demonstrated the switches to open and close all the windows and curtains automatically.

The private gym was another surprise. All the equipment was linked up to Internet cameras because the fitness instructor was based in the States. "He can monitor your progress over the web and he adjusts the resistance on your machines accordingly. Or of course you can use the manual option if you so wish," Lauren continued. The house was furnished for optimum effect and so naturally the TV and sound systems were utterly up to the minute. Dave positively drooled as he watched the way the television screen rotated so as to follow the person holding the remote control. He walked over and back across the room several times just so as he could watch the TV rotate. Eventually Sue pulled him out of the living-room and into her favourite room, the kitchen.

Resembling the bridge of the *Starship Enterprise*, every possible cooking aid had been added. There was a halogen hob for instant heat, three separate ovens and two microwaves. "They have fuzzy logic chips installed," Lauren enthused, "so they won't burn food!"

"I prefer oven chips," Dave teased.

"Ohmigod, that's huge!" Sue saw the fridge before Dave did. It was even more modern than his own top-of-the-range one at home.

"There are no others like these in the country," Lauren explained. "They were shipped in from the US especially."

The utility room was the same size as the kitchen. It was home to another large oven, a chest freezer and a further two sinks. Beyond that was the laundry room. "It has two large washer-driers and a built-in ironing board," Lauren explained, "but this feature is one of my favourites!" She slid open a press. "This is a laundry chute from your family bathroom upstairs. No more lugging laundry down to wash. Just drop it into your chute. Who knows? The kids might even do it for you, it'll be such fun!" She laughed.

"It's more likely that Guy and India will shove their little brother down the chute!" Dave said. He began to realise that maybe it had been a mistake to take Sue with him to view the houses. It was obvious that she was falling in love with this one. "Honey, we still have five other houses to see and remember we are only here to have a look!"

But it was too late.

"Oh, Dave, the space! Don't you think it's marvellous? The dining-room is twice the size of ours and so is the drawing-room for that matter. Come on, let's have a look upstairs!"

Everything was as Dave had expected. The master en-suite had a steam room as well as a Jacuzzi.

"What, no sauna?" Dave teased Lauren.

"That's outside in the pool house," Lauren replied.

"Oh, Lauren, what's the guide on this one?" asked Sue.

"They're all guiding one and a half to two million, Sue. After that it's up to you and the other bidders."

"Speaking of the other bidders," Dave asked, "who else has been in to see the house?"

Lauren became animated. "There's a rumour going around that Chris De Burgh is here."

Sue nodded in agreement. "I think I saw him earlier."

"Wow! He hasn't been in to me yet. OK, let's see, you're my fifth couple. You already know Bob and Cindy. I had two other couples that just looked rich. I don't know who they were – I'm sure I could find out for you if you like – and I had a man called Raymond Saunders in. Do you know him?"

"Yeah, of course. He's the beef baron, isn't he?"

"That's the one. He's very good-looking."

"You'll find as you get older, pet," Sue Parker winked at Lauren, "that the richer they are the more attractive they look."

Dave blinked at his wife. "What's that meant to mean?"

"Nothing, handsome!" She turned to Lauren and whispered, "Always best to keep 'em on their toes."

Sue and Lauren giggled conspiratorially.

"Hey, I thought we were talking about Raymond Saunders," Dave said. "His money is in beef and land. Isn't that right? Is he married?"

"Widowed," Lauren answered. "I got the run-down from the girls in the office when he phoned in to make his appointment to see this place. He has three kids a little older than your bunch, I think. Anyway, it's very sad – his wife died last year and now he has to bring them up alone."

"That won't last long," Sue remarked cynically.

"Well, it's funny you say that, because he was looking

around the house with his nanny!" Lauren explained. "Can you imagine taking a nanny along to make a decision on a house purchase?"

"Maybe advice isn't the only thing she's giving him!" Dave chuckled.

Sue Parker paled visibly. Less than three years ago, Lauren's mother Saskia had discovered that her husband had been bedding their au pair for some time. It had literally torn the family apart and was the talk of the village for months afterwards. Naturally Edu, the au pair in question, disappeared pretty fast but Sue didn't think that Saskia had ever really recovered.

Trust Dave to blurt out such an insensitive remark. She kicked him in the heel and he realised what he had done. "Ah shit, Lauren, I'm sorry. I didn't mean to upset you."

"Relax, Dave. I'm well over Dad. Anyway, Edu was an au pair, not a nanny." She laughed at Dave's discomfort. "Really, I am over it."

"Phew! Sometimes I'm a real klutz."

"I agree, Lauren," Sue was eager to move the conversation along, "it is a little odd to bring a nanny along to view a house but she probably has a good idea of what would suit the children. Did they like the house?"

Lauren thought about this for a moment. "I don't think they were happy with the fact that the swimming-pool was so close to the house. Kids' safety and all that. Personally I don't see a problem. Just teach your kids to swim. Robin is practically swimming already!"

"Couldn't agree more," Dave added. "If you have a pool, you just teach your kids to swim as soon as possible and make sure that they know about how dangerous water is."

"Anyway," Lauren added, "if they want a house with the pool a little distance from the house, they can buy number one or number six!"

The threesome continued their walk around. Although Sue had no plans of moving when they came to view the development, she had now fallen in love with the house they referred to as number three. As they walked around the pool at the back of the house, Dave asked Lauren about the numbers on the houses.

"They're just for reference now. I assume that everybody will give their own home a name."

Sue looked over the back fence of the property and realised that she could see over to Innishambles and beyond, to the far side of the valley. "Valley View," she smiled. "This house should be called Valley View."

Dave knew he was beaten. There was no way he would be able to change her mind. They bade their goodbyes to Lauren and glanced over the other houses. Sue barely looked at them. Having seen all they wanted, they left Patricia at the front gates of Ballymore Glen and climbed back into Dave's car.

"Oh, Dave, that was marvellous."

Here we go, he thought. "I thought we were just going for a look," he tried.

"Oh yes, but that was before I actually saw them. Don't tell me you weren't impressed."

"Well, yes, I was actually. It's just one and half, probably two million euro to secure one of them. Jesus, Sue, that's a lot for a house!"

"Perhaps, but you're forgetting that we'll be able to

sell our own and it should fetch a strong price off the back of these. What do you think?"

Sue Parker had a terrific ability to make the most implausible scenarios seem quite reasonable when it suited her argument.

"What do you think our house would be worth?" Dave asked, trying to work out the sums.

Sue wasn't sure. "Gosh, I have no idea but I'm sure I could get a few estimates next week."

"Well, that would be a good start. Let's do that and then discuss the matter further," he suggested.

"Oh Dave, you're wonderful!" Sue hugged him as he tried to drive the car away from Ballymore Glen.

"Hang on," he laughed, gently protesting. "I haven't promised anything. OK? I haven't promised anything."

Sue became demure and looked at him sheepishly. "No, darling, I understand that. You haven't promised anything."

When Dave returned to the job of driving, he heard her softly say, "Not yet!"

CHAPTER 6

As the Parkers drove away from Ballymore Glen, the Condons pulled up.

"Are you sure this is the place, Arthur?" Camilla Condon asked her husband. "We're in the middle of nowhere."

"Of course it is. Can't you read, woman?" He gestured to the huge *For Sale* signs posted up on either side of the gates.

"She has a point about this place, Pa! We are in the back of beyond! Why can't we live in Dublin?" one of Arthur Condon's seventeen-year-old boys piped up from the back seat of the car.

"Oh, I don't know, Seb. This place might have its charms," Max elbowed his twin brother in the ribs and pointed to the Jerry Hall look-alike who was waving at the redhead holding the clipboard. The blonde bombshell was mounting the steps of a private plane parked on the driveway.

"Good Lord, that's a plane," Camilla Condon spluttered as their Volvo pulled up outside.

"Well done, Ma," Seb sighed.

"Did you see her?" Max enthused. "If she lives here, I think I'd be able to find a way or two of amusing myself."

"Now, Max, don't even think about fraternising with her," said his father. "That's why we're here in the first place. Remember?"

"Don't remind me," Max moaned from the back seat.

Arthur Condon parked his old Volvo on the grass verge outside the gates of Ballymore Glen. He looked older than his fifty years, probably due to a life of partying a little too hard. He had lost most of his hair and filled out considerably in the last decade, but what he lacked in physical appearance he amply made up for in joviality. Arthur was always able to see the funny side of a situation, often to the frustration of his wife. There was little doubt that the boys had inherited their wild and feckless ways from their father. The big difference between Arthur and his twin boys however was that Arthur had the uncanny ability of *getting away with it*. The twins were always caught. When they were just thirteen, Camilla had found them drinking and cavorting with their baby-sitter. She was furious. Arthur on the other hand gave them a lecture on being more discreet. It was academic really because the boys ignored both their parents. They continued to live life to the fullest and they continued to get caught. That was why they were now in Ballymore Glen. Arthur had built up a very successful legal practice in Epsom in Surrey. His heart attack three years earlier, however, had forced him into early retirement. Although the practice continued to make him money, there was no real need for him to stay in Surrey or indeed England. When the boys were expelled from yet another public school there was only one real solution in Arthur's mind. He decided to move the family back to his homeland. At first Camilla and the boys thought he was joking. Arthur had indeed been born in Ireland but had left it when he was a baby and he hadn't been back since. He often talked of his 'homeland' but nobody took him too seriously. Not until now. Arthur had seen an advert for Ballymore Glen in the Sunday papers the previous week and had promptly booked a ticket for the car and four passengers on the boat to Ireland. Now here they were.

"The houses are rather nice," Camilla commented. She was still not sold on the idea of moving countries. "Their Bishop of Llandof really is rather spectacular!"

"You see a bishop, Ma?" Max asked incredulously.

"No, the plant, darling," she explained impatiently.

Patricia strode up to them as they tentatively walked in through the large private gates.

"Hello," she smiled, introducing herself and checking the Condons off on her precious clipboard. She explained that there was a guide posted at each house for their convenience and no, private planes were not permitted to use the driveway as a runway.

"Hello, precious!" Seb appeared beside his mother.

His effect on Patricia was visible. She blushed violently, her pink cheeks clashing wildly with her auburn hair.

"I wonder could you be my personal guide?" he said as he kissed her hand.

"Sebastian!" Arthur called after his wayward son as the Condons headed off towards the first house.

"Perhaps some other time," Seb suggested as he kissed Patricia's hand again and gave her one of his smouldering stares.

Max had other plans. "Hey Seb," he called his brother,

"I can feel another opportunity coming on." He smiled wickedly as he whispered his plan to Sebastian.

For several minutes Seb and Max followed Arthur and Camilla around the first house. They "Oooed" and "Aahed" at all the interesting bits. Then gradually they began to look at other rooms in the house.

"Stay near," Camilla called to them absently but the boys were gone.

"OK," Max rubbed his hands together. "So many houses, so little time! Pick a number, Seb."

"I rather liked the little redhead at the front gate."

"Come on, brother, how can you get anywhere with her if she has to stand at the front gate all day. Now, pick a number, other than number one of course – we can't exactly *explore* that one with Ma and Pa in it."

Seb had a look around. "Well, what do you want?"

Max thought about it. "I haven't had a good shag in days. I could do with a few." His eyes lit up. "I know, I'll take the even numbers, you take the odd. Let's see how many shags we can get into our first day in Ireland!"

"Now you're thinking," Seb agreed.

The boys gave each other their habitual high five and headed off to houses two and three. Max ran up to the front door of number two. It was wide open and a cute little blonde girl stood just inside clasping a bunch of brochures.

"Quick," he whispered urgently, "we haven't got much time."

"Oh hello," Francesca Murray smiled at her new guest. "Can I show you around?"

"I rather hope so." He smiled at her charmingly as he took her by the hand and pulled her upstairs.

Seb Condon, who some argued was the better-looking of the two, used a slightly softer approach. At home, their friends teased them both about being so utterly wicked to young ladies, but of the two Seb was a little more gentlemanly. He took his time and enjoyed himself. With Max it was wham, bang – shit, is that the time? Seb was known by his friends as Sublime Seb while his utterly remorseless twin brother was known as Mad Max. It was difficult to see which of the boys was the better-looking because they were actually identical twins. There was, however, one striking difference. Sublime Seb had sultry, dark brown hair and Mad Max's was blond. They had been small and stocky when they were young but suddenly, around the age of twelve, the two shot up. Now they were both over six foot tall. Long and lithe, their physical appearance was definitely inherited from their mother. The boys looked like racehorses. They were as hyperactive as racehorses too. They each had straight hair, which seemed to be the bane of their mother's life. They insisted on wearing it short at the back but with long fringes, falling lazily into their eyes.

"You'll go blind," Camilla tried to talk reason to them regularly.

"The girls love it," Max tried to explain to her equally regularly.

As usual, Seb's dark fringe fell casually over his left eye as he walked up to house number three.

Lauren sat on a chair inside the door reading the house brochure.

"*Knock, knock!*" Seb gave her a lopsided grin as he stood in the door frame.

"Oh, I'm sorry. I didn't see you standing there. I was

miles away." Lauren was flustered to see such an attractive young man standing at the door.

"Do you not want to be here?" he asked playfully. "Perhaps this is not such a good buy after all!"

"Oh, of course I do. Ballymore Glen is a wonderful place to be," Lauren tried to reclaim some sort of control and get back into her sales pitch.

"Ah yes, Ballymore Glen," Seb looked around the front hallway of number three as if he was a prospective buyer.

"Yes, Ballymore Glen," Lauren echoed. She considered asking him if he was thinking of buying himself but as she thought about the extortionate viewing fee she decided to keep her mouth shut. "Can I show you around?"

"Yes, please. What's your name?" Seb looked straight into her eyes in a way that made her very uncomfortable.

"I'm Lauren. What's your name?"

"I'm Seb. Well, Sebastian, but please call me Seb."

"You're not Irish, are you, Seb?"

"No, I'm English. Is that a problem?"

"God no," Lauren laughed, admiring Seb's long body and thinking how nice it would be to have somebody like him as a neighbour.

"Are you from around here?" he interrupted her thoughts.

"Yes, actually, I live very close. You can even see my house from upstairs –" she trailed off when she saw the look in his eyes.

"Upstairs?" he whispered.

Lauren nodded mutely. Seb took her by the hand and smiled gently at her.

"Well then," he said. It was barely audible. "Let's go upstairs."

Lauren couldn't believe this was happening to her. It had to be a dream. Gorgeous guys didn't walk into your life and take you by the hand and lead you up the stairs. It just didn't happen.

Seb walked into the nearest bedroom he saw, holding Lauren's hand ever so gently all the time. To his delight all the rooms were furnished. Beds were so much more comfortable than the floor or the ground.

He took Lauren in his arms as if it was the most natural thing in the world to do.

"You said you lived close," he whispered into her ear. "Is it this close?"

Lauren could smell his aftershave. She didn't trust herself to talk so she just shook her head.

He held her a little more tightly and whispered into her ear again. This time he let his lips brush up against her earlobe.

"Is it this close?"

She shook her head again.

Then Seb looked deep into her eyes. "Then, Lauren, it must be this close," he brought his lips down onto hers and kissed her gently. She didn't fight him.

Lauren's mind was spinning. This was definitely the craziest thing that had ever happened to her. Five minutes ago she had been bored to tears sitting at the front door of number three and now here she was, in the master bedroom of this palatial building, being gloriously covered in kisses by this beautifully spoken, sultry sex-god. What the heck, she thought, life is too short not to live on the wild side every now and then. I'll probably never see him again, even if he does buy this house – Mum's probably going to sell Innishambles. Their gentle

89

kisses soon turned into an industrial necking job. It felt like Seb had three pairs of hands. They were everywhere. She didn't even feel him undo her bra strap, but it was definitely undone. When she stopped kissing him for a moment to look at him accusingly his wicked grin only succeeded in making her laugh. Then he began to slide his hand inside her pants.

Lauren adored the sensation, but sanity prevailed.

"Hang on," she pleaded breathlessly, "this is crazy."

"Why?" he grinned, unwilling to lose the momentum.

"Why? Seb, you're asking me why? Look, we barely know each other and yeah, this is a little wild, but if you think I'm going all the way with you, you're sadly mistaken."

"Why ever not?" Seb looked genuinely shocked.

"You're not in bloody Soho now, sunshine!" she barked as she climbed off the bed they had somehow ended up on and began to right her clothes.

"Sebastian! Maximilian!" A woman with a very strong Surrey accent called from the driveway. It was so loud they could hear her from the bedroom. Seb jumped up and started to tuck his shirt back into his trousers. "Sorry, gorgeous, I have to go. Perhaps we can continue this delicious meeting at a later date."

He took her hand gallantly and gently brushed the back of it with a kiss. Then he turned her hand over and softly kissed the delicate white skin on the inside of her wrist. The action made her shiver with pleasure. He saw her reaction and grinned, "Until next time," and then bounded down the stairs. Lauren ran to one of the bedrooms at the front of the house to watch him go. She was sorry now that their little encounter was over. It had been delicious. As she watched him run out of the front door of number three, a nearly identical young man, only with blond hair, was running out of number four. He was still pulling on his shirt.

"What the – ?" Lauren was confused. They had to be twins, they were so alike. Was the other guy up to no good with the girl next door? Stephanie Butler was in number four – surely not! That's disgusting, she thought, suddenly feeling a lot worse about her little session. The woman who had called the boys was visibly chastising them as she dragged them off to view number ten across the road.

Confirming her darkest fears, the boys gave each other a high five and followed their mother.

It was strictly against the rules to leave your designated house but Lauren didn't care. She had to talk to Stephanie Butler in number four. Things had been very quiet in the last half hour. There had been no more prospective buyers through her house. A quick chat wouldn't do any harm.

She left the door to number three open and ran as fast as she could across the beautifully manicured lawns and over the wall that separated the two houses. By now she was crying to herself.

"Steph, are you OK?" Lauren asked.

"Yes, of course I am. Why wouldn't I be?" Stephanie snapped as she tried to hide her face.

"Steph, I'm sorry, it's just I had this, well, this weird experience with a client just now and then –" she stalled trying to find the right words. "Well," said Lauren, "I think his mother called him and he ran out of the house and met up with another guy coming out of your house."

Stephanie looked up at Lauren hopefully. "Oh, Jesus, Lauren. You too? We are right idiots, aren't we?"

"Why?"

"Oh, your one didn't tell you? They were twins – Seb and Max. They were having a competition to see who could shag the most girls in one afternoon. Can you believe that? The bastards!"

Lauren couldn't believe it. She collapsed onto the chair next to Stephanie.

"The fuckers," was all she could muster.

"Naturally Max didn't say anything until after –" she couldn't finish her sentence.

Then Lauren realised what Stephanie was saying. "Ohmigod, you went the whole way with him, Steph?"

"Well, yeah, you did too, didn't you?"

"No."

"Ah, come on, Lauren, I don't believe you got all that upset over saying 'no' to him!"

"I did – I didn't. I mean I did say no. I didn't bonk him," Lauren tried to defend herself but Stephanie chose not to believe her.

"Yeah, whatever you say, Lauren, but you could at least be woman enough to own up to it. Little Miss-Goody-Two-Shoes!"

"Stephanie, I swear! Nothing happened. Or rather it did. But it wasn't that much if you know what I mean."

"No, I don't." Stephanie sniffed. "Well, you'd better get back to your house before you're caught mitching on top of everything else."

Reluctantly Lauren went back to number three. She was just in time as another couple were walking up the driveway to view it. Distracted though she was, Lauren was pretty sure that the guy who wore the dark sunglasses was in fact Chris De Burgh!

What was left of the afternoon passed by relatively uneventfully. Finally, Patricia went around each of the ten houses with the minibus, to collect the various guides.

Lauren was the third collected. She went down to the back row to sit beside her older sister's friend, Francesca Murray. Then it occurred to her.

"Hey, Fran, if you were in number two, did you have a visit from a young Etonian type earlier on?"

"Visit?" Francesca laughed. "The man took me to heaven and back again!"

"What? Did you have sex with him?"

"You bet your sweet ditty I did! Max was his name. He called himself Mad Max and with good reason," she chuckled. "He was the best I've had in ages." The twenty-one-year-old sighed. "Ah, it's true what they say about younger men! He was only seventeen, but what assets!"

The minibus had stopped to let Stephanie Butler get on.

"Don't talk about it any more. He visited Stephanie after you and she doesn't have such liberal views. OK?"

Francesca laughed. "Why get your knickers in a knot over it? It was fun! God, people can take life too seriously!"

Stephanie got on the bus and looked mutinously at the two down the back. She chose to sit beside Elizabeth O'Dwyer, the girl who was showing house number one.

"Stephanie!" Francesca called her.

Lauren tried to keep the peace. "Fran, please don't."

Stephanie turned around to face Francesca.

"What did you think of the blond bombshell?" Francesca laughed.

Stephanie looked horrified. She hastily turned her back on Francesca and Lauren and looked dead ahead.

"Ah, Stephanie, where's your sense of fun? He was a good shag, wasn't he? Mad Max!"

Steph had heard enough and couldn't ignore it any longer. She marched down to the back seat.

"Could you please keep your voice down, Francesca? I don't think it's a bragging matter."

"I do. He was the best I've had in weeks. I tell you, he could teach the Wicklow guys a thing or two!"

Lauren was waiting for Stephanie to take a swing at Francesca but to her amazement she heard Steph start to laugh. It went from a light chuckle to a splutter and from a splutter to a big belly laugh. Quite suddenly the two girls who had enjoyed Max's 'attention' that afternoon were in hysterics, laughing together. Lauren was quietly amazed at how easily Stephanie's mood had changed. Shakespeare was right – *nothing's either good nor bad but thinking makes it so.*

"He's still a bastard," Steph said as she wiped away the tears, only this time they were tears of laughter.

"Hey," Francesca defended him, "it takes two to tango!"

"Yeah? Well, I mightn't have danced if I'd known I was his second waltz of the afternoon!"

"Look at it this way," Francesca continued. "I only warmed him up for you."

"Revved him up more like!" Stephanie burst out laughing again. "God, he knew what he was doing!"

"And that gorgeous blond hair!"

Francesca moved forward so she could whisper to

Lauren and Steph. Patricia was busying herself collecting the rest of the guides.

"I actually think you got the best of him because unless I'm very much mistaken, he also managed a quick *union* with Patricia just before they left. He must have been fairly knackered by then." They all crumpled into laughter again.

Lauren however was shocked to realise that she was the only one who hadn't gone through with it, so to speak.

Stephanie read her thoughts. "What are you saving yourself for, Lauren?" She giggled. "Why did you stop Seb from making you happy?"

Lauren thought about it. "I don't know really. I suppose I'm just so used to saying no, it never really occurred to me to say yes, although it was a lot of fun."

Francesca looked at her friend's baby sister. "In fairness, Lauren, you're still a bit young. Damn it, you're still at school! We're all a few years older than you. I forgot about that. Sorry, I shouldn't be exposing you to my wicked ways!"

Lauren was stung. "I'm old enough! I'm doing my Leaving this year."

Francesca winked at her. She didn't want to start a fight so she dropped the subject of age. "Hey," her eyes lit up, "imagine getting the two of them together!"

To Lauren's amazement, the minibus had pulled up outside Innishambles. As she disembarked, Patricia spoke to her. "I'm not sure if there'll be another viewing day. If there is, can you come?"

Lauren could hear Francesca and Stephanie explode into laughter down at the back of the minibus as they took the double meaning out of Patricia's question.

"Oh, I think I could make myself available," Lauren smiled.

"Great. I'll count you in. You know the lay of the land now."

The two girls down the back were practically falling around laughing.

"A great lay, by all accounts," Lauren mumbled.

"What did you say?" Patricia looked suspicious.

"A great day by all accounts, Patricia. Please do count me in."

CHAPTER 7

Raymond Saunders didn't even notice the admiring glances that he was getting as he helped Jayne Mullins with her chair in Dali's restaurant, but she did. Jayne returned the looks with something more reminiscent of a proprietorial wolf than a gracious dinner companion. The message Jayne sent out was clear: 'He's very much spoken for. Get on with your own life.'

Oblivious to the goings-on, Raymond sat down opposite his nanny, "What did you think of Ballymore Glen?" he asked.

"I liked it a lot, Raymond. However, I would be worried about moving the children so far out of town."

"Yes, I agree, Cedar Close in Cabinteely was very nice too and of course it's so convenient to the city. It's just that there is so much space in Ballymore Glen. The kids could really spread their wings. They might even like to get a few ponies."

"What makes you think they even want ponies, Raymond?" Jayne laughed. "Your children are used to the city. I'm genuinely worried about how they would

handle the move, especially after the year they've had."
She touched on the one subject that made Raymond
Saunders pale. Any reference to his late wife Caroline
made him vulnerable and Jayne knew what she was
doing.

"Yes, perhaps you're right. OK, you prefer Cedar
Close. It's crazy that the two houses could be going for
the same money, isn't it?" Raymond's eyes sparkled. "I
mean there's a tiny garden in Cedar Close and acres of
land in Ballymore Glen with a tennis court and a pool!"

"But it's miles away," Jayne continued to argue as she
began to study the menu.

Raymond sighed and picked up his menu too. "Of
course you're right, Jayne. You're always right. Where
would the kids and I be without you?"

"Out in the middle of the country, it would seem," she
laughed as she flirted gently with him.

The restaurant was frantically busy as was the norm
for a Friday night in Blackrock, but the waiters were
unfazed and in control of the situation. Raymond had not
even had a reservation. He hadn't even realised that he
was hungry until Jayne mentioned that she was starving.
The kids were safe and happy with his in-laws and so he
gave Dali's a ring. One of the advantages of producing
the best beef in the country was that he had a good
relationship with most of the top restaurants. When the
restaurateur heard that Raymond Saunders was looking
for a table, he quickly produced one of his best.

Raymond's motto for life was: "Produce the best
quality, play fair and you won't go too far wrong." It had
served him well. He had a good reputation in Ireland and
in Europe where he was now doing more and more

business. Jayne kept his home life running smoothly. She had been with the Saunders family for the last four years and Caroline had liked her. Then again Caroline had liked everybody. She could never see the bad in anybody. She had always looked for the good in people and usually found it. Caroline was terrifically popular and Raymond used to tease her that she loved other people more than she loved him. She was a real people person. She would stop and talk to anybody anywhere. It used to drive Raymond mad because he was quite shy and he would feel awkward when she stopped the car to pick people up at a bus stop when it was raining. Her friends used to call her Meg because she looked like Meg Ryan. She had short blonde hair and big blue eyes. Caroline Saunders was the light of Raymond's life. Since she died, the light had gone out. All three children had her spirit and vivacity which Raymond was grateful for. Only now, without her to guide them, they were considerably more moody and difficult. When Caroline was diagnosed with pancreatic cancer at the ridiculously young age of thirty-five, she simply didn't believe it. Raymond and she only had a few precious months together before she died and Jayne had been a tower of strength. She moved into the house and started to spend a lot more time with the children. Jayne became a surrogate mother while Caroline was still alive. This gave Raymond and his late wife a few more precious moments together but now, with hindsight, he realised that perhaps the children suffered from not having had enough time with their mother. The truth was that there was never enough time when somebody was diagnosed with cancer. Jayne had tried to console him but Raymond was still racked by guilt. He felt guilty because he couldn't save his wife, guilty because he didn't share Caroline more with his children when she became ill, and he still felt guilty now because he didn't ever seem to get enough time with the kids.

After Caroline died, Jayne didn't move out.

"You look worried," Jayne said.

"I'm sorry. Not much company, am I?"

"Are you thinking about Caroline?" Jayne asked gently.

"Yeah, and the kids. It's just all so difficult to know what to do."

"I'm here."

He looked at her as if she was telling him something he had forgotten.

"Yes, you are, and you're the wind beneath my wings, Jayne."

"Fish or fowl?"

"What?" He didn't understand.

"What are you going to eat, Raymond? Don't forget you love the sea bass here."

"That's right, fish it is." They placed their orders and settled down with a nice bottle of Sauvignon Blanc. If Raymond didn't notice the admiring glances that he was receiving, he did notice the looks that Jayne attracted.

"Hey, you're getting the serious one-two from that table over there, Jayne," he whispered over their starters.

Jayne giggled. "Is he cute?" she asked, not wanting to turn around.

"How the hell would I know? Is he cute indeed? Actually, it's *they* and not *he* but you'll have to turn around and have a look yourself."

"I couldn't possibly do that. That's playing far too easy. You know that it's different for girls!"

"How's a guy to win?" Raymond sighed helplessly but he smiled at her as said it. He knew that this was the time to bring up a matter that had been on his mind for some time now.

"Speaking of admiring glances, Jayne . . ."

She looked straight at him, hearing the change in his tone. "Yes?"

"Well, there is something we need to discuss."

Jayne held her breath. She had done everything she could think of. She ran Raymond's house as efficiently as possible. She minded his children, minded him. She even took his two disgusting Rottweilers to the grooming parlour once a month.

"Jayne, you're such a help to me and the kids, I don't know quite how to say this . . ."

She held her breath. Say it, say it, her mind begged him telepathically but her face stayed utterly blank and her body language was calm.

Raymond was oblivious to her thoughts. "It's just that, I don't want you to miss out on your own life because you're baby-sitting me and the kids so well."

Shit, she thought to herself. Remaining composed, she laughed. "Ah relax, Raymond! I'm not missing out on anything."

"But that's just it. You are. Look at you, Jayne. You're gorgeous. You're young and full of life. You have beautiful long blonde hair and big blue eyes. OK, you're a little too skinny –" he smiled, "that's something we'll never agree on! But you're so good-looking and God knows you're amazing with kids. You should be out there living life. Otherwise it will pass you by. Believe me, you're talking to one who knows."

"Finished?" she asked as she finished her own starter. Then she replied. "Firstly, thank you for all your compliments. I'm glad you think I'm such a fine thing, but you're leaving out one very significant point. I'm very happy. I don't want to go out with one of those yobbos over there." For the first time she glanced over at the table that Raymond had referred to earlier and confirmed her suspicions. They were yobbos. Nobody could stand up to Raymond Saunders in her eyes. That was her problem. Jayne knew she had a serious challenge in her boss, but she didn't see how she had any choice. He was quite simply the only man for her.

"Well, OK, those guys may not be to your liking, but what about some other guy?" Raymond asked, genuinely perplexed at her lack of libido.

"Oh, the right man will come along. Wait till you see." She winked at Raymond.

"Not if you're out with me all the time," he laughed.

"You know not the place nor the hour," she teased.

As their main courses arrived, Jayne decided to take the chance. After all, he had brought the subject up.

"What about you?" she asked.

"What about me?"

"Have you thought about getting involved with anybody else yet?"

Raymond burst out laughing at the ridiculous notion. "Are you joking?"

"Of course not!" She looked indignant.

"Ah, Jayne, I'm sorry –it's just, well, I'm not exactly Mr Eligible any more, am I?"

"Why ever not?"

"Hello, Jayne! I have three kids and you above all

people know what a full-time job they are and I also have enough emotional baggage to start an airline strike."

"That's rubbish. The kids are terrific and of course you come with emotional baggage. Who doesn't?"

"Well, the truth is I don't want another person in my life. I can't imagine anyone being able to replace Caroline." He looked sombre.

"I understand," Jayne said gently, "but you can't spend the rest of your life alone, Raymond. That would be a double tragedy. To be honest, I don't think Caroline would approve."

Raymond looked at Jayne sharply. "With all due respect, Jayne –"

Damn it, she thought hastily – she had pushed it too far. "I'm sorry, I shouldn't have said that." She looked at her food guiltily.

"No, I'm sorry. I know you mean well, it's just – hell, I'm not quite ready for that hurdle yet."

"Look," she said, trying to change the subject, "you haven't even tried your sea bass. Try it and tell me if it's as good as usual."

"Raymond? Raymond Saunders? Is that you?" A very high-pitched voice filled the entire restaurant, causing half the patrons to look at Raymond's mortified face.

"Oh Christ, it's Cassandra Booth-Everest."

"Who?"

"Ah, she's one of the landed gentry set in Meath. Major PITA."

"Major what?"

"PITA," Raymond whispered. "Jasmine taught me that last night. Pain in the ass!"

Jayne erupted with laughter as Cassandra Booth-

Everest descended upon their table with the purpose and speed of a D-Day torpedo.

"Raymond, you bad bad boy! What are you doing here?"

Raymond stood to greet the lady, gently embracing her and attempting to kiss her on the cheek, only she air-kissed him from about ten inches away and so he didn't come anywhere near her heavily made-up face.

"And who do you have here?" Cassandra looked down her rather generous nose and three chins at Jayne, who had remained sitting.

"Cassandra, this is Jayne Mullins. Jayne, this is Cassandra Booth-Everest."

"You bad bad boy," she repeated at Raymond, utterly ignoring Jayne. "Why didn't we see you at the hunts earlier this year?"

"Cassandra, I've never hunted," Raymond laughed.

"Why ever not?" she asked incredulously. "Everybody should hunt. Do you hunt?" Cassandra momentarily turned her attention towards Jayne.

"No, I'm more of a roller-blader myself," Jayne smirked. She and Jasmine, Raymond's nine-year-old daughter, had tried to teach Raymond the finer points of roller-blading the previous weekend.

"You should try it sometime, Cassy," Raymond smiled.

"I rather think not," Cassandra dismissed them. "Raymond, tell me, when can you come out of mourning? Is that what they call it these days? I would love for you to come to one of my social evenings."

Jayne was horrified at the way this objectionable woman was attempting to smooch up to her boss.

"I'm not in mourning, Cassy," Raymond said rather curtly. "I am however a father of three and, as such, not much of a social evening kind of guy." His slightly acerbic tone was lost on Cassandra.

"Nonsense. Lots of my guests are on their second significant others!" Then her eyes flashed as if something had just dawned on her. "Oh, I see, you and Jennifer here . . ." she let the suggestion hang.

"It's Jayne actually, Cassy, and no. Jayne is my nanny. She minds Jasmine, Edward and Francis for me. She's a treasure." He smiled down at his dinner companion.

"Really, Raymond, you shouldn't take your house staff out to dinner. They will get notions above their station." Cassandra was horrified and totally indifferent to the fact that Jayne could hear what she said.

Jayne, on the other hand, couldn't believe what she had witnessed. Her anger flared faster than her self-control. She stood up and faced Cassandra.

"How dare you speak about me like that? My relationship with Raymond is absolutely none of your business. And as for notions –"

"Ladies, ladies," Raymond was acutely aware of the entertainment that they had become for the restaurant. He glared at Jayne to make her sit down again and began to guide Cassandra away.

"Where are you sitting, Cassy? I'm sure your guests are waiting for you."

"Really, Raymond! I think you should get rid of that girl. It's quite obvious that she has already got above herself."

"I'll talk to her later."

"Yes, yes, do that. Now, about my social evenings.

You really must come. Eligible men are so hard to come by these days, especially attractive ones. Georgie and I have just moved into a darling new house in Cabinteely. You must come and visit."

Raymond spotted George Booth sitting in a corner table. He was surrounded by a grey cloud of cigar smoke and talking to two people Raymond didn't recognise. As he guided Cassandra towards her husband's table he asked casually, "Where have you bought in Cabinteely, Cassy?"

"Oh, it's an utterly new development. *Très chic*, you know. They're called Cedar Close. Perhaps you know them?"

"Yes, I do, as a matter of fact." Raymond smiled at her as he deposited her into her seat.

"Raymond Saunders! Well, I'll be damned," George Booth waved his arms above his head in a futile attempt to disperse the cigar smoke. "Haven't seen you in an age! Come, come join our group."

Raymond actually thoroughly enjoyed George Booth's company and had to admire the man for taking on the challenge of Cassandra as a wife, regardless of how many millions she had brought as a dowry.

"George, good to see you," he pumped his hand. "I'm afraid I can't stay, however. I'm actually dining with someone."

"He's dining with his nanny," Cassy whispered loudly to her table.

"You old dog!" George laughed conspiratorially at him.

"No, it's not like that, folks. Actually we were house-hunting ourselves today – that's why we're only getting back to town now."

Cassandra nearly fell off her seat in excitement. "Oh Raymond, there are still some houses available in Cedar Close. Come and live near us! We could see each other every day! Wouldn't that be just divine?"

"Divine," Raymond copied her, realising that there was now no way he could live in Cedar Close. Cassy wasn't the worst – she was really quite harmless but not the sort of person you wanted to live next door to.

Jayne was in a foul mood by the time Raymond returned.

"How do you know that fat slag?"

"Now, Jayne, that's not very nice."

"What a bitch!"

"Yes, she was a little hard on you. Sorry about that. She is kind of yester-world."

"I've never come across her before. How do you know her?" Jayne could not be appeased.

"Look, Jayne, I know her from school socials, if you must know. Her father practically owns County Meath. They're massive beef producers. I do a lot of business with him."

"She looks like a fine heifer herself!"

Raymond had to laugh. "She is rather generously proportioned."

"Generous? I'd say her milk yield would challenge the national milk quota! Kind of unfortunate her surname is Everest, isn't it? I mean, she is the size of a mountain!"

"Actually," Raymond explained as he poured them both some more wine, "her great-grandfather, or was it her great-great – anyway one of them – was the first up Mount Everest from some particular aspect. To be honest, I can't remember the whole story. He went up the east or the west side or whatever. Anyway, he was the first person ever to do it and so he changed his name to Everest by deed poll to mark the occasion."

"If his wife looked anything like Cassandra, I'm not surprised that he went off climbing mountains," she scowled.

Raymond was relieved to see that she was calming down. "Look, I really am sorry. She's a bit thick."

"A bit? So where does the Booth bit fit in?"

"Her husband is George Booth."

"So she was Cassandra Everest before she got married?"

Raymond nodded.

"I bet she was considerably easier to mount than her namesake."

"And a lot less frosty," Raymond winked at Jayne.

As the night wore on Jayne relaxed. She even had dessert at Raymond's insistence.

"You know if I look at food I put on weight," she wailed.

"You're too skinny, Jayne. Please have some."

She sighed, not as resolute as usual because of the amount of wine in her system. "Oh, OK, just this once and just for you." As they moved from wine to Irish coffees, Jayne felt her head begin to spin a little.

"I think I'd better visit the ladies'," she explained as she attempted to stand.

"Are you all right?" Raymond was concerned.

"Ferfectly pine," she answered.

He laughed and watched her as she concentrated very hard in order to avoid bumping into any of the tables between her and the ladies' loo door.

Jayne pushed open the door and saw Cassandra applying yet another layer of cherry-red lipstick onto her chubby lips. Even her lips are fat, Jayne thought mutinously.

"Oh hello," Cassandra said she as saw Jayne in the mirror. She appeared to have forgotten the altercation earlier. "Raymond told me that you were house-hunting this afternoon. You must try and convince him to buy a house in Cedar Close. We've just moved in. Wouldn't that be fun? You could mind my two little angels too!"

Jayne couldn't believe it. Her face must have reflected some of her horror because Cassandra added, "I would pay you, of course."

"Did you tell him that you had bought in Cedar Close?"

"Yes. Why?"

But Jayne had gone.

She stumbled out of the loo, completely forgetting that she hadn't even peed.

"When were you going to tell me that they lived in Cedar Close?" she demanded of Raymond as soon as she got back to the table.

"What's wrong?"

"The mountain – Everest! She lives in Cedar Close."

"Oh yes, so it would appear."

"When were you going to tell me that?"

"I don't actually know, but it wasn't going to be tonight. You were a little too – well, I know that you're not her biggest fan."

"She's a horror! Jesus, Raymond, we can't live next to that! And she has kids – God knows what they must be like."

"Do you hate her enough to actually go off Cedar Close?"

"Yes."

"Are you telling me that you would now prefer to live in Ballymore Glen?"

"Yes."

"Christ, but you're fickle! What about being miles out of town and the kids having to change schools?"

"They'll get used to it!"

"I don't believe this. Well, as it happens, I much prefer Ballymore Glen. So that's it. Decision made. We're moving to Ballymore."

CHAPTER 8

"I want this house the cleanest it has ever been! Lauren, where are you? Kelly, what are you doing now?" Saskia issued commands around Innishambles that would have made any field marshal proud.

"Where the blazes is Tiffany? She's been gone ages. It doesn't take that long to do a little shopping and pick up a few bunches of flowers!"

Lauren joined Saskia in the hall.

"Mum, will you please calm down? You're panicking. The house looks terrific. Tiffany and Robin only left ten minutes ago."

"I'm not panicking, am I? God, I'm sorry, Lauren. It's just that I've never sold a house before and the idea of putting our home on show terrifies me! I just want people to see it at its best – you understand, don't you?"

Lauren smiled sympathetically at her mother. She wanted Saskia to calm down, but she couldn't bring herself to say that she understood. The girls were still at loggerheads with Sas for putting the house on the market in the first place.

"Everything will be fine, you'll see," she soothed Saskia. "What's Tiffany buying that's so important anyway? The house is bursting with polish and Cif."

"No, she's buying flour and sugar. I completely forgot," Saskia explained. "I read somewhere once that a house is more desirable if there is s smell of freshly cooked bread in the kitchen."

"Oh, Mum," Lauren laughed, "don't tell me that you're going to have Vivaldi's *Four Seasons* playing in the drawing-room too."

"No, Bach," Saskia looked uncomfortable.

"Oh yeah," Lauren laughed, "and everybody that comes in will light up a great big cigar!"

"What are you talking about?" Saskia looked perplexed.

"Bach's *Air on a G String* – even I know that that particular piece of music was destroyed thanks to a cigar ad!"

"That reminds me, will you please light all the fires?"

"All of them? Are you mad? The house will be boiling!" Lauren argued. "Mum, it's the summertime! The sun is even shining today."

"Well, OK, just light the study so and the drawing-room. Oh and the dining-room and my bedroom, please."

"People will see through this. I promise."

"No, they won't. We're selling an ideal here, a way of life. Not just a house."

"You've been reading too many of those sell-your-own-house books!"

For the first time that day Saskia laughed and relaxed. "Well, Lauren, we may as well give it all we've got. We obviously want it to go for the highest price."

"Well, I think it will go for millions," Lauren said.

"You should see those ones down the road that I was showing yesterday. If they can make up to two million, we definitely can!"

"I'd dearly love to see them, Lauren, but I'm not forking out one hundred euro a head until I've seen how popular Innishambles is. Maybe nobody will come."

Lauren could see her mother beginning to fret again.

"Look, Mum, if nobody comes it's not the end of the world. We can go on living here for ever. It's OK."

"No, it's not bloody OK!" Saskia snapped. She looked shell-shocked.

Since receiving Nicolas's phone call, Saskia had realised that there was now absolutely no way that she could turn back. Selling Innishambles had seemed like the smartest move as a way to raise money. That way she could buy a place in Dublin for Tiffany and possibly an apartment in the sun too. She was also convinced that she didn't need such a big house what with Tiffany and probably Kelly moving up and on too. But what had recently seemed like the *smartest move* now felt like the *only move* open to her. With Nicolas totally broke, she had no choice. Nicolas's phone conversation had eaten into her. It had all come as an enormous shock. Little did she realise when she was making the decision to sell that Nicolas was actually completely out of money. The knock-on effects for the village of Ballymore were going to be appalling. Kelly and Barney were going to be out of a job for starters. Obviously Nicolas was not going to be able to subsidise her lifestyle as he had been doing in recent years. Quite the opposite – she was going to have to support him until he got back on his feet again – whenever that would be, she thought in despair. She felt dreadfully guilty about the fact that he had supported her so generously for some time. Little had she realised that he was actually frittering away his nest-egg on their day-to-day living. Well, it was payback time. He had supported and minded her when she needed him and now she would do the same thing for him. One thing she had certainly learned in the last few days was that when she did get them out of this mess, she was going to look after the business and money side of things, not Nicolas! She shivered now as she wondered how the heck she was going to make ends meet.

Lauren saw the uncertainty in her mother's eyes.

"Mum, what's wrong? It's obvious that something is really eating into you."

Saskia looked at Lauren. She couldn't hold it in any longer. Now, at the end of her tether, she let everything spill out to her daughter.

"Lauren, Nicolas has absolutely no money. When I phoned him last Monday, he finally told me the truth. He has gone bust. The man is deeply in debt – I don't know what's to become of him."

Lauren was stunned. "I thought he was loaded!"

"Didn't we all, and I have to admit I drew great security from that. Nicolas paid for all those holidays that he and I took. As you know, your father has supplied well for your schooling and living costs but in truth we have been spending considerably more. Nicolas has been paying for that. Now I feel dreadful. All his money has gone. As for us, we have to learn how to live within our means. I mean *really* within our means."

"Oh shit, this is not good," Lauren fell onto the seat in the hall, "especially with Kelly. Oh shit, shit, shit."

"What about Kelly?" Saskia sensed something serious.

"What? Oh nothing!" Lauren swallowed hard. Kelly had told Lauren and Tiffany that she had quit her job but that was all she had said.

"I know something is up," Saskia persisted. "Last Monday morning Barney told me that Kelly was more or less on her last chance. That evening Kelly told me that it was all sorted out and that she had a week's holiday. I'm not a fool. Something is going on."

Lauren looked at her mother. "This is one you need to discuss with Kelly. I'm not getting involved."

Saskia wouldn't let go however. "Look, Lauren. Have Kelly and Barney had a fight? She's been like a cat on a hot tin roof all week."

"I don't know. Honestly, I don't."

"Well, what do you know?"

"I know that you need to talk to Kelly. That's all."

Despite her frustration, Saskia admired Lauren's steadfast loyalty to her sister. The girl was completely soundproof.

The first indication that Tiffany and Robin were back was the yapping of Woody and Wilma who had been kicked out of the house for the morning. They were utterly fed up and, as if to indicate their disgust, they had taken up residence at the front door with all the attitude of two Rottweilers. Dudley and Dexter ignored their new competition for the position of guard dogs and busied themselves sleeping in the late August sun.

"Hello, Mummy!" Robin barged through the back door and into the kitchen where Saskia and Lauren had come to greet them. "I was talking to Daddy!"

"What is she talking about, Tiffany?"

"I was talking to Dad on the mobile," Tiffany said, feeling decidedly guilty. "Robin heard me call him Dad and wanted to talk to him. She didn't even know who it was – just a voice down the phone."

"You didn't do any explaining then," Saskia asked nervously.

"No, not at all. She thinks she was talking to a man by the name of Daddy, I swear."

"Fine," Saskia replied in a slightly frosty tone. She felt the pressure of introducing Robin to her natural father growing. "I just hope you weren't driving at the time. It's very dangerous."

"Yeah, but it looks cool." Lauren laughed irreverently as she began to unpack the cooking things.

"He wanted to know about the house," Tiffany explained, unable to keep the truth from her mother. "He was a little," she searched for the right word, "shocked."

"Yes, well, it's actually none of his business what we choose to do with it."

"What *you* choose to do with it," Lauren corrected her.

"That's enough, Lauren. Are all the rooms upstairs clean? Where in hell is Kelly?"

"I'm here, Mum. I was cleaning out the stables as you ordered, remember?" She looked as white as snow.

"Kelly, love, you're not well. You'll have to go and see Doctor Harrington," Saskia tried softly.

Lauren and Tiffany looked at their older sister.

Robin picked up the atmosphere. "What's wrong, Kelly?" she asked in her little-girl voice.

Kelly looked around at her family – even the dogs, who had managed to regain entry with Tiffany and Robin, were looking at her.

She burst out crying and collapsed into a chair by the kitchen table.

"It's over. It's all over!"

Saskia rushed to the side of her firstborn. "You and Barney, is that what you mean, pet?"

"No, Mum, my life! It's over! It would be better if I were dead."

"Hush, pet, nothing is ever that bad. Nothing. Come on, tell me what's wrong?"

Saskia pulled a chair over to Kelly's and hugged her daughter, willing her to open her heart. Kelly looked up at her mother. Usually her beautiful brown eyes were big and bright and full of life – today they were full of tears. Slowly one dropped down onto her clear young skin. Kelly wore no make-up but the tear still left a narrow little track. Saskia rubbed it away gently. It broke her heart to see her daughter in such pain.

"OK," Saskia continued, "I give you my word, I will not be in any way angry or judgemental of what you have to tell me. It doesn't matter, it just doesn't matter. Tell me what's wrong, Kelly, and we'll take it from there."

"I'm pregnant."

"You're what?" Saskia jumped up.

"You heard me. I'm pregnant."

"Oh Jesus, Kelly, is this a joke? Please tell me this is a joke! You're not that stupid! How many times have I told you to be careful? Christ, I'm blue in the face trying to get you to the doctor's. I don't believe this." Saskia paced up and down the kitchen, Woody and Wilma following her every step.

"So much for not being judgemental," Kelly scowled as she studied the wood grain of the table.

117

"You must be joking! I thought you were going to tell me that you and Barney were finished or that you wanted to leave your job or something."

"Oh yes, that reminds me. Barney and I are finished and I quit my job," Kelly replied matter-of-factly.

"OK, now I know you're joking! Kelly?"

"No, Mum, I'm not joking." Kelly stood up from the table and looked her mother straight in the eye. "This is very definitely not a joke. I have been doing some thinking about it, however, and the solution as I see it is I'll get a job in Wicklow. If it's OK, I'll live at home, wherever that is, for the next eight months and after the baby is born I'll move out. I'm not sure where yet, but we'll get something small in Wicklow – the baby and me. I'm sorry I've let you down so badly. I've probably let everybody down. Guess that's just typical of me. Well, I'm sorry but what's done can't be undone. I'm not having an abortion, much as Barney would like one."

Tiffany, Lauren and Saskia all gasped.

"Nor am I giving it up for adoption. This is my baby and I'll stand over my responsibility."

Saskia stood and watched in wonder as she realised her eldest daughter was transforming into a woman before her very eyes. The tear-washed eyes were strong and clear now. The jawline was firm and resolute like her father's. Kelly's fists were slightly clenched, prepared to fight with anybody who challenged her plans. Saskia smiled. This was so typical of Kelly. She was a beautiful fragile girl, but faced with some serious resistance, she fought back like a terrier.

Saskia's mind flashed back to her own pregnancy test, just a few days earlier. How could she judge her daughter when she was nearly in the same boat herself? Staring at Kelly now, Saskia realised that she wasn't really angry with her. In fact, she was proud of the woman her daughter was becoming.

"I'm sorry," Saskia started, looking at Kelly, "you are absolutely right."

Kelly was stunned into silence at their mother's sudden turn-about. All the girls looked at her in shock. Saskia took a deep breath and continued. "Kelly, I totally respect your decisions and they are all yours to make. I accept your entire plan and ask only that you consider delaying your plans to move out of the family home."

"Delay by how long?" Kelly looked suspicious.

"Oh, maybe ten or fifteen years!" Saskia smiled tentatively at her daughter. "Your sisters and I would love another baby to play with, darling!"

"Oh Mum," Kelly flew into her mother's embrace and hugged her, almost suffocating Saskia in the process.

"Christ, I'm glad you told me," Saskia commented as things settled down and the girls set about making the bread. "No wonder you've been so sick of late. But Barney . . ." she trailed off.

"He's a bastard!" Lauren spat out.

Kelly glared at her sister for an instant, finding it difficult to let go of her loyalty towards the man. "Yeah, I never would have thought."

"I can't believe it, to be honest," Tiffany added gently, through a cloud of fine flour. She was kneading the bread mixture at the table.

"Believe it, Tiff," Kelly said. "He said that a termination was the only solution."

"Bloody, bloody men," Saskia grumbled as she fed

Robin some lunch. "You can't rely on them for anything." Quietly she wondered how the heck they were going to feed another mouth. Richard definitely wouldn't bankroll this one. In fact, he would be furious. That was another day's problem. "Look, girls, the estate agent will be here in half an hour. Tiffany, can you get that bread into the oven? Lauren, can you do a quick once-over on the house and, Kelly, are you up to checking the outside?"

"Of course, Mum, I'm not an invalid."

"OK, well, as soon as the bread is cooked and the estate agent gets here, we'll move out. I'll just pop the lilies into various vases around the house."

The thirty minutes flew by and the girl from the estate agent's arrived. Saskia was in a blind panic. "Girls, out now! Everything is ready."

Lauren intercepted her mother at the front door as she was trying to get all four dogs into the back of the Land-Rover at the same time – not an easy job.

"Mum, can I have a word?"

"Not now – will you help me? Grab Dexter, where's Woody gone? Those bloody dogs, they get so excited."

"I wonder why," Lauren commented under her breath as she gently guided Dexter into the Land-Rover. "Mum, Tiffany and I want to stay here. Is that OK with you? We want to keep an eye on the house. I asked the girl showing the house and she thinks it's a good idea. There's a lot of valuable stuff here, you know."

Finally getting all the dogs in, Saskia closed over the back door of the car. "Oh, I hadn't thought of that. Are you sure it's OK?"

"Positive."

"Well, all right then, it's probably a good idea. Now

where the hell are Robin and Kelly? My God, if this is just trying to get out of the house for a couple of hours, what are we going to be like when we have to get out of Innishambles for ever?" Saskia laughed nervously.

"Good bloody question, Mum." Lauren couldn't help herself.

Presently Robin and Kelly arrived.

"Now, you have the number of the manor. If there are any problems, just give me a call," Saskia told her middle daughters.

"Goodbye, Mum," Tiffany laughed.

"You'll make sure that the fires stay blazing, won't you?"

"Home is where the hearth is," Lauren nodded. "Goodbye, Mum. Go!"

Reluctantly, Saskia squeezed the accelerator and drove down the lane, out of Innishambles.

"I've got something to do," Tiffany said as soon as her mother's car was out of view, and she ran back into the house.

Lauren went for a wander around her dear old home. She had been born into Innishambles and found it difficult to digest the fact that she would be leaving it soon. She knew every nook and cranny in the building.

The hall was very large and airy. The first room to the right was the study. It was the room they kept the computer in now and it doubled up as a sort of library. The view from the two windows overlooking the front of the house was spectacular. For the first time in Lauren's life, she truly appreciated the beauty of Innishambles. There were a further two windows in the study overlooking the garden to the side of the house. Even that little garden was probably bigger than the front gardens in Ballymore Glen.

"Are we mad?" she whined. "Why do we have to give this up?" Instantly, however, her mind turned to the shocking news that her mother had just dropped on her. Nicolas – broke – wow!

The fire crackled merrily. Richard had worked in the study when he lived in Innishambles, but no one did now. The deep green colour was sombre but it gave an air of relaxation and it was a terrific room to curl up in, with a good book. Opposite the study was the drawing-room. It was a huge reception area and it was great for throwing parties. The double doors led into the dining-room.

"Mum!" Lauren laughed now as she noticed that her mother had set the entire table for a formal dinner party. The crystal and silver shone, while the two fires roared a welcome in each reception room. "This place will be like a furnace in no time," she commented to herself. She had never seen the living-room so tidy and told the estate agent as much as she passed through that room. Upstairs, all the bedrooms were neat and tidy. There were fresh sheets on all the beds and the air was drenched with the scent of fresh lilies. Lauren casually looked out Kelly's bedroom window. She admired the paddock at the front of the house. Mooner and Polly were enjoying the long August grass and Saskia's gardening skills had been utilised to the maximum on the front lawn. The borders were full of colour. Delphiniums danced, sunflowers swayed and roses – Lauren thought about it. "Rocked?" she asked herself out loud. Then she noticed the Volvo driving up the lane.

"Ohmigod, house-hunters!" she screamed. She tore

down the stairs. "Tiffany, they're here!" she called for her sister, needing the moral support. She ran into the kitchen. "Tiffany, who are you on the bloody phone to at a time like this? They're here! The house-hunters are here."

"OK, Dad, I've got to go. Some people are coming. Yeah yeah. I'll see you soon. Bye." Tiffany hung up.

Lauren stopped dead in her tracks.

"Dad? You were talking to Dad?"

"Yes, it's no big deal."

"Tiffany?"

"OK, OK, look, I had to tell him. It just wasn't fair. He didn't even know that the house was on the market."

"All he had to do was open a bloody paper and he would have known," Lauren replied sharply.

"Yes, well, that's why I phoned him this morning and he was very grateful. He asked me did I think it would be OK if he came and had one last look before it was sold."

"Actually, that's kind of sweet."

"I'm glad you think so, because I've just phoned him to tell him that the coast is clear. Mum's gone."

"You little cow! You told me that you wanted to stay to look at the house-hunters – ohmigod that reminds me. Tiff, some are at the door right now!" Lauren grabbed her sister's hand nervously.

"Honestly, Lauren, you're the one that was showing houses all day yesterday. Just look calm and pretend that you've been employed by the estate agents to keep an eye on the valuables –" Tiffany stopped mid-sentence when she saw the young man who walked in.

"Well, well, well, we meet again! Hello, Lauren," Sebastian grinned at her from under his perpetually long dark fringe. He stood in the door frame of the kitchen as if he owned the house. Leaning slightly on one hip he had his right hand in his jeans pocket and held a navy linen jacket casually over his shoulder with the other.

Seb looked from Lauren to Tiffany. He smiled at them wickedly and said, "Delicious!"

CHAPTER 9

"What are you doing here?" Lauren spluttered at him.

"Really, Lauren, you did a better sales pitch yesterday."
Seb grinned lasciviously as he walked into the kitchen
and looked around.

"Oh, this is different. I'm not showing this house.
Look, forget it, this house isn't for sale."

Seb looked at her. "Hang on, you say you're not
showing this house? Ah, now I see. You live *this close*!" He
referred to their conversation of the day before. "Lauren,
is this your house? Are you leaving Ballymore? It won't
be as much fun without you."

"Go away! This house isn't for sale."

He crossed the room to her and tried to take her hand.
"Shhh, Lauren! If you have to sell your rather beautiful
house, wouldn't it be better if somebody you liked was
sleeping in your bed?" He did that thing with his eyebrow
again.

Lauren was annoyed with herself because she could
not control the effect he had on her.

"This is infinitely nicer than the ones we saw

yesterday," Seb continued. "Who owns the two nags out the front?"

"They're not nags. Polly and Mooner are members of our family. Don't talk about them like that," Lauren defended Kelly's horses. She glanced at Tiffany who looked like she was about to pass out.

"Tiff, are you OK? You look like you've seen a ghost?"

"More like a skeleton from the closet," she mumbled, as she grabbed her sister for support.

"You know what you two need?" Seb volunteered.

"Space!" a strong voice as low as a baritone's boomed from the door of the kitchen. "That's what my daughters need."

"Oh hullo," Seb was unfazed. "You must be the owner of this fine house."

"No, actually I'm not. Now why don't you go and find something outside to amuse yourself with. Can I suggest the river? You look like you could do with a little cooling off."

Sebastian knew he was beaten.

"Nice to meet you," Seb grinned confidently at Richard Dalton as he meandered out of the room, still with his jacket draped over his shoulder.

Richard watched the young man as he headed back outside into the August sunshine.

"Daddy!" Tiffany ran into her father's arms.

"Hi, princess," he hugged her back. "Hey, steady on. You weren't in any real danger, you know!"

Lauren, although glad to see her father, was a little sad to see Seb go yet again.

"I'm not sure that you should have been quite so rude, Dad – he might be buying our house!"

"Well, I don't think he will be doing the actual buying. I dare say it would be his parents," Richard reasoned. "And anyway, I'm sure he's heard a lot worse." Richard recognised the effortless charm that the young man wore like a second skin. It was a mantle he had worn for a long time himself. He also knew how dangerous it was for young ladies.

Richard wrapped an arm around each of his daughters' shoulders protectively. "Now to matters much more serious. How are my girls? Are you sure the coast is clear? I don't want to upset your mum."

Tiffany had only slightly regained her composure. "The coast is clear, Dad – she won't come back for two hours. You made terrific time. How did you get here so fast?"

"To be honest, I was just up the road, waiting for your call! I left Dublin straight after you phoned just to make sure I would be here on time. OK, then, why don't you girls give me the guided tour? God, I loved this house! Why is she selling it?"

Tiffany explained. "She says that she wants to buy something smaller and easier to run. But we know the truth, don't we, Lauren? She really wants to buy somewhere out in her blessed Puerto Banus, so she and Nicolas can have fun in the sun!"

Lauren bit her lip, remembering the explanation her mother had given her only an hour earlier.

Tiffany continued, "She also wants to buy an apartment in the city for me to live in when I'm in college."

"But that's ridiculous – you can commute, or you can live with me if you like."

Tiffany looked at her father, wide-eyed with hope. "God, Dad, do you think Edwina would mind?"

Richard winced. Of course Edwina would bloody mind. Edwina minded everything! She was the constant martyr. Everything was a problem to Edwina but Richard needed her so he kept peace with her – most of the time. She had only come to Kelly's party and remained polite because Richard insisted. He had explained that it was all part of his plan to get Saskia back. Like it or not, Saskia was the mother of his children and they were a family. He had to get her back. He wanted things like they were before she got all uppity and, to do that, he was going to have to give her a little attention and work on her a little. Only when she heard this did Edwina agree to come. The cruel, bitter truth was that now that they were gone from her life, Edwina desperately missed her granddaughters. Richard was her only child and so the Dalton girls were her only grandchildren. They were all she had. So, with a massive amount of effort, she had managed to be nice to everyone.

On the other hand, Richard considered the advantages of his daughter living with his mother and himself. Edwina regularly drove him nuts with her constant questions. "What time will you be home? Where were you last night?" Perhaps if Tiffany lived there too it would lighten the atmosphere. If Edwina heard the front door open at five am, he could claim that he was wrapped up in bed. It must have been his daughter! He would promise his mother that he would deal with Tiffany later. The biggest advantage was blindingly obvious, however. It would bring him closer to his ultimate goal – Saskia! Yes, there were definite advantages to this situation.

Tiff was exhilarated. "Can you imagine if I lived with you through the week and here for the weekends. That would be amazing!" she gushed.

"You're forgetting one thing," Lauren interrupted her. "It won't be here."

"Maybe she won't have to sell it if we don't have to buy a place in the city," Tiffany argued.

"Well, actually, there's more to it than that," Lauren continued hesitantly.

"What's wrong?" Richard asked.

"Oh, Daddy, it's such a mess!" Lauren began to cry. Slowly she told Richard and Tiffany everything that Saskia had told her earlier, about Nicolas being broke.

Richard listened quietly, nodding to indicate that he was taking everything in. He could barely hide his delight. This was too good to be true. Mr Bloody Wonderful had fallen on hard times. About bloody time!

"I think Nicolas and Mum are breaking up anyway," said Lauren.

"How can you say such a thing?" Tiffany snapped at her sister.

"Come on, Tiff, don't say that you haven't noticed. When was the last time he phoned her? They used to phone each other three times a bloody day."

"He's in the States. It's expensive."

Lauren laughed. "OK, well, what about the flowers? He used to give her a big bunch every Friday. I haven't seen him do that in ages."

Tiffany again defended her mother's boyfriend. "You said yourself he was broke."

Richard watched the girls talk together. This was the best news. He had bided his time and watched from a distance for over two and a half years. Now, at last it looked like there just might be an opportunity presenting itself. If Nicolas was on the way out, Richard Dalton was on the way back in. He had successfully seduced Saskia once before. He was sure he could do it again. It was time for a little bit of history to repeat itself.

* * *

As Saskia left Innishambles, it occurred to her that she had no idea how she was going to spend her time in the manor.

"I'm just going to get the papers, girls," she explained as she pulled the Land-Rover up outside O'Reilly's. "Kelly, are you OK? You look ill."

The girl shrugged. "I'm just scared of bumping into Barney."

"Do you want me to talk to him?" Saskia offered through clenched teeth.

Kelly looked at her mother and laughed. "I don't think he would survive that."

"Well, you do realise that he has responsibilities towards you and the baby?"

"Mum," Kelly's eyes glassed up, "not now, please."

Saskia nodded and squeezed her eldest daughter's hand.

"I do understand, really I do. We'll talk when you're ready. Have a little rest now. We had a hectic morning." She turned and got out of the Land-Rover. As Kelly watched her go into the shop, she wondered how the heck her mother could possibly know what she was going through. Saskia was separated from Richard now, but they had had a terrific twenty years together before their break. How could she possibly think that she understood what Kelly's situation felt like? It was completely different.

The little bell above the door tinkled as Saskia walked in.

Maureen O'Reilly scurried into the shop from her back room. The O'Reilly home was above and behind the shop and so she could relax in her kitchen, watching the television or doing whatever it was that Maureen did between customers.

"Saskia, it's yourself! I see in the paper that your house is on view today. Is it busy up there?"

"I don't know, Mrs O'Reilly. I left before anybody arrived," Saskia answered patiently.

"And you don't think that maybe you picked a very bad time, what with those lovely *new* ones for sale up in Ballymore Glen?"

"We didn't know about those when we picked our dates, to be honest."

"Oh, I gather they're lovely. Very very modern. Not like your old place!"

Saskia's patience was wearing thin. "Who told you that Ballymore Glen was lovely, Mrs O'Reilly?"

Maureen fumbled. "Barney!" she announced.

Saskia could feel the hairs on the back of her neck stand on end.

"And how the hell would he know? Has he been in them?"

"I don't know."

"Yes, well, Lauren has and she says that they're only slightly above average," Saskia lied.

"Was it milk you wanted?" Maureen O'Reilly hated being beaten in a conversation, especially when it was gossip –her speciality.

"The papers please, Mrs O'Reilly. *The Times* and *The Independent*. Thank you."

They both turned to look at the door as the bell tinkled, heralding the arrival of another customer.

"Barney, it's yourself," Maureen greeted one of her favourites.

Saskia suddenly realised that she was not ready for a confrontation with this man. She still couldn't believe that he wanted Kelly to have an abortion. Saskia threw the money on the counter and strode past Barney, barely acknowledging him.

"What's wrong with her?" Barney asked Maureen.

"Ah, she's got the hump because I was implicating that maybe Ballymore Glen would have nicer houses than Innishambles."

Barney grinned at her creative use of the English language, but knew better than to correct her. He also knew that it would take more than an insult from Maureen O'Reilly to upset Saskia Dalton.

"Are you OK?" Saskia asked her eldest as she climbed back into the car and threw the papers onto the back seat beside Robin.

"Yeah, why wouldn't I be?" Kelly saw her mother's distracted face.

"Barney just walked into O'Reillys – didn't you see him?"

"Ohmigod no, I was just resting here with my eyes shut. He must have walked straight past me!"

"Well, if we move fast, you won't have to see him."

"Papers," Robin announced gleefully as she began to pull the pages apart energetically.

"Ah Kelly, can you save what's left of *The Times* while I get us out of here?" Saskia threw the car into reverse and hit the accelerator. The car whizzed back. Even the dull thud did not register with Saskia until she heard the screams of Sue Parker. Dudley and Dexter were also whining loudly and scratching at the back door of the Land-Rover.

"What the heck is wrong with her?" Saskia snapped as she stopped the car. Barney, who had been walking out of O'Reilly's shop dropped his shopping and ran to the back of Saskia's jeep. Sue Parker had beaten him to it.

It was only as Saskia got out that she realised to her horror – she had hit Guy Parker. He lay motionless on the road beside Saskia's rear inside wheel.

"No, please no!" Saskia screamed. "Dear God in heaven, help!

It was as if by some divine intervention: as Saskia screamed, Guy came round.

"Hey," he whimpered as he tried to sit up. "What happened?" He rubbed his little head.

Saskia saw Barney's shoulders drop with massive relief but Sue Parker wasn't so convinced.

"Guy, are you OK? Can you see me? Where does it hurt? How many fingers am I holding up?"

Guy looked at his mother a little strangely. She was acting very oddly. "One finger and one thumb, silly," he answered. DJ, who had been hovering beside his mother, began to protest.

"Sweeties," he demanded, losing interest in the incident.

Saskia stood beside her neighbour, willing Guy to be OK.

"Mummy, look,"Guy announced proudly, "I'm bleeding!" He rubbed his head and sure enough there was blood on his fingers.

"Ohmigod," Sue looked from him to Barney.

The vet studied Guy's head. "It's OK, Sue. This is only a superficial scratch. He really does seem to be fine."

"Are you quite sure?" Sue asked urgently.

"It's a very small cut but it might need a stitch or at least a tetanus shot. Look, can you take him to Wicklow General?"

"What about India and DJ?"

Barney looked at his watch. "I can take care of them for a while if you like."

"Oh, Barney could you? I'll phone Lisa and tell her what happened. I'm sure she'll take over from you if I end up taking a long time. Would that be OK?"

"Fine," Barney smiled. In truth, now that he was single, he had no idea how he was going to spend his weekend. Usually he and Kelly went out for a ride together or maybe caught a movie. Now that he was alone again, he was lost. Barney's eyes moved from Sue and Guy Parker up to Kelly. She looked pale and thinner if that was possible. She looked away as Barney almost caught her eye. Then carrying her little sister, she walked away from the scene. She must really hate me, he thought. Saskia interrupted his thoughts.

"Sue, Barney, is there anything I can do?" She crouched down beside Guy to talk to them. "I'm so dreadfully sorry. I didn't see him at all," she tried to explain.

Sue reached over to her friend and touched her arm. "Sas, he is a constant nightmare. He has no road sense. I'm always screaming at him to keep his eyes open and watch out for cars."

Guy was enjoying the attention and not remotely phased by his bump. "Hey, am I going to have to go to hospital?" he asked gleefully, interrupting Saskia and Sue's conversation. The two women looked at him and laughed.

"Sas, he'll live."

"But I'm so sorry," Saskia continued. "If there's anything I can do –"

Barney scooped Guy up and put him in the back seat of the Parkers' car making sure he was well strapped in. Then he took India and DJ by their hands.

"How would you two like some sweeties?" he asked playfully. They didn't need to be asked twice.

"Be good for Barney," Sue said as she got into her car. "I'll be home soon." Then she took off for Wicklow hospital.

Saskia, Kelly and Robin watched the car drive away as Barney headed back into O'Reilly's with his two new charges. As she turned around Kelly saw him walk into the shop. How could he hold those two little people's hands and spend a lifetime dedicated to healing, and yet suggest that she terminate his own baby?

The Dalton women climbed back into the Land-Rover and slowly headed up to Rathdeen Manor.

Having retrieved his own shopping and bribed the two Parker children with a criminal amount of sweets, Barney then walked to the Parkers' house, playing with the two youngsters all the way. He couldn't help but wonder what it would have been like to have had children with Kelly.

* * *

Sue Parker was relieved to see that James Harrington had arrived at the hospital before her. She had phoned him from her car. The waiting time in the accident and emergency ward could be hours in Wicklow and she bloody well wasn't going to wait to see if her little boy was going to be OK. James would help her skip the queue. He was standing at the emergency entrance waiting for their arrival.

Guy Parker was whisked straight past all the poor unfortunates who hadn't phoned ahead and was seen to immediately. He was thoroughly enjoying himself. He was made sit on a bed with wheels on it and it was glided into a private examination room. A team of medics descended upon him like a pack of hyenas. Although Sue knew she was in the right place, she felt strangely alienated as she stood next to him and held his hand while the medical people did their bit.

James took control. He shone a small torch in Guy's eyes and played with the little boy as he examined him. He asked him questions about his breathing and asked him to move his hands and feet in various directions. Guy had no problems with any of the doctor's requests. Much to his annoyance, his head had stopped bleeding. Upon examination, however, he was delighted to hear Dr Harrington say that he would need a few stitches.

Sue watched James at work. He really was terrific with children.

He also looked so suave and in control. She couldn't help noticing his long delicate hands, his smooth complexion and his utterly devastating eyes. In his white coat, she trusted him completely. She wasn't sure that the delectable Dr Harrington knew what effect his sincere eyes had on his patients or their mothers! Stop it, she told herself. You're here because of Guy! What kind of woman fantasises about her doctor when her son has just been hit by a car? A woman who's not getting enough attention at home, her mind answered back before she could stop it.

"All right, young man, I'm just going to have a chat with your mummy. Will you mind Nurse Eileen here for me while I make sure your mum is OK? You gave her an awful shock!"

Guy nodded gleefully as James and Sue walked out of the room.

"James, thank you so much for overseeing Guy personally for me."

"Not at all, Sue, that's what I'm here for. It's going to be OK, that's the first thing you have to digest. He has a small cut on his head and we'll have to give him a stitch or two there. I would also suggest a cranial x-ray, just as a precaution I assure you. Other than that, Guy is absolutely A1. He's a tough little soldier. How are you?"

She warmed to his concern. "Oh, I'll be all right. Is there anything I can do?"

"Yes, stop worrying! I want to take a blood sample from Guy." He saw the worry on her face increase. "It's just for his files, Sue. It looks like he got away with it, this time, but if your son was ever in an accident again, at least I'd know what blood to have on standby!" James laughed as he said this and so Sue didn't panic too much.

"You don't need to give him blood now, then?"

"No, it would appear not but I do think it would be prudent to keep him in hospital overnight, just for observation. If he suffered from some internal injuries or internal blood loss this would be the best place for him to be."

Sue covered her mouth with her hand. "Oh, James, you don't think there's any internal damage?"

He gently guided her to a quiet seat where they couldn't be overheard.

"Sue, all indications are that Guy is absolutely fine. He's not complaining of any pains or bumps or anything. In fact, he's full of fun with the nurses but this is just a precaution because he's so small to have been hit by a car."

Sue's eyes glassed up again. James put his arm around her shoulders. "Sue, where's Dave?"

"I haven't even spoken to him yet. I did try to phone him but he's out of mobile coverage. You see, he's in Egypt and the bloody mobiles don't work between here and there."

"That's tough on you," James smiled sincerely. "You need somebody to mind you at this time."

Sue thought she might lose it altogether if she didn't get away from him fast. All this sympathy was going to make her cry. Why couldn't Dave be this attentive and loving, she thought angrily.

"Come on!" He stood up and took her by the hand. "I don't think our little soldier is going to be quite so brave for his stitches and his tetanus! He'll want to hold your hand."

Sue rose and went back to Guy's bedside.

* * *

Arthur and Camilla Condon had seen all they needed to see.

"This house is infinitely nicer than the ones in Ballymore Glen, Arthur," Camilla enthused. "The house has such character and charm. As for the gardens, they are quite, quite exquisite."

"You know, old girl, for once I think we're actually in agreement!"

They approached the young lady showing the house.

"How much do you want for the house and the land?" Arthur asked.

"Well, sir, this is only the first day of viewing. This house is to go to auction at the end of September, in a month's time."

"Come, come, girl! Let's not beat about the bush now. How much do you want?"

"I'm not at liberty to say, sir. I don't know if the vendor has even decided on the reserve yet. The guide is five million euro, that's all I can tell you." She was giving nothing away.

"Well, here it is, I'll offer six million euro," Arthur announced triumphantly.

Camilla Condon nearly fell over. She was pretty sure that their house budget was around the four million euro mark. Even allowing for currency fluctuations, surely they didn't have this much to play with?

Arthur continued. "As a gesture of my absolute resolve in this issue, I am willing to give you a ten per cent deposit right now."

In an expansive gesture, Arthur swung the briefcase that he had been holding very protectively all morning and banged it down on the marble-top table in the front hall of Innishambles. He clicked the two brief-case fasteners simultaneously and they snapped open.

Camilla and the young lady showing the house gasped in unison.

"Feast your eyes, ladies! It's all there, six hundred thousand euro – cash. It's ten per cent of my offer." He closed the case again and held it out to a now very nervous estate agent.

The young girl stared at the case and then at him mutely. Nothing like this had ever happened to her before. Nothing like this had ever happened to anybody in the agency before. "Sir," she stuttered, "couldn't you possibly hang on to the deposit? I have no security with me," she stammered. "What if I lost it?"

Arthur looked at her with highly arched eyebrows. "Yes, what indeed? You would be in a sticky wicket, wouldn't you?" Then he heaved a great big sigh. "OK, then. I'll hang on to it for you but hear me on this: today is Saturday. The offer is only valid until Monday at five o'clock. After that I retract it. I'm looking at other properties too, you know."

"I'm very sorry, sir. I don't have the authority to accept or turn down your offer. I'm just showing the house. I'll notify my boss, Mr Bingham, as soon as I get back to the office. He can contact you immediately, if that's OK."

"Oh, very well," he grumbled, then he added as an afterthought, "Oh, and I'll be looking for a very short close. Two weeks at the most."

He and Camilla walked out of the house arm in arm.

"Really, Arthur, you are so masterful," she giggled as she squeezed his arm. "I had no idea!"

"What ho, there's plenty more where that came from, old girl!" He smirked, squeezing her arm back, recognising the fact that his wife was flirting with him. He was going to have a good night.

The truth was, Arthur was just using an old trick he

had heard about through his own practice in Epsom. It was a well-known ploy among the big property players. If you wanted to be taken seriously, flash a lot of cash. Nine times out of ten, the minion showing the house wouldn't take the money but it did usually have the effect of blowing all other prospective buyers out of the water. The agents at the house were often foolish enough to stop showing the properties, saying it was sold! It had certainly worked like a charm for him today! And it looked like it had even worked on his lady wife too . . .

"Sebastian, Maximilian, where are you?" he yelled for his boys.

The boys casually sauntered around the side of the house.

"This one's not bad," Sebastian offered.

"I like it too," Max added.

Richard watched them go from his old bedroom window.

Lauren was still with her father but Tiffany had sneaked downstairs to get a better look at the house-hunters. There were three other couples who had come to view the house, but they were of no interest to Tiffany. She only cared about the Condons. She had overheard the entire conversation between Arthur and their estate agent.

She looked at the blond boy who walked alongside Sebastian. There was now no doubt. Her worst nightmare had just become a reality.

CHAPTER 10

"Hi, we're home!" Robin yelled as she arrived back into Innishambles.

She was the first to appear. A little convoy of dogs – Woody, Wilma, Dudley and Dexter – followed her. Kelly wasn't quite so fast or sprightly.

"Hi," she mumbled.

"God, what's wrong with you? I thought you'd be dying to hear all the gossip about who was here in your absence," Lauren teased her eldest sister.

"We had a bit of an accident," Kelly explained just as Saskia walked into the kitchen.

"Is everybody OK? Mum, are you OK?"

"I'm fine, love. We're all fine. It's just – well, I had an accident and – er – I reversed into Guy Parker."

Lauren began to giggle. "You're not serious?" Then she saw the solemn faces. "Ohmigod, you are serious! Is he OK? I mean is he hurt?"

"Just a cut on his head. He's OK. But Sue has taken him to the hospital for a check-up."

142

"We bumped into Guy Parker!" Robin announced gleefully.

"Oh Christ," Lauren gasped.

Saskia began to get upset again as she thought about the accident.

"Look, will you girls mind Robin? I'm going into the study. I want to try to phone Sue on her mobile. Perhaps there's something I can do."

"Mrs Dalton, a word please," the young girl showing the house intercepted Saskia before she reached the phone in the study. She was fit to burst with her good news. It wasn't every day you were offered six million for a five million euro house. This man was definitely serious. She was sure the Daltons would be happy. Saskia had no choice but to stop and listen, such was the girl's euphoria.

She listened carefully. "Well, obviously I'm delighted, provided the offer is genuine and legal. I've never heard of someone handing over such a huge deposit at a first viewing. That said, if this is a real offer, I'd be mad not to accept. Can you get Oscar Bingham to tell this man's lawyer to talk to mine and, if everything is above board, we accept!"

The young girl practically danced out of the house. Saskia's mind had already turned to her next task, however. She had to call Sue. She settled into the stillness of the study. The room was oppressively hot with the fire burning. She dialled her friend's mobile.

Guy had howled when he got his injection but now the experiences of his day were beginning to catch up on him. Sue watched over him tenderly as his eyelids began to close. When her mobile began to ring, she hoped that it would be her husband returning one of her umpteen messages. However, the small screen printed out the name Saskia Dalton. They rang each other so regularly, their phones had the numbers in their memory banks. For an instant, Sue considered letting the phone ring out but then she thought of how her old friend must be feeling.

"Saskia, hi," she answered her phone, as she walked out of Guy's room. She didn't want to keep him awake if he was ready to doze.

"Oh, Sue. I'm so glad that I got you. I'm so sorry – is there anything I can do? How are things with you?" Saskia was almost ranting, she was so upset.

"It's OK, calm down. Dr Harrington assures me that Guy is going to be fine. They took an X-ray and he just got two stitches at the crown of his head. He also got a tetanus, which he wasn't too happy about. Bloody sore things, but other than that everything seems to be OK."

Saskia exhaled loudly. "Sue, thank God! Are you coming home soon?"

"Well, they want to keep Guy in for observation but they're telling me that it's just a precaution."

Saskia groaned, " I really am so sorry."

"Look, will you please stop saying that!" Sue eventually snapped as she found a hospital seat to collapse into. "I know it was an accident. You didn't actually mean to do it. The truth be known, Sas, Guy has always been a devil for running out on the road. I guess today I just wasn't fast enough to stop him."

Saskia heard her old friend's voice began to quiver.

"Oh now, Sue, don't even think about blaming yourself for this one. That would be nuts. Where is Dave?"

"That's the worst part. He's in bloody Egypt. He's looking at some real estate out there and I can't contact him."

"Do you want me to come in to the hospital for some moral support?" Saskia offered.

"Oh, Saskia, that's very kind of you but no. I think I just need to stay near Guy for the time being."

"I understand. I really am so so sorry, Sue."

"It's OK. Sometimes these things just happen. At least he got away lightly, just a few bumps and bruises."

"Thank God for that. Look, if there's anything I can do . . . Just call if you want help with the other kids, whatever."

"Thanks."

Sue felt drained as she cut the phone line off. Then she tried her husband again. Still no coverage.

"Damn him," she fumed.

"Still unable to get hold of Dave?" James Harrington sat down beside her.

"Oh James, where the heck is he?"

"In Egypt," James smiled. "Now tell me, have you even had a cup of coffee?"

"No, now that you mention it, I haven't."

"Guy is still asleep after the trauma of the shot. I'd say you have about twenty minutes before he wakes up! Come on, I'll buy you a sandwich and a coffee. How about that?"

"You're a dote," Sue smiled into his luxurious, welcoming eyes.

* * *

145

"Six million euro?" Kelly gasped as Tiffany repeated the conversation that she had overheard.

"You shouldn't listen to other people's conversations," Saskia chastised her daughter automatically.

"Well, I'm happy I did this time!" Tiffany laughed lightly.

"What are you going to do about the offer, Mum?" Lauren asked, fearing the worst.

"Well, we'll have to accept it, of course," Saskia replied.

"What?" the girls gasped in unison. Thinking and talking about selling Innishambles was one thing. Actually doing it was another matter altogether.

"Can't we at least have a little time to think about it?" Kelly whined.

"Girls, you heard Tiffany. The offer is only good until the day after tomorrow." She paused to get a little courage and then ploughed on. "Look, I may as well tell you. I've told the estate agent to accept the offer."

The girls looked at their mother mutinously so Saskia kept talking.

"OK. Here's what I propose. We go and have a look at Ballymore Glen. Perhaps you girls might like to live in one of those houses. We can also buy a place in Dublin for Tiffany and there should be enough money to buy somewhere in the sun too."

"I want to live with Daddy next year. He says it's OK," Tiffany blurted out.

The kitchen went quiet and deadly still.

"You what?" Saskia gave her daughter a steely stare.

"You heard me. I want to live with Daddy. I've discussed it with him and he says he would love me to live with him Monday through Friday."

Usually the girls did not talk about their father to their mother. Saskia had not forgiven Richard for all the dreadful things he had done to her, but it was looking more and more like the girls had.

Saskia felt betrayed. Richard had had a long-term affair with their au pair right under their roof in her beloved Innishambles. He had also had an affair with his public relations executive and he had even managed to virtually sexually assault their neighbour, Sue Parker. On reflection, it was amazing that Sue even spoke to the Dalton family still. After all his sins, how could the girls be so forgiving? Saskia's temper flared with a mixture of jealousy and fear that she was losing her girls to him.

"You little witch! That's why you were talking to him this morning!"

"Don't call Tiffany a witch!" Kelly defended her sister. "Just because you hate your ex-husband doesn't mean we have to. He's our father and he's not as bad as you make him out to be!"

"That's only because I've defended you from the worst things he did."

"He's still our father!" Kelly's eyes flashed in defiance at Saskia.

"Oh, Mummy," pleaded Tiffany, "I'm sorry! I won't live with Daddy if it upsets you this much. It's OK!"

Saskia however was still staring at her eldest. She really was the living embodiment of her father. Their faces were so similar, only Kelly had finer features and more feminine lines. Deep down Saskia knew that it would be impossible to keep the girls away from the man who had made them the women they were. She sighed deeply.

"I'm sorry, girls. It's true, Kelly. Richard is your father

and you have a right to be with him, and, in Tiffany's case," Saskia crossed the room and hugged her younger daughter, "if you want to live with him and he's happy to have you, I can't stand in your way."

"Oh Mummy, I said I won't do it if it upsets you this much."

"I won't lie. It is going to take some getting used to on my part but you have a right to have a life with your father."

Kelly flopped into the sofa, a triumphant grin on her face.

"I wonder though, Kelly," said Saskia, "will you be as understanding with your child when he or she wants to spend time with Barney in a few years?"

Kelly's face went ashen. She stood up and ran from the room as the tears began to stream down her cheeks.

"Mum, that was a little harsh." Lauren, who had been watching the pantomime, got involved for the first time.

"She shouldn't dish it out if she can't take it," Saskia sighed.

"Yeah, but she's full of hormones. We have to cut her some slack," Tiffany agreed with Lauren.

* * *

The shrill of Sue Parker's phone was most unwelcome when it rang out over her and James's second cup of coffee. The nurses had assured her that they would come and fetch her if Guy woke. She was enjoying the time out.

"Yes," she answered it shortly.

"Sue, is that you? It's Penny, in Egypt!"

"Oh hello, Penny, have you heard from Dave in the last few hours?" Sue asked her husband's personal assistant.

"No, I haven't. I just got back to the hotel and I picked up his messages so I knew that you had called, er, quite a few times. Is everything OK?"

"No, it's not actually, Penny. Guy has been hit by a car. I'm in the hospital as we speak."

"My God! Is he OK?" Penny was horrified.

Sue really wanted to exaggerate the situation but she couldn't with James watching her across the canteen table.

"He's OK. He's in good hands." She smiled at her handsome coffee companion. "It is ridiculous that I can't contact my own husband though. Where the hell is he?"

"He has gone out on a field trip. There's a consortium of business men looking at buying out an entire shopping complex on the outskirts of Luxor. He's with them. To be honest, Sue, I don't expect to see him until much later, if not tomorrow. The trip finishes off with dinner in some posh hotel tonight and I dare say it will be a late night."

"He'll probably phone home at some stage," Sue replied.

"Only if he can get to a phone. You know the bloody mobile phones don't work over here."

"Yes, well, if he does check in with you, will you tell him to ring me on my mobile?"

"Absolutely. Look, can you tell me about Guy's injuries so I can at least pass that on to Dave. He'll be beside himself when he finds out."

Sue was so fed up with being unable to contact Dave herself she decided a little upset would do him no harm. Maybe he would be more contactable in the bloody future.

"Just get him to call me, Penny. Tell him Guy is in no danger but he should call me if he wants an update."

"OK," Penny backed off when she heard the edge in Sue's voice, "but please do give little Guy my love."

"Of course I will," Sue answered, knowing that she would do no such thing. Penny Shorthall had got significantly too big for her boots since she had started travelling with Dave on international business.

"Everything OK?" James asked as he watched Sue close her phone.

"Well, I'm afraid Dave is totally uncontactable. That was his PA and she doesn't even think she'll see him for the rest of the day."

"Is she out there too?"

"Yes."

"Nice work if you can get it."

"Yes, it is, I suppose." Sue felt a stab of jealousy towards Penny – not for the first time, she realised.

"You're a very understanding wife, Sue." James placed his hand over Sue's on the table.

The physical contact was like a bolt of pure electricity coursing through her system. She felt herself jump with the sensation, but James's hand didn't flinch. He held hers confidently and boldly.

"Yes, well, what choice do I have?" she responded.

James burst out laughing as if she had said the funniest thing he had ever heard.

She looked confused. "What's so funny?"

"You. What's so funny is you. 'What choice do I have?' Indeed!"

"It's true," Sue defended herself. "Dave works very hard. I have no choice. I stay at home and mind the kids."

She looked at James, slightly perplexed as he stared at her. "OK. I have help. Lisa is a terrific nanny but I don't really have a choice as to how hard Dave works."

James stared at Sue with more intensity than she could bear. She began to shift in her chair a little uncomfortably.

He leaned over the hospital canteen table so nobody but she could hear what he was saying. "You, dear lady, have all the choice in the world. Sue, you are without exception the singularly most attractive woman I know." He smiled at her and she smiled bashfully back.

"You have more style in your little finger than most women have in their entire bodies. Nobody I know could hold a candle to you."

It had been quite a while since Sue Parker had heard such flattery and she was enjoying it.

"Oh James! Perhaps a few years ago, but not now after three babies –"

She made a feeble attempt to argue with him, hoping he wouldn't stop.

"Sue, you still don't get it, do you? You're three times more interesting and more mysterious now that you've had three children."

She liked the idea of that. "You're like a mysterious forest or maybe an Amazonian river, full of rich deep luscious secrets."

Sue was shocked to feel a definite churning in her groin. He was getting to her.

"James, you're just being nice to me because I've had such an appalling day."

"No, Sue, I'm not." He gave her a penetrative stare. "If you were my woman, I wouldn't let you out of my sight."

Involuntarily, Sue's mind wandered to what James

would be like in bed. God, what am I thinking? "James, I could be your mothe – well, your older sister."

"What an older sister!" he grinned devilishly. "Have you ever had a younger boyfriend?"

"No. I've never had another boyfriend. Dave was my first love. We met in college."

James looked utterly shocked. "You mean Dave is the only man you've ever been with?"

"Yes, James. I'm one of those women who only knows one man."

"That's tragic."

"Thank you very much!" she answered indignantly.

"No, I don't mean it like that. It's just tragic that you were never with somebody else, for reasons of comparison if nothing else."

"Whatever do you mean?"

"Well, lovemaking is a little like handwriting. No two people ever do it exactly the same way. It's good to shop around a little before you settle down, if you know what I mean."

"I do, but I didn't."

"Did Dave?"

"Well, of course! Actually, I'm not sure. I'm sure he hasn't been doing anything since we got married, of course, but before we met. Well, we were very young. I think he had some experience. We've always fudged around the subject." Sue began to feel uncomfortable. She was discussing her most intimate details with this rather gorgeous man.

He sensed her change of mood. "Sue, I didn't mean to upset you. It's just that you're the most classy, beautiful lady I know and it would sadden me to think that you didn't realise how special you are." He squeezed her hand again.

"There you are, Doctor!" A large masculine frame towered over them.

"We've been paging you for the last five minutes. Didn't you hear?"

"Oh hello, Matron." James reluctantly stood up. "Sue Parker, this is Matron. She keeps all of us on our toes, don't you, Matron?"

The Matron ignored his efforts at charming her. "We've been looking for you because the results are back from the blood lab."

"Is something wrong?" Sue asked, rising to her feet nervously, instantly forgetting the conversation she and James had been having.

The Matron softened when she saw Sue's panic. "No, Mrs Parker, but there is something we need to keep an eye on. Did you know that Guy is blood type O negative?"

Sue looked surprised. "No, I had no idea. Is it very rare?"

Dr Harrington explained, "It's not something you see every day. You or perhaps Dave is O negative because Guy must have inherited it from one of you. Do you know if you are O negative?"

"Me? No – well, I don't know what blood type I am."

"A simple blood test will tell us," James reassured her. "If you are O neg, would you mind giving us a pint now? We can hardly get a pint from Dave just at the moment!" He smiled, trying to keep Sue from worrying.

"Does Guy need blood?" Sue asked.

Again James tried to calm her. "Your son is in good nick. It's just a precaution. I must make sure we have some fresh blood in stock in case he does, but I don't expect we'll need it."

Sue nodded mutely.

The Matron spoke to Sue. "If you come down right now, I can take a sample. I'll go and get ready. If you join me just outside Guy's room in a few minutes we can get the results straight away."

"Certainly," Sue smiled.

Damn Matron, James thought furiously. I nearly had her. Another fifteen minutes and I could have got her. Sue Parker would have been a nice little notch on my bedpost. Still, he reflected, the game's not over yet. He put his arm protectively around Sue's shoulder.

"You've been through a lot, Sue. You look exhausted. Are you trying to do a little too much at home, do you think?"

"It has been fairly crazy recently, Doctor." But Sue's mind was somewhere else altogether. How could she not have known that Guy was O negative?

He squeezed her shoulder. "Please call me James. Listen, when we get Guy fixed up and safely dispatched home tomorrow, I want you to come in to my clinic. We don't want you getting ill now, do we?"

"OK, James." She smiled at him as they walked down to the accident and emergency ward and to Guy's private little room together. It was nice to feel minded.

CHAPTER 11

Following the phone call to the hospital, Saskia's mood did lift significantly. Guy was going to be OK and so was Sue. Then, of course there was the small matter of six million euro for Innishambles.

"Six million euro," she said aloud to hear what it sounded like. It was such a huge sum. "Thank God for telephone banking," she smiled as she dialled her branch and transferred ten thousand euro of her savings into Nicolas's account. Safe in the knowledge that more money was coming soon, she was happy to help Nicolas out. Hell, she could afford it! She had already transferred ten thousand, the previous Monday, to cover poor Barney's bouncing cheques. This was for the following month. That gave her another few weeks to sort out the Rathdeen Manor mess.

She tried Barney at Peartree Cottage first but there was no reply and so she tried the Parker household. Lisa answered the phone. She was laughing as she picked up the receiver.

"Barney, stop it! Hello, Parker residence."

"Lisa, is that you? It's Saskia Dalton here. How is everything?"

"Oh we're fine, Saskia. Barney here is keeping all of us amused. DJ is climbing all over him and India and I are enjoying the show. Good news from the hospital too! Guy has done no permanent damage and Sue is even coming home tonight. They'll keep Guy in for observation though, just as a precaution."

"Yes, I was just talking to her. It's a terrific relief. I wonder could I have a word with Barney, please?"

Saskia really didn't want to speak with him. She secretly hoped that Lisa would say it was impossible. She felt he was treating Kelly appallingly. If it hadn't been for the trouble with the Rathdeen Refuge accounts, there was no way she would be speaking to Barney Armstrong – damn Nicolas!

Lisa was oblivious to all of this. "No problem, Sas. I'll get him now."

Barney came on the phone. "Hello, Saskia."

"Hello, Barney." She got straight to the purpose of her call. "I'm sorry I didn't get back to you faster but at last I've got to the bottom of that bank mix-up. It has been sorted out so you can rest assured that you can issue next month's cheques for the staff. They'll be fine now." She tried to sound confident.

"And what about the following month?" Barney wasn't appeased.

"Really, Barney, it was just a clerical error. I expected some modicum of understanding from you." There was no way Saskia was ready to come clean with Barney Armstrong about Nicolas Flattery's financial situation!

"I think I've been incredibly understanding, actually.

That's one of the advantages of a close-knit team. Speaking of which, will we be seeing Kelly back any day soon or has she really gone for good?" Barney mentally kicked himself for asking but he had to get some news of her. The last week had felt like an eternity.

Saskia was shocked and appalled to be dragged into their personal lives. "Well, Barney, that's something I think you would have to discuss with her. Although I hardly think she's in any fit state to be riding or mucking out dog-shit."

"There's absolutely nothing wrong with 'Kelly's state' as you put it, although I do sometimes wonder about her mental state!"

"How dare you, Barney? I warn you, you're on very thin ice. There's only so much I'll take from you –"

"From me? Jesus, this is rich. She's the one that ridicules me in the middle of her party and then decides that a day's work is too much for her delicate constitution and then she blows me out and quits her job. How does that make me the ogre?"

Saskia was furious. "Well now, Barney Armstrong, Mr Holier than Thou. Let me see. How did you put it – ah yes, a termination, wasn't that it?"

Barney winced, remembering his pretty tragic linguistic skills when it came to breaking up with the woman he loved. "OK, Shakespeare I'm not but she agreed with me."

"She most certainly did not! Kelly wouldn't have an abortion if her life depended on it!"

"A *what*?"

"You, Barney, are lower than I ever would have believed! Jesus, you're lower than my ex-husband and

157

that's saying something!" Saskia slammed the phone down in fury.

"Barney, are you OK? You've gone very pale." Lisa was sad to see that it looked like their cosy little domestic situation was melting away.

"Lisa, can you handle the kids by yourself for a few hours?"

"Of course, silly, that's what I'm paid for."

"Thanks, I've got to do something." His mind was racing. Saskia had definitely said 'abortion'. What the hell did that mean? Could it be possible that Kelly was carrying his baby? Surely not. She would have told him. He racked his mind to try and remember their exact conversation. He remembered Kelly calling him a murderer, but wasn't that a reference to the little mutt he had put to sleep a few weeks earlier?

"Where are you going?" India asked Barney.

"I have to see a girl about a dog," he smiled.

* * *

"You've been in a frightful mood since you met Sebastian Condon this afternoon, Tiffany. What's the matter? Do you think he's cute?" Lauren asked her older sister.

"Fuck off!" came the rather hostile reply.

"Jeez, that's a bit harsh," Lauren giggled. "So you do fancy him?"

"I've never even met the shit before, so just shag off!"

"Christ, for a guy you've never even met before, you're a bit nervy about it."

"Just leave me alone," Tiffany snapped as she jumped up and ran out of the room.

"What's wrong with her?" Lauren asked huffily.

"Beats me," Kelly answered without taking her eyes off the television.

Suddenly Dudley and Dexter jumped up and shot off towards the door.

"Nix," both sisters yelled in unison. There was obviously somebody making their way to the front door of Innishambles and neither one of them wanted to answer it.

"I said nix first," Lauren whimpered.

"Yes, but I'm exhausted," Kelly smirked and patted her dead-flat tummy.

"You cow, are you going to milk this pregnancy thing for the next eight months?"

"I may as well get some advantage out of it!"

With that the doorbell rang. Lauren let out a long groan and rose to answer it. Secretly, however, she was glad to see that Kelly was beginning to get used to the idea of being pregnant.

"Barney, I didn't think we'd see you around these parts!" Lauren didn't even attempt to hide her surprise when she saw who their visitor was.

"Yes, well, here I am," he answered with a slightly unsure grin.

"I'm not sure how welcome you'll be but you'd better come in."

"Is Kelly here?"

"Yeah, she's in the drawing-room watching the telly. Mum has taken Robin out for a walk up to the Taylors'."

"Next door? Long walk!"

"Yes, well, Robin's legs aren't too long just yet."

"And Tiffany?"

"Actually, now that you mention it she's in a sulk upstairs. Why don't you go and have a word with Kelly and I'll go and see if I can shake Tiff out of her mood. Deal?"

"Deal," Barney looked a little more comfortable.

Lauren turned and began to climb the stairs two at a time but Barney called after her.

"Lauren!"

"Yes?"

"Thanks for not turfing me out on the spot!"

"It's OK. Just get it right this time, Barney. I mightn't be so obliging next time!"

"I'll try."

He took a deep breath and knocked on the drawing-room door. Then he popped his head around as Kelly looked up at him.

"What the bloody hell are you doing here?" She shot to her feet. "Who the hell let you in? Lauren? I'm going to kill her." She started towards the door that Barney had just walked through but he backed into the door frame, blocking her escape route.

"Three years, Kelly. It's been three years. Do you not think I deserve at least three minutes of your time now?"

She stopped in her tracks, but more because she wouldn't be able to get past without touching him.

"What do you want?" she asked aggressively.

"Are you pregnant?"

"What?" her voice weakened.

"You heard me. Are you pregnant?"

"You already know the answer to that. Is this some kind of a joke, Barney? Because if it is, I'll –" her eyes began to glass up.

"Jesus. You are. Christ, Kelly, I had no idea." He took a few steps towards her but stopped short, uncertain whether she would welcome his embrace.

"What the hell do you mean you had no idea? When I went over to tell you, you said that you already knew, you said that you wanted an abortion!" Her tears began to flow softly down her cheeks.

"Christ no, Kelly. A baby, *our* baby? Never in a million years! Even if you didn't want me in your life any more . . ." he trailed off.

"What are you talking about?" She looked at him and realised that his eyes were awash with tears too. She had never seen him cry – Barney was usually laughing.

"Please, come and sit down." He reached out his hand to take hers. "My God, a baby!"

Tentatively she took his hand. "But you knew, Barney! You said you did!"

"Jesus, Kelly, did *we* have a convoluted conversation! I admit I was fairly hot under the collar last Monday when you trotted into work after lunch. I thought that you were just playing Lady of the Manor. That's why I was so annoyed." Then he continued a little sheepishly, "I also had this idea that you wanted to break up with me. That's what I was talking about when I suggested a termination."

"Holy shit. You wanted to terminate the relationship?" She laughed through her tear-stained eyes. "What planet are you from? Terminate? From now on I'll call you Arnold Schwarzenegger – Mr Terminator! Whatever happened to just plain breaking up?"

She had settled back into her armchair again and he knelt beside her.

"My God, a baby," he repeated, still in shock.

161

Kelly's face suddenly clouded over. "Barney, you wanted to break up with me? Do you not love me any more?" Her eyes flooded with anxiety again and Barney thought his heart would break.

"Christ no, Kelly. I love you more than life itself. This has been the most wretched week of my life. I suggested we break up because I thought it was what you wanted."

"What?"

"Last weekend at your party. You called me a – well, that doesn't matter now, but it was pretty obvious that you didn't want to be with me. I reckoned that you needed to spread your wings a little. Maybe I was holding you back . . ." He looked at her nervously.

"This would be after my twenty-one Red Bulls and vodka?" she smirked a little sheepishly.

"Well, yes."

"I'm sorry I was so mean to you." Then a thought struck her. "Oh God, Barney, I was drinking like a sailor. I even had a joint! I didn't realise I was pregnant."

He looked at her tummy. "Can I, would it be OK if I –?"

"Of course you can feel my tummy. There's actually nothing to feel."

Ever so gently Barney placed his hand on Kelly's flat stomach. His smile stretched across his face and lit up his eyes.

"Our baby," he said. "You and me, Kelly, our baby."

Kelly looked at his face, animated and happy. Her emotions were so confused. There was no doubt that she had been thinking about breaking up with him before her birthday. Barney had been right when he sensed that. They had been growing apart. She wanted to live life a little and be young. He was already past that. Now however, it looked like she was past that too. If she was going to be a mother, she was going to have to start acting like one. Kelly thought of her mother. Saskia had hardly put her children first when she turfed Richard out. It was all so confusing.

"What's wrong? You look upset," Barney fretted.

"What? Oh no. Actually I was just thinking about Mum."

"My God, I've just remembered! That's why she gave me a look that would kill in O'Reilly's earlier."

"Mum knows and so do Lauren and Tiffany and now you. That's it."

Barney placed his strong warm hands squarely on her shoulders. It had a tremendously reassuring effect on her. "Hey," he beamed, "I want to tell the world. This is terrific news. The woman I adore is carrying my baby. I want to shout it from the rooftops!"

"Easy there, Romeo. Dad might not be so impressed. We're not married, you know. This baby is going to be illegitimate."

Barney's face darkened. He hadn't thought of that. In a flash he changed his position from a kneeling one to a genuflection. His face became very solemn.

"Kelly Dalton, you know I've asked you this before, but now I'm even more serious if that's possible. Will you do me the honour of being my wife?"

Kelly didn't need to think. Her eyes filled with tears for what felt like the umpteenth time that day. She threw her arms around her old boyfriend's neck.

"Yes, Barney, I will marry you. Yes, yes, yes!"

He started to smother her face in kisses. "Christ, I love you, Kelly."

"I love you too," she laughed, "Daddy!"

He looked at her for an instant. "Daddy? I like that. Daddy! Wow!"

"Hey, I want to tell Mum before I tell anybody else – let's go and find her."

"You want to walk over to Taylors' now? Do you think you're up to it?"

"Barney, I'm only a few weeks pregnant! I think I can manage a little walk still! Look, if it makes you happy, we'll go by the road. That way is a little flatter. OK?"

"OK, but I must warn you. I am going to fuss over you something awful for the next – how many months?"

"I don't know actually. I think it was that time the condom slipped, do you remember?"

He burst out laughing, "Yes, I do, and you were so freaked out. Look at us now. Don't worry, we'll get you to a doctor soon and he'll be able to figure the whole thing out." Barney stopped talking and looked into his girlfriend's face. "Kelly, you know, you've made me the happiest man on earth."

* * *

Jayne Mullins was not so happy. She had driven around Ballymore three times and that had taken all of five minutes.

"Not exactly a roaring metropolis," she grumbled to herself.

She hadn't even woken up until lunch-time, following her dinner with Raymond. She also had a roaring hangover. He had laughed at her weakened condition and promptly gave her the rest of the day off.

"It's a Saturday – I don't have any particular pressing

work to do. Look, it will do me good to spend the day with the kids. You give a few friends a call. Get out and enjoy the last of the summer sun."

Jayne didn't want to get out and enjoy the bloody summer sun. She wanted to be with Raymond. Her great plans on seducing him over the long and lazy summer months were rapidly fizzling out. Forced to leave the house, she spent a few hours blowing her substantial wages in the end-of-summer sales in Brown Thomas. Feeling marginally better after a little retail therapy, she had a brainwave and decided to check out Ballymore again. In doing so, she went from a bad mood into a filthy mood. The place was an absolute dive. There wasn't even one clothes shop. The pub looked like it should be shut down by the health authorities and the newsagent's resembled something out of biblical times. Feeling dreadfully sorry for herself, she decided to drive along the other roads that exited the tiny village. The first one she drove out passed by the Rathdeen Refuge. Even Jayne had heard about that place – it was owned by some Hollywood guy. At least some of the neighbours would be interesting. Eventually that road took her into another little village, Rathdeen. Yawn. She headed back to Ballymore and out the road opposite the Rathdeen road. A whole lot of nothing out that road too. Although even Jayne had to admit that it was very very pretty in the summer evening light. Again she drove through the tiny village. Nothing had changed. Jayne took the first left. It was the only road remaining. Now there was nothing left to see. A couple were walking along the road together arm in arm. They were obviously in love. Jayne continued to watch them in her rear-view mirror as she drove past. The man was gently caressing his lady friend's tummy with his free hand.

"Bitch," Jayne thought. "She's pregnant!"

The misery of her own situation hit her again.

"How can I compete with a bloody ghost?" she wailed to an empty car. "Caroline, what the hell did you have that I don't have? At least I'm bloody well alive! Surely that stands for something."

It was obvious that this road went nowhere too and so, begrudgingly, Jayne did another U-turn. She drove past the loving couple again. They were still laughing and talking and even kissing.

I fucking hate them! she screamed.

She turned onto the road for Wicklow and Dublin and drove past Ballymore Glen. Her little visit had been quite futile because with the huge front gates closed, it was impossible to see anything anyway.

At least, she reflected, bloody Cassandra Booth-Everest wouldn't be around here to bother her. She was relieved to have escaped living near that snobby bitch. Christ, somebody like her living nearby would have definitely hindered her chances of becoming the next Mrs Raymond Saunders. In fact, on reflection Jayne thought that was one advantage of living out here in the bloody sticks. There wouldn't be too much competition. With just herself and Raymond and of course the kids, there was a much better chance of seducing him. This thought cheered her up a little.

"Yes," she said out loud. Then she pretended that Raymond was sitting beside her. "Just you and me and all this fresh country air. Perhaps that's what we need, darling, to get your juices going again – a change of scenery."

Jayne crunched the gears aggressively and accelerated towards home and Raymond.

* * *

Cathy Taylor wasn't as fast on her feet as she used to be but she was still rudely healthy for someone who had celebrated her eightieth birthday some years ago. There was little that surprised her at this stage in life. Cathy acted as everybody's grandmother in Ballymore. She had minded Saskia through her divorce. Over the years she had practically adopted Barney who never knew his own mother. She cooked and cleaned for Nicolas Flattery after his wife went back to the States to be with her lesbian lover. Even Sue Parker often visited looking for a shoulder to cry on or just an ear to listen. Cathy didn't say much. That was the reason for her popularity. She had the ability to listen and sound interested no matter what the story was, whether it was little Robin telling her about a dream she had had or Saskia slowly breaking the news that she was about to become a grandmother. Cathy never judged and rarely gave advice. She would instead guide with questions, leading her guests to their own conclusions. That is what she was doing this evening.

"How do you feel about becoming a grandmother?" she was asking Saskia as the banging on her doorknocker interrupted their chat. Robin was playing on the floor. Slowly the old woman shuffled to the door.

"Is Mum here?" Kelly asked, barely able to contain herself.

"Hi, Cathy," Barney beamed at her.

If Cathy's body was slow, her eyes were quick. She saw his arm around Kelly's waist and knew that, like so many situations in life, the one she had just been listening to Saskia talk about had just resolved itself.

"Come in, children! Saskia is here, *a grà*. Come in, won't you and don't be standing at the door. Barney, you're very welcome too. Come in, come in."

Kelly and Barney went past Cathy into her small kitchen where Saskia had risen to her feet. She had heard Barney's voice and was ready for a fight.

"Mummy, I have the most wonderful news. Barney has asked me to be his wife and I have accepted. We're going to be married!"

Saskia's face went ashen – she fell back into the chair.

"No," she whispered. "You can't! Not like this. It can't be."

"Mummy?" Kelly looked shocked and Barney was speechless. Then Kelly got cross. "What kind of congratulations is that?" she yelled. "Why aren't you delighted? Jesus, Mum, there's no pleasing you!"

"No, you don't understand. This is wrong. You can't marry Barney just because you're carrying his child."

Barney and Kelly glanced at Cathy whose eyes were downcast. She obviously knew already. Then the old lady gently took Robin by the hand and guided her out the back door of the cottage. This was not a conversation for young ears.

"Look, Saskia," Barney tried to take control after Robin and Cathy were out of earshot, "I understand where you're coming from. You probably don't trust me after my actions this week but I have to tell you there was a big misunderstanding! It's not like it seems – honestly it's not. Kelly and I love each other. Surely you know that? And the baby? Well, that's just helped us clarify the situation."

168

But Saskia was not for bending. "I won't have it. I forbid this marriage."

"What?" The blood left Kelly's face. "Mummy, what are you saying?"

Barney spoke. "Now look here, Saskia. Kelly and I are going to get married. We're not children –"

"You're not a child, Barney," Sas spat, "but she is! Kelly is still only a child. Damn it, she has just turned twenty-one. To marry her would be stealing her youth – believe me, I know."

"'You know, you know!' What the hell do you know?" Kelly snapped at her mother angrily.

"Don't you get it?" Saskia laughed almost deliriously. "History is repeating itself. I got pregnant with you and that's why your father married me! He trapped me when I was too young to know any better and that one mistake cost me my life!"

The room went deadly quiet.

"What?" Kelly's body froze with shock. "That's not possible. I've just turned twenty-one and you're twenty-two years married!"

"No, Kelly, if I was still married to that man, I would be twenty-one years and six months married. We got married when I was three months pregnant. It was his idea. Your father was always a great long-term strategist. He never wanted you to know. He realised that sooner or later you would want your birth cert so we couldn't lie about your age. You would need to present your birth cert when you needed your first passport for example but we could pretty easily lie about how many years we were married. You weren't likely to ask to see our marriage cert and even if you did I would just have said that it was lost.

So that's exactly what we did!" Saskia's eyes were huge. She looked a little crazy as she ranted on. "You're the reason I married that bastard! Don't inflict the same blame on your child!"

"Right. That's it. I've heard enough," Barney interrupted. "Come on, Kelly, I'm taking you out of here! We'll go back to Innishambles to collect a few things and then go back to Peartree Cottage."

Kelly was in too much shock even to speak. She let herself be led by Barney out of the little house.

On hearing the front door of her little cottage bang shut, Cathy gave Robin the job of finding all the eggs in the yard. When the child was totally immersed in her chore, the old woman went back in to Saskia.

Keeping Robin outside had been a wise move because Cathy found her neighbour in floods of tears.

"I swore I would never tell her, Cathy," Saskia cried. "I swore! I didn't want her to have to feel the burden of guilt."

"I think I'll brew another pot of tea so." Cathy shuffled over to the Aga slowly.

CHAPTER 12

James Harrington offered Sue a lift home. She was sorry to have to say that she had her car with her. His attention was very gratifying and the fact that Dave hadn't made contact yet was really fraying her nerves. Even more upsetting, however, was the fact that Matron had confirmed her suspicions. Sue Parker's blood was A positive. She couldn't give blood to her own son – her own flesh and, well, *not* blood it would seem. Luckily, as it turned out, there was no need for a blood donation. Guy had woken in fairly good form after his brief nap and wolfed back two and a half hospital dinners.

"I really think he could go home with you now, Sue, but it is standard practice to keep minors in after they've had a bump on the head."

Sue had to agree that there seemed to be nothing wrong with him. When she asked him if he would like to stay in hospital for the night as a special treat, he was unstoppable.

"Pleeeeeeese, Mummy, can I stay? I promise I'll be good. You go away and come back tomorrow!"

Sue looked down at her adorable three-year-old. He was far more independent than India or little DJ. She gave him a big hug and said that if that was what he really wanted, that is what she would do. A large part of her longed for him to be less independent, more needy, but her little boy wasn't interested.

Dr Harrington had witnessed the conversation and laughed. "He really is a little fighter, isn't he?"

Sue had to agree. I sometimes wonder if he needs me at all," she sighed.

James donned his concerned doctor mantle again. "Sue, of course he needs you. In fact, it's a sign of terrific parenting skills that he's so confident and happy in his own company. Look, how would you like a drink? I think you could do with relaxing a bit – Doctor's prescription for the poor unsung hero – Mummy!"

Sue was surprised at his offer. Surely that was way beyond the call of duty! Equally surprising was how attractive she found the offer but naturally she should decline. It wouldn't be proper, would it?

Suddenly her mobile rang. She smiled at James and walked a few feet away for some privacy before answering it.

"Sue, it's Dave! Penny's just filled me in. My God, how bad is it? I'll try and catch an earlier flight."

"There's no need for that. Slow down, Dave! Jesus, where have you been? I couldn't get hold of you anywhere."

"Ah, Sue, not now! Tell me what happened."

"Well, basically Saskia Dalton reversed into Guy." She knew that she was exaggerating appallingly but she was angry with him for being so uncontactable.

"Oh, dear Jesus, how bad is it?"

Then she felt guilty when she heard his genuinely terrified tone. "Look, Dave, he's going to be fine. To be honest, she barely tipped him. He thinks it's all a big game. Dr Harrington is here and he's given him a complete check and Guy is A1 – honestly."

"Sue, I'm so sorry I'm not there. I'll fly home as soon as I can. Are you still at the hospital?"

"Yes, I'm just outside Guy's room with Dr Harrington. They want to keep him in for the night, just as a precaution, mind you. He's having a ball, Dave. Look, don't worry about changing your flights. You're due to come home late tomorrow night anyway, aren't you?"

"Yes, but that means I won't see him until Monday morning at the earliest."

"That's time enough, Dave. Really he's going to be back to normal by then. He got two stitches in his head – there won't be a scar because it's under his hair – and he got a tetanus. That's the height of it."

"Can I talk to him?"

Sue brought the phone in to her three-year-old and listened to Guy's animated explanation of the day and how he ended up in Wicklow General hospital. Next Dave asked Sue if he might have a word with James. She handed the phone to her doctor who had been hovering at the door and he stepped out into the corridor. She would have preferred to be able to hear what James was telling Dave about Guy. She quickly gave her son a special kiss and hug goodnight.

"You're sure you want me to go home?" she asked him one more time.

"Yes!" he yelled in exasperation. "Go home to the others! I'll see you tomorrow."

She tussled his hair and laughed. "OK, big boy. See you tomorrow and be good for the nurses."

She hurried out in time to hear the conclusion of James' conversation with Dave. "Really, Dave, he'd be up and about right now if we let him! By the time you get home, it'll all be over – forgotten," James's tone was warm and reassuring. They said their goodbyes and the doctor handed the phone back to Sue.

Again she walked away for privacy. She had to ask. She was terrified of the answer but she had to know the truth. She wished she knew what James had said. Had he mentioned the business about Guy's blood type? Sue braced herself and kept her tone as light as she could. "Dave, by the way, what blood type are you?"

"I'm A positive."

"Are you sure?"

"Of course I'm sure. I'm a regular blood donor. A positive. Why?"

"Oh, it's nothing. I was just wondering." Her legs went weak. Obviously, James hadn't mentioned anything about Guy's blood type.

"What were you wondering, Sue?" Dave's voice had an edge to it.

Christ, she thought in a panic, he can read my mind – keep your voice level.

"It's nothing really." Her head was spinning. Change the subject, change the subject, she thought wildly but she couldn't think of anything to say.

"Honey?" Dave filled the silence. "Is something wrong? What is it?"

Think, her mind screamed. She blurted out the first thing that came into her panicky mind. "Dave, what do

174

you think about getting away for a while? Just you and me. Don't you think a holiday would be nice?"

There was a pause. When Dave spoke his voice was full of anger. "Jesus, Sue, what are you thinking of? One of your children has just been hit by a car! I would have thought your mind would have been on Guy! Oh, yeah, and only last week you set your eye on a house that I thought you wanted which I might remind you cost two million. I'm working all the hours that I can but it's just not enough for you. You can't have it every way, new house, lavish holidays – what's next? What do you want? Blood?"

Blood? Why had he suggested that? Christ, could he know? Had James said something after all? Damn it, she should have listened to their conversation. She was in a mad panic. She had to get off the phone. She needed time to think.

"Sorry, bad idea," she replied quickly. "Look, James, eh Dr Harrington is calling me for something. I have to go. Everything really is fine here. If things change I'll call you. OK?"

Dave let out a deep sigh. "Fine, Sue. Goodbye."

There was an incredible finality is the way he said goodbye. It was as if it was forever. Sue had to get off the phone. She clicked it shut without saying goodbye.

James, who had caught the end of the conversation, was intrigued to hear that she was lying to her husband. He certainly wasn't calling her. Then he saw her face. She was as white as a sheet.

"Come on, you need a drink." He took her by the arm and gently guided her to the warmth and security of his car. She didn't argue.

"Is there a pub in Ballymore?" he asked as they drove out of the hospital car park.

"Yes, The Hitching Post, but that's miles away. Let's just go somewhere near. I'll have to come back to get my car anyway." She was starting to regain some of her composure.

He let her calm down a little and then he asked gently, "Everything OK?"

His voice was so calm, so warm. James was so caring. The turmoil of her day caught up on her. Her three-year-old had been hit by a car and now to her utter horror, she had discovered that neither she nor her husband had blood that was compatible with her son's blood type. There was only solution. Richard Dalton was Guy's natural father. Saskia's ex-husband was Guy's father. Shit, shit, shit, shit. Could life get any worse?

"Sue, you really don't look too good! Can I help you at all?" James was trying to get her attention. He had glided his BMW into the car park of a small hotel she knew and liked and cut the engine.

Sue's eyes blinked. It looked like she was heaving her mind back to the present with a mammoth effort.

"Do you know, James? I've had a hell of a day. Let's have a drink or three!"

"Music to my ears," he laughed lightly.

Sue made herself smile brightly as she walked into the bar with James. Her mind was clear again. She had one objective here. She needed to know what the good doctor had said to her husband. She had to know how much Dave knew. If there was any way of keeping the horrible truth from him, she would find it. It was Operation Charm James time.

Having phoned Lisa to ensure India and DJ were wrapped up for the night, she joined James in the bar. He was sitting at a discreet table at the back of the lounge but rose to greet her as she crossed the room. "Now, what will you have to drink?" he asked, as he admired her long legs crossing elegantly when she took her seat.

They sat and talked comfortably over a drink and then another and then a third by which time Sue reckoned he was mellow enough to pump for information about his phone conversation with Dave.

She smiled at him. "You know you really are very kind to look after me like this."

"Not at all," he argued. "It's always a pleasure to be in the company of a beautiful woman."

"You charmer!"

"It's true," he continued as their drinks arrived. "You're a spectacular woman. Dave is a lucky man."

She spotted her chance. "Did he seem OK on the phone to you?"

"Yes, fine. Why?"

"Oh nothing. I assume you filled him on Guy's condition?"

"Naturally."

"Anything else?" she asked absently as she pretended to concentrate on her white wine.

"What are you talking about?"

She didn't dare ask about the blood types specifically. James might twig to her situation.

"Oh, don't mind me," she laughed it off. "I'm just fretting about Dave. He's so far away. I don't want him to have to worry unnecessarily – about anything. I'm sure you understand."

James didn't but he damn well wasn't going to admit as much.

"I assure you, my objective in talking to Dave was to ease his concerns over his son. It's my belief I did that."

James sounded very solemn.

Sue reached out and touched his hand. "I'm sorry, here you are being so nice to me – bringing me out for a drink after my appalling day and I'm giving you a hard time about my husband. Forgive me, James. I'm not very gracious, am I?" She granted him one of her most demure looks.

It worked. He was totally smitten by her.

"You know, I think you're the most beautiful woman I know." He looked straight into her eyes.

"Oh, James, you're just saying that!"

He moved a little closer. "No, I certainly am not. Look at you, Sue. You look like a model. You're always dressed impeccably but it's more than that. You've got such class."

Sue had stopped protesting and was listening. Dave certainly hadn't talked to her like that in quite some time. He took her hands and studied them.

"I mean, Jesus, you're perfect. Look, even your nails are beautiful."

"That's just a French manicure," she scoffed gently. "Anybody could have that done."

"But they don't and you do. Don't you see?" He gently touched her cheek. "That's exactly what makes you so spectacular. You make the effort that other women don't."

Their eyes locked. Sue knew what was coming next. She could sense it. The space between their faces was closing. Ohmigod, he's going to kiss me, she thought wildly – a brief flash of reality entering her slightly misty mind. In a microsecond, Sue Parker sobered up and willed her mind to clear. Ever so gently she moved her body so James kissed her on the cheek. She looked around the lounge.

"Richard Dalton," she announced loudly, "fancy meeting you here!"

Richard, who had just entered the pub with Oscar Bingham, looked quite startled. They hadn't actually spoken to each other since Saskia and Richard had broken up almost three years earlier. Richard had disappeared from their lives so he was easy to avoid.

This was a strange place to bump into each other.

Richard was surprised to hear her calling his name so jovially. He was quite certain that she had avoided him at Kelly's twenty-first party. Now she was being extremely friendly. He crossed the bar to say hello.

"Hi, Sue. How are you?"

"Fine," she lied, hiding the rising tide of panic that she felt. Her mind raced – Christ, from the fat into the fire! On the one hand I have an over-friendly GP and on the other I have my best friend's ex-husband who happens to be the true father of my child. This was rapidly turning into a real-life nightmare. "You know James Harrington, don't you?"

Richard smiled and took the doctor's hand. "Of course. How are you, James?"

"Well, thanks," James answered a little shortly, annoyed at having been interrupted.

Richard called Oscar Bingham over.

"I have some more prospective buyers for you!" He laughed good-naturedly and did all the necessary introductions.

James was momentarily distracted when he heard that Oscar was the estate agent handling Ballymore Glen.

"We're very happy at the rate they're being snapped up," he said.

"Who is the developer behind it?" James asked.

At this question, however, Oscar's expression became unreadable. "That, I'm afraid, is confidential information. I can tell you all about the builders, they're a highly reputable firm of –"

"Ah no, James was trying to figure out who's making so much money out of our precious Ballymore," Sue interrupted him.

"I'm afraid he's a very modest businessman," Oscar smiled. "Likes to keep his business affairs private!"

"So it's a man!" Sue laughed.

"You could be here all night, Sue. I've been trying to weasel it out of him for the last few hours," Richard interrupted. "Now, can I get anybody a drink?

Sue glanced at her watch. "Gosh, is that the time? I really must go." Then she turned to James, "Thank you so much for minding me and taking me for a much-needed drink. I'm all right now – really." Then she turned and gave a brief explanation to the other two men as to why she was having a quiet drink with James Harrington on a Saturday night. The last thing she needed now was more tongues wagging!

James however looked crestfallen. He wasn't doing very well at seducing Sue Parker. Usually he was a great deal more effective than this.

"Sue –" He stood up.

"No, James. You've already done so much for me today. I really appreciate it. It's a short stroll back to the car and the fresh air will do me good." She hugged him and whispered into his ear, "We'll talk tomorrow."

He looked at her and nodded, knowing he was beaten by circumstance.

* * *

If she had been breathalysed, Sue wasn't sure whether she would have been just over or just under the limit. She was certainly pretty close to the line. That, however, was not what she was thinking about as she sped towards Ballymore and her home.

"If I can just get home, I'll figure this thing out," she reasoned to the empty car. "There has to be a way out. It will all go away." Her speed was way above the legal limit but she gave it scant regard. She felt that she had had all the bad luck one woman could get in a day. If only she hadn't taken the children down to O'Reilly's. If only she had bloody well walked. Then they would have been slower and their paths wouldn't have crossed with Saskia Dalton. She reached the gates of her house and took a deep breath – relief. She was home. Suddenly, on a last-minute impulse, she swerved the car in to the side of the road just before she drove in. If Lisa was still up, she would want details and updates on Guy's condition. Sue couldn't face being polite to her just yet. Thankfully, Lisa had already agreed to stay the night. Hopefully she would go to bed early and so Sue wouldn't have to face her. She cut the car's engine, took the keys out of the ignition and then she began to cry. At first they were little tears but quite quickly they grew into great big drops as she wept. The true gravity of her situation was beginning to sink in.

Her three-year-old son was in fact the product of a

drunken encounter with Richard Dalton. In truth, for a long time after Guy's birth Sue had had her suspicions but, after Dave and she had managed to put that bad time behind them, she had always been successful in suppressing her qualms. Any time in the small hours of the morning when the doubts crept in, she always chased them away. But sometimes Guy would look at her, his jawline set in determination or his eyes flashing with mischief, and she would catch her breath. He looked so like Richard. The problem was – or was it a blessing, she now wondered – well, either way the fact was that Richard and her husband looked very alike. They had similar stocky physiques. They were both slightly sallow and although Richard Dalton was perhaps slightly more handsome, David had a fine strong jawline too.

She loved her husband and she loved little Guy. She had only contempt for Richard Dalton but there was no denying the situation. Richard had to be Guy's father. Dave quite simply couldn't be. He was A positive, she was A positive and Guy was O negative. Frantically, Sue wondered who she could talk to. Her husband was obviously not an option. She couldn't talk to her best friend either. Saskia was too close even if she and Richard were separated. The fact remained that Sas was married to Richard at the time that Sue became pregnant with Guy. Sue had never felt so alone. Then she thought of visiting Cathy Taylor. Cathy was a terrific woman when it came to lending a shoulder to cry on. "No, it's too late to visit Cathy," Sue reasoned out loud and so for a long time she just sat there and cried. Her weeping gradually softened and eventually stopped. "I know what I need," she decided. "A cigarette!" Until recently she had abhorred cigarettes.

Why had she suddenly changed, she wondered. It was now so dark, she reckoned it was safe to bring the car into the driveway. She wouldn't be seen and the odds were that Lisa was in bed by now, anyway. Sue wouldn't smoke in her car so she parked it and got out. The night was still warm and the ink-black sky seemed vast. She looked at the stars in wonder. She walked over to the wooden bench on their front lawn and sat down.

Then she began to search through her enormous Mondi bag. She threw her make-up bag onto the ground along with her Filofax, her hairbrush, cheque books and sunglasses.

"Where the bloody hell are they?" she mumbled at her bag. Eventually, after a few more minutes of rummaging, she found her Silk Cut. Sue hadn't smoked since college but just a few weeks ago she was in a petrol station and saw the boxes of cigarettes neatly stacked on the wall behind the counter.

She had her petrol and her newspaper and, just as she was about to pay for them, she hesitated and smiled at the young man behind the counter.

"I'd also like a box of Silk Cut and a box of matches please." It didn't sound like her own voice. She didn't feel like it was her, but the shop assistant didn't seem at all shocked.

"Which ones, lady?" he asked, managing to remove all interest from his voice.

"What do you mean?" Sue was confused.

"Silk Cut Purple, Mild, Extra Mild or Blue? Regular or extra long?"

"Oh, I don't know. I haven't smoked for ages, you see."

He looked at her for a second and then pulled out the extra long purple box.

"These ones would suit you." He almost smiled but didn't.

After her wild and reckless purchase, Sue went to Bewleys for a coffee and to try out her cigarettes. The first thing that struck her was the smell in the smokers' section of the coffee shop. It was vile. She sat down with her coffee and lit up. It tasted disgusting. She put it out almost immediately and hadn't smoked since.

Tonight, as she looked up at the stars, she decided to try again. She lit up a cigarette and inhaled deeply. This time it was nice.

"What a day," she said aloud to the stars. She was tired and her joints were beginning to ache. "It's one I'll certainly never forget. Today is the day that my darkest fear became a reality. My husband is not the father of my son."

* * *

Oscar Bingham was well and truly inebriated. It took all Richard's powers of persuasion to convince his friend that what Oscar really needed was to go home to his lady wife. Eventually Richard managed to pour him into a taxi. He assured Oscar that he too was going home but in truth he had other plans. They had managed to convince James to stay with them after Sue's sudden departure. Richard smelt an opportunity and he never liked to let one of them pass him by. It was closing time as Richard managed to get back to James Harrington.

"Ah, James, I'm glad you're still here," Richard beamed at the slightly sozzled doctor. "It's my bloody palm pilot,"

184

he lied comfortably. "I seem to have lost it. Did you see it anywhere around the table?"

"Your pilot? You have a pilot?" James asked incredulously.

"No! A palm pilot," he repeated. "It's an electronic diary. It's a small black and silver thing, about the size of a calculator. It's not just my diary, however, it's also my contacts book, my virtual right hand."

James made a feeble attempt to look for it under the table that he was sitting at. The fact that he didn't really know what he was looking for didn't seem to bother him.

"Has Oscar gone?" James asked as Richard pulled up a seat next to him. Richard nodded.

"Sure I may as well join you for one more, so," Richard said companionably. After a little charm and a big tip, he managed to secure a double whiskey for James and a Diet Coke for himself from a reluctant barman.

"Cheers," James raised his fresh glass to his new drinking companion.

"To life, love and happiness," Richard toasted.

"Shag love," James grumbled.

"Oh? It can't be all that bad, a good-looking lad like yourself," Richard coaxed.

"No, only the dregs are left," James examined his glass and then continued. "All the best ones are gone. Take Sue Parker for egshample," he slurred slightly.

Richard leaned across the table to whisper, not that it really mattered because the bar was empty at that stage. Even the barman had disappeared from behind the hotel bar counter. "Yes, you should!" Richard said simply.

"What?"

"Take Sue Parker," Richard grinned wickedly.

At first James looked surprised but then his face broke

into a wicked grin. "I bloody well wouldn't mind taking her, y'know." He took another large gulp of whiskey.

"Well, I'm not telling you your business now," Richard spoke quietly over his Coke, "but that woman wants you."

"Eh?"

"Oh, yes. It was so obvious."

"Really?"

"If I was an indiscreet man, I'd say she was mad about you!"

"Do you think? Well, you know, it's funny," James tried to balance his chin in his hand but his elbow slipped off the low table. "Oops!"

"Mind yourself there."

"Er, yeah. No, strictly between the two of us, she was giving me loads of come-on signals. I really thought that she was keen and then suddenly – bam – she froze me out, right here in the bar."

Richard nodded sagely, "Ah, there's a very good reason for that."

"There is?"

"Yes, James. I walked in. She doesn't want to be seen!"

"Now that you mention it, I wanted to take her to the pub in Ballymore and she didn't want to go there. I guess this place seemed private."

Richard smiled. This was like *giving* candy to a baby, it was so easy. "Don't forget she's a married woman. She has to be quiet about a rendezvous, if you know what I mean."

"I suppose she was happy to be here with me until she saw you and Oscar Bingham walk in," James reasoned.

"I rest my case. I reckon she's ready for you all right,

James. You just have to be more discreet. Get her someplace where nobody can see you, boy."

The younger man drained his whiskey glass and sat up. "You know something, Richard? I think you're bloody well right. I'll get her, all right. It just has to be in the right location!"

"That's my boy," Richard smiled, realising that this was indeed a nice opportunity. Dave Parker had all but destroyed Richard financially a couple of years ago. What better way to get back at him? Destroying his marriage would be sweet revenge indeed.

CHAPTER 13

When Kelly woke on Sunday morning, it took her a few minutes to get her bearings.

"Are you OK?" Barney, who had been sitting on a chair next to the bed, looked anxiously at her.

"What? God, I have the most awful headache." Then she remembered her fight with her mother and all the trauma of the night before.

"Hush, Kelly. Don't upset yourself again. It will all get better from today, I promise. It was a hell of a shock that you got last night. Saskia was a real bitch to drop it on you like that."

Kelly sat up in Barney's bed and rubbed her head. Despite what her mother had said to her, she wasn't comfortable thinking of her as 'a bitch'. That was going too far.

"Why does my head hurt?" she asked.

"I'd guess it was all the tears last night. You will be better today, really," he added reassuringly.

Kelly looked around her. Nina, Barney's mongrel, was snuggled up beside her. "Did you sleep in here last night?"

Barney looked a little sheepish. "Eh, no, I slept in the living-room. I thought you had enough on your mind without having to fight me off too."

"Oh, Barney, you're so good to me. I can't believe my head is so heavy. I feel like I clubbed all night."

"Well, I did give you a little whiskey to help knock you out. You got fairly worked up once or twice."

"Whiskey? What about the baby?" Kelly's eyes flooded with worry.

"It's OK. It was only a drop. It won't do the baby any harm, I promise."

"Barney, I still can't believe it. This morning it feels more like a dream than a reality. Can you believe that Mum was pregnant with me and that's why she married Dad?"

"Honey, don't start to dwell on it again. It'll drive you mad."

"Do you really think it's my fault that her life was ruined?"

"Please, Kelly, this is how you ended up getting so freaked out last night. Don't start it all over again."

"I have to talk to Dad."

"Why don't you and I go to Dublin? We can walk around Grafton Street. Hey, I can buy you some maternity clothes!"

Kelly looked at him in shock. Then she burst out laughing. "Barney, I won't be needing any of those for quite a few months yet."

"How about some breakfast?" he continued, anxious to keep her mind off her wretched family.

"Do you know what I'd really like?"

"What?"

"A bloody good shag!"

"Now that, Kelly, is music to my ears."

She giggled and moved over in the bed to let Barney climb in.

"I guess it's true what they say. Pregnancy increases a woman's libido. The good news is we don't have to use protection either," she laughed.

"No," Barney agreed. "I don't think there's much likelihood of you getting pregnant."

* * *

Sue Parker was getting back into Wicklow General Hospital around the same time as Barney was getting back into Kelly.

She looked utterly gorgeous as she walked into its quiet foyer. Her golden tan shone on her arms and long legs. A stranger would never have guessed that she was the mother of three. This Sunday morning the real irony was that she had made absolutely no effort to look good. Usually, Sue would take great care and think out what she was going to wear but today was no ordinary day. This was the first day in the rest of Sue Parker's miserable secretive life. She didn't care what she looked like. All she cared about was her marriage and that it was in great danger unless she could keep Guy Parker's blood type a secret from her husband.

Sue had simply thrown on an old cream linen dress. The line still managed to accentuate her slim waist and generous bustline, however. The sleeves were short and the neckline a simple round cut. It was, like so many pieces in Sue's wardrobe, an Escada; thus it hung on her like it was made for her personally. There was a matching bolero jacket, but she hadn't bothered with that this morning. It was turning out to be another hot day anyway. As with all Sue's outfits, she had bought the matching shoes and handbag at the same time and so today, despite all her indifference, she looked like a million dollars.

Following a night where she had got practically no sleep, she had decided that James Harrington couldn't possibly have been making a pass at her. It was the drink. She wasn't used to alcohol. It always did funny things to her. James was far too good-looking and young to be chasing her. Yes, she told herself firmly. It was all just her imagination. He was a lovely man, who also happened to be extremely attractive. If he was a little over-friendly the night before, it was probably just the booze on top of the trauma of their day. Who knows, perhaps she had even inadvertently led him on when she was trying to charm him for information about his telephone conversation with Dave. Anyway, she went home by herself and left him in the pub with Oscar Bingham and bloody Richard Dalton. That would have made it abundantly clear to the good doctor that she was most definitely not available. Then she halted abruptly.

"James, I didn't expect to see you here this morning." She was momentarily caught off guard.

So was James. She looked fantastic. He had the most appalling hangover following what had turned out to be a wildly debauched night of drinking and then clubbing with Richard Dalton. The two men had ended up in some dive of a disco in Wicklow. Being a Saturday night all the local slappers were out. Richard and James had picked up two disturbingly enthusiastic young girls who were easily impressed by a little flash cash. James remembered with a shiver that he shagged one of them and then swapped with Richard. God, it had been a wild night! Richard had crashed out in his place in Wicklow town and to James's knowledge he was still happily asleep there – lucky bastard!

"Sue!" His broad smile concealed how bad he felt. "How are you?"

"I'm fine, thanks. I've just come to collect Guy."

James began to walk with her and gently took her arm in a protective manner. "Did you get some rest last night? It was a big shock for you yesterday."

"Yes, thanks. I slept like a log and I spoke with Dave again," she lied.

James's face cooled at the mention of Dave Parker.

Sue continued, "Everything is fine now." She was on edge speaking with him. Had he figured out her secret? "Look, James, I'm sorry I was such a basket-case on you yesterday. I'm OK now. Thank you for minding me so well yesterday evening."

"You do have to carry a lot on your own, Sue," James sighed. Sympathy was the one thing that she reckoned she could not bear. She knew that a dose of sympathy could reduce her to a blubbering mass of pink cheeks and tears quite quickly.

James knew this too, however. "It's not easy to carry on with three children and keep it all together, is it?"

To her enormous frustration, she could feel her eyes filling up with tears.

James looked at her. "Sue, you're not OK, are you? Come in here for a minute." He quickly side-stepped her into an empty room. "Do you want to have a good cry? It might do you all the good in the world. Here, tell me all

about it." He gently took her into his arms and she began
to sob on his shoulder.

"Oh, I'm such a fool," she cried. "I don't know if I can
go on and I'm trying so hard to keep it all together. I can't
even keep my bloody children safe, James! What kind of
a mother am I?"

"It's OK," he soothed as he hugged her, softly stroking
her exquisite hair. "You just need to go easier on yourself.
You're a marvellous mother, Sue." He looked into her
eyes. "I know you're a marvellous mother. I see the
attention you give those children." He wiped a tear from
her cheek. "You should trust me. I'm a doctor."

He smiled at her and Sue realised, to her shock, that
she did not want to leave the security of his arms. The last
twenty hours had been sheer hell. There was nobody she
could talk to and yet here was this wonderful man telling
her that she herself was wonderful. Was it possible that he
had figured out her problem and was trying to advise her
on how to handle it? She loved the way he was so attentive
to her needs. Why couldn't Dave be more like this?

"James, you're very good to me," she began.

"Nonsense. I am, however, concerned about you." He
tightened his embrace as he said this. "Are you looking
after *you*?"

Sue sighed. "When there's time."

"If something happens to you, what will happen to the
children, Sue? This is serious. We do need to give you a
medical and make sure that you're in good shape."

"A medical? Good heavens, James, I'm not ill. I'm just
a little – oh I don't know." Sue stopped, distracted. Was it
her imagination or did she feel a definite firming up in Dr
Harrington's trousers?

James stepped back and placed his hands on her shoulders. "Now, Sue, I don't want any excuses. We're going to give you a total medical. I insist, as your doctor." He smiled as he said it. "Now to matters more pressing. Let's go and see how that son of yours is and get him home with you." It was only as they left the little room that Sue realised it was in fact a chapel. There was no way Dr Harrington would have got a hard-on in a church. It was obviously her rampant imagination again.

Within an hour all the correct forms had been filled in and James had waved Sue and Guy off the premises. The little fella had had a lucky escape, but James's mind was on his mother. He was determined to seduce her. Fuck, she was gorgeous and so natural with it! She genuinely didn't seem to have the slightest idea that she was so beautiful. He had got so turned on by her in the chapel, all he wanted to do was take her there and then. It took all his restraint not to kiss her when she was in his arms but he knew that it was the wrong place and the wrong time. There was only one thing he could do now. He went off to find Nurse Eileen – she was always game for a quickie. She didn't even mind if he called her Sue while he gave it to her. Thankfully, Eileen was on duty in Out-patients.

"Eileen, could I see you for a minute?" He granted her one of his best killer smiles.

She looked at him hopefully. "What is it, Dr Harrington?"

"If I could just *have* you for a few minutes. Shall we say at the door to the chapel in five?"

"Certainly, Doctor," she smiled at him, knowing exactly what he meant.

James turned on his heel and walked away. He was going to fuck Sue Parker if it was the last thing he did.

Feeling considerably better than she had earlier, Kelly sat up in bed beside Barney.

"I have to talk to Dad. I have to find out if Mum was telling the truth."

Barney sighed. He had reckoned that this was what was going to happen.

"Do you want to meet him or would you prefer to have the conversation on the phone?"

"Well, I want to do it now. So I guess the phone is what's easiest."

He sat up beside her. "OK, pet. Just let me go to the loo and I'll be right back."

"Actually no, Barney. If it's all right with you, I think this is something I need to do by myself."

He looked a little hurt. "Oh, OK, I guess. So what you really want is for me to make myself scarce. Is that it?"

"Would you mind dreadfully?"

Barney smiled at the girl he loved so much.

"Not at all, honey. I'll go and give Owl his oats, now that I've had my own!"

"Thank you for being so understanding."

Barney pulled on a pair of jeans and an old jumper as she watched him from the comfort of his bed. Then he kissed her on the forehead.

"I'll be just outside. If things get a little hot for you, just yell."

"OK."

"I love you."

"I love you too," Kelly replied and realised that she

meant it. From deep within her very soul, she really meant it.

He left and she phoned her grandmother's house.

"Dalton residence," Edwina answered in her usual condescending manner.

"Gran, eh, hi. It's Kelly. How are you?"

"I'm absolutely fine, girl," she managed to answer in an incredible tone of disapproval. "I've been to Mass and seen to my dahlias. Never better."

It would never occur to the old bat to ask me how I am of course, Kelly thought.

"Did you enjoy the party last weekend?" she said, trying to make conversation.

"Dreadful music. I don't know how you're not all deaf. Really, why your mother lets you listen to it, I will never understand."

Kelly was remembering why she hated her grandmother so much.

"Is Dad there?" she interrupted before Edwina got on a roll about the vices of modern pop culture.

"I think he's still sleeping,"

"I really need to talk to him. Could you wake him, please?"

"Your father works very hard. He needs his rest, child."

"And I need my dad. Can you just knock on his door?"

"Well, really!" Edwina put the phone down but Kelly could hear her droning on about the insolence of the younger generation. After a few moments she came back.

"He must have gone out when I was at Mass. He's not there now," Edwina answered shortly.

"Oh . . ." Kelly was at a loss. "Well, if he comes back in, could you get him to ring me please? Oh, I'm – er, in

Barney's house. Here's the number –" As she rhymed it off to Edwina, she sent up a silent prayer that her gran wouldn't twig to the fact that she had in fact spent the night there.

"Have you tried his mobile?" Edwina asked.

"No, I didn't think of that."

"That's the problem of the younger generation these days. They never think."

Kelly had had enough of her. "Thanks, Gran, bye." She rang off without waiting for a reply. She wrapped Barney's huge winter dressing-gown around her and plodded out to the back yard where Barney and Owl were.

"Wow, that was fast," he said cheerfully.

"He's up and out already," Kelly explained miserably. "I don't feel like trying his mobile – who knows where he is or who he's with." The back garden of Peartree Cottage was drenched in sunlight and it was pleasantly warm but still Kelly shivered.

"Your dad? Up early on a Sunday?" Barney looked shocked.

Kelly blinked as the reality of the situation sank in. She put her hand to her mouth as if that would stop her crying but it was too late. "God, Barney, how could I be so stupid? He isn't up and out already. He never came home last night, did he?"

"Hush now, don't upset yourself about stuff that you don't know to be true."

"I think I'm going to barf!" Kelly ran back inside Peartree Cottage, with Barney hot on her heels.

"That'll be the morning sickness," he explained proudly to her back as she ran into the bathroom, then shut the bathroom door in his face. She didn't have time to explain that it was actually the notion that her father was out cavorting that made her nauseous. Not the pregnancy.

Presently she reappeared.

"Feel any better?" he asked.

"I wasn't sick."

"How about a nice big breakfast? I could run you up a fry in no time. Rasher, sausage, eggs? Would you like some beans and fried mushrooms on the side, and of course some fresh bread?"

Kelly winced. "Do you have any orange juice? If I eat what you're suggesting I'll definitely be ill."

Barney looked crestfallen. "Eh, no. We'll have to go out for that. Tell you what, why don't you get back into bed and I'll make the trek to O'Reilly's for your juice, my fry and the Sunday papers."

"That sounds like a plan." Kelly climbed back into bed with Nina for company, and Barney took a quick shower and then headed out for the goodies. As he closed the front door, he didn't hear the phone ring.

"Barney, that's your phone," Kelly yelled after him but it was too late – he was obviously out of earshot. She came out to the living-room and looked at the phone ringing. What if it was something important? Or worse again, Saskia. Then Kelly thought, it could be Richard. Nervously she answered Barney's phone.

"Eh, Armstrong residence."

"Ah, Kelly! That's a bit rich," Richard laughed. His head pounded like there was a brass band in residence but he wasn't going to let his daughter know that he was hungover

"Dad! Hi! I thought you were out."

"Well, it's funny you should say that. I am! I had some stuff to do early this morning, nothing too pressing though. But Mum, thankfully, had the good sense to call me. She thought that you might need me for something. Is she right?"

"Were you out on the town last night, Daddy?" Kelly wanted to be convinced that her worst fears were unfounded.

"Kelly, moi? Never! Now that we're on the subject, however, what the hell are you doing in Barney's house this early on a Sunday morning?"

"Oh Daddy, so much has happened and I hate Mummy. She told me that you got her pregnant and you two got married just because of me. Is that true? Is it all my fault?"

Richard was stunned into silence for an instant. His tone changed into one that Kelly rarely heard him use. It was ice cold and clinically precise.

"Is Barney with you, Kelly?"

"No, he's just gone down to O'Reillys to get some, er, breakfast stuff."

"Honey, we need to talk but face to face would be better. I can be there in half an hour. Can you wait that long?"

"Just tell me, is what she said true?"

"No. It quite simply isn't true. Now sit tight, we'll talk soon. OK?"

"Why would she lie to me?"

"Kelly, I want you to listen to me very carefully. What she said is not true. We both love you very much. I'll be there in thirty minutes. Sit tight, OK?"

"OK, Daddy. Thank you."

"I love you, honey."

"I love you too."

Following his conversation with his daughter, Richard cancelled his plans of going back to sleep. He looked around the room that he had been sleeping in. Thankfully the woman he had picked up the night before had had the good sense to slip out under cover of darkness. He found her note and phone number next to the bed. Richard laughed aloud.

"In your dreams, bitch!" He crumpled the paper into a ball and threw it towards the bin in the corner of the room. James Harrington had turned out to be a good drinking buddy. Some years younger than Richard, they had worked well together, pulling women. It had been a wild night all right. He vaguely remembered James saying something about having to work this morning, poor bastard! Richard would have gladly slept for a few more hours if his bloody mother hadn't tracked him down on his mobile. Still this was too good an opportunity to miss. He had to make the most of it.

He showered and dressed quickly and next he wrote a short note to James, thanking him for the bed and promising to repeat the party again some time in the near future. Then he left. First things first, he thought, as he started up his Merc.

"Innishambles," he spoke to his voice-activated phone. "Let's see what Saskia is playing at because there's no doubt – the game's afoot."

CHAPTER 14

"What exactly are you playing at?" Raymond Saunders laughed at his three children from over the top of his Sunday newspaper. They had marched into the kitchen, dressed in an array of clothing from their dressing-up box.

"We're getting married, of course, what does it look like?" Jasmine, his nine-year-old, replied snootily.

"Yes, Jasmine. I can see that, but I would have thought that you would have made a much prettier bride than your younger brother!"

"Edward wanted to wear the dress," Jasmine explained simply. "Anyway, I'm taller so I should be the Daddy and I want to run the business stuff so I should definitely be the Daddy."

Raymond put his newspaper down. "Darling, you can run the 'business stuff' as you so eloquently put it and still be a beautiful young lady."

"I don't want to be a beautiful young lady," Jasmine scowled.

"I do!" her eight-year-old brother piped up.

201

Raymond had been very nervous about Edward's obsession with girlie clothes and all things feminine, but Caroline had insisted that it was just a phase and Raymond was to give the boy time and room to grow. It was one of the last things she had said to him on her deathbed. "Let Edward grow his own way – don't try to knock it out of him. He'll find his path." Raymond had promised his wife that he wouldn't push Edward and he intended to stick to that promise and so, yet again, he smiled at his son for his childish comments and ignored what he said. Instead he concentrated on Jasmine.

"Why don't you want to be a beautiful young lady?"

"I just don't," she looked at the floor.

"But you are a beautiful young lady already," Raymond tried.

Jasmine looked at Raymond in terror.

"No, I'm not. I couldn't be."

"Why not?"

She mumbled something as she studied her fancy-dress shoes. Raymond noticed painfully that they were in fact a pair of Caroline's old stilettos. He gently took Jasmine's hand and pulled her towards him.

"Why do you not want to be a beautiful young lady?"

"You said Mummy was a beautiful lady and look what happened to her! I don't want to go to heaven, Daddy, even if Mummy is there."

Raymond took a deep breath and tried hard to control his emotions. Were Jasmine to see her father cry, it would hardly help the situation.

He pulled her close to him and hugged her tightly.

"It's OK, angel, you're not going to heaven – not for a very very long time. I promise."

"How can you promise that? You said that nobody knows when they're going to go to heaven. That's what you said when Mummy got sick and no matter how many times I begged her not to go she still went," Jasmine sobbed into her father's shirt.

"I know, darling. We all miss Mummy dreadfully. I think we will always miss her but you know that she's looking down at us right now, minding us from heaven."

"I want her to mind us from here," Jasmine whined.

"Well, do you think she could mind us if we were in McDonald's?" Raymond asked playfully, trying one of his oldest tricks – distraction. The child psychologist had explained to Raymond that it was bad to ignore the children's feeling of grief. The trick was to help them live with and through it. With time and lots of love and patience it would get easier.

Jasmine looked at him suspiciously but the boys jumped into the air at the mere mention of their favourite fast food.

"Of course she could look down from heaven into McDonald's," Jasmine answered carefully.

"Well then, I think that's where we should all have a huge lunch. What do you think?"

His daughter nodded almost imperceptibly. Her platinum hair and big blue eyes were so like her late mother's, it made Raymond catch his breath. He missed his wife. Francis broke Raymond's daydream as he tore through the house yelling "McDonald's!" Edward danced off to find a suitable coat to wear over his bridal gown.

"Eddy, you're not going to McDonald's in a dress! I want everybody dressed in regular clothes before we go anywhere," Raymond laughed goodnaturedly.

"Daddy, will I wake Jayne and see if she wants to come?" Jasmine asked, being as considerate as always.

"Not this morning, love. Why don't we just go alone? You, me and the boys, what do you say?"

"I say that's a great idea."

Within half an hour of this conversation, the four Saunders were digging into quarter pounders with nuggets on the side and a Fillet o'Fish, just in case anybody got hungry again, and of course a mountain of French fries.

"This was a great idea," Francis informed his dad.

"I'm glad, Francis. What do you want to do next? Go to a movie?"

"There's a new Dalmatians movie out," Jasmine said hopefully. The boys groaned.

"How about the new *Return of Pokemon* one?" Francis suggested.

"No way," Jasmine made a face.

"Well, the weather is probably too nice to go to the movies anyway." Raymond was trying to avert the fight he could see brewing. "Tell you what, let's go on a magical mystery tour!"

The three children regarded their father suspiciously.

"Where?" Edward asked.

"It's meant to be a mystery," Jasmine explained impatiently.

"OK, well, this is just an idea now," Raymond started. "It's just a thought, but I was wondering if you guys would like to move house?"

They looked at him in stunned silence.

"But why?" Francis asked.

"Well, I've seen this house in a place called Wicklow and I think you would really like it."

Raymond didn't want to tell them his real reason for moving. He didn't want to explain that everywhere he looked in their home there were painful memories of Caroline. It was just too difficult to stay there. It was Raymond's psychologist who had suggested he move house. He knew he had to move on and that meant he really had to move house.

"I like our house," Jasmine scowled.

"Yes, but this house in the country is much bigger and it would mean the boys wouldn't have to share a room any more. You guys would each have your own room!"

As expected, the boys were relatively easily won over. They exploded into cheers and gave each other a high five. Jasmine was more difficult.

"I already have my own room."

"Ah, yes, but you have to share when we have visitors. You won't have to do that in the future. This would be a room just for you. You wouldn't have to share it with anybody, ever."

As expected, this caught her attention.

"What else does it have?"

"Oh," Raymond pretended to be disinterested. "Nothing else, just a tennis court and a swimming-pool."

The boys looked at their father incredulously. "What?" they asked in unison. "Did you say a pool?"

"Yep."

"*Yeaaaah*!" Another round of high fives.

"Like our own pool, a private pool?" Even Jasmine was now enthralled.

"Our very own pool, Jas, although you will have to share that with your brothers and perhaps any visitors that come to the house. Now what do you think?"

"I think we should go and have a look." Coming from Jasmine this was a hell of an acceptance. She was queen of negotiation. Raymond dearly hoped that she would one day come and work with him.

"Do you think that there'll be any other young boys living there, Daddy?" Francis asked with a mischievous grin. Out of the three Saunders children, Francis was the best at finding trouble.

"I'm sure there will be," Raymond smiled back.

"Jayne will be coming with us, won't she?" Edward suddenly asked, his face contorted with concern.

"Of course she will," Jasmine answered impatiently.

Raymond looked from his son to his daughter. "Well, the answer is yes, Edward, she will come with us but I'm fascinated that you're so certain she'll agree, Jas. What makes you so sure?"

"Daddy, it's obvious. Jayne is in love with you. She'll go anywhere with you."

The boys groaned at the mere mention of girlie stuff like 'love'. Raymond burst out laughing.

"I think you're a little off the mark there, angel. Jayne is our nanny. She loves all of us just the same but she doesn't love me in the way you're thinking of."

"No, Daddy, she loves you in the husband-wife way. Once when I was going to the toilet late at night, I passed by her room and she was crying, well groaning sort of and saying your name, even though you weren't there. In fact you weren't even in the house. It was when you were away on business."

Raymond nearly choked on his nugget. "I'm sure you've made some sort of mistake, honey – now finish up your food."

206

"No, I didn't make any kind of mistake. I know what I heard. I think she was pretending that you two were kissing and stuff if you know what I mean." Jasmine wrinkled her nose in disgust.

The boys began groaning their father's name and giggling.

"OK, that's enough now, gang. Eat up and shut up." He looked around, hoping that nobody had seen or heard the conversation. It was OK on that front.

"I think she wants to be your new wife," Jasmine added matter-of-factly, as she examined the remains of her burger.

"Now you're really being ridiculous," Raymond spluttered. "OK, she may have had a bad dream one time that you happened to overhear but I think I would know if Jayne wanted to marry me, Jasmine."

"No, Daddy," Jas continued patiently as if she was talking to a four-year-old. "If Jayne wanted to marry you, you would be the *last* to know."

* * *

Saskia did her best to ignore the phone but whoever it was obviously had no intention of giving up.

With any luck, it will be Kelly phoning me, she thought, feeling wretchedly guilty about her outburst the previous evening. She knew she would have to call over to Peartree Cottage later to apologise properly, but not just yet. The day wasn't turning out very well and it was only eleven thirty. Lauren and Tiffany were having some terrible cat-fight and Lauren had stormed out of the house to "get some fresh air". She had taken Dudley and Dexter and little Robin too. She had seemed utterly fed up as she mumbled something about there being at least one sister she had who still talked honestly to her – even if she was only three. It was obviously a pretty bad argument between Lauren and Tiff, which was very unusual.

Tiffany was still sulking in her room. It was clear that the girl had no wish to answer the phone.

"Hello," Saskia said.

"Just what exactly did you say to our eldest daughter about her being the cause of our getting married?" Richard thundered down the phone. Introductions were unnecessary.

"What right do you have to ring me and ask such things?" Saskia snapped back.

"Saskia, what the fuck is wrong with you? We agreed that we would never tell her the truth. Why now?"

"She didn't tell you then?" Saskia's tone was softer. She knew that this was going to be a blow to her ex-husband.

"Tell me what?" he demanded impatiently.

"Richard, there's no easy way to break this to you. Kelly is pregnant."

"What?"

Saskia heard the car swerve and a car-horn blasting Richard.

"You're driving. Would you consider pulling in to the side of the road for a minute, Richard?"

He had in fact just done that, hence the loud beeping.

"She's bloody pregnant? Barney's, I assume?"

"Yes. Look, she has been miserable for the last week about it. Barney broke up with her when he found out. He wanted an abortion."

"Barney? I don't believe it," Richard snorted. "Barney is a wuss, a softy!"

She ignored his comments and continued. "For some reason, I don't know why, they've changed their minds and now all is sweetness and light and they want to get married."

"And you saw fit to pick that moment to tell her how stupid she was being and not to make the same mistake you made. Is that it?" Richard was beginning to fill in the blanks for himself.

"Exactly," Saskia's guard was back up. "Just because she's made one significant mistake, there's no point in making an even bigger one!"

"Is that what we were, Saskia? A big mistake. All twenty-one years?"

She didn't say anything. Richard sighed.

"I know I fucked up, Saskia. I know I behaved like a royal prick to you over the last few years, but how did that cloud your judgement so badly? Do you not remember any of the good times? None at all?"

Again she didn't dare to speak.

"I guess not," he concluded. "Look, I'm going to Peartree Cottage now. This thing has to be sorted out. Whether you like it or not, I'm going to tell Kelly the Mills and Boon version of her slightly early arrival into our lives. Do you hear me?"

"Yes."

"I'm going to tell her that you just got a little emotional last night and you exaggerated. OK?"

"No, not OK, Richard. I don't think she should marry him and I can't stand by –"

But Richard cut in. "Listen here, Saskia, I don't intrude much upon your life these days because that's the way you like it but I will have my say on this matter. What *you* think Kelly should do with her life is not the issue here. What *she* thinks she should do is what we need to think about. Maybe Barney did behave like a prat when he first heard she was pregnant. He wouldn't be the first guy to do so, but it sounds like he's fairly happy about it now. What we need to do is give them all the understanding and time they need to make the right decision. There's a bloody baby coming and they have to deal with that. Do you hear me, Saskia?"

He spoke so authoritatively that she relented.

"I suppose so," she whispered.

"Good. Now do you want to come with me this morning or do you want to sit this one out?"

This question caught Saskia completely off guard.

"I – I don't know. What do you mean?" she spluttered.

"Well, we're her parents, damn it – I think it would be better if we put on a unified front here, especially after your little outburst last night. What do you think?"

Saskia's mind raced. She had nothing to wear. Richard! Here! Soon? Oh, Jesus. Cop on, Sas. She panicked even more. Why do I even care what I wear in front of that shit of an ex-husband?

"Saskia?" Richard interrupted her thoughts.

"Where are you?"

"I'm, er, just outside Wicklow." Richard had no intention of telling Saskia where or how he had spent his previous night and so he continued to press her. "Will I collect you or not?"

"Why don't I meet you at the cottage?" Saskia suggested, trying to think on her feet.

"Good idea, that way I can smooth the path a little before you get there." His voice had softened somewhat.

"Saskia, I know it must have been a hell of a shock for you – hell, it is for me too, but to tell her after all this time! What were you at?"

"I don't know, Richard. I swear I don't know what came over me."

"Bloody hormones," Richard grumbled. It was his way of explaining the inexplicable, having lived with four women for the best part of twenty years.

Two minutes later, Saskia was under the shower, frantically trying to make her hair look like the ones on the television commercials. She pulled out her pull-everything-in knickers and panicked over what else to wear.

At the same time as she was running around her bedroom practically naked, Richard was pulling up outside Peartree Cottage.

He knocked on the pretty little front door.

Tentatively, Kelly opened it. When she saw that it was Richard, she threw it wide open.

"Daddy, I'm so glad to see you!" She flung her arms around him and he hugged her back, a big bear hug.

"It's good to see you too, sunshine. Now let's get inside before people start to talk," he laughed. "Where's Barney?"

"I'm right here." Barney came out of the kitchen, his voice strong and proprietorial. He had returned from O'Reilly's with enough food for an army. "But if you two want, I could take the dog for a walk." He was sensitive to the fact that Kelly wanted to do this alone. What Richard Dalton wanted was of no interest to Barney. That man had already done enough bloody damage to his family. Barney still hadn't forgiven him but this he kept to himself.

"Would you mind?" Richard asked.

Barney looked at Kelly for her response. She nodded at her fiancé. "Back in twenty minutes," he smiled and kissed Kelly on the cheek.

Richard shook Barney's hand and clapped his back. "Congratulations on getting engaged," he smiled warmly.

"Thanks, Richard. See you soon." Barney winked at Kelly. Then he and Nina headed out.

Alone with his first-born, Richard smiled at her. "This gives us a little time to talk, sweetheart."

Kelly looked at her father. "Daddy, there's something I have to tell you," she stuttered.

Richard decided to make it easy for her. What was the point in dragging it out?

"I gather I'm going to be a granddad," he smiled down at her.

"You know?"

"How many times have I told you that daddies know everything?"

"Oh, Daddy, it's such a mess," Kelly continued without missing a beat. "Mummy said that she got pregnant with me by accident and then she got married and it was the biggest mistake she ever made and I shouldn't make the same mistake and now I don't know what to think."

Richard took her hand and led her to Barney's big armchair. He sat her down and sat on the coffee table next to her.

"Hey, hey, sweetheart, the first thing you must do is relax. You're going to be fine. I have to tell you – your mum was overwrought last night. You gave her a heck of a surprise. I don't think she was quite ready to become a grandma, let alone mother-of-the-bride and now that I mention it, the idea of granddad doesn't exactly do it for me." He laughed good-naturedly.

"Oh Daddy," Kelly had the decency to look suitably embarrassed, "I'm sorry to drop it on you like this."

"Yes, well, I didn't exactly come down in the last shower, but that doesn't mean that I'm not surprised to discover that my little angel has, in fact, lost her innocence."

Kelly continued to look embarrassed. "Sorry."

"Kelly," Richard took her chin in his hand, gently tilting her face towards his, "as luck would have it, your parents *were* in exactly the same position some years ago, so we're going to be the last ones to judge you."

Kelly's face contorted in anguish. "So Mum was telling the truth!"

Richard cut her off before she began to spin off into a blind panic again.

"OK, let's set the record straight. Your mother was a little emotional last night. That's the first thing. Secondly, you know she and I have had a particularly nasty divorce. I was a real bastard to your mother over the last few years of our marriage. God knows why, Kelly – I ask myself that every day, but that's not what we're here to discuss today."

Kelly had never heard him talk so honestly about his life before.

"What we are here to discuss," he continued, "is you. When you dropped into our life, slightly earlier than expected, of course we were surprised and a little scared. I'm sure you know exactly what I'm talking about. Anyway, after we got over the initial shock, Sas and I decided to get married. Your mum and I *were* madly in love. We wanted to be together. We were very very happy for a long time. You need to know this, Kelly. You may have altered the date that Saskia and I got married but I know in my heart and soul that we would have got married sooner or later anyway. We were very much in love."

Kelly looked at him incredulously. "What happened to change all that?"

Richard heaved a great big sad sigh. "Damned if I know, but I do know that in the early days – more – for the best part of our married life your mom and I were very happily married."

"What if that happens to Barney and me? We might start out great and then after twenty years it could fall apart."

Richard laughed hollowly. "Thanks for rubbing it in, Kelly!" Then his tone changed. "Ah honey, I can't help you on the answer to that. You'll need to seek the advice of somebody who is still happily married after twenty years." His tone softened even more. "This is a huge decision and one that you have to make by yourself. Your mum and I can only guide you."

"I'm not sure that she'll ever even talk to me again," Kelly moaned.

As if on cue, the door bell tinkled.

"Speak of the devil!" Richard smiled.

"Ohmigod, is that Mum?"

"She's here because she loves you and she wants to help," Richard soothed his daughter. "Can I let her in?"

Kelly nodded nervously.

CHAPTER 15

On Sunday evening Dave Parker was still in Egypt. He looked at the clock over the bar counter. It was time to get going if he wanted to catch his flight. The truth was he didn't want to catch his wretched plane. Dave was in a very dark mood. He had barely slept the previous night, following his phone call from Sue. He had phoned her again at lunch-time that day and found that Guy was home. Sue was supernaturally happy and he knew why. She was putting on one big act. "Everything's fine here, Dave. Honestly!" That's what she had said. As he thought about it now he got even more steamed up. How could she say "honestly"? The one thing she wasn't being was honest. James Harrington had been so nonchalant when he talked about Guy's blood type. He explained that Sue wasn't O negative and Guy was – so obviously Dave must be. After all, Guy had to inherit it from one of his parents! Dave's fingers tightened around his glass. Then Sue had come back on the phone and casually asked him what blood type he was. From that moment Dave was in freefall. Why wasn't Sue panicking? Why wasn't she asking the same questions as he himself was? How come Guy was O negative and neither of his parents was? He buried his drink and ordered another. There was only one plausible answer. Sue was covering up. Dave could hardly believe it. They had been through such a tough patch some years ago when Sue thought Richard Dalton was Guy's father. When they eventually got through it together, the one thing they vowed was "no more secrets" – so much for that bloody vow.

When his barman returned he grabbed the gin and tonic like it was a lifeline. He needed to dull his senses. It was so obvious and yet so painful to face. Richard Dalton really was Guy's father! Even more painful, however, was the fact that Sue knew and was trying to hide it from him – the one man she claimed to love more than anyone else in the world. *Ha!* It festered in his mind and he dwelt on it as if replaying the scenario over again and again might change the outcome. It didn't. An O negative child had to have an O negative parent. When he had said to Sue on the phone that he was A positive she hadn't reacted. That was her bloody chance. He had given her an opportunity to come clean and say that something really weird was going on, that maybe the hospital had made a mistake. But now he knew that there was no mistake. Sue Parker was covering up the fact that Guy was not his son. She knew and she was keeping it a secret from him. Dave's mind spun in a rage. Was she still having an affair with Richard Dalton? It would explain the rift that had been developing between him and Sue over the last few months. The anger swelled even more. Christ, was he minding and supporting Richard Dalton's bastard son under his own roof! Dave fantasised about murdering Richard. How could it be done?

"How are you?" Penny had walked up behind him.

He spun around and summoning all his willpower he pushed the dark thoughts aside – for later.

"Tired." He rubbed his eyes.

"Anything to do with all the boozy lunches that have been part of this particular junket?" she teased gently.

Dave looked at his PA and smiled. "It's funny – for a country that's meant to be dry, it's amazing how much booze I've been offered. Mind you, they know how to charge for it!"

"Gosh, you really are a bit maudlin, aren't you?"

"I was just thinking how nice it would be to stay on here for another twenty-four hours and enjoy the facilities of this gorgeous hotel. Christ, we've been here for the entire weekend and this is the first drink I've actually had here, in the bloody hotel."

"Forget the hotel, you should see some of the temples here. Luxor is absolutely fantastic. Dave, you'd get a much better feel for Egypt if you actually went out and looked at the place instead of looking at business proposals all day."

"You have a point there."

"It's a pity you can't stay for a few more days and have a look around the city, maybe even take a cruise down the Nile?"

"What, all alone?"

"Well, I could hardly stay with you if it was pleasure instead of business. What do you think, Mr Parker?" she teased him.

"Christ no, Penny. I'm sure you want to get home as soon as you can."

Now it was Penny's turn to sigh. She dragged the bar

stool next to Dave's under her bum and plonked her head into the cup of her hands.

"I'm dreading going home. Sean and I have broken up again."

"Ah Jesus, not again, Penny? I thought you two were definitely for the long jump this time."

"Huh," she laughed sadly, "so did I. That's the main reason we've broken up. Sean has a bit of a problem making that particular jump."

"Here, let's have a drink to your new-found freedom."

"Damn sure I'll drink to that."

Dave called the waiter over. He was a friendly-looking guy who spoke fluent English. He had introduced himself to Dave when he brought him his first gin and tonic. That was three drinks ago and Dave's private pain was beginning to dull.

"Penny, this is Omar. Omar, this is Penny. What will you have to drink, Penny?"

"Gin and tonic, please."

Omar granted them a huge white smile and went off to find some tonic water.

"No ice," Dave called after him. Then he said to Penny, "Have you been OK since you got here? You know, tummy problems?"

"Yeah, I did exactly what you said. No ice, no water other than bottled, and everything has been fine, touch wood." She knocked on the exquisite cedarwood bar counter. "Egypt really is beautiful, Dave. Do you think you'll go ahead with your development here?"

"Well, I must say it's looking very positive. The local labour is intelligent, relatively cheap and they have a very good outlook."

"They all speak fluent English too," she added as Omar returned with her G&T.

"*Shukran*," she smiled at him.

"Ah, you speak Arabic," Omar smiled. "*Afwan*."

"What does that mean?" Dave whispered as soon as Omar turned his back.

"Jesus, Dave, all the time you've been here and you haven't even picked that up? *Shukran* is 'thanks' and *afwan* means 'you're welcome'."

"Ah, thanks. Er, *shukran*!"

They laughed and drank a little.

"I must say I'm a little surprised, Dave. You're usually in a huge rush to get home. Especially this week, what with little Guy's accident yesterday – I thought you'd be catching an early flight if anything."

Dave's face clouded over for only an instant, but it was enough for Penny, who knew her boss well, to understand that all was not well in paradise.

"Well, he's fine now. To be honest, I think Sue got a little melodramatic."

"Ah, right so," Penny tried to drop the subject. "Well, cheers!"

"How do they say cheers in Arabic?" Dave asked.

Penny giggled. "They don't – remember, they don't drink!"

"Omar!" Dave shouted to his new friend. "Two more G&Ts and no ice!"

"No problem," Omar smiled back.

"We're going to miss our plane," Penny cautioned.

"We can catch a later one."

"What about Guy?"

"He's fine. All a storm in a teacup," Dave said as he

raised his glass to eye level and swirled the clear liquid around to form a whirlpool.

Penny watched her boss. "Well, I think I should try and put a call through to Sue to tell her you've been delayed."

"Whatever."

Penny now knew that it wasn't her imagination. Dave and Sue Parker, the proverbial Romeo and Juliet of the retail industry, were having problems.

"You line them up there, Dave. I'll go and make the call."

It took her the best part of twenty minutes to rejoin him, by which time he had said hello and goodbye to a further three G&Ts. They were making him feel better.

"I thought you might have changed your mind and gone to catch the plane without me," Dave laughed.

"No, I just phoned Sue and told her about a last-minute trip you had to do around Luxor and that there was no way out of it – you'd catch a flight out tomorrow. Now come on!"

"Where?"

"Dave Parker, you're not going to make a liar out of me. I'm going to take you on a trip of Luxor by night!"

She took him by the hand as he downed the last of his drink and they headed out into the dry heat of the city.

As they exited the hotel, Dave admired the ornate architecture. "Isn't it funny that they call this place the Old Winter Palace. I mean there isn't really a winter in Egypt, is there?"

Penny nodded in agreement. "Well, in case you haven't noticed, that's the New Winter Palace next door so I guess coming up with new names is not their strong point!"

She pushed Dave into one of the horse-drawn carriages that were Luxor's answer to taxis and she greeted the driver.

"*Mesaa al khayr, Karnak Temple. Shukran.*"

"Jesus, you speak fluent Arabic, Penny."

"Not quite," she laughed, "but enough to get you to Karnak Temple. It would be criminal to come to Luxor and not see this temple."

The little horse was a bag of bones and, as his driver urged him into a canter, Dave was sure that the animal would fall over from exhaustion on the job.

"Can you get him to slow down?" Dave whispered.

"I don't know how to say slow down in Egyptian!"

Dave tapped the driver on the back and smiled, "Can we slow down?" He gestured with his hands, as if he was pulling in the horse's reins.

The driver smiled widely, revealing a practically toothless mouth and nodded, urging the horse on faster.

"Jesus, I think we're all going to be killed," Dave laughed nervously.

"This is nothing, wait till we get down into the town. It's bedlam down there. Whoever is bravest has right of way!"

"Ah shit!" Dave winced and wondered what he was doing there.

As the little bony nag clip-clopped into the city of Luxor, so did a thousand other little horses and traps. They all looked ancient and the carriage interiors were decorated with bright and garish colours. The mosques began to broadcast their strange lament, urging the Muslims to prayer. The sound travelled clearly through the hot night air, but to Dave's ear it sounded like somebody in considerable discomfort. As they travelled through the back streets, he watched all the action. People bartered at stalls for spices and lighters and even kitchen sinks. The noise level was high and jovial. Men slapped each other on the back; women talked among themselves, their bodies totally covered in black shrouds. The most striking assault on his senses however was the fantastic aroma of burning spices.

"Has he taken us through the residential quarter?" Dave asked.

"No, Dave, this is the main street. Isn't it wonderful?"

Dave looked at Penny in amazement. She was enthralled by what was around them. It seemed to energise and invigorate her. Quite suddenly his mind's eye flashed to a vision of Sue sitting beside him. She would love this, he thought. Then he thought of Guy and his mood darkened. Thankfully a loud noise brought his focus back to the present.

"What is that racket?" he asked but Penny was craning her neck to try and see what it was too.

"Oh, Dave, look, it's a wedding!" Penny gushed.

Dave tried to look but it was practically impossible as the street was totally backed up with little ponies and traps and the wedding cavalcade was in the square ahead of them. Horns of every sort beeped loudly. He caught a brief glimpse of the bride in the back of the first car. After that, all the cars that followed had men dangling out of the windows – whooping and cheering. It struck Dave that there were no female revellers in evidence. In Ireland, you could be quite sure that there would be as many women as men hanging out of the car windows – probably more.

"Doesn't it bother you that women are treated as second-class citizens here?" he asked as their trap began to move again and they bounced towards the Nile.

"I don't think they're treated badly – they're just treated differently. What's more they respect our beliefs – I've had no grief for not being covered from head to foot in fabric."

"Well, don't get lulled into a false feeling of security, Penny. The Egyptians may be very tolerant of our debauched western ways but you wouldn't be so lucky in Saudi Arabia, for instance, or, God forbid, some of the even more fundamentalist countries."

Penny looked at Dave and smiled broadly. "But I'm not in Saudi, Dave. I'm in Luxor. I'm in Egypt! The air is hot and alive with sound. The smell of strange spices fills my head and the beauty, my God, the beauty –" Just then, the pony and trap pulled over to the side of the road and Penny continued, "This, Dave, is Karnak Temple."

Even Dave was momentarily stunned.

"My God, it's huge!"

"Not bad for a couple of thousand years ago, is it? When our fore-fathers were living in mud shacks, this is what the Egyptians were doing."

She gave the driver a heavy tip and told him to wait which, amazingly, he understood perfectly.

Dave and Penny walked around the ancient and huge temple of Karnak. It was even more spectacular than the last time Penny had seen it because that had been during the day, and at night it was lit up in a way that made the columns look even more magnificent and domineering.

"Look, it's a mini-sphinx!" Dave laughed as he pointed to a small sphinx, measuring no more than three feet in height.

"Well, there was a time when there were thousands of them. They lined the entire route from here to Luxor Temple three kilometres away."

"What, the whole way?"

"Yep, on both sides of the road."

"They must have been going cheap at the temple discount store!"

Penny gave him a dig and laughed. "They've built the city on top of them now so it can't really be excavated."

"Still," Dave continued a little more seriously now, "Hollywood and Liz Taylor didn't really do it justice – I mean the temples are just so huge, aren't they?"

After Karnak Temple, their little pony and trap took them to the equally impressive Luxor Temple. Many different kings and even a queen or two over the course of thousands of years had built it. The sky was pitch black and the stars seemed huge and so bright. It made Dave forget all about home. Ballymore seemed like a distant memory. It felt totally insignificant out here.

As they were just about all templed out, Penny began to yawn.

"Penny, thanks for showing these things to me. Sometimes I get so wrapped up in the business side, I forget to come up for air. I saw Egypt as a business opportunity. Don't get me wrong, I still do. It's just that you've reminded me what a beautiful, rich, exciting culture there is here too."

"Good, now let's go and get some food, I'm starving!"

"Old Winter Palace, *shukran*," Dave commanded their driver in his best Arabic accent.

Omar was still on duty when they got back.

"Hello, friends."

"Hello, Omar. Rack 'em up!"

"Say again please."

"Two G&Ts," he laughed.

"And no ice!" Penny and Dave chorused together.

They went into the large dining-room. Dave felt considerably better than he had earlier. He actually felt like he was on holidays. All the other businessmen in his consortium had returned to their various homes around Europe. He was the only one left. He looked at Penny. She was actually quite attractive but far too young for him, of course.

Firstly, they tried the local brew, a white wine called Obelisque, but it didn't go down too well and so Dave and Penny returned to the safety of their G&Ts.

The night wore on and they got more and more relaxed.

"You and Sean will get back together, you'll see," Dave tried to console her over some sort of nougat dessert.

"I know. I even know he loves me but what he really needs is a little shove," Penny said morosely.

"That's it! You need to make him jealous."

"He knows me too well. He would know that I was only going out with somebody to make him jealous."

"You could invent an Egyptian lover," Dave suggested.

"Omar?" Penny laughed.

"He's your man!"

"He's engaged! He told me earlier when you were at the loo. Jesus, everyone's engaged but me!"

"Ah, Penny, hang in there. You're a wonderful girl. Sean will come to his senses soon. You'll see. Tell you what – let's have a bottle of champagne to cheer you up."

Penny looked at him and managed a small smile. "Dave, you're so kind to me."

"Ah, don't start that now. You keep my life running like clockwork practically all the time. You're a treasure."

"That reminds me, I bought the kids little Egyptian outfits as your present from here. They're absolutely gorgeous. You did well this time, Dave!" She winked at him and laughed. She always bought his presents for his family. "And I was going to suggest a pair of Alexandrite earrings for Sue. They change colour in different light. It's just that I wanted you to see them before I bought them. They're in the hotel shop."

"I'll see them tomorrow. Thanks, Penny. You're the best."

He looked at her with such appreciation that Penny thought she might burst out crying. Sean had never looked at her like that.

"I think it's time for bed," she said simply. "I'll let you have a sleep in, in the morning, and then we'll get an afternoon flight to Gatwick or Heathrow. From there, we'll just hop on the next flight to Dublin. How does that sound?"

"Like a bloody good plan."

CHAPTER 16

They headed out of the dining-room and up in the lift together.

"Oh," Penny suddenly remembered, "the outfits for the children! Will I give them to you now?"

"Yeah, why not?"

They made their way to Penny's room and she invited him in.

"The place is a bit of a mess, sorry."

"Hey, this is nothing. You should see the state of my room. Although I must say the housekeeping here is excellent."

"Here they are," Penny produced a bag bulging with different fabrics.

"Let's see what you got." He pulled out an exquisite, midnight-blue scarf. It was feather-light and almost transparent.

"What's this?" he laughed.

"It's for India – she wraps it around her body like so," Penny wrapped herself in the blue, as Dave pulled out the head-piece. It was covered in tiny shimmering gold disks.

"Very exotic," he laughed as he placed it on Penny's head and she covered up most of her face in true Egyptian style.

"Exotic, you say? Do you think I could get a night job as an exotic dancer in one of those clubs at home?"

"Easily!" Dave laughed as he jumped to his feet and began to dance with her.

Under the influence of the gin and tonics and then the bubbles, Penny began to dance a little more suggestively.

"Mademoiselle, you dance beautifully," Dave said in his deepest, most Arabic accent.

"Thank you, master of ze harem," she teased.

He wrapped his hands around her body and squeezed. She wound her arms around his torso and began to stroke his back.

"Do I please my master?" she whispered.

"Oh yes," Dave replied, his voice getting even deeper. "More than you know."

She lifted her face towards his and looked into his eyes. In doing so, the light blue fabric covering her mouth slipped, revealing her soft full young lips.

"Penny?" he whispered.

"Yes," she said and brought her mouth up to his.

His embrace got stronger as he opened her mouth with his lips and pushed his tongue inside. He was hungry and urgent with her.

Penny loved it. In truth, she had fancied her boss for the three years that she had worked for him but never in her wildest dreams had she thought anything would happen. Dave was devoted to Sue. Well, not tonight, it seemed. Her mind swam with lust and drink. What the hell, she thought, we'll figure it out in the morning.

She began to tug at Dave's shirt. It was a light linen shirt because the Egyptian weather was so hot. As soon as he felt Penny pulling at his clothes, he took her hand and guided her towards the bed.

He gently broke away from her mouth to lift her top over her head. Penny saw his face for a moment. It was no longer that of her boss – this was a man drunk with lust and with one thing on his mind. Fine, she thought. I'll shag him senseless!

She climbed onto the bed and stood in front of him so her belly-button was at his eye level.

"So ye want to fuck?" she asked him boldly.

Dave stopped momentarily, stunned by the change of mood. He had to look up to her. His mouth was open and he just nodded.

"Right so, but if we're going to do this, we're going to do it right, Dave Parker! We're going to fuck for Ireland! Deal?"

He grinned at her, like the cat that got the Baileys and nodded happily.

"Strip!" she commanded from her position of authority. He did what he was told and she tore off the rest of her clothes.

"Now," she said, "Are you ready, Dave? Or should I call you Mark Anthony because I'm your Cleopatra?"

Dave jumped onto the bed and pulled her down on top of him. She happily straddled him and kissed him passionately. Penny was a very vibrant and enthusiastic lover, positively athletic in bed – not what Dave was used to at all. He enjoyed stroking her. Her body was still young and firm. For an instant he wondered how his own compared to Sean's, probably not too favourably.

Penny had other things on her mind however. She wriggled down on his body and began licking him hungrily.

"Oh, Jesus," he groaned. It had been so long since Sue had given him a blowjob, he had forgotten how good they were. "God, that's good," he moaned as he lay back and let her do the work.

"Don't you dare come on me, Dave," she laughed as best she could, with a full mouth. "Not yet!"

"Jesus, you're good at this," Dave moaned again. "But what about you?"

"Do you want to lick me too? Do you like that or do you hate it?" she asked simply as if she was asking about black or white coffee.

Dave's head was spinning a little. "What are you saying?"

"Do you want a sixty-nine or do you just want me to blow you?"

"Oh, yeah. Em –" He couldn't get over her bluntness. This girl was wasted doing shorthand!

"I'm game for a sixty-nine if you want," she added happily, but then she moved back down his body again, so he didn't reply.

Even in his drunk state, he could not help comparing Penny with Sue. They were so different it was unbelievable. Sue's body was significantly better, but she would never have the nerve to stand up in the middle of the bed, with her hands on her hips and her legs apart, and boldly lay down commands. Sue was a shy lover. Penny was not. She was voluptuous, curvy and full of fun and he liked it.

Of course his secretary's body was a great deal younger. By how much, Dave wondered, his mind now swimming with the heady cocktail of drink and sex. How much younger than him was she? Christ, how much younger than Sue was Penny? He tried to focus, Penny, Sue, Sue, Penny.

"Oh shit!" He bolted upright in the bed, forcing Penny to stop. "God, Penny, what are we doing?"

"Well, Dave, I would have thought that that was obvious!"

"I mean – this is insanity. You know I have a wife and three kids at home! You're practically married to Sean and here we are doing – doing," he stuttered, "this!"

"You mean having sex?"

"Well, *this*. We shouldn't be doing this. I'm sorry, I've only just come to my senses."

"That's about the only place you've come!" Penny snorted. "Jesus, Dave, your timing isn't the best, is it? You could have said this twenty minutes ago, I would have thought. I mean, you're a big boy now."

Dave pulled himself to the side of the bed and began to fumble for his clothing.

"Ah Penny, Christ, I'm sorry for being such a dickhead but you know that this is wrong."

"Nice dickhead though!" she grinned at his still hard cock. Dave looked at her in horror and then saw the smirk on her face.

"OK," she sighed. "It's not going to happen. It would have been wild though."

"Yeah, Penny, you're a wild woman, I mean you're terrific. How is it you're so uninhibited?"

"Why? Should I be inhibited?"

"People often are, when it comes to showing off their bodies! I don't know, maybe it's an age thing," Dave laughed.

"Well, at nineteen I don't have to worry about that just yet."

"What?" Dave swung towards her. "You're twenty-three, aren't you?"

For a moment Penny looked panic-stricken but then she shrugged as if it didn't matter any more. She looked at her boss. "Dave, I lied to you. I'm nineteen – sorry."

"That's impossible." He jumped away from her. "Christ, you've been working for me for three years. You hardly started when you were sixteen!"

"I'm afraid I was. I had to lie because I knew that you wouldn't take me on if I told you the truth."

"But you had three years' experience with Eircom before I employed you."

"No, it was three months. The guy you phoned for a reference was my sister's boyfriend at the time."

Dave got annoyed. "You mean our entire working relationship is based on a lie?"

"Hey, Dave, relax the bod a bit. Our work relationship is not based on a lie. The last three years have been the best of my life. Working with you has taught me so much I would never have learned at some stupid old third level."

"That's crap for a start. You need a good education."

"This from the man who quit college after one year!"

She had him there. "Still, you shouldn't have lied to me, Penny. I probably would have given you a chance anyway."

"Not as your PA," she argued, "and anyway, you're the one who's always telling me 'if the facts don't fit the pitch, *rearrange* them'!" He looked at her as if thinking for a while and then a smile broke out on his face. "Penny, you're amazing. You're absolutely right." He had sobered up now. "But why are you telling me all of this now?"

"Well, I didn't actually mean to. I forgot that you thought I was older than I really am. Hey, maybe the fact that I'm still a teenager is why I'm so uninhibited. Our generation take what we want when we want. We're not shy and retiring, like all you forty-somethings and, Dave, and we certainly don't take it lying down!" Penny knew he was forty-three because she had helped Sue to organise his fortieth birthday just after she started working for him.

"Nineteen? I could be your father, you know."

"No. You're older than my father."

"Ouch, that hurt!"

"Sorry."

"No, *I'm* sorry. I shouldn't have let this situation develop. You're not married. I am."

"Well, it looks like you needed to blow off a little steam, if you'll pardon the pun."

He laughed. "You get some sleep and let this old man get back to his own bedroom. I'll see you in the morning, for breakfast – say around nine o'clock?"

"Fine, Dave," she smiled.

Dave got up and gave her a paternal kiss on the forehead.

"Good night, Penny," he whispered.

"Good night, Dave."

He walked across the bedroom to the door but, just as he opened it, she called him again. He turned to see her sitting in the middle of the bed wrapped in a single sheet and still looking considerably more than her nineteen years. He suppressed his urges and smiled.

"There is one consolation," she said.

"Yes?"

"You're a lot cuter than my dad!" She gave a naughty smirk. She might as well have punched him in the stomach.

"Thanks," he managed as he headed out into the hall. He walked back to his room feeling old and very lonely. He realised as he opened his bedroom door that he had forgotten the Egyptian goodies for his kids. "God, I'm going senile too," he sighed morosely.

He looked at his watch. It was only eleven thirty. They had started drinking too early. That meant it was only half past nine at home. He could easily phone Sue, but the guilt choked his throat. How could he talk to her and sound normal? He couldn't even remember what Penny had used as an excuse for his not being home so it would be dangerous to phone her now anyway. Dave fell onto his bed. He thought about Penny. Sean was a lucky man. Then he thought about Sue. Oh Jesus, what have I done? What was I thinking? He slipped into a troubled sleep.

As the night hours crept away, Penny's mood crashed deeper and deeper into despair. Sure, she had been so cool and confident with him but that was all an act – a stupid, dumb act! She lay in her bed and began to cry. Never in her life had a man actually stopped her mid-blowjob. He must have been really repulsed by her, she thought. How could she possibly compete with the exquisite creature that he was married to? Penny cried into her pillow and wondered how she could feel more miserable. Did he really believe that crap about her being uninhibited, about sex meaning nothing? How could he? He was just pretending to believe her to make it easier on himself.

234

Penny could count her lovers on one hand. She knew she was good at blowjobs because Sean told her she was. He made her do them all the time and although she didn't really like them, she thought Dave might. To be stopped mid-blow, however – oh, the humiliation! His dick had been literally in her mouth when he pulled it out and jumped up panicking about his bloody perfect wife at home. How could he be such a bastard? Penny's older sister was right. All men really are dicks, even her totally wonderful, adorable boss, bloody Dave Parker.

She knew her eyes would be all swollen in the morning, but she didn't care. Dave was so thick, she could probably fob it off as some insect bite. She got up and fumbled for her cigarettes. One of the beauties of Egypt was you could smoke absolutely anywhere.

"Brilliant country," she snapped and then burst out crying again as she thought about her tour of the city with Dave.

How could he have been such a bastard? She was going to give him everything. She had really given it the works, standing up on the bed like that, being so forward. Then it occurred to her that maybe she'd been too forward. Maybe she'd scared him. Sue Parker didn't seem like the type to hang out of the chandeliers.

"Fuck him," she howled at the empty room as she paced up and down, wrapped in a single white sheet and dragging deeply on what she reckoned was an imitation Marlboro. The box looked authentic enough, but at thirty pence a box, it wasn't particularly likely to be the real McCoy.

"A bit like Dave bloody Parker," she sniffed. "Looks real enough, but as soon as you put him between your lips, nothing!" She laughed, a little menacingly. "I wonder what Sue would make of his little escapades," she thought evilly as she eyed the Egyptian tobacco masquerading as her beloved Marlboro. "I wonder if she would be impressed if she knew that PA stood for *Penis Assistant*." Penny's mind began to play with the possibilities of this new development. She could blackmail him. She could just tell Sue Parker and do serious damage to his marriage, perhaps even destroy it altogether. There was definitely something wrong between Dave and Sue already. She, Penny, could be the straw that broke the Egyptian camel's back! She could exaggerate what actually happened and pretend that they have been having an affair for ages. Penny started to get giddy.

"Either way, Dave Parker," she spoke to the cigarette, as if it was him, "you don't treat me like you just did and get away with it!" She stubbed the cigarette out with considerably more force than was needed and then she went to bed.

CHAPTER 17

Sunday evening in Innishambles had been considerably frostier than it was in Egypt.

"Look, Tiffany, if you don't tell me what the hell is wrong with you, I'm going to tell Mum about the time you electrocuted all the tropical fish in the aquarium."

"You wouldn't dare!" Tiffany looked horrified. "That was all a terrible accident!"

"Tell that to the fish!" Lauren needled her sister. "Oh, I forgot! You can't – they're all dead!"

"I didn't know that the water was already heated automatically," Tiffany whined. "I thought a hairdryer was a gentle way of heating it up indirectly."

"*Indirectly* being the relevant word, Tiff."

"I didn't mean to drop it."

"Ah well, I'm sure they didn't feel a thing!"

"Who didn't feel a thing?" Saskia walked into the kitchen and into her daughters' conversation.

"Woody," Lauren lied smoothly. "I was cutting out some of his bigger tangles yesterday and he looks great now." Then she turned to Tiffany. "Well?"

Tiffany looked hassled and upset. She motioned with her head that they should go outside.

"Mum, Tiffany and I are going for a stroll – we'll be back soon, OK?"

"Fine," Saskia was delighted to see that their fight seemed to have come to an end. "But don't go too far. We have to think up things to do for Robin's birthday and I want to talk to you two about Ballymore Glen. We have to make a decision soon. The houses are bound to be popular. I don't want to lose the house of our dreams just because we dragged our heels."

Lauren groaned. "What do you do at a three-year-old's party?"

"Just don't be gone too long," Saskia repeated.

"Come on, Tiffany," Lauren smiled. "We haven't had a good chat in ages!"

"Are you OK with Mum accepting the offer on the house?" Tiffany asked as they headed out into the late afternoon sun.

"I do understand that it's just too much money to turn down. I mean six million! God, that's a lot even for dear old Innishambles. What do you think?"

"Well, obviously I'm gutted to see it go but I had no idea that those houses in Ballymore Glen were going to be so luxurious. Jesus, they're amazing, aren't they?"

"You're forgetting you're talking to the guide. I even know the codes to most of the safes and all the front gate codes!"

"How do you remember them all?"

"Easy. They're all one, two, three, four."

Tiffany laughed, "OK, that does make it a bit easier!"

"Now, Tiff, are you going to tell me what's been

bugging you or is Mum going to hear about the smoked fish?"

"Ah Lauren, can't you leave this one alone?"

"You know it's always better out than in. Look at Kelly. This time last week her life was falling apart and now she's madly in love and preparing for the wedding of the century. She even managed to get Mum and Dad back together again, under one roof."

Tiffany snorted. "For a matter of minutes."

"Still. I think it's a start."

"Lauren, you're not harbouring any silly notions of Mum and Dad getting back together again, are you? I mean that's plain crazy. She could never forgive him for all the shit he did to her and anyway she's in love with Nicolas Flattery."

Lauren looked at her older sister. "How can you say that? You're the one who arranged for Dad to come back and see Innishambles. I thought you were trying to get Mum and Dad back together. Jesus, Tiffany, you even want to live with him in Dublin! How can you say he's a shit?"

"I didn't say he's a shit. I said that he did a lot of shitty things to Mum. Now that you mention it though, I do think our dad is a shit. I mean, come on, Lauren, he was shagging our childminder for years. Have you forgiven him for that? You know he had a lover called Robin? That's how our little sister got her name. I'd say he would make a lousy boyfriend but that said he is still my dad. I'd love to live with him because I like him as a dad. But I'd hate to see him back with Mum. He hurt her so badly last time, it would kill her if he did that again."

Lauren looked at her sister incredulously. "I didn't know about Robin. Do you mean his PR woman? I didn't realise that they actually had an affair! I guess I just thought they flirted."

"Oh God, Lauren! I'm sorry. I didn't mean to drop that on you like that."

"No. It's not your fault. We never really discussed it back then. It was all brushed under the carpet. Anyway, I think Nicolas Flattery is doing a damn good job of breaking Mum's heart again, so she doesn't need Dad back in her life."

"Why do you think that?"

Lauren looked at her sister. "You should have seen her face when she told me that Nicolas had gone bust. She looked utterly crushed. She's been let down again by yet another man. I'm telling you, Tiff, she'll never trust him again. I think Nicolas and Mum are no more. I mean, he has practically moved back to the States. The only question is what's going to happen to the refuge. If he's broke, who's going to bankroll that place? God, you don't think Kelly and Barney and the baby will have to move away, do you?"

"Lauren, where do you get these notions? Everything will work out fine. Mum and Nicolas haven't broken up. You'll see."

"You're just an incredible romantic, Tiff. That's your problem." Lauren looked at her sister. "Now to you. You know, you're great at shifting the conversation when there's a subject that you don't want to discuss but you're not getting away with it this time. Why are you so freaked out for the last couple of days?"

Tiffany groaned, but she accepted that her little sister knew her too well. She would never get away with keeping this one a secret and she wasn't sure that she wanted to anyway. It was too big a burden to carry.

"Lauren, I don't know if I can talk about it."

"Well, maybe I can help. Does it have something to do with the Condon twins?"

Tiffany looked horrified. "What makes you say that?"

"Well, you nearly fainted when you saw Seb Condon breeze into our kitchen."

Tiffany burst out crying, "Oh, Lauren. I'm such an idiot and such a slut. You'll hate me when I tell you."

Lauren couldn't believe her sister. Never in her wildest dreams would she have thought of Tiffany as an idiot or a slut.

"Sis, if ever there was a couple of words that don't describe you, it's them!" Slowly she guided her older sister to the bench in the walled garden. The lavender that surrounded it was still in full bloom and the garden looked wonderful, full of late summer glory.

"Now, come on, tell your little sister what's wrong. Are you pregnant?"

Tiffany stared at Lauren for an instant and then burst out laughing. "No, I'm not quite that bad."

"That's better. Let's see more of those smiles. Now tell me what's so awful that you are this upset."

"Well," Tiffany started slowly, "you're nearly right. When I saw Seb, I nearly died. That's because I thought he was his brother, Maximilian."

"You know Max? How?" Lauren asked.

Tiffany sighed. "Puerto Banus."

"God, that was years ago. Fair play to your memory. I don't think I'd remember a face from that long ago. Or do you have a good reason for remembering him?"

Tiffany studied the ground and nodded almost imperceptibly.

Lauren sighed, knowing that this was going to be bad. "OK, Tiffany, so you know him perhaps a little too well. You're not the first and I'm sure you won't be the last. Why don't you start from the beginning and tell me everything. I promise I won't judge you. I'll try to help."

Tiffany looked at her sister for a while. "You're a great sister, Lauren. Please don't think badly of me, OK?"

"OK."

"Well, it all started one night in the middle of the holiday. Nicolas and Mum were being pains in the ass. They were so lovey-dovey. I felt like a gooseberry with my own mother and her new boyfriend. It was horrible. The first two nights I had to stay in and baby-sit Robin and the next night we all went out together. That was even worse than staying in. Robin acted up in the restaurant and she made an awful scene. Anyway it was mortifying."

"So the holiday was pretty appalling."

"About as bad as you can get."

"So where does Max fit in?"

"I'm getting to it. Hang on to your hat. Anyway the next night Mum asked me to baby-sit again and we had a fight. I said that I wasn't there just to be her free slave and stormed out."

"Nice one."

"Well, she deserved it," Tiffany spat with what was still quite a lot of contempt. "Anyway, God has punished me enough for it."

"Ah Tiff, spare me! What happened after that?"

"You don't know the port, Lauren, but it's fantastic. The people are all so beautiful and so rich. Everybody is so glamorous."

"I would love to see it."

"The popular part of the port is in the shape of an L so what most people do is walk along the shops and restaurants and admire the boats and the yachts."

"Are there many?"

"Oh, Lauren, you should see them! They're magic! All the richest people in the world keep their boats in Puerto Banus for a few weeks in the summer." Tiffany's eyes sparkled at the memory. "Some of these boats have helipads on the roof, they're so big. They all have at least two or three jet skis casually suspended from their sides. Most of them have a full complement of staff for cooking, cleaning and of course running the boats."

"Ah, so they're not the sort of boats you see in Dun Laoghaire?"

Tiffany snapped out of her daydream and looked at her sister. "Ah Lauren, this is really a different world. Then, in front of the berth, where the beautiful people keep their beautiful boats is their parking spot. That's where they throw their Lamborghinis or their Ferraris. It's the most exciting and decadent place I've ever seen."

"I think I'd like to see it after all."

Tiffany's eyes darkened. "No, you don't. You don't want to mix with those people. They destroy ordinary people like us. They feed on our very souls."

"Steady on there, Tiff. You've been reading too many of those scary novels again. What are you on about?"

"I was walking along admiring these boats when I spotted one called *Tiffany*, which made me smile and slow down a little. Then I saw this guy. His T-shirt was soaking wet and so was his beautiful blond hair and he was laughing. He ran off the boat and grabbed my hand. 'Quick, hide me,' he said and he pulled me after him."

"Was that Max?" Lauren asked softly. She could see that this was not easy for Tiffany.

Her sister nodded as she continued. "As we ran down a little back street I turned back to see a gorgeous girl with long blonde hair and even longer brown legs run off the boat. She was holding a bottle of Dom Perignon and shaking it. He told me later that she had been spraying him with it."

"Whatever you're into. Personally I'd rather drink it!"

"Lauren, this is serious."

"Sorry."

"Anyway we got talking and I told him my name was Tiffany, like the boat. He started to make all these suggestions like being my captain, raising my mainsail and dropping his anchor between the sheets."

Tiffany turned to Lauren, "Did you know that the ropes on a boat are called the sheets?" Lauren nodded and so Tiffany continued. "Anyway, to cut a long story short, he took me for a few drinks in Sinatra's. It's a bar just at the entrance to the port. Christ, everybody knew Max. He smiled effortlessly at them and shook hands casually. Everybody seemed to like him. It was only after they had gone that he admitted to me rather sheepishly that he couldn't remember how he knew them."

"Sounds like a bit of a prat," Lauren mumbled.

"No, you don't understand. He was the coolest man I had ever met. Everybody wanted to be near him. They wanted to shake his hand and talk with him. He was the innocent one. He couldn't help it if he looked so cool and devastatingly good-looking."

Lauren realised sadly that Tiffany was still obviously

madly in love with this jerk. She was now talking nineteen to the dozen.

"And as for the girls! Jesus, Lauren, every girl between the ages of fifteen and forty-five said hi to him as they walked by. I must admit he did look fantastic. His skin was dark brown from the Mediterranean sun and his hair was bleached white. His eyes were as blue as the sky – even the bloody champagne that hardened in his hair only acted as a gel and made him look fantastic!"

"Sounds pretty good," Lauren encouraged her sister.

"Too good," Tiffany agreed. "Then he asked me to join him for dinner. He said he didn't want to go back to the boat yet, not until Annabel had calmed down. He swore that there was nothing between them. They were just sailing buddies. Evidently *Tiffany*, the boat, belonged to Annabel's dad and they were taking the thing from England to Corsica with him, stopping off in Puerto Banus for a few days."

"Wow, some life!"

"Yeah, the twins sail a lot. They've competed in Cowes loads of times. Did you know that?"

"How the hell would I know that, Tiff?"

"Anyway, we went to a lovely restaurant and proceeded to drink our heads off."

"Ah."

"Yeah, then he took me to a terrific beach bar he knew on the Playa de la Siesta, but surprise, surprise it was closed. Well, it was after midnight and there was no one on the beach!"

"So you ended up alone on a hot summer's night on this dark deserted beach? Is that what you're saying?"

"Oh Lauren, don't think so badly of me. I still haven't

forgiven myself. It was all so magical at the time. He had the bottle of champagne that we had ordered for dessert and the night was hot. The beach was deserted and one thing led to another."

"Tiffany, I wouldn't ever judge you. I'm jealous, that's all."

"No, Lauren, you don't understand. I had sex with him. Full-on sex. Jesus, I didn't even know his surname."

"Wild! OK, now why are you angry with yourself?"

"Ah, Christ, Lauren, why do I bother? I've just told you I had sex with a complete stranger on a beach, in public for God's sake, in the south of Spain and you don't see why I'm angry with myself and him?"

"Tiffany, I can't think of a better way to lose your virginity, especially if the guy knew what he was at and I think it's fair to say that Maximilian Condon would have had quite a good idea of how to keep a woman happy."

"That's not the point."

"So what is?"

"That was it. There was nothing more. We fell asleep on the beach and woke up in the morning. He was friendly but in a fairly distant way. He offered to walk me home but I felt awful and said no."

"At least he offered."

"Lauren, he didn't even ask me my surname, not to mention my phone number. He didn't want them. I was just a few hours' amusement to him."

"Now I think I'm beginning to understand."

"Don't you see? He totally used me. It's barely a step up from rape."

"Now stop just there, Tiffany. Get off that particular train of thought, because that's crap. It was a one-night stand between two consenting adults – admittedly one was perhaps a little more consenting than the other but you can't accuse him of something like rape. Did you at any point say that you wanted him to stop?"

"Not exactly."

"Honey, if we had a penny for all the women in the world who regretted sex after it had happened, we would be rich women. Welcome to the club!"

"How the hell would you know?"

"I lost my virginity to Connor Cantwell."

"No way!"

"Way!"

"Shit, I never knew."

Lauren continued, "I guess it was a little different because we were going out with each other, but I have to say, Tiff, what you did sounds like an experience to remember."

"I wish I could forget it. I wish it never happened."

"Why?"

"Lauren. I feel so used. I feel like I was his mount for that night. He was probably back in Annabel's arms by lunch-time the next day or in the arms of some Italian lover by the following night."

"Well, you did say that you didn't want an escort home," Lauren suggested.

"OK, but I did give him plenty of opportunity to ask for my number or something. He didn't want to know. I made myself forget about it over the last few years and then – Christ. What are the odds of him buying our house?"

"Maybe it's fate."

Tiffany's eyes filled with hope. "Do you think so, sis?

Do you really think that maybe in some crazy way God is bringing us back together?"

Suddenly Lauren realised that she had said the wrong thing. "Look, Tiffany, everybody knows that your first love is never your final love. Why don't you chalk it up to experience and go and find another man?"

"I've never seen anybody to compare with Maximilian Condon, and anyway, look at Mum and Kelly. They have both ended up with their first loves. Maybe I should too."

"Mum? Ha! She and Dad hardly lived happily ever after. Surely you don't want to end up in her situation."

"Max and I wouldn't end up like that," Tiffany scowled.

Lauren knew that her sister was living a crazy daydream. Max was not the settle-down type and probably never would be.

"Look, Tiffany, I'm glad you told me and believe me it's not nearly as bad as it could have been. We'll figure something out. Try to stop feeling so miserable."

"How can I stop feeling so miserable? I doubt he even remembers me while he occupies my every waking moment. Why do you think I haven't even looked at a man since that holiday?"

"I thought it's because you were studying."

"Yeah, but why do you think I was studying? I couldn't bear to go out into the world again and now he's bloody well come into mine. This sucks."

"Don't worry. We'll sort it out."

"You think?"

"I know," Lauren lied.

CHAPTER 18

Lauren was delighted to get another day's work out of Ballymore Glen. First thing on Monday morning, around eleven a.m., which was the crack of dawn for a teenager on summer holidays, Patricia Doyle from Bingham auctioneers phoned frantically looking for Lauren to 'show number three' as she put it.

With another school year looming just in front of her, it was good to earn a little extra cash. She had every intention of blowing everything she earned on clothes in the end of summer sales.

"Lauren, thanks for getting here so fast." Patricia was fussing around the office like an old mother hen. Then she addressed all the girls together. "Now can I have everyone's attention, please? Firstly, I hope you all have your Bingham uniforms on and in perfect condition." She cast a critical eye over her little troop. "Secondly, I would like to thank all of you for making it here on such short notice." She glanced at her watch. Patricia had only started phoning around for the girls mid-morning but they were all here, spruced up and ready to go, even though it was just lunch-time. Not bad, she thought. "Now just to inform you of some changes since you last showed these houses. Bob Bolton and his wife, I'm sure you remember her, well, they have bought number one. Number seven has also been sold so obviously those houses are no longer on show. We also expect at least one booking deposit today and we are expecting a lot more visitors and house viewers, so let's go and sell some houses!"

Lauren was surprised to hear how fast they were selling and so she decided to put in a quick call to Saskia.

"Mom, are you serious about buying one of the houses in Ballymore Glen?"

"Yes, of course I am." Saskia replied, somewhat surprised to hear from her daughter. "Most likely the sale of our own house will go through today and we'll need somewhere to live so we'll have to start thinking about it soon."

"Well, you better think faster because the houses in Ballymore Glen are being snapped up faster than you can say boom economy. Two are already sold and one is expected to go today. That's three houses in three days, Mum. You'd better come and see them today and bring your cheque book!"

Saskia was stunned at the speed the house market moved. She wasn't ready for it. She had assumed that Innishambles would take a matter of months to sell. After that it would take a few months to close the sale and then she planned to look around for a house. In Saskia's mind, that was to happen after Christmas. Here she was, all in the space of a matter of weeks, selling and now being forced to buy if she wanted to live in Ballymore Glen. Damn it, she hadn't even seen them yet!

"OK, Lauren. Thanks for letting me know. Can you please put me through to Patricia? I think it's time I made an appointment to see these super houses."

"Patricia, this is for you," Lauren held the phone in the air.

Nobody was happier than Francesca Murray to have Patricia distracted because she knew she was about to get a right dressing-down for failing to wear the correct Bingham uniform.

"Thanks," she smiled at Lauren. "I owe you one. I think Miss Goody-Two-Shoes was about to go ballistic because black leather trousers aren't part of the Bingham dress code!"

"Well, she has a point, Francesca. What happened to your little navy number?"

"Ah Jesus, Lauren, I felt like a right prat in that last week. Hey," she smirked mischievously at her friend, "I bet I can shift more houses in black leather than in the old navy uniform."

"Well, it's funny you should say that, Francesca, because there is something I need to discuss with you."

"Sure, what's up?"

"Well, it's to do with your innate talent for shifting!"

"You have my attention!"

Lauren hesitated. "It's kind of delicate and strictly confidential."

Francesca heard the change in her tone. "Is everything OK? It's not Kelly, is it? She's OK?"

"What do you know about Kelly?" Lauren asked.

"Everything. She called me last night. I knew about the baby already. She told me that as soon as she discovered herself but she phoned me yesterday to tell me about her

251

and Barney getting back together again. Don't tell me there's more trouble afoot!"

Lauren was shocked. "Jesus, I had no idea you knew about that when we were messing around together last Friday."

"Why would you?" Francesca asked simply. Kelly had often said that Francesca was her best friend in the world and the most secretive person but it was only now that Lauren realised how good she was at keeping mum. She now knew that Francesca was the one to help her with her other sister.

"No, it's nothing to do with Kelly. She and Barney are the proverbial Romeo and Juliet. Actually it's about Tiffany."

"Is she OK?"

"No, definitely not. Tiff is different from the rest of us, Francesca. She really feels things. Kelly and I and even little Robin just kind of get on with life but Tiffany is really sensitive and she is hurt too easily."

"Has somebody hurt her?"

"Promise you won't say a word."

"You know I won't," Francesca answered shortly as she guided Lauren to the quietest part of the large open-plan office. "What's wrong, Lauren?"

"It's was Max bloody Condon."

Francesca burst out laughing, "Jesus, he's one fast mover!"

"No, that's what makes this worse. She met him years ago in Spain and he hurt her really badly way back then."

"What did he do?"

"Well, he took her virginity but he didn't take her number and she thinks that it was practically rape!"

"Heavy!"

"Yeah, there's no talking to her. I want to get him for hurting her but I don't know how."

"Look, Lauren, haven't you heard? All's fair in love and war!"

"But this is Tiffany," Lauren pleaded. "She's so soft and so nice to everybody all the time, Francesca. I genuinely think if it was Kelly or me or anybody else I know, I'd just tell them to buck up and cop on but Tiffany is made of different stuff. It's killing me to see her so hurt like this. She's been carrying it around for the last three years. It has really affected her badly. Did you know that's why she's become such a swot? She's just hiding behind her books."

"Maybe that's a blessing," Francesca moaned as she thought about her own lousy Leaving results.

"Francesca, I know you can help me. Please, think about it!"

Patricia Doyle interrupted their conversation. "Ready, girls, let's go! Everybody on the bus!"

"Jesus, I feel like I'm back at school," Francesca muttered under her breath.

"Will you help me?" Lauren persisted as they headed out.

"Look, I don't really see what I can do. Like I said, all's fair. Tiffany is a big girl; she'll just have to grow up, Lauren. This is just one of life's knocks. I'm sorry."

Before Lauren could plead any more Patricia had grabbed Lauren's arm. "Miss Dalton, I've just had a chat with your mother. It appears she's coming to view Ballymore Glen this afternoon. Isn't that wonderful?"

"Eh yeah," Lauren replied as she watched Francesca

get caught up in another conversation with some of the other girls on the bus.

"Can you believe it, you could be actually living in one of those exquisite houses?" Patricia continued to rattle on but Lauren wasn't listening. There had to be a way to get Francesca to help.

* * *

Saskia Dalton was most concerned about Kelly. Sunday morning had taken a lot out of all of them. Richard and Kelly had talked most things out by the time Saskia got over to Peartree Cottage and Barney arrived back from his walk soon after.

With a considerable amount of charming from Richard, Kelly eventually agreed to move back into Innishambles. Saskia apologised for her outburst and agreed that she had exaggerated considerably. She also admitted that the divorce with Richard had clouded her judgement and memory of the early days. If marriage was what Kelly and Barney wanted then they should go for it. Richard studied Saskia as she spoke, almost telepathically telling her what to say.

A mere twenty-four hours later, Saskia was still drained. Seeing Richard had had a profound effect on her. He was absolutely right about how Kelly should be handled. She needed to be loved and supported, not screamed at. How was it that Barney and Richard seemed to know what to do and she, Saskia, was making such a mess of things? Eventually, after everybody had said their piece, Barney cooked up a huge fry for the four of them. It had turned into a lovely family celebration.

"Saskia, you were hungry," Richard laughed as he

watched his ex-wife mop up the final bits of the fried egg with her bread.

"Gosh, I think I was."

"I didn't think you liked black pudding?" He looked confused.

"I didn't but I seem to now."

Richard shrugged and laughed. "Kelly is the pregnant one but Saskia is the one with the food fetishes!"

She shook herself out of the memory. No matter how she tried, however, she couldn't keep Richard out of her mind. He was like a different man from the one she divorced. He was soft and approachable now. He was quite, she searched for the word – loving.

"Ha," she laughed aloud, "isn't that *why* I divorced him? He was *too* bloody loving!" She felt the hatred build up in her again. No, she was right to divorce him. Richard shagged everything around him. That's *why* they got divorced. "And don't you forget it!" she said aloud to her reflection.

"Don't forget what?" Tiffany popped her head around her mother's bedroom door.

"Oh, don't forget to look at the space they have under the stairs."

"Who? What are you talking about, Mum?"

"I am talking about Ballymore Glen, Tiff! How would you like to saunter up there for a little look at those houses with me?"

"I'd love to. Will we take Kelly and Robin too?"

"Absolutely – we should all have a look if we're all going to be living there!"

"Won't that cost a fortune?"

"Money is no object!" Saskia laughed recklessly. In

truth, she was most concerned about money but this was a necessary expense. Moving from Innishambles to Ballymore Glen was how she was going to raise much needed capital – surely she was doing the right thing.

Tiffany was delighted. "Cool, I'll tell the other two and grab my jacket."

"Relax, we're not going for another hour," Saskia called after her daughter. At least that's one girl I don't have to worry about, she thought with relief. She was a good girl and a hard worker.

Tiffany bounded back into the room with her jacket on. "What did you say?"

Saskia laughed. "I was just telling you to take your time. We're not going for another hour." She stroked Tiffany's hair. "Gosh, you've suddenly become so grown up. What happened to my little girl? I'll really miss you when you're at college, Tiffany."

"Oh Mum! I'll still come back at the weekends and during the holidays."

But Saskia knew that this was the beginning of the end. The weekends in Dublin would look a lot more attractive than the quiet ones in little old Ballymore and the working holidays abroad would start soon. Her little girl was leaving her. She hugged Tiffany hard and pushed the sudden feeling of loneliness back down.

"Mum, Mummy, you're squishing me – I can't breathe!" Tiffany laughed good-naturedly. "Hey, I have to go and look at my stuff. I have to think about what I'm bringing and what stays here. Did you discuss with Dad what bedroom I'll be in?" Tiffany was prattling slightly now.

"Why don't you phone him?"

"Oh, Mum, you're the best. Thanks," and she flew out the bedroom door.

Saskia sat on the bed, feeling very alone. Her little chicks were definitely leaving the nest, she thought. Kelly had moved back home for a while but she was getting married soon enough and then she would be gone. Tiffany would be in Dublin in a matter of weeks and the house would be very lonely with just Robin and Lauren. Before she could get too maudlin, however, Robin came rushing in to her with Dudley and Dexter in tow.

"Mummy, Tiffany said we're going to see our new house now! Are we?" she asked hopefully.

"Yes, honey, soon. Come on downstairs and we'll get a coffee and fruit juice and then we'll go. I promise."

* * *

It was pandemonium in Ballymore Glen. The entrance fee had only served to make the properties even more interesting. All morning Patricia's phone had been ringing and so she was forced to tell people to simply turn up at the gate with the viewing fee and then they would be admitted. She had already taken a couple of thousand euro at the entrance and her head was dizzy with zeros when Raymond Saunders arrived.

"We were here only last Friday, Patricia. Today I'm bringing my children to have a look at a particular house. Surely you don't expect me to pay again?" He gave her one of his best just-a-friendly-guy smiles and it worked.

"Oh, what the heck! Go on in, Mr Saunders. You've already paid once."

Jasmine, Edward and Francis charged through and Jayne followed at a slightly more feminine pace. As they headed up towards number six, Raymond walked beside her.

"Are you sure you'll be happy out here?" he asked Jayne nervously.

"I'm positive," she smiled at him.

"You won't be lonely?"

"With these three to keep me busy?" she laughed.

Raymond had given much thought to what Jasmine had said. Was it possible that Jayne, their nanny, was in love with him? Surely not! She was so young and good-looking. Then again he wasn't exactly over the hill himself. She was terrific with the kids and maybe it would do them good to have a mother figure in their life again. Raymond knew he didn't love Jayne but he had had his life with Caroline. Anything he did at this point would be for the sake of the kids. He didn't expect to fall in love again, but maybe providing a mother for his kids was the right thing to do.

"Are you ready?" he asked the children playfully as they walked up the long private road of Ballymore Glen. As promised, Raymond had taken them down to the complex the previous day but they were unable to see inside, such was the security. Today the children were fit to burst with excitement.

"Which one is it?" Jasmine asked, beginning to lose patience.

"*Da-da!*" he gestured with hands pointing to number six.

The Saunders children looked at the huge gates. They were already open.

"Can we go in?" the boys asked in unison.

"Of course. There's a girl at the door – she'll show you around."

The children ran ahead, much to the horror of the Bingham auctioneer rep who was standing at the door.

"What do you think?" Raymond asked Jayne.

"I remember it well from Friday. I think it's a perfect choice, Raymond."

"Do you want to look around it again?"

"Yes, certainly, but I do think it will make a perfect home for us – eh, for you."

"Us, Jayne. You're part of our family too, of course." Raymond felt there was a double meaning to everything he said in view of Jasmine's revelations. But, then again, what if it was all in his daughter's head?

"Are you all right, Raymond?" Jayne asked as she studied his face. She touched his arm lightly.

"Yes, yes, I am. It's just a big move, you know." He forced a smile, gently pulling his arm away. "Come on, let's have another look around. I need to grab the master bedroom before Jasmine stakes her claim!"

* * *

"OK, now I'm completely confused! Which ones have we seen and which ones haven't we seen?" Saskia asked in exasperation.

"Oh Mum, what are you like?" said Tiffany impatiently.

"It's easy for you," Saskia complained. "You have a natural inclination for numbers and a great memory."

Tiffany couldn't help smiling at such praise. Even if she knew herself that it was true, it was still nice to be told. She spoke to her mother slowly. "We've just done it backwards. We've seen ten, nine, and eight. Seven is already sold. We've seen six, five – that was the one you liked most because of the traditional kitchen – and we've just come out of four. We only have Lauren's, that's number three, and Francesca Murray's number two to see. Number one is gone as well to that wild American couple Lauren told us about. Remember?"

"Oh yes, the couple with the plane."

Kelly, Robin, Sas and Tiffany did the tour of number three with Lauren acting as their guide.

"They really are the most amazing houses," Kelly sighed wistfully and then added, "God, I'd love to live in one of them."

"What about dear old Peartree Cottage, Kelly?" Lauren asked.

"Flog it! I'd much rather one of these state-of-the-art ones."

"What do you think, Mum?" Tiffany asked a very pensive Saskia.

"Well, we haven't signed off on our own yet. We won't be doing anything until that's done. I just don't know," she replied honestly. "They are very nice inside. It's just that there's something missing."

"People and people's stuff!" Lauren suggested, still in her sales-girl mode.

"I thought you wanted her to stay in Innishambles," Kelly whispered to Lauren as they returned to the front door. "Stop trying to sell her one!"

"That was before," Lauren explained.

"Before what?"

"Before we knew that Nicolas was bankrupt, silly!" Tiffany said it before she realised what she had done.

"What are you talking about?" Kelly asked, no longer whispering.

"Oh, shit!" Lauren commented rather unhelpfully.

Kelly looked from one family member to another. They all looked suitably guilty, except for little Robin who was happily playing with the automatic curtains.

"Hello! Would somebody tell me what Lauren is talking about? Nicolas is bankrupt? What about the refuge?" she asked hotly.

Saskia slowly guided Kelly out of number three.

"Look, honey, it appears that Nicolas has a few financial difficulties. I'm sure it will be OK."

"'Bankrupt' doesn't sound like 'a few financial difficulties', Mummy! What about the refuge? What's going to happen to that if Nicolas is in trouble?"

Saskia could see the panic rising in her eldest daughter's eyes.

"OK, here's what I suggest: we'll fly through the last house and then we'll go home and have a long chat about it. Let's just handle one situation at a time. OK?"

Kelly nodded mutely.

Francesca Murray did her sales pitch, but she knew it was falling on deaf ears. Saskia tried to sound interested but she kept glancing from Kelly to Tiffany. Lauren had to stay in number three because she was working.

Francesca showed them her state-of-the-art fridge freezer and they smiled. She showed them her swimming-pool but they were elsewhere and when she showed them the super saturator steam room without a reaction, she knew it was pointless. One of the most gratifying bits about this job was the *oohs* and *ahhs* that the house-hunters rewarded the guides with. Francesca didn't get one *ooh* or *aah* from the Dalton women.

"What's wrong?" Francesca asked Kelly as they finished off the tour.

"I think my life is over," Kelly grumbled, glaring at Tiffany.

"What did you do, Tiffany? What's wrong with your family?" Francesca asked.

"Oh, you know. I'm just so silly sometimes. It's all my fault, of course. If I just kept my mouth shut, everything would be OK. The sooner I'm gone from here the better, Francesca."

As she waved the Daltons off, Francesca was gripped by a deep desire to help them. Kelly was her best friend and she was absolutely miserable. It was obviously affecting the entire family – and poor, poor Tiffany, she was carrying around so much guilt for some stupid bonk that happened years ago. This was utterly ridiculous!

While the house was quiet, she rushed over to Lauren in number three for a moment.

"Lauren, I've been thinking about what you said this morning."

"Yeah?"

"Of course I'll help you. Tiffany is a lovely girl. She doesn't deserve to carry around that much guilt."

"Francesca, you're the best!"

"Hey, we still have to figure out what we're going to do!"

"Let's go for a drink later and talk about it, OK?" Lauren suggested.

Francesca smiled, "Perfect! Maximilian Condon isn't going to know what's hit him!"

CHAPTER 19

Tiffany was filling her third suitcase. She had packed practically everything she owned.

"You're only going up from Monday to Friday of each week," Lauren grunted as she sat on her elder sister's bed and watched her pack.

"I know," Tiffany defended her actions, "but I need all this stuff."

"Mrs Puddleduck?" Lauren held up Tiffany's oldest and most raggedy toy.

"Definitely Mrs Puddleduck!" Tiffany snapped her special 'friend' away and shoved it into the case.

Kelly stuck her head around the bedroom door.

"What are two you doing?"

"Just getting the stuff together that I'm taking to Dad's."

"Christ, that's a lot of stuff, Tiff. How long are you going for?"

"That's what I was just saying," Lauren agreed.

"Look, if you guys are going to comment on every bloody thing that I put in my case, you can shove off. If you're just here for company, fine!"

"Sorry! God, you're sensitive today," Kelly teased. "I'm the one who's meant to be sensitive!"

"How are you feeling?" Lauren asked her eldest sister. "Any more morning sickness?"

"No. In fact I feel totally normal. I'm going to make an appointment to see Dr Harrington next week. I want to find out when the baby is coming."

"Now there's a man!" Lauren grinned.

"I don't know," Kelly looked pensive. "There's something about him. He's too smooth or something."

Lauren and Tiffany looked at Kelly aghast.

"Hormones," they both said together.

"You always thought he was totally gorgeous, Kellser," Tiffany argued.

"Yeah, I still think he's gorgeous. It's just something about him," she sighed. "Oh, I don't know. I don't know anything any more."

Tiffany looked at her sister. "Kelly, I'm really really sorry about dropping the Rathdeen Refuge thing on you like that. I forgot that you didn't know."

"I'm more fed up that you both knew and didn't tell me for so long."

"Well, you had quite a bit on your mind already," Lauren defended her silence. "Have you said anything to Barney yet?"

"I don't know what to say. 'Hey, Barney, my mum's ex-boyfriend has gone bust and that leaves you and me with no job' – I don't think so!"

"Maybe you could break it to him more gently," Tiffany suggested.

"How?"

"I don't know. Is there any way the refuge could be

saved? Could you get a government grant or something and buy it?"

Kelly's eyes brightened. "Hey, there's a thought! Just because Nicolas Flattery isn't around, it doesn't mean we have to go under."

"That's the spirit," Lauren encouraged her older sister.

But then Kelly slumped down onto the bed again. "But that would never work. The house alone has to be worth the same as this. If it's worth six million, where am I going to get that sort of money?"

"Come on, don't lose hope. You don't want the house. You want the refuge. Rent out the bloody house to foreign diplomats or something and concentrate on the refuge."

Again Kelly's eyes brightened. "Hey, we could do one of those Hidden Ireland houses or something like that. You know, charge people a fortune to stay for the night and have an authentic Irish breakfast in the morning!"

"Now, there's an idea," Tiffany agreed. "Those old houses make a mint."

"Who am I fooling? I could never figure out the business side of things. I'm thick," Kelly moaned.

"Kelly Dalton, stop that self-pity crap right now," Lauren commanded. "You're the one who came up with the idea of selling those dogs to the Mount Eden mums and you're the one who suggested the kennelling facilities and pooch parlour. You're a natural at making money, a chip off the old block. Now start believing in yourself and get a plan together. What is Mum always saying: believe in –"

"The Power Of A Woman!" The girls chorused their mother's favourite expression.

"OK, but I'll need you two to help me. I don't want to

say anything to Barney until I've come up with a rescue plan. Deal?"

Tiffany and Lauren looked at their beautiful older sister. "Deal," they agreed.

* * *

Sue had barely seen Dave since his return from Egypt. He had got back to Ireland mid-afternoon on the Monday and had gone straight to the office instead of coming home. He arrived home late that night and left early on Tuesday morning. While she was profoundly grateful not to have to look him in the eye, she was deeply disturbed by his actions. Usually after he had been away for a couple of days, he would make it his business to get home early enough to play with the kids and spend some quality time with her. If that wasn't possible, he would take the following morning off to be with them. It wasn't unusual for Penny to phone and say that they had been delayed – in fact that was quite normal. But in view of Guy's accident she did think that he could have made some sort of effort.

When she got up, she found a parcel in the kitchen. There was a little Egyptian belly-dancer outfit for India and Aladdin outfits for the boys. At the bottom of the bag was a beautiful pair of Alexandrite earrings for Sue. She nearly cried when she saw them. She knew that Alexandrite changed colour as the light changed from day to night and couldn't help comparing it to how her marriage was changing, equally fast. Sure, they had been having a slightly rough time for the last few months, but that was nothing to her latest discovery. For the thousandth time, Sue wondered how she would find the inner strength to

hide this big ugly truth from Dave. To tell him that Guy
was not his was simply not an option.

Sue had played that scenario out in her head a few
times and each time the result was the same. Fights, blame
games and ultimately a break in the family. There was no
way Dave would be able to accept Guy under his roof
once he discovered that he was Richard Dalton's son –and
only son at that. Guy would come to represent everything
that Dave hated in the world – Richard's incredible greed,
his absolute selfishness, the fact that he had sex with Sue.
What if Richard wanted to be involved in Guy's
upbringing? Sue could feel the tears coming again. There
was one thing she was certain of: no matter who had
fathered Guy, she loved him with all her heart and she
would not see her three children split up. No, she decided
for the hundredth time that morning, there was only one
solution to keep the family together and happy. She must
tell nobody.

When India changed into her belly-dancer's outfit she
looked utterly divine. She had her mother's long and
graceful limbs. She looked like a little Egyptian princess
in the gear. She was in terrific sprits because summer
camp was over and school didn't start again for another
week.

"Mum," Guy whined from the sofa, still playing the
part of the wounded soldier very well. "The video is over
– can you change it, please?"

"I'll do it," Lisa, ever-efficient, was on the scene. "What
video do you want to watch now?"

"Thanks, Lisa." Sue forced a smile. "I just need to do
some things in my room. I'll be back down soon."

Sue mounted the stairs with a heavy heart. To add to

all her grief was the lingering worry as to why Dave was avoiding her. It was very unlike him, she thought. A new dull panic began to rise in her stomach.

When she heard the phone ringing, she jumped.

"Please God, let that be Dave," she said aloud. Maybe he was ringing her to tell her he loved her. He used to do that all the time. Lisa knocked on her bedroom door. "Sue, it's Dr Harrington on the phone."

"Oh, thank you, Lisa. I'll take it now," Sue sniffed. She sat down on the side of her bed and made herself smile. "I'm fine. I'm fine. I'm absolutely fine!" she said aloud to herself and then she picked up the handset.

"James," she smiled into the mouthpiece.

"Sue! How's Wicklow's most glamorous woman?"

"I'm fine, absolutely fine." She lied well.

"Are you?" His tone turned into his most concerned Dr Kildare voice.

"Yes, really. Everything is fine here. Guy is getting on great and of course I have Lisa. Where would I be without Lisa?"

"Still, Sue, you did look very tired when we met at the weekend. I would like you to pop in and I can give you the once-over."

"Really, James, that's not necessary. I feel fine these days. It's Guy I'm worried about." Sue knew what that bloody man really wanted and he was beginning to become a bit of a nuisance.

"Oh, that little trouper? Nothing would slow him down! Look, come in for a little chat and we'll take it from there."

Now that Guy was out of trouble, Sue wasn't really interested in seeing James Harrington. Life was too complicated already.

"Really, James, I'm as fit as a fiddle. Thank you for minding Guy so well over the last few days and indeed you minded me very well too but now that the situation is better, so am I."

"Well, obviously if you're sure –" James stalled.

"I'm sure. You really are very kind."

"Nonsense. Just minding my patients." His voice was like syrup.

"No, I'll stay in touch about Guy and if I feel at all unwell I'll call you."

"Very well. Goodbye then, Sue,"

"Goodbye, James." She put the phone down crossly. James Harrington really was beginning to push it too far. Saturday night she excused because he had a little drink taken and perhaps she had inadvertently given out the wrong message. Sunday morning? OK, he had been very kind to her when she burst out crying but now with yet another phone call, she felt sure that the doctor was after more than her blood pressure.

"If Dave was around, this bloody well wouldn't be happening!" she barked at her reflection. She yearned for some love and attention from her husband, not her GP.

James Harrington slammed the phone down. "Fuck, fuck, fuck! I *will* have you, Sue Parker!" he shouted into the air. So near and yet so far, he thought. That was what was so tantalising about this particular quarry. The joy of taking easy quarry had worn off recently. Now he enjoyed the hunt. Sue Parker was well worth waiting for. He wanted to have her and he knew he would.

* * *

Penny didn't go into Dave's office. She used the telephone intercom system so he wouldn't have to see her face.

"Sue's on line four," she said.

"Oh, right. Thanks, Penny," Dave mumbled as he picked up the hand-piece.

"Sue, how are you?" he asked in the voice he reserved for clients he was trying to humour.

"Thank you for the earrings. They're beautiful."

"Ah, you got them. Great. No problem. How are the children?"

"Everybody is fine. They miss you," Sue said. She didn't trust herself to say she missed him.

"How's Guy?" Dave asked.

"He's fine, fine, absolutely fine," Sue repeated her morning mantra.

The line went quiet. Neither of them could think of anything to say and then they both started to talk together.

"Will you –?"

"Have you –?"

They laughed like two strangers talking on the phone for the very first time.

"You go first," Sue suggested.

"I was just wondering have you given the children their gifts yet?"

"Oh, yes, I'm sorry, I meant all of us. We all love our presents. India in particular is delighted."

"Ah, right." Silence again.

"Oh," Dave remembered, "what were you going to say?"

Sue took all her courage in her hands. She had to face him sooner later – better to get it over with, surrounded by children. "I was just wondering if you were going to be able to get home this evening in time to see the kids?"

"Ah, Sue, em, I'm not sure. Things are pretty hectic, you know. I have to get a feasibility study together as quickly as possible following the Egyptian trip," he lied.

Penny chose this moment to walk into his office with the feasibility study. He accidentally caught her eye as she dropped the manila folder on his desk. Penny sensed the colour in her face rise and ran out of the office.

Sue felt misery flood into her at the idea of having yet another day before she would see her husband face to face.

"I quite understand," she lied. "Well, I just wanted to touch base. Don't work too hard!" She tried to sound jovial.

"No, no," Dave laughed absently as he watched Penny go. "Give the kids a kiss for me, will you?"

Sue felt her throat tighten. She wasn't sure whether she would be able to talk – no kisses or hugs for her. Christ, was it possible that he knew?

"Of course, goodbye then." She hung up without waiting for his 'goodbye'.

Dave Parker looked at his phone and thought about his wife. Sue, beautiful, graceful, serene Sue. How was he ever going to be able to look her in the eye again? What the fuck was he thinking of in Egypt? Could he possibly hide it from his wife? If he told her, she might leave him. Then again, he forgave her her indiscretion with Richard Dalton but that was before he – No! He would not let himself dwell on the blood-type mystery again. It was so soul-destroying. He buried his face in his hands. Avoiding her was the easy short-term solution, but he was miserable and desperately wanted to hold her again.

Then Dave glanced at the manila folder.

"Penny!" he called his PA. He left his desk and went out to her office.

"Penny?" he called again softly.

She looked up at him. He came over and sat on her desk.

"How are you?" he asked gently.

"Grand, why wouldn't I be?"

"Well, I was referring to Egypt."

"What about it?"

"Ah, Penny. You know what I'm talking about. I was wondering if you are OK about *us*?" he whispered.

Penny gave a slightly forced laugh. "What *us*?" she ridiculed him. "Sure, nothing happened. Remember?"

Dave grinned and raised his hands in defeat. "Sorry, sorry. God, you emancipated women take the biscuit." He laughed and walked back into his office, feeling marginally better.

It's considerably more than the biscuit I'll be taking, Dave Parker; Penny fumed as she watched him saunter back to his desk. I won't be happy until I have the entire packet of biscuits!

* * *

Raymond couldn't believe how nervous he was. This was ridiculous! He was a highly successful businessman with a fantastically profitable beef-export business. His other interests would make him a multi-millionaire in their own right. How could he be scared of one woman? He talked to his nanny many times every day. It was no big deal. Most evenings they sat and watched the television together so this was no different. He started hesitantly.

"Eh, Jayne. I see there's a new *Star Trek* movie out."

"Is there?" she replied, not taking her eyes off the episode of *The Sopranos* she was watching. "You're not a trekky," she added absently.

"No, no, I suppose I'm not."

This time Jayne did stop and look at him. "Raymond? Are you OK?"

"What? Oh, yes. I was just wondering if you'd like to go to see *Star Trek* some night?"

"What? Out? You and me? We usually wait until it comes out on video, don't we?"

"Yes, but I thought we could do with a break. You know, we could go to one of those omniplexes and have a burger and chips and then go see the movie."

"What about the kids?" Jayne asked. She kept her tone light but her mind was racing.

"Oh, they won't mind."

"No. I mean, who will mind them?"

"I was thinking Caro's mother could –" Raymond stopped, suddenly unsure if that was the most sensitive thing to do.

"I might be able to get a friend to pop in for a few hours tomorrow night," Jayne suggested softly.

"Yes, that might be better."

"That sounds like a lovely idea, Raymond. It would be good to get out of the house for a few hours." Jayne grinned broadly at him.

"Great," Raymond beamed and stood up to leave the room. He looked like a man who had just been through a massive ordeal.

Jayne realised that that must have taken a lot out of him.

"I'm just going to do some work in the study," he added as he headed out of the living-room.

Jayne grabbed the cushion that lay next to her on the sofa.

"Even the mighty may fall," she whispered into the fabric as she hugged it tightly, "and he's definitely starting to fall. At last!"

Chapter 20

The room was surprisingly small for such a big event. The four white walls felt like they were closing in on Saskia. At most, it measured ten foot by ten foot. *My en suite bathroom is bigger than this,* she thought to herself. Well, it won't be *my* en suite for very much longer, she realised suddenly. The walls were blank, with no paintings or decorations of any kind.

Saskia sat alone with Barry McCourt, her solicitor. He was a good friend and a damn good solicitor.

"Are you OK?" he asked sensitively. "Can I get you a tea or a coffee?"

"Perhaps a glass of water please, Barry?" She couldn't believe how emotional this was turning out to be.

"Even the divorce papers didn't affect me this much," she laughed as he handed her a glass of iced water.

"I think you were psyched up for that. This has all happened so fast. It's a big move, Saskia."

"That's exactly what it is. It's just all so sudden."

"As your solicitor, I should tell you, you've done terrifically. That price has exceeded all previous prices in the area. You should be very happy to sign these documents. As your friend, however, I have to ask you – are you sure you're doing the right thing? Money isn't everything and that house is your *home*. It has been your home for the best part of your life and the girls' entire lives."

Saskia looked into his eyes. He looked so concerned.

"Oh, Barry, you old romantic! Life must move on," she said with more joviality in her voice than she actually felt. "You should see the houses in Ballymore Glen. They are absolutely divine. The developer has thought of everything. The girls and I have discussed it. We're going to buy number five in there and I'll still have loads of money left over. We need to buy a few properties, perhaps an apartment or two that we could rent out. I need to generate – what do they call it? 'An income stream'."

Barry burst out laughing, "All right. You seem to have it all thought out. There's just one more thing. Do you mind what happens to Innishambles in the future?"

"Why do you ask?"

"Well, it's not a given by any means, but the Condons' solicitor did say that they were planning to develop the land."

"What are you saying? They're going to build houses on it?"

"That's exactly what I mean."

"They'll be lucky! To answer your question, I would be very sorry to see Innishambles compromised but they can't tear it down, even if they wanted to. It has a preservation order on it. It's a listed building. Surely they would know that?"

"Oh, I'm sure they do. No, I rather got the impression

that they were going to try to build something similar to Ballymore Glen on some of the land."

Saskia thought about this for a while. "Well, Ballymore Glen only took twenty-five acres to build and it has been a huge success. So I guess they could do something similar with part of the Innishambles land without compromising the actual house and the surrounding gardens," she reasoned out loud. "It is a fifty-acre estate – there should be enough room to develop some of the land without interfering with the house. Anyway, I don't really have any choice, do I?"

"Not if you sell it."

Saskia's mind flashed back to her conversation with Nicolas. There was no money left in the kitty. She was too broke to have concerns about the future of Innishambles.

"I suppose we can't stop progress, Barry," she smiled at him.

"In that case let's get this done."

Within half an hour, Saskia was out of Barry McCourt's office, having signed away her once beloved Innishambles. Barry pumped her hand at the front door of the office and then hugged her.

"You've done very well, Saskia. Hey, you're a multi-millionaire now.

"I don't feel any different," she said.

"Maybe that's because you haven't actually seen the money yet. It will be in your account this afternoon. You could amuse yourself and phone in just to check the balance on your account!"

Saskia laughed. "Yes, that would be a first. 'Your account is six million euro in credit, Mrs Dalton. Is there anything else I can do for you?'"

"You know, it's very decent of them to let you stay in the house after the money has changed hands. That is very unusual."

"I know – that was a conversation between Camilla Condon and me. She's very nice, a little frosty at first, but underneath it a nice woman. I told her we would be out by next weekend. If push comes to shove, we could move into the manor for a few weeks."

"Do you think you will be able to move into Ballymore Glen soon?"

"I think they're ready to move into today. I assume if I buy it this week, we should be able to move in fairly fast."

"Yes, well, get them to send the contracts to me first of all and I'll get straight to them. Being brand new, it should be straightforward enough. OK?"

"Thanks for everything, Barry." She hugged her old friend again and left for home.

September had arrived in a burst of sunshine and Innishambles looked glorious as Saskia drove up the old driveway. She admired her army of chestnut trees that flanked the private road. The clematis tumbled down carelessly and bloomed merrily. Getting the garden in Ballymore Glen to look as glorious as this would be impossible. Saskia suppressed her feeling of unease. Selling Innishambles was the only choice she had. Originally she thought she had to do it to free up enough money to buy a place in Dublin for Tiffany. When the real estate agents came along, however, they were so convincing. She had to get it on the market quickly, before things got too crazy in the winter selling season. They told her to put it on the market practically straight away to get ahead of the posse and as usual she did what she was told. Saskia kept telling herself that if nobody bought it then she could keep living there, but then, of course, she had discovered that Nicolas was broke. He wouldn't be 'minding' her the way he had been. Now the biggest irony was that it looked like she wouldn't have to buy a place in Dublin for Tiffany because she was going to live with Richard. She sighed and thought philosophically: things must happen for a reason.

Dudley and Dexter barked a loud welcome to her as she pulled up on the gravel outside the house. Saskia glanced at her watch. Cathy Taylor was minding Robin for the afternoon to let Sas get in to the solicitor's office in Dublin. Before she collected her youngest daughter, however, Saskia knew that there was one other thing she had to do. In truth she was dreading doing it. Surely that wasn't healthy. Nicolas was meant to be her boyfriend. Why didn't she want to talk to him? Was she cross with him?

"Yes, bloody furious," she answered herself aloud.

"A cup of tea first," she announced to Woody and Wilma who were warming themselves next to the Aga, despite the warmth of the day.

Saskia sat at the kitchen table, nursing the steaming mug, and tried to gather her thoughts. She was surprisingly addled considering she was now such a wealthy lady. Phoning Bingham Auctioneers was the more pleasant of the two phone calls, so she happily made that one first. Patricia took her call.

"Is number five in Ballymore Glen still on the market?" Saskia asked.

"Oh yes, Mrs Dalton, and what an exquisite house it is too. That's the most traditional home in the development with the '*olde worlde*' kitchen and –"

"Yes, it is rather gorgeous," Saskia interrupted her, just as Patricia was about to go into her sales pitch. "What do I need to offer you to secure the purchase of the house?"

"Well, as you know, Mrs Dalton, it's open to tender –"

"Just give me a figure, Patricia. I have the money. I just want to know how much you want."

Patricia wasn't used to such horse-trading and got a little flustered. She put Saskia on hold and immediately Oscar Bingham came on the phone line to deal with her "in person", as he said.

Within two minutes, Saskia had made a verbal offer of two million euro on number five, Ballymore Glen. Oscar Bingham had, in turn, accepted her offer and the property was now *sale agreed*. He promised to courier the contracts over to Saskia's solicitor within the hour. If Saskia wanted to, she could sign within a matter of days and, once the full sum of money was deposited, she could move in at her leisure. The viewing fee would be returned to her in due course. As she hung up she felt a surge of excitement.

"Bloody hell, Woody, I've just bought a house!" Feeling great and wanting to share it with somebody, Saskia felt brave enough to phone Nicolas.

She punched out the thirteen-digit number she knew off by heart and waited.

"Hello," Nicolas answered the phone himself.

"Good morning," Saskia smiled lightly. She could tell by the muffled tone of his voice that she had woken him up. It was eight a.m. in LA.

"Oh, good morning, Saskia. How are you?"

"Good. In fact I'm very good. I have good news for you."

"Unless you've won the lottery, it can't be good."

"Well, not quite the lottery, but I have come into a little money! I've sold Innishambles."

"What?"

She could sense him straightening up in the bed.

"I've sold Innishambles, so I've taken the liberty of throwing a few grand into the Rathdeen Refuge account until we can sort something out."

"Jeez, that's fantastic! But, Saskia, that house was your home. I thought you would only leave Innishambles in a box!"

Saskia laughed. "In a coffin? I guess there was a time I thought like that too, Nicolas. But things change. I realise now that I have to start taking control of my life. I must sort out my, er, our financial situation."

He ignored her reference to their joint financial difficulties. "How much did you get for the place?"

"Well, that's the good news – six million euro."

Nicolas let out a low whistle. "So the Celtic Tiger continues to roar," he said, referring to the booming Irish economy. "Hey, I wonder how much the refuge is worth then?"

Saskia felt a cold chill slide down her spine. If he sold Rathdeen Refuge, he would have no base in Ballymore. What would become of their relationship? What would become of Kelly and Barney? Saskia suppressed the tension she felt rising.

She tried to change the subject. "How are things going with you?"

"Eh, Sas. I've been meaning to ring you."

281

"Oh yes?" She could feel that something was coming.

"I've been offered a job."

"Oh, that's wonderful!"

"Eh, yeah."

"What's wrong? You don't seem too happy."

"Well, it's a television soap."

She understood that this was a big come-down for the man who had once been the toast of Hollywood.

"Hey," she tried to sound positive, "regular money. That'll be nice!"

"It will be regular, but it won't be particularly *large*!" he grumbled.

"You mean it's not that well paid?"

"Not really, Sas, but shit, I have to do something. This is crazy. I'm getting further and further into debt. Nick Junior's college fees are due soon. I've got to take it."

"Ah, Nick Junior is going to college after all," Saskia laughed. There had been many arguments between father and son on the boy's future.

"Yeah, he got accepted into the LAAA thanks to a lot of string-pulling," Nicolas said.

"The what?"

"The LA Academy of Acting."

"Like father, like son!"

"Nah, he's determined to direct. They do directing courses there too."

"Well, you'll enjoy getting back to work again, Nicolas," she continued, trying to sound positive.

"The thing is, Saskia –" he stopped himself.

"Is something wrong?"

"I don't think I can really afford to keep the refuge going. It's been costing me a fortune. I have been thinking

about it for a while now and, Jeez, six million! Do you
think the refuge is worth that? Heck, it must be. It has
about the same amount of land."

Saskia suppressed the urge to slam the phone down on
him. "Nicolas, I have just told you that I'm pumping
money into your bloody refuge to keep it going and here
you are, talking about selling the damn place. Why am I
trying to keep it going?" She didn't let him answer however.
"Oh, yes, that's it. I remember now. You 'had a dream'–
no disrespect to Martin Luther King. You had a bloody
dream of saving all the poor animals in Ireland and if I
remember correctly all the deer in England too."

"Sas –"

"And then again there is the small matter of the staff of
the refuge, not to mention Cathy Taylor who still goes up
there once a week to give the house an airing for you."
Saskia paused for breath but not long enough to let
Nicolas get a word in. "Do you think you can just waltz in
here and turn all our lives around and waltz back out
again, Nicolas? We let you in. We embraced you. Well,
actually I did a good deal more than embrace you and
what now? You've just had enough. Is that it? Will the last
person to leave Ballymore please switch out the light?
You absolute shit. The going has got a little tough so you
just go."

"Saskia, I don't have any choice. I can't afford to keep
the refuge going," Nicolas gasped.

"Screw you!" she snapped and hung up on him.

It took her almost half an hour to cool down. How
dare he? How bloody dare he? She was utterly torn. What
should she do? There was no point in her throwing more
money at the refuge if it was going to be shut down in a

few weeks anyway. This would destroy Barney. He would be right back to square one in his practice.

"And what about Kelly and the baby?" she asked aloud. She thought she might cry. Nicolas hadn't made any reference to *her* involvement in his life. It was becoming pretty clear, however, that there was no part for her to play in his new life in LA. The sound of the phone ringing made her jump. She thought about ignoring it but couldn't.

"Hello," she said in a small voice.

"I'm really sorry," Nicolas said.

"Yeah."

"No. Really I am. This is a big day for you. I can't believe you've sold Innishambles. Congratulations."

"Yeah, thanks."

"Hey, I don't suppose you want to buy the refuge, do you?"

For a minute Saskia's mind raced. "Wow, do you think I could? How much do you want for it?"

"How about six million?"

"Ah Jesus, you didn't pay anything near that for it, Nicolas. My God, you didn't even pay two million back then, did you?"

"I bought it derelict," he defended himself. "I spent my entire fortune renovating that place. I'd sell it to you for whatever the market value is. Sorry, Sas. I couldn't afford to give it to you cheaper than that. I'm broke, remember?"

"Yes, I understand, really I do. As to its value, I really have no idea of what it would be worth, Nicolas, but I do know that I couldn't afford it. I have to buy a considerably cheaper house because I need to generate an income with the rest of the capital. The girls and I need some money to live on. I'll need to invest very wisely."

"Well, buying the refuge wouldn't be buying wisely," he laughed miserably.

"I'm sorry, Nicolas, that your dreams didn't work out," Saskia said softly.

"So am I. Anyway, I thought Richard was meant to be financing your lives."

"Not at the rate we seem to go through it." Saskia thought back to how ridiculously generous Nicolas had been with his money over the last two years and felt guilty for her outburst. "I'm sorry I screamed at you. It was just the shock. I mean, selling the refuge – it's a big step."

"So was selling Innishambles."

"Ultimately I had no choice."

"Ditto." Nicolas continued in a small voice, "I'm really sorry that it's come to this."

"Do you want me to put it on the market?" Saskia asked.

"Would you? Please. Saskia, I wish there was another way."

"So do I. That reminds me – we have some other news! Barney and Kelly are engaged."

"Hey, that's terrific! Oh, I think I'd better have the decency to phone Barney myself, Saskia – you know, to tell him about the refuge."

"Well, I'd better warn you because I'm sure he'll tell you anyway. He's going to be a father!"

"Oh shit – not the best time to become unemployed."

"Em, no."

"Gawd, I feel just awful about this."

"Yeah, so do I," Saskia added. "Well, don't lose hope just yet. Let me put the refuge on the market. Perhaps another millionaire will come along and decide to continue running it as the Rathdeen Refuge!"

"I hope he has deep pockets."

Saskia laughed awkwardly.

"Sas, there is one other matter that we haven't discussed."

"Oh?"

"Us."

"Oh."

"Yes."

Saskia waited and said nothing.

"I still love you."

"Do you, Nicolas?"

He became indignant then. "Heck yeah! Why, did you think that would change?"

"Well, you never call any more and you have moved half a world away. If I remember correctly that was only meant to be a three-week bookselling trip."

"Don't mention the bloody book. I wish I had never tried that. It's cost me three precious years and my entire bank balance."

"Well, what about us?" Saskia tried to get him back to the matter in hand.

"I do still love you. You've got to believe me, Saskia."

"OK, I do believe you for what it's worth but I don't really see what we can do about it. We are literally half a world apart. I mean, it's not exactly intimate."

"Would you move over to LA?" he asked hopefully.

"Nicolas, be reasonable."

"What's wrong with that?"

"I'm a mother of four little women. My eldest is about to become a mother herself – I can't leave them."

"Well, surely if she's about to become a mother herself, it's time she got a life of her own."

That hurt Saskia. "The others still need me. Anyway Ballymore is my home."

"Is it? I thought you had just sold Innishambles, Saskia." There was an edge to his voice.

"We're moving to Ballymore Glen. I've just bought number five."

"Oh, you didn't say that." He sounded a little stung.

"I simply can't go, Nicolas. Tiffany is about to start college. Lauren is in Mount Eden and Robin is about to start in Montessori. It's frantically busy here. I can't just up and leave."

"Well, neither can I."

"So that's it then."

"Yeah, I guess that's it."

"We're breaking up. Aren't we?" she asked.

"I guess so," he said.

"I'll miss you," Saskia sighed. As she said it, she realised that it was painfully true. "I'll put the house on the market as soon as possible."

Nicolas's voice was small. "I'll talk to Barney today. Can you tell Kelly?"

"Sure."

"Thanks, Sas."

"It's OK." She was anxious to get off the phone quickly. "I have to go now."

"I'll call soon," he said.

But she knew he wouldn't.

"Goodbye, Nicolas."

287

As Saskia hung up, Wilma jumped onto her lap. The little Yorkie sensed that her mistress needed some extra attention.

"Well, Wilma, so far today I've sold this house for six million. I've bought another house for two million and I've broken up with my boyfriend. I think that's quite enough for one day, don't you?" She tried to sound positive. "Let's go and collect Robin from Cathy's house."

Saskia felt low and tired as she headed out of Innishambles. Her body was exhausted and she needed a cuddle. With deep regret, she realised that she was alone again. Was it her, she wondered. Was she incapable of sustaining a relationship? Then she chastised herself for letting herself think such things.

"Stop it, Saskia," she admonished herself. "Nicolas is in LA and I can't move over there. That's why we've broken up. And Richard wasn't worth keeping!" As she thought this, her eyes twinkled with mischief. "But Richard is in Ireland. That is a plus!"

CHAPTER 21

Nicolas phoned Barney as soon as he finished talking with Saskia. He didn't want his old veterinarian friend to hear anything second-hand.

Barney was utterly shellshocked with the news that the refuge would have to be sold off. No matter how many times Nicolas explained it to him, it still didn't register. The American had said that it was just too expensive, it was devouring money, and the land had become too valuable in the booming Irish economy. Barney worried. What was he going to do now? How was he going to support Kelly and the baby? The one small consolation was that he wouldn't have to break it to Kelly. Nicolas had said that Saskia was doing that.

It didn't take Kelly long to make an appearance. "Hi, Barney!" She smiled tentatively, checking out his mood.

His heart melted when he saw her mop of dark curls falling around her shoulders and her huge dark eyes brimming with concern.

"Well, at least one part of my life is absolutely perfect," he smiled and opened his arms to welcome her.

She happily rushed into his embrace. "Oh, Barney, I'm so sorry about this place. It's all so sad. Can you believe it?"

"Well, obviously I'm gutted, but I guess, with hindsight, I should have seen this coming for the last few months."

"Why?"

"All the bouncing cheques! Nicolas was very frank with me on the phone. Now I even feel a little sorry for the guy. It's all gone, all his money. What a bummer."

"Well, I think he was very reckless. He shouldn't have made this place so big if he wasn't going to be able to sustain it."

Barney looked at his fiancée. "God, Kelly, but you're a hard taskmaster. There's more of your father's blood coursing through your veins than you'd care to admit to."

"And what's that supposed to mean?" She looked at him warily.

"Well, you always see the business angle. Here I am thinking 'poor old Nicolas' and you're blasting his business acumen!"

Kelly looked hurt.

"Hey, honey, I think that's terrific," said Barney. "You're a businesswoman. In fact, why don't you divert some of your energy and that brain you have into finding out how and where we can offload some of these animals and what's the most efficient way to wind up the refuge?"

This time Kelly's lower lip began to quiver. "Oh God, then it really is going to happen, Barney? We have to close down?"

"I'm afraid so, Kelly. I can only pay wages up to the end of this month. We'll have to be closed by the thirtieth of September."

"What if we could get another sponsor, somebody else to bankroll us?"

"Yes, that would be wonderful, but it's as likely as winning the lottery."

But Kelly's mind was working overtime. "Mum knows that reporter Brian O'Malley. Perhaps he could do a piece on the refuge. You know, a plea to the nation. It might give us some help."

"Well, I guess we've nothing to lose – only the property is going up for sale straight away so we would need to move fast." Then Barney's tone changed and he looked at Kelly. "Now, onto matters more interesting – how's our baby?" He patted her still flat stomach.

"I'm going to make an appointment with Dr Harrington for sometime this week. Do you want to come?"

Barney looked a little uncomfortable. "This visit will just be a check-up, won't it?"

"Yes, why? Are you getting a little squeamish, Barney Armstrong? You're the vet. You know all about the birds and the bees for God's sake!"

Barney blushed. "Birds and bees I can deal with – but ladies? Well, that's another matter! I'd love to go when you're having your scan though. I gather you can see the baby's head, arms and legs with an ultrasound. That must be amazing. I can't wait to see him or her!"

Kelly laughed at him, which, in turn made him laugh. He hugged her tightly again. "God, I'm so glad we got through that little confusion we had. I love you so much, Kellser, and now we have a baby too. That just confirms our life together." He took her face in his hands and gently kissed her. "Together forever?"

"Together forever," she agreed and kissed him again.

"You know I'm feeling a lot stronger these days. If you like I can come back to work now."

"Well, you know that the cash is about to run out so there's no future in it. But of course I could do with your help. Why don't you do office stuff today? Phone your contact, Brian O'Malley, try and figure out where we can offload our animals and get on to the ISPCA and the other organisations that bring animals to us. Tell them about our situation. They're going to have to find other refuges."

"Jeez, why did I offer?" Kelly moaned but she was smiling at the same time. "Hey boss, can I phone Dr Harrington first?"

"Oh yes!" Barney grinned like a Cheshire cat. "Please do."

* * *

James Harrington had got on the phone to Dave Parker.

"James, I meant to phone you. I wanted to say thanks for the terrific job you did with Guy, poor little mite."

"Not at all, Dave. He's a great little fella." James coughed to clear his throat and continued. "Actually, I'm phoning about Sue, Dave."

"What about her?"

"Well, I was wondering – have you noticed her acting a little strangely of late?"

"No stranger than usual!" Dave laughed and instantly regretted it. "How do you mean?"

"It struck me when you were away that she seemed quite stressed," said the doctor. "It could be nothing, but do you think she could be a little down in herself?"

"No. She seems fine to me," Dave replied evenly.

"Just the same, I think she should come in and have a chat with me."

"Well, why don't you phone her?"

"That's just it, I phoned her yesterday and she point-blank refused to see me. Often when people, particularly busy mothers, are down or perhaps a little depressed, they don't want to discuss it with their doctors. In fact, she may be doing her damnedest to hide it from you too. She may be in denial, Dave. This only drives the problem underground and it gets worse and worse if it's not seen to."

Dave began to get seriously concerned. "Jesus, James, what are you saying? Do you think Sue has some sort of chronic depression that she's hiding from you and me?"

"I'm not saying anything just yet other than that I'm concerned about her stress levels. Do you think you could get her to come in and see me?"

"I'll see to it," Dave promised.

As he hung up, Dave Parker felt even worse than he had done all that week. Here he was avoiding his wife because he had been messing around behind her back and, to make matters worse, it now looked like she was suffering from depression. His pricking around in Egypt would definitely push her over the edge, if she ever found out . . .

* * *

On Wednesday evening, Jayne Mullins looked better than she ever had. Her hair shone and her skin glowed, but that was nothing new. What had changed was the light within. For years she had lived in the shadow of Raymond Saunders, the mighty businessman. Five years ago, he had it all: the beautiful wife, three gorgeous children and a business that was growing faster than the Internet. He was in the Sunday papers almost every week and when she heard about the job vacancy in his home for a nanny, she didn't need to be asked twice. What Jayne didn't know, however, was how drastically his life would change over the course of the next few years.

It didn't take long for Jayne to fall hopelessly in love with her boss. It wasn't hard; he was gorgeous, successful and extremely nice. Then Caroline got sick. The sicker she got, the more desperate Raymond became and the more Jayne fell for him. When Caroline did die, Jayne was determined to take her place in the family home. She adored Raymond. Unfortunately, the kids were part of the package. She was already living in the house. All that remained was for him to notice her and eventually fall in love with her.

Now, at last, it seemed to be happening. The *Star Trek* experience, followed by a burger and chips, had been the most romantic of her life. Raymond was so unsure of himself. For a bastion of the beef industry, he was a puppy with her that evening. Unlike an ordinary date, he didn't have to come and collect her and so when the baby-sitter arrived, he rather awkwardly offered Jayne a drink.

She laughed at him and took him by the arm.

"Let's just get out of here," she said and guided him to his own front door. The film part of the date was easy because they sat in silence in the darkness. After that they headed to their old favourite, McDonald's.

"I guess I should have taken you somewhere a little posher, Jayne," he suddenly thought, halfway through his quarter-pounder.

"Nonsense, this is just perfect," she smiled. There would be time enough for expensive restaurants when she was his wife, she thought confidently.

"Are you sure you're happy to be seen with an old fella like me, Jayne?"

"Of course," she laughed. "You're not *that* old, you know. A friend of mine is going out with a guy considerably older than you."

"Who's that?"

"Oh, you don't know her."

"Hey, I thought I knew all your friends."

"No, Raymond, not all of them," she flirted. It was impossible that he would know that particular friend, considering she had just made her up.

"I like you," she risked, in an attempt to continue the conversation as they walked out to Raymond's Merc 500.

"I like you too." Raymond glanced at her.

She was staring at him, waiting to catch his eye. He looked into her eyes and was drawn in.

Then Raymond Saunders took Jayne Mullins in his arms and kissed her. It was a soft kiss but his arms were strong and reliable. She felt her body press against his and desperately wanted to kiss him passionately. That however would be fatal. She knew that. She had been this patient; she could wait a little longer. She let him control the kiss and decide how long it lasted. Unfortunately for her, it wasn't that long. He gently broke away from her and looked into her eyes again. She grinned at him dreamily, leaving him in no doubt. She was ready when he was.

"Are you OK with this?" he asked with a look of incredulity on his face.

"Yes, Raymond, I am," she smiled and willed him to kiss her once more.

He obliged. In the middle of the car park, he kissed her again, this time a little harder. She wanted to melt into him, to hang onto his beautiful torso and squeeze him tightly, but again she kept her body soft and compliant and gently embraced him. This time when he broke the kiss he grinned at her like a little boy. He gently tapped her on the nose with his index finger. "Come on Jayne. Let's go home!"

All the way home she prayed that he would offer her a drink and then take her to his room. She was so ready to make love to him! But it was not to be. Raymond paid the baby-sitter and met Jayne in the drawing-room.

"Eh, would you like to go out for a meal sometime soon?"

"Yes, that would be lovely!"

"Great. Well, goodnight then and thanks for a lovely evening." He smiled at her from a safe distance, across the drawing-room. He made no effort to kiss her.

Back to the house and back to the old rules, Jayne thought furiously, but she kept her face serene.

"Goodnight, Raymond," she smiled at him as he left. Then she fumed all the way to bed herself. Why did he have to respect her so much? She would have loved to get down and dirty with him then and there.

"Bloody men," she spat as she pulled out her vibrator.

* * *

Oscar Bingham called Richard Dalton on his landline. Edwina answered the phone.

"Dalton residence," she said in her usual clipped tone.

"Hi, Edwina. Is Richard there please? It's Oscar Bingham."

"One moment please and I'll just see if he's in," she replied in her best business voice.

God, what an eejit, Oscar thought as she put the phone down. He knew that Richard was there. He worked from home and as such he was usually there but Edwina always said the same thing. "I'll just see if he's in," Oscar mimicked her rather unflatteringly as he waited. Edwina was such a pain and a transparent one at that.

"Oscar, hi," said Richard. They heard Edwina put the receiver down on the phone in her front hall.

"Richard, I have good news for you. We've sold another of your beautiful houses in Ballymore Glen."

"You're playing a blinder, Oscar!"

"Thanks, but I think this one will particularly interest you."

"Oh?"

"Yes, the buyer."

"Who is it this time? Do I know him?"

"It's a her, Richard. Your ex-wife has just bought number five."

Richard said nothing for a moment. It wasn't a great shock. He knew that she was selling Innishambles.

"How much did you let it go for?"

"As per your instructions, I played inside the one and a half to two million window, so I think you'll be happy to hear that she paid top dollar, two million euro on the nose."

Richard kicked himself. It wasn't Oscar Bingham's fault. Richard knew that she could have been screwed for another half million. Saskia was no businesswoman. The only thing his ex-wife knew about was how to destroy families. Damn it, she had sold Innishambles for six million. That woman had too much money. That was the bloody problem.

"Well done, Oscar. I appreciate your call. Any other prospective buyers?"

"All of the houses have generated a considerable amount of interest. I'd say they'll all be gone in a matter of weeks. You're a very wealthy man, Richard."

Richard laughed amiably. "Not if you knew how much I had to pay to build them!" he lied.

"One other bit of news that might interest you."

"Yes?"

"Saskia has instructed me to put Rathdeen Manor on the market."

"What?"

"Yes, she says she's acting on behalf of Nicolas. I have to go out there later this week to put a value on the place."

Richard's mind began to race again. "OK, Oscar, now this is very important. I need you to put a very conservative value on it. Do this for me, Oscar, and I'll make it seriously worth your while."

"Dave, you're already paying me a more than generous fee. I hear you."

"Seriously now, what do you think it's worth?"

"Jeez, it's hard to say but Innishambles went for considerably more than we anticipated. We would have to put a similar price tag on the manor now. Ballpark figure? About five million euro."

"Shit," Richard let out a low gasp. "OK, Oscar no higher than four million. Do you hear me?"

"Christ, Richard, she won't believe that! Don't forget that she could get a second valuation."

"I'll try and cut her off at the pass," Richard snapped. "Do you hear me now? No more than four million."

"Whatever you say, boss," Oscar hung up, feeling lousy. Saskia Dalton was a nice woman but Richard was practically bank-rolling Oscar's life at this stage. He knew that he couldn't cross Richard Dalton.

Richard on the other hand was elated. He had heard from the girls that Saskia planned on buying a place in the sun and a place in Dublin and now that she had bought number five, admittedly for only two million euro, she would soon run out of money – silly bitch. When was she going to realise that she needed him? Saskia had no business brain. She was going to whittle away all of her capital and then she would have to come back to him. This would teach her. He would show her and now it looked like he could deal with bloody Nicolas Flattery at the same time. If they believed that it was only worth four million, he himself could snap it up for a song. Jesus, the land alone was worth more than three million or at least it would be as soon as he had worked his magic on it and got it rezoned. With his friends in high places, that wouldn't be too difficult. He would build another Ballymore Glen on the land. His brown-envelope method of doing business was as effective as ever. Back-handers were the only way of doing business in Ireland. Only this time, Richard had the good sense not to let anybody know what he was up to, least of all Saskia.

"Fools!" he cried, slightly manically. "Bloody fools!"

Edwina knocked gently on his study door at the top of the stairs.

"Is everything all right, Richard?" She popped her head around the door. "I heard you shouting."

"Get lost, Mummy dearest! Can't you see I'm working?" he snapped at her.

Edwina closed the door again quickly and rushed to her room. He had turned into such a brute. Her tears flowed freely as she sat on the side of her bed, a truly broken woman. Edwina knew that Richard was a man possessed and he definitely had something cooking. She just didn't know what it was.

CHAPTER 22

"This is absolute madness," Lauren complained. "Kelly only had her twenty-first less than two weeks ago and now it's another party for her!"

"Not just her," Saskia said. "It's Robin's third birthday party, it's Kelly and Barney's engagement party, and it's Tiffany's going-to-college party. Oh, and it's our house-moving party too. They're all rolled into one!"

"Usually people have parties in their *new* houses, not their old ones," Lauren continued to grumble.

"Yes, well, we have to have a party for little Robin, and Kelly needs a lift what with the refuge up for sale."

"Is it up for sale already?" Tiffany asked, astonished.

"The signs will go up today and it will be in the papers next week. I had a long conversation with Oscar Bingham this morning."

"Yeah, he must think you're a regular property tycoon, Mum," Tiffany laughed. "This is your second large house to sell in a month and you've bought one of his blessed Ballymore Glen houses! Any news on when we can move in there?"

Saskia sighed. "Well, it's going to be pretty close but Barry McCourt is working on the contracts as we speak. It looks like we can move in on Saturday week. That's the day we give the Condons the keys to this house!"

Lauren saw Tiffany's face cloud over at the mere mention of the Condons and so she started to complain loudly, to divert attention from her sister. "In fact now that I come to think about it, I'm the only one who doesn't have a share in this party!"

"What has you so emotional, pet?" Saskia asked. "I'm sorry you're not directly involved in this one. Tell you what, why don't you have your own party in the new house once we're settled? How does that sound?"

"Better," Lauren grumbled, but she was grinning at the same time.

"Tiffany," Saskia turned to her other daughter, "what date does college start?"

"Well, it's the week after next but I'll be up there for quite a bit next week checking out the different varsity clubs and learning where all the rooms are," she replied, barely able to contain her excitement.

"My heavens, it has crept up on us very quickly. Robin starts Montessori next week too and of course you're back to Mount Eden, Lauren." This caused another groan from her younger daughter which Saskia duly ignored.

"It's all happening at once – as usual," she said.

"Are you sure you want to throw this party tomorrow night, Mum?" Tiffany asked.

"Yes, yes, quite sure. To hold it off for another week would mean having a party in this house the day before we move – not a good idea. Now I really must start phoning around to get everybody here for tomorrow night. And I must contact the house-moving people. When is that for again?"

"Saturday week," Tiffany and Lauren replied in unison.

"Mummy, are you sure you're OK?" This time it was Lauren who was asking.

"Yes, I just seem very forgetful these days," Saskia smiled vacantly and left the kitchen, heading for the study.

"She's acting a little weird, isn't she?" Lauren looked at Tiffany.

"Yes, she is. I can't figure out why either. She's been going to bed really early and getting up very late. You don't think she's ill, do you?"

"Ohmigod, I hope not. Not Mum!" Lauren covered her mouth with her hands. Then she stopped and dropped them again "Hey, you've got me at it now – worrying. There's nothing wrong with Mum. Come on – let's take the hounds for a walk. They're dying for one and you'll be cooped up in college soon enough. You need all the fresh air and exercise you can get!"

Tiffany perked up at the idea of college. "Yeah, I can't wait. It's all going to be so different, and as for living in Dublin, I'm really looking forward to it!"

"Don't let Mum hear you saying that," Lauren laughed. "You know how fond of Edwina and Dad she is. Here, you round up the dogs – I just want to ask Mum something," She left Tiffany out at the back door and ran back into Innishambles to find Saskia.

"Mum, just a thought," she said, walking into the study.

Saskia was sitting at her desk, looking for phone numbers. She looked up when she heard her daughter's voice.

"Yes, pet?"

"Well, wouldn't it be a nice idea to invite the Condons? They're buying Innishambles and this way they could meet their new neighbours. What do you think?"

"I think it's a lovely idea but I don't know how to contact them."

"Barry McCourt will." Lauren had it all thought out.

"You are clever! Yes, that's a nice idea."

"What's a nice idea?" Tiffany came into the room surrounded by dogs.

"Taking Robin with us to give Mum some space," Lauren said before Saskia had the chance to say anything.

Sas smiled. "That's a lovely idea. She's up in her room playing happily. She's such a contented child!"

"Sure aren't we all?" Lauren laughed.

"Not a bit of it!" Saskia looked shocked. "You were by far the most demanding, Lauren. You insisted on sitting on my lap morning, noon and night. You wanted to be the centre of attention all the time!"

"What about me?" Tiffany asked.

Saskia's eyes glazed over as she looked down the tunnel of time. "You were always a Daddy's girl. You were good as gold during the day – quite like Robin actually. But at night when you heard Richard coming in the front door you would tear off to greet him and you would stick to him like glue all evening."

Tiffany and Lauren looked at their mother as her face suddenly snapped out of her daydream.

"Yes, well, that was a long time ago. Now, are you off for a walk or are these dogs going to be driven mad with the anticipation?"

A few minutes later, Tiffany, Lauren and Robin were

heading out into the September sun, with Dudley, Dexter, Woody and Wilma for company.

"Let's go to the river," Robin begged her older sisters.

"You and your river! You're obsessed with it. What are you going to be when you grow up? A sailor?" Lauren laughed, cuddling her baby sister.

"Or a marine biologist!" Tiffany suggested.

"Eh, yeah," Lauren laughed. They walked in companionable silence for a while enjoying the last of the summer sun. The valley was full of mid-morning light and the air was full of sound. Little birds chirped merrily, their bellies full of grain and even the cows seemed quite vocal.

"What do you think they're talking about?" Tiffany asked as they heard a particularly loud 'moo' from the field next to them.

"God knows. Maybe it's a girl-cow blasting a boy-cow out of it!"

"That would be a bull," Tiffany laughed. "Lauren, sometimes I wonder about you."

"Yeah, bull, whatever. Speaking of boys and girls, however –" Lauren looked at Tiffany.

"I wondered how long this would take." Tiffany glanced at her sister and then continued, "I'm OK, I guess. Out of sight, out of mind and all that."

"But he's buying our house. Doesn't that upset you?"

"More than you can imagine, Lauren, but I just keep concentrating on college. If I think about it –" she bit her lip to stop it quivering. It was obvious to Lauren that her sister was anything but OK.

"Fuck that bastard for hurting you so badly," Lauren spat.

Tiffany elbowed her sister and nodded towards Robin. "Mind your language," she frowned. Then she turned to her baby sister, "Robin, if you want, you can run ahead with Woody. We'll keep an eye on you."

Robin was delighted with the extended freedom and tore off with the terrier.

Happy that her baby sister was out of earshot, Tiffany spoke freely. "Oh, Lauren! Why was I so stupid? If I just hadn't gone out that night. If I'd offered to baby-sit for Mum and Nicolas – this is my punishment, you know!"

"Tiffany, that's rubbish. You were just – well – unfortunate."

"Unfortunate? Is that what you call it? I think about that guy every day – hell, very minute of every day. How could he do that? How could he have sex with me and never want to see me again? How could he be that intimate and not even notice that he doesn't know my surname?"

Tiffany was on a roll now, so Lauren just let her sister talk while she watched Robin run ahead with the dogs.

"He's such a bastard. I swear, Lauren, guys should be taught at school how to treat girls – and certainly not like he treated me! I don't know if I'll ever be able to trust a guy again. I don't know how I'm ever going to get over him." The tears began to rush down her cheeks. Lauren stopped to hug her.

"Hush, Tiff. He's just not worth it. I know that sounds like some old cliché, but he's not. You're so kind and thoughtful. You're always the one who remembers everybody's birthday in our house! We're shagged next year!"

This made Tiffany laugh a little. "I'll text you to remind you."

"You see? Still minding the family, even from afar." They started to walk again but Lauren continued, "And as for your brains? My God, Max and Seb don't have one between the two of them."

Tiffany laughed again.

"Trust me, sister," Lauren persevered, "you're too good for him."

"Well, if I'm too good for him, how come he didn't even want to see me a second time?" Tiffany wouldn't be consoled. "No, Lauren, I'm afraid I wasn't nearly good enough for him," and she began to cry gently again. "Max is a god and I'm a mere mortal."

Lauren had run out of arguments. Fuck him, I'll get him for this if it's the last thing I do, she fumed to herself.

Saskia didn't have that much organising to do. One quick phone call to Kelly's friend Francesca and all of Kelly's friends were sorted out.

"You leave that to me, Mrs Dalton, I'll round up the troops. I'm so happy for Kelly and Barney. They're terrific together."

At the ripe old age of three, Saskia reckoned that little Robin would be satisfied if the Parker children came. In truth, Saskia's youngest didn't really have any other friends but all of that would change when she started Montessori. She should also invite the Taylors, of course, because Cathy Taylor was like a grandmother to Robin. This brought Saskia to a matter she had been pushing out of her mind since she started to think about the party.

What about Robin's real grandmother and indeed her father? It just wasn't fair to lock them out of her life. Reluctantly, Saskia phoned Edwina Dalton's number.

"Dalton residence." Edwina was as dependable as the Irish rain. Her condescending air was ever-present.

"Hi, Edwina. It's Saskia."

"Oh, hello."

"How are you?" Saskia tried to make polite conversation.

"Well, I'm fine now. My ears were quite badly damaged by my last visit to Innishambles. The music was really too too loud."

"Ah, well, I was just phoning to invite you to another party but perhaps it would be too loud for you too."

"Another party? You're certainly very flash these days, Saskia. What are we celebrating this time?"

The 'we' really annoyed Sas. She wondered for the hundredth time why she even made an effort with this bloody woman.

"Why, Barney and Kelly's engagement, of course. I assumed Richard told you." She couldn't stop herself being a little bitchy – Edwina deserved it!

There was silence from Edwina. Her son obviously hadn't told her. Whyever not? "He's frightfully busy these days, you know – what with all his business." Edwina tried to regain some ground.

Saskia had no idea what line of business Richard was in any more but she didn't dare ask Edwina.

"Well, the party is on tomorrow night. Will we count you in?"

Edwina sniffed. "Such short notice – really."

"We only decided to throw the party today and what with the house sale it has to be done very quickly," Saskia tried to explain.

"The what?"

"Edwina, we've sold Innishambles."

"I had no idea!" The older woman was so shocked she didn't even hide her surprise this time. A lifetime ago she had thought Richard and Saskia utterly mad to move out of Dublin's suburbs but, over the years, even Edwina came to think of Innishambles and Ballymore as home even though she had never lived there.

Saskia could tell that her ex-mother-in-law had been utterly stunned by the news. "God, I'm sorry to drop it on you like this. Why don't you come tomorrow night and I'll fill you in on all the family news because there is quite a bit at the moment." Saskia thought about Kelly's pregnancy and felt sure that Richard hadn't imparted that particular nugget yet either. As usual, the dirty work would be left to Saskia.

She continued, "It's also a third birthday party for Robin and it's Tiffany's going-to-college-party."

"Richard told me that she wants to live with us." Edwina was delighted to impart the one small bit of news that she was aware of.

"Yes." Saskia tried to keep her teeth from clenching.

"Perhaps we should make an appearance – for the girls' sakes," Edwina answered.

"Good, we'll see you tomorrow night then."

"Yes."

"Do you think that will be the two of you?" Saskia asked, trying to sound as casual as possible. She didn't want to sound like she cared really, but she desperately wanted to know whether or not to expect her ex-husband.

"Oh, I can't speak for Richard, as you know, Saskia. He's so dreadfully busy these days."

Edwina had the upper hand again, damn her.

"Yes, well, we'll expect him if we see him."

"That would be best. If he's free, he'll come. If he can't, he won't," Edwina concluded.

This annoyed Saskia even more but she tried to hide it as she said goodbye. Now she would have to hang on tenterhooks until the following night. Darn this, she fumed.

"Mummy, where are you?" Kelly yelled as she came into Innishambles through the back door.

Saskia came out to greet her eldest. "Is everything OK?" she asked, delighted at the distraction.

"No, it certainly isn't OK. I phoned your old friend Brian O'Malley yesterday and he said he'd get back to me sometime so I thought he was just politely telling me to sod off. Well, I was wrong! He's coming up to the refuge *this afternoon* with an entire news crew," Kelly wailed, but her eyes were bright with excitement. "I can't believe it, Mum. I thought he might just take a phone interview or something but he said the refuge was newsworthy especially because it used to belong to Nicolas Flattery."

"Slow down there!" Saskia tried to catch up with what her daughter was saying. "You contacted Brian O'Malley? Why?"

"Oh Mum, I wanted him to do a news piece on the refuge. Maybe we can get another sponsor or the public to donate money to keep it going."

"Clever, I'll give you that." Saskia followed Kelly up the stairs.

"Yes, but look at me, I'm a mess! I could be on TV and my hair is in bits and I have nothing to wear."

"Of course you do," Saskia tried to soothe her daughter. "Come on, I'll help you find something clean. You'll look a million dollars by the time those cameras roll!"

Even Barney couldn't believe the transformation. Kelly arrived back to the refuge at three o'clock, the same time Brian O'Malley was due. Brian had arrived early, however, and had already enjoyed quite a long chat with Barney. Despite her boyfriend's strong protestations, Kelly still rode Mooner. She galloped into the refuge and pulled up her massive horse in the middle of the courtyard. Various dogs barked her a welcome and Mooner, who always liked a bit of drama, let out a loud whinny just in case anybody managed to miss their arrival.

Brian's jaw hit the ground. She was gorgeous. Kelly dismounted Mooner in one easy, fluid movement. Not so fast, however, that Brian O'Malley and his entire news crew missed the tightest little ass in a pair of jodhpurs you were likely to see. She wore a pink cotton blouse and a riding hat, but her dark brown curls danced down her back freely and no hat – riding or otherwise – was going to be able to hide the biggest eyes he had ever seen.

"Hi, you must be Brian! I'm really sorry you got here before me." She beamed at him and thrust out her hand to shake his. Her manner was at odds with her image. Brian thought she looked cool, calm and aloof but she spoke and acted openly. Then, to his intense dismay, Kelly reached over and kissed Barney on the lips, "Hi, darling! Miss me?" She smiled at him with love in her eyes.

Ah hell – the good ones are always taken, he thought,

as did half his news crew. He took her hand and shook it. "Hi, you must be Kelly. It's lovely to meet you too. You're not late. We were early actually, sorry."

His cameraman could barely contain his laughter. Brian O'Malley, newsman extraordinaire, was apologising for being early! That was a first.

Kelly took Brian around the refuge while his film crew took tea and then Brian wrote down a small news piece. He talked it over with Barney and Kelly, to make sure all the information was accurate, as his camera and soundman got organised, and then he did his piece straight to camera.

Rathdeen Refuge, in the village of Ballymore in Wicklow, is in trouble. It was the brainchild of actor and philanthropist Nicolas Flattery, more famous for his part in the film Freedom *than anything else. Sadly however the refuge and the original house, known as Rathdeen Manor, have proved to be too expensive for him to maintain and so the lands and the spectacular house, equipped with swimming-pool and tennis court, are for sale. What's to become of the refuge, however? Well, it isn't looking good at the moment. Rathdeen Refuge will have to be closed at the end of this month unless some other source of income can be found. With all the animals that the refuge has found new homes for in the last three years, what they really need is a sponsor with a big heart and an even bigger wallet! Brian O'Malley, RTE News. Ballymore.*

"And cut," the producer announced. As far as Kelly could see it was the first thing she had said all day but then she spoke again. "OK, folks, that's a wrap. Some cut-aways of strays – the more pathetic-looking the better and then home time."

Kelly couldn't believe how fast the actual filming had taken.

"Is that it?" she asked Brian.

"That's it," he smiled back at her. "Just some cut-aways and we're out of your hair."

"What are cut-aways?"

"A posh way of saying some other pictures so the viewers won't have to look at me all the time!" He winked conspiratorially at Kelly.

The cameraman took some footage of the refuge and a few of its residents. Then he filmed Mooner, which the horse thoroughly enjoyed while Brian explained to Kelly,

"The longest part is getting the story accurate. Doing the bit to camera is fairly straightforward once the crew are on the case." He laughed, elbowing his soundman. It was obvious that they were a tight team.

"I often wondered when I watch you on the news whether you had those cue cards or whether you kept it all in your head," Kelly said. "You must have a great memory."

This led to loud laughter from the rest of the film crew who were packing up the equipment.

"Ignore that lot!" Brian laughed. "Sometimes I get it wrong, but usually it goes fairly smoothly."

Barney walked with Brian to his car. "I hope you get some sort of backing to keep this place going," said Brian. "It's a magnificent setting and you are doing great work."

"Thanks, Brian. Who knows? This news piece might do the trick."

"Well, if we've helped, that's good. It'll run tonight as far as I know. The news is fairly quiet at the moment so we were glad of the story."

"Six o'clock tonight," Kelly gasped in disbelief, glancing at her watch. It was four-thirty already.

"Well, if I get out of here fast enough to get it back and clean it up," Brian laughed as he waved goodbye and drove off.

"What a life," Kelly swooned.

"What a woman," Barney said as he stood behind her and wrapped his arms around her. "Now that, Kelly Dalton, was a good day's work. You single-handedly put the refuge on the national news this evening. I'm proud of you!"

She turned to face him so she could hug him too. Then she kissed him. "I'm proud of you too!" she smiled.

"But you got all scrubbed up in case you were filmed and they didn't even interview you," Barney said with concern. "Are you upset about that?"

"No way," Kelly laughed. "It's the refuge that I want on TV really – not my mutt! Especially in this condition!" She looked at her tummy and stroked it. Then she smiled at Barney as she realised once again that, yes, she was delighted to be pregnant with his child.

CHAPTER 23

Innishambles was deadly quiet. Even the dogs had the good sense to stay silent. Saskia looked around the drawing-room. Barney was sitting back in one of the armchairs, with Kelly on the armrest, staying close. Lauren and Tiffany were sitting on the sofa, eyes glued to the television, and Robin was on the floor watching with interest – not quite sure why but caught up in the mood. They had rushed in as soon as they heard the familiar jingle of the main RTE evening news.

Lauren, the least patient of the girls, was the first to lose interest. "Are you sure it's going to be on tonight?"

"Yes," Kelly whispered urgently. "Now shhh!"

Saskia looked out the window of the drawing-room. Mooner and Polly were grazing in the field and the shadows were starting to creep across the gravel driveway. Evening was coming. The end of another day. Where was the time going? Her baby was starting school and her eldest was getting married. She would be a grandmother soon. Richard began to invade her mind again. He had been doing that quite a bit since she had spoken to him at Kelly's birthday. He was so charming, so nice – cut it out, she thought angrily to herself. Why was she thinking about him so much lately? He was still the same shit who had been unfaithful to her – and so many times, not just once. He had been involved with their old au pair for years. He had even had sex with their neighbour and of course there was that piece of work from Corporate Affairs, his PR girl – the one called Robin! Saskia could feel herself getting angry again and she started to polish the ornaments on the table beside her with an old tea towel she happened to be holding.

"Here it is, here it is!" Tiffany and Kelly squealed in unison. Then everybody "shushed" together.

Brian O'Malley reported the plight of the Rathdeen Refuge to the nation. Everybody watched in absolute silence, not moving a muscle.

"Christ, it was short," Lauren complained as soon as it ended.

"Well, I think it was wonderful," Barney smiled at his fiancée and kissed her. "You're a hell of a hustler, Kelly Dalton."

"What do you think, Mum?" Kelly watched her mother anxiously.

"Well, pet, I agree with Barney. You've done terrifically but I'm not sure Nicolas will be glad to hear his name on the television."

"Sure, he'll never know," Lauren argued.

"Perhaps, but outside of that, it's terrific publicity, Kelly," Saskia continued. "I think it was a great idea and it may well help you to get another source of income."

"I didn't realise that the 'for sale' signs had gone up already," Tiffany said sadly.

"Yeah, they went up today as the crew were filming stuff around the refuge," Barney added sadly. "It really is ending."

"Have you had a chance to think about what you'll do, Barney?" Saskia asked softly, hoping that she didn't sound too much like an interfering mother-in-law.

"Well, Sas, to be honest, I'm still getting used to the idea of closing up the refuge, but I guess I'll go back to what I used to do."

"And that was?" Lauren asked, not remotely embarrassed.

"Well, I'll work from Peartree Cottage, my house, and visit farmers on their farms. It depends on the demand but when I need a surgery, I'll rent one. Eventually I'll probably try to buy into a practice in Wicklow. That'll cost a heck of a lot though," he sighed.

"I'll be very sad to see the refuge go," Tiffany said.

"Me too," added Lauren.

"Where's Nicolas?" Robin asked Saskia innocently.

The other girls and Barney looked at Sas for her response. She looked at her family and decided that it was probably better to be honest.

"Well, the good news is that Nicolas has a job!"

"And the bad news?" Tiffany asked.

"I'm afraid that job is in LA, so he won't be coming home for, er, for a long time."

"How long, Mum?" Kelly asked.

"Well," she stuttered, "eh, Nicolas and I have decided that his life is really over there and I'm afraid my life is very definitely over here so, well –"

"You've broken up," Tiffany helped her.

"Well, yes." Saskia stared at her shoes.

The girls gathered around their mother and hugged her, even Robin.

"Oh Mummy, I'm sorry it didn't work out," Lauren said.

"Yes, Mummy, you deserve a good man," Tiffany added.

"Nicolas was – is a good man," Saskia defended her ex-boyfriend. "It's just that we live so far apart." Surrounded by so much love and sympathy, Saskia thought that she might cry. "Now, now, girls, I'm fine." She forced a smile. "Nicolas and I can still be friends. The truth is both our lives are just too busy! Now, come on, let's think about tomorrow night. What else do we need to do to get organised for this party?"

"Pass the Parcel," Tiffany suddenly said.

"What?" Lauren didn't understand.

"Robin will need 'pass the parcel' for her and her little friends. I can do those now. Come on, Robin, you can help me." She winked at her mother and took her youngest sister off in search of newspapers and little toys.

"Mum, are you sure you're OK? About Nicolas, I mean?" Kelly looked at her mother.

Because Tiffany had had the intuition to take Robin out of the room, Saskia was able to be a little more frank. "Obviously, it would have been lovely if it had worked out, honey, but it didn't."

"I know what you mean, Mum," said Lauren. Always one to speak her mind, she didn't stop now. "If you still love each other, though, why don't you move over to LA?"

"What? And leave you crowd here to your own devices? I don't think so!" Saskia smiled. "Or would you like to move to LA, Lauren?"

The girl thought about this for a while. "Actually, it

could be fun. Robin and I could move and Kelly and Tiffany could stay here."

Saskia's mind raced. Could she really do it?

"No way," Kelly moaned. "I don't want to lose my mother, not now not ever."

Saskia snapped out of her emigration fantasies. They were utterly ridiculous. She looked at her daughters. They were so precious, much more so than any man would ever be. "Perhaps I wasn't what he wanted after all."

"Mummy! Don't put yourself down like that! It's his loss," Lauren snapped. This reminded her very much of what she was saying to Tiffany these days. "I guess that's the difference between real love and a crush," Lauren concluded. "Real love lasts a lifetime."

Saskia's mind instantly rushed to Richard. Jesus, she thought, what am I doing still thinking about the man I divorced years ago?

The phone started to ring.

"That'll be some rich millionaire, wanting to save the refuge," Lauren laughed as she sprang up to answer it. "Ah no, it's only Dad."

Saskia's heart skipped a beat.

Lauren raised the handpiece to Kelly. "He wants to speak with you."

Then Saskia's heart sank into her belly. What the hell is wrong with me, she snapped at herself. I know it's just a rebound thing.

"Bloody hormones," she mumbled and then smiled at the memory of Richard saying the same thing.

* * *

By lunch-time Friday, the house was chaotic. Robin had

changed her mind and no longer wanted a Barney birthday cake. Now it had to be a Teletubby cake. Lauren was doing her best to convert a purple dinosaur into a purple Teletubby and pass it off for Tinky Winky. Robin, however, was deeply suspicious.

Tiffany was *still* packing.

"Are you taking everything you possess?" Saskia asked her, slightly impatient.

"I don't know what I'll need," Tiffany tried to explain, "so I really need to take everything." The boxes were mounting at the front door because Richard, when he phoned to accept the party invitation, also offered to take some of her stuff back to Dublin with him.

"That load isn't going to fit in your dad's two-door, especially if he has his mother with him."

"Dad isn't driving a two-door any more. He's bought a four-door, but it's still a Merc," Tiffany added as she pranced up the stairs for yet another box of stuff she couldn't live without.

"Poser!" Lauren shouted from the kitchen.

Kelly appeared at the door. "Right, I'm off." She looked beautiful.

"God, Kelly, I never looked that good when I was pregnant," Saskia laughed wistfully.

"Thanks, I must say I feel absolutely fine. I don't even *feel* pregnant. Is that normal?" she asked her mother.

"Perfectly," Saskia caressed her eldest's hair. "Dr Harrington will talk you through everything today. You can tell him that you have full insurance – thank you, Richard! You'll also have to choose an obstetrician – he can advise you – and then you'll have to decide where you're going to have the baby."

320

"Ohmigod, I'm going to have a baby!" Kelly put her hands over her mouth. "It still hasn't sunk in."

"To be honest, pet, I don't think it ever does until you're actually holding the little person in your arms," Saskia replied, still stroking Kelly's hair. "Are you sure you don't want me to go with you?"

"Where the hell is Barney?" Lauren yelled from the kitchen.

"Yeah, where the bell is Barney?" Robin tried to imitate her sister.

"He's wimping out so I'm doing this bit by myself. Nothing will happen today anyway," Kelly continued, half convincing herself. "He's only going to tell me what date to expect the baby and have a chat with me. Isn't that right, Mum?"

"Yes, honey, that's absolutely right. Now off you go and enjoy the visit. He's a very nice doctor."

"And a bit cute," came the comment from the kitchen.

"I'll tell him you said hi, Lauren. OK?"

"Yeah," Lauren enthused. Then she appeared at the door, covered in purple icing sugar. "Hey, why don't you invite him to the party tonight?"

Kelly looked at her mother for a comment.

"If you want to, you can, pet," Saskia agreed.

"To use your phrase, Mum, 'we'll see'." She slipped into her green Barbour jacket and headed out the door. "Oh, Mum, I forgot to ask, could I borrow the car?"

"I thought you girls were meant to drive the Micra and leave me my car," Saskia laughed.

"That old thing doesn't even move any more."

"Since when?"

"Please, can I drive your car? It's so much more comfortable."

"OK," Saskia gave in, "seeing as it's such a special occasion. Good luck with Dr Harrington."

* * *

James had had a horrific afternoon. Three strep throats, one tonsillitis and yet another visit from that fat slag who thought she had a deadly virus every time she got a cold. His one consolation was that Sue Parker was his last patient of the day. He would enjoy her.

The next patient in his diary was Kelly Dalton. Now there was another cutie, only too young for him. He stepped into his waiting-room.

"Miss Dalton," he announced confidently, in his utterly-sincere-totally-trustworthy doctor voice, but there was no sign of her. The only person in his waiting room was Sue Parker. She looked up at him politely. "Hello, James."

"Oh, hello. You're early."

"Yes, I am a little and no sign of your other patient. I guess I could queue skip!" She smiled coolly. In reality, Sue was hopping mad to have been so manipulated.

Dave had phoned her and begged her to make an appointment to see James. He had said that he was worried about her and to do this for him. Sue agreed because she wanted to please him. She didn't dare tell him about James' unwanted flirtations. Things were strained enough between Dave and herself.

"Come on in," James laughed. "Sometimes patients don't come in if they start to feel better."

"That's dreadful." Sue looked surprised. "Would they not phone your secretary to cancel?"

"Some don't." James looked hurt.

"Gosh, James, that really is bad!"

"Enough about me. How are you, Sue?" He guided her over to his patient's bed.

"James, really, I am fine. I'm only here because you got David on the case. That was very bold of you."

"We're both worried about you. Now if you can sit here and roll up your sleeve, please. I'm going to take your blood pressure." He walked around his desk and sat down for a moment. "I have your family files here, Sue, and there is something I think you should be aware of."

She held her breath.

"Sue, did you know that Dave is in fact blood type A Positive too?"

She didn't trust herself to talk as he looked up so she just shook her head.

"Yes, it's extremely unusual. Both you and he are A positive which can in some very unusual circumstances result in an O negative baby. It's just something you need to know because it means that neither you nor Dave can give blood to Guy." Still, Sue didn't speak. "As I said, it's not really a problem because Guy can get blood from other sources, should the need arise. Just be aware. OK?"

This time she nodded but the feeling of elation was beginning to tingle in her toes. It reached her knees and then the pit of her stomach. James was still talking but she wasn't listening!

"It's most unusual that neither parent *blah blah blah . . .*"

Her shoulders felt lighter and then her head. Her bloody head had been throbbing since she discovered that Guy was O negative and here was James Harrington telling her it was 'no big deal'. She dared to speak as

James crossed the room to her with his blood-pressure thingy.

"What are the odds that two positive blood-type parents could have a negative blood-type child?"

"Gosh, I don't know but you are the first case I've come across. At a guess I'd say a thousand to one! But it's not impossible. Not by any means. God, if it were impossible –" he laughed, "Well, then, that would raise all sorts of scenarios!" He gave a sinister laugh. "Things that wouldn't even cross the mind of a lady like you, Sue."

"No, no, quite." She was still in shock.

"Still," he continued, "it might be a good idea to get India and DJ checked out. If they are O negative too it would be good to be informed."

Again she nodded. All of her worries were for nothing. She smiled to herself. Here was James trying to take her blood pressure. Doubtless it had been very high up until that last little gem of information! But everything was going to be just fine now. She was wearing an exquisite navy silk jacket but it was difficult to pull the sleeves up.

"It's not a problem. Just take it off," James said, trying to sound as uninterested as possible. He wasn't even looking at her. Instead he fiddled with some machine beside her. "You know you haven't had a medical since you were pregnant with DJ?"

Then he looked up and caught his breath. Sue was wearing a white silk one-piece. Under her jacket, it had looked innocent enough, but now with the jacket removed, he could see it for what it was – underwear! James tried to control his breath while he took her blood pressure.

"So how have you been? Any dizziness, difficulty sleeping, tendency towards tears recently?"

Sue looked at him in astonishment, "Yes, how did you know?"

"Sue, I'm your doctor." He sat beside her on the little bed and took her hand. "Do you want to tell me anything?"

"Really, James," she pulled her hand away, "I'm fine. You know that Guy caused me a few grey hairs with his accident. I'm suffering from nothing more than the strains of motherhood." She tried to sound more convincing. Forget about Guy for the moment and get yourself out of this situation, she told herself. She was becoming very uneasy in James' company.

James took her hand again. "It's more than that, Sue. You know it is."

She felt desperately uncomfortable with her jacket off. "Look, if you must know, things have been a little strained at home. They're getting better now, though."

James couldn't control himself and raised his hand to her face.

"God, you're gorgeous, Sue! He shouldn't treat you like that. I would never let you out of my sight –"

She looked at him in shock. "James, what are you talking about? Are you crazy?" She jumped to her feet when she saw the look on his face.

"I'm fine. My marriage is fine. You on the other hand are getting way too friendly. James? Snap out of it!" She grabbed her jacket and got it back on at lightning speed.

James had gone too far to stop now, however. His mind flashed back to his conversation with Richard Dalton. He had to seize the moment and take control. He stood up and tried to take her hands again but she pulled away. "Sue, come and live with me. I'll mind you. You

325

know how I feel about you and I think if you're honest with yourself, you'd admit that you love me too."

"Love? Hello? James, what the hell are you talking about? You're my children's doctor. Correction, you *were* my children's doctor. Wait till the Eastern Health Board hears about this!"

She flew out of the room without waiting for his reply.

As she rushed out the front door of the surgery, she nearly knocked Kelly Dalton down.

"Do you have an appointment with Dr Harrington?" she asked Kelly.

"Yes, I'm a little late –"

"Don't let him lay a hand on you. Seriously, Kelly, don't let him touch you. He's a pervert!"

"Oh, OK!" Kelly smiled weakly at her totally freaked-out neighbour. Jesus, half the women in Wicklow were fantasising about Dr Harrington giving them one and there was Sue Parker calling him a pervert. That woman was really losing it!

"See you tonight," Kelly called after her neighbour but it was too late. Sue was gone.

* * *

Sue cried all the way home to Ballymore. What was wrong with her? How had she managed to get it so wrong about Guy? How could she possibly have thought that Richard Dalton was his father? Why had she kept it all from Dave? Did she not trust him? And even more upsetting, why was it that her husband didn't seem to want to spend any time with her lately?

She was obviously sending out all the wrong signals to the other men in her life, but she couldn't keep her own husband's attention. She felt hot and cold at the same time.

"Damn this thing," she snapped at the air-conditioning as she punched the digits. She tried to get it to cool down two minutes after she had just got it to heat the car up. *"You, stupid, stupid machine!"* she screamed, willing it to comfort her. As she looked at the panel of options for different levels of heat, she took her eyes off the road. It only took an instant for her beautiful Mercedes to career off the tarmac and onto the grass verge next to Ballymore Glen. The German suspension wasn't any match for the tufty grass of Ballymore and the car bounced along until Sue slammed on the brakes. No harm done and uninjured, Sue bent her head over her steering wheel and cried.

Dave didn't plan on coming home early when he phoned Sue to ask her to visit James Harrington. She reminded him of the party in Innishambles that night, however, so he was on the road to Ballymore at the same time as his wife. When he saw Sue's car in the ditch, just outside the village, his first reaction was panic. God, had she crashed? Or worse still had she tried to do herself harm? Maybe James Harrington was right about Sue's state of mind. Dave quickly parked his car behind hers and jumped out, rushing to her car door.

"Sue, my God! Are you OK? What happened?"

"Dave, I'm sorry. It's all my fault. I'm so sorry. I don't know what was wrong with me."

"Shhh, honey, you have nothing to be sorry for." Christ, he thought in a panic, was she going to tell him the truth at last? In that instant, Dave realised that he would rather not know – he just wanted life to return to the way it had been, happy and uncomplicated. He wrapped his arms around the woman he loved more than life itself and held her tightly. All other thoughts he forced out of his brain for the moment. "Are you hurt?" he asked, as her tears began to subside.

"No, no, it wasn't a crash or anything. I just took my eyes off the road for a second and the car swerved."

"Thank God. I would die if anything ever happened to you, Sue."

"Would you?"

"God, yes. You know that, don't you? Sue, you're everything to me!"

She wiped her eyes and her nose with her sleeve, something Dave had never seen her do before. She looked like a four-year-old.

"I thought you were going off me," Sue said in a little voice.

"Whyever did you think that?"

"Well, you've been spending more and more time in the office and away from me and the kids."

"It's just work. I'm sorry. I have to work to keep us in the style that we expect these days."

"Is that all it really is, Dave?"

His gut twisted in anguish and guilt as he remembered Egypt. "Yes, Sue. That's all it is. I love you more than life itself, I promise you."

Sue let out a little laugh. "I'm sorry I've been such an emotional wreck. I don't know what's wrong with me."

"Didn't James Harrington talk to you about that?"

For a brief second, Sue toyed with the notion of not telling him, but she realised that she had to be honest. A long time ago they had agreed: 'no more secrets'. Sue knew that she had to come clean and live with the consequences. "Dave, there's something I need to tell you about James."

CHAPTER 24

"Barney, is there any chance that you could help me here and stop looking into space like some lovesick lamb," Saskia pleaded, but her voice was light and she chuckled as she looked at him.

"*Why do fools fall in love?*" Barney sang, doing his best Diana Ross impersonation. He swept across the room and tried to engage Saskia in a dance.

"No way, not now. Look, I can't get the kegs open. That's a 'boy job'. Will you do that and I'll go and check on the ice?"

Barney knew he was beaten – temporarily. "God, Saskia, you're a tough boss! I'll do the kegs if you stop fretting. Everything will be fine. You've enough drink here to drown the village of Ballymore."He looked out the window. "Look, even the weather is going to stay fine. You can feed everybody outside and that way the dogs can eat anything that falls on the ground. It just gets better and better!"

Saskia looked at her future son-in-law. "You know, I don't think I've ever seen you so happy, Barney. I'm very glad for you."

"Thanks, Sas. To be honest I don't think I've ever been so happy. As you know, I don't really have any family of my own and I've always loved your family. The girls are like sisters to me – well, except Kelly of course." He laughed again. "The only woman I've really ever loved has agreed to marry me. She's carrying my baby and as if all that weren't enough, the phones didn't stop ringing all day with donations for the refuge! Things are starting to work. I know we'll get through this problem with the refuge!"

Saskia wasn't so sure. She continued tentatively, anxious not to upset him on such an evening. "It is terrific about the donations, Barney, but do you think it will be enough to sustain the refuge indefinitely?"

"I'll have to talk to the makers of K9 first. I don't know how far their generosity goes."

"What did they offer?"

"Well, as you probably know they're the biggest manufacturer of dog food in the country. They've agreed to 'sponsor the refuge'. That's all they said. I don't know if they meant the entire place or just to a certain price. I'll have to talk details with them sooner rather than later."

"Well, it does sound terrific. Just don't build your hopes up until you've seen the colour of their money."

"I hear you, Sas, but nothing could put me into a bad mood today!"

Dudley and Dexter, who were pretty frantic with all the commotion in the house anyway, started to bark wildly.

Lauren got to the front door first.

"Hello, Parker family," she greeted her neighbours.

Dave Parker walked in, holding DJ in his arms. He

331

had actually been planning on finding some excuse not to come to the party because he wasn't ready to see Richard Dalton face to face just yet but that had proved utterly impossible after he had seen the state Sue was in. Sue followed behind with Guy and India. Robin came rushing out to greet her friends.

Saskia had agreed with Sue on the phone the day before that the children would come a little earlier than the other guests. That way, they could have the kiddies' party out of the way first. Cathy and Frank Taylor arrived early too because they loved Robin like their own grandchild.

"Who's for a drink?" Barney asked expansively. Tiffany started up a game of Pass the Parcel, while Lauren got busy with the soft drinks. Robin was in seventh heaven. As she ripped open presents she sang, *"Happy birday to me, happy birday to me!"*

The doorbell rang again. Saskia was closest to it and glanced at her watch. "My gosh, it couldn't be some of Kelly's friends already, could it?"

She should have known better, however, because Dudley and Dexter were going particularly ballistic. She opened the door.

"Hi, Sas," Richard smiled at her.

"Oh, Richard and Edwina, welcome. Please come in. Dudley, Dexter, quiet," she tried to pacify the animals but they were too excited to see their old master.

Richard bent down and gave each of them a good scratch. "How you doin', guys? Are you looking after all the women in this house properly?"

Dudley growled back good-naturedly as if to say he was doing just that.

Saskia's heartbeat was racing. "They obviously miss you," she smiled.

"Not half as much as I miss you," Richard replied, but he didn't look up from the dogs.

"Daddy!" Tiffany came running out from the kitchen. "Welcome! Look at all this stuff! Do you think it will fit in your car? There's an awful lot of it –"

As Tiffany spoke, Saskia went off into her own dream world. Could Richard have said what she just thought he said? Surely not. She was hallucinating. It was the dogs barking that confused her. The place was getting very loud and chaotic now. That was it. She had misheard him. Or had she?

"Saskia, where's your drink?" Barney cut into her thoughts. "What will you have?"

She came back to reality with a thud. "I'll have a gin and tonic, please Barney – actually, make it a double!"

Having loaded Tiffany's belongings into his car, Richard joined the Taylors and the Parkers in the kitchen along with his mother, where Robin's party was in full swing.

Sue was particularly buoyant. She was drinking gin and tonics like they were soda waters and the effects were beginning to show. Unused to drink, she was quite skittish and loud. She winked at her husband across the kitchen and mouthed the words, 'I love you.' Dave Parker winked back. His heart was breaking. Sue was like a bird, a very beautiful, very fragile bird. His conscience decreed that he had to tell her about his little encounter with Penny, but he was scared that she would snap when she heard, or worse, kick him out. If he told her, she might not forgive him but if he didn't tell her, he would be breaking

333

their one golden rule – 'no secrets'. Then his mind flashed back to why they had that particular golden bloody rule. Sue once kept a big secret from him. She had once been unfaithful – well, she had had that encounter with Richard Dalton. That brought Dave back full circle. Guy had to be Richard's son. Why the fuck was *he* worried about keeping secrets? She had enough of her own. Either way he lost. It was killing him. Why had he been such a fool? As for James Harrington – Dave could feel his blood pressure rising: James would live to regret the day he ever set eyes on Sue. As if all of this wasn't enough, Richard Dalton had turned up. Why was he hanging around so much these days? Dave was at a complete loss on how to handle that situation. God forbid that Sue was involved in a cover-up! For an instant his mind went to a horrible place and he wondered if she and Richard were in it together? Surely not, surely not his beautiful queen – she couldn't be having an affair with Richard. Then again Edu, the Daltons' au pair, had been a lovely girl and she had carried on with Richard for years and nobody knew about it.

Dave was not enjoying the party at all. He very much liked the Dalton women. The girls were really lovely and Saskia had become a good friend over the years but Dave knew that there was some reason Richard Dalton was back in Ballymore. Please God, don't let it be my wife, he prayed silently.

To make matters worse, Richard, strangely enough, didn't appear to bear any grudges towards the man who had nearly destroyed him financially as he crossed the room to pump Dave's hand.

"Dave, good to see you. How are things?" he asked as if they were old friends.

"Fine thanks." Dave's tone was cool and distant. Something was definitely up. Richard smiled casually. It unnerved Dave that his old enemy was so relaxed in Innishambles. Richard definitely had some sort of agenda. Nothing was ever as it seemed with that man. Then it hit him. Richard was acting like the host. My God, Dave thought, horrified. Richard bloody Dalton is trying to weasel his way back into Saskia's life. It's Saskia, not Sue he's after.

A bunch of Kelly's friends arrived in on top of the kiddies' tea party. Francesca was at the front of the gang. She flounced in with a big bunch of flowers for Kelly.

"Hi, Barney! Congratulations!" She threw her free arm around him, clutching the bouquet in the other. "Look, I'm really sorry about Kelly's twenty-first. I didn't mean to come between you two love-birds."

Barney looked at his fiancée's best friend. "Fran, you're a great pal to Kelly. It's all water under the bridge at this stage, but please – no more joints. OK?"

"Mum's the word, Barney!" Francesca winked at him. "She's told you?"

Fran giggled and nodded. "Double congrats," she whispered and hugged him again, squashing her flowers in the process. "By the way, where is your fiancée?" She tried to un-squash her bouquet.

"Well, actually, I was just beginning to wonder the same thing," he said, looking down the long driveway of Innishambles and glancing anxiously at his watch.

Saskia was beginning to worry. "Where the heck is Kelly? Tiffany, would you mind saddling up Polly for the kids and I'll start to think about food for the adults. I can't drag it out for much longer."

Suzanne Higgins

"Mummy, look, the Condons are here," Lauren called to Saskia. Then she rushed off to find Francesca.

"Lauren, hi," Francesca smiled. "Your mum certainly knows how to put on a party. I've only been to two good parties this summer and your mum has thrown both of them!"

"Good, I'm glad you've been enjoying yourself, because now there's work to be done!" Lauren smiled wickedly as she dragged Francesca away from the punch bowl.

Seb and Max glided into the drawing-room with the ease and comfort of a pair of cheetahs walking among a flock of gazelles. Lauren walked into their path bravely. "Seb, hello again. Welcome!" She put out her hand to shake his.

He took it and kissed it. "Hello, delicious." He smiled at her from under his dark fringe. "I'm glad you're here." His voice was dripping with charm. She had other things on her mind however.

"I don't think I've met your brother yet," she smiled, taking her hand back from Sebastian and thrusting it in the other boy's direction. "How do you do?"

Max studied her from head to toe. "How do you do?" he repeated to her, only a lot more suggestively.

Seb laughed at his brother. "Max, this is Lauren, the lady who currently owns Innishambles. Lauren, this is my brother, Max."

"Max," Lauren appeared calm and indifferent to their charms, "I think you know my friend Francesca." Max looked confused for an instant and then, slowly and gradually, a devilish grin spread over his face.

"Yes, I know you, Francesca." He took her hand and

336

kissed it. "If I'm not mistaken, you showed me the charms of one of those houses in Ballymore Glen."

"Got it in one." Francesca locked his eyes into hers. "Have you had the guided tour of Innishambles yet?"

Max raised a single eyebrow from under his long blond fringe, "No, now that you mention it, I haven't."

"If you think Ballymore Glen had character, wait till I show you the hidden and numerous charms of Innishambles," Francesca purred as she took his hand. Then she quickly whispered into Lauren's ear.

"Is Tiffany ready?"

"As ready as she'll ever be," Lauren whispered back.

"Remind her for me: cool, cool, cool!"

"Cool, cool, cool," Lauren repeated as she turned away. The plan was in motion. She had to tell Tiffany.

Seb was standing next to Lauren. "What about you and me?" he asked hopefully.

"What about us?" Lauren looked at him.

"Well, unless I'm seriously mistaken, we have some unfinished business to see to ourselves."

She gave him a polite but impersonal smile. "Yes, Sebastian, you are seriously mistaken. Our business is well and truly finished. The account is closed due to lack of interest on my part. Thanks, anyway." She patted his cheek and turned on her heel. Sebastian looked at her back as she walked away. It was his first ever rejection. It didn't feel very nice actually. Hell, why didn't she want him? How odd!

To the back of Innishambles was the original cobble-stoned courtyard. Polly and Mooner's stables looked over the yard and this is where Lauren found Tiffany, surrounded by children. She lifted India Parker onto Polly's broad back.

"Why don't the rest of you kids go and play hide and seek in the walled garden until it's your turn on Polly?"

"There are lots of hiding places there," Robin agreed.

"I'll call you when India has had her turn and then the next person will get a go. OK?"

"Yeah!" they all cheered together and ran off like a pack of wolf pups.

Lauren turned to her sister. "Tiff, the wheels are in motion!"

Tiffany looked terrified. "Oh, Lauren, this will never work. He'll see right through me!"

"Stop it!" Lauren cut across her. "We've been through this a million times. Francesca says it's absolutely foolproof. It works every time but only if you play by *the rules*. Now are you going to play by the rules or not? Remember it's as easy as joining the dots. She said that you just take it one step at a time.

"Baby steps, baby steps," Tiffany repeated to herself manically. She was walking Polly around the yard in broad circles with India happily perched on top of her back. The clip-clop of the big horse's hooves were a reassuring familiar sound to her

"Why are we taking baby steps?" India asked indignantly.

"We're not," Tiffany smiled at the five-year-old. "Lauren and I were talking about something else. Something you won't have to worry about for a few years yet."

"What are you talking about?"

"Survival," Lauren laughed, trying to lighten her sister's mood. "Now, Tiffany, focus! What's the first step? What did Francesca tell you?" She wanted to go over it one more time.

"I have to play it very cool and pretend that I've never met him before," Tiffany repeated the first part of the plan.

As if on cue, Francesca and Maximilian sauntered out the back door of Innishambles.

"Just remember, one step at a time," Lauren whispered as she walked away, praying that Tiffany would survive.

Francesca boomed from halfway across the courtyard, "Oh, Max, I don't think you've met Tiffany yet, have you?"

"No." He smiled at her as they approached.

Bastard, Tiffany thought. She wanted to yell it at his face, to scream it at the top of her lungs but she looked up at India instead.

"Baby steps," India whispered, not quite understanding why she was saying it, but sure it was important. Tiffany looked at the five-year-old in shock and then grinned and winked her. She could do this.

Francesca spoke. "Tiffany, this is Maximilian Condon. He's buying Innishambles."

"Hello," Tiffany said indifferently. He took her hand to shake it, but rather predictably kissed it instead. Polly chose that moment to rear her head and so Tiffany pulled her hand back from Max so she could grab hold of the reins.

"Are you the horsy one?" Max asked amiably.

"God, no!" Francesca burst out laughing. "Tiffany is the globetrotter and the whiz kid. She's off to Trinity College next week!"

339

"So not just a pretty face," Max said, concentrating on Tiffany. She didn't trust herself to look at him and so she saw to Polly.

Francesca cut in again. "The Med won't be the same without you, Tiff. Cannes, St. Tropes, Puerto Banus –"

Puerto Banus? That's my next cue, Tiffany thought frantically. This is all happening much faster than it did in rehearsals! Francesca was staring at Tiffany for what felt like an eternity.

"Been there, done that," Tiffany said her line loudly and clearly, like an amateur actress, and then she turned on her heel and walked away with Polly and India. Ordinarily Tiffany would never turn her back on anybody mid-conversation, but this is what Francesca had insisted she do. It seemed so rude to Tiff.

"Wait, Puerto Banus? I've been there a few times," Max spoke to her back. "Maybe we've met before?"

Tiffany stopped dead. She turned and looked back at him. She made her eyes start at his feet and slowly rise to his face. Then she said her next line as per instructions from Francesca.

"I've never met you before," she drawled, sounding almost contemptuous. This time she could have won an Oscar.

Max felt the definite edge in her voice. It was like a bucket of cold water had been thrown over him. It was as if she didn't like him, but that was ridiculous – she didn't even know him. As she walked away with Polly and India, Max turned to Francesca.

"She's a bit bloody cool. What's her problem?"

"Tiffany? Oh, don't mind her. She's got very high

standards in men. Max, don't waste your time with her. Now come in –"

But Max interrupted her. "Hang on a minute. What exactly does that mean?"

"What does what mean?" Francesca pretended to be confused.

"Do you think I'm not good enough for Tiffany Dalton?"

He knows her bloody name now, Francesca thought wickedly. "No," she pretended to look uncomfortable, "it's not you, per se. It's just, well, Tiffany tends to date older guys – you know, more sophisticated."

Max looked affronted. He tried to defend himself. "I haven't had any complaints in the past!"

"She wouldn't complain. She just wouldn't be interested in you," Francesca explained. "Now, come on, I need another drink."

"Yeah, I think I could do with one myself!"

Tiffany sneaked a glance as they linked arms again and headed back into the house. She felt weak with relief. He had held her hand, had actually kissed it. She put her hand to her cheek and then kissed it.

"What are you doing now?" India asked.

"I'm damned if I know," Tiffany answered honestly.

Inside the house, Lauren yelled at Saskia from the front door. "Mum! James Harrington is here!" Then she turned to the dishy doctor. "Maybe you can tell us where the hell Kelly is."

"Hasn't she come home yet?"

"No. We thought she was going to see you and then coming straight home. What did you do with her?"

"Well, I think she'll have to explain that one to you. Patient/doctor confidentiality and all that." He smiled at Lauren. She would be real cute too in a few more years.

Lauren sent him towards the drawing-room as she went to the study to put his coat with the others.

In truth, James had other things on his mind. He wanted to clear things up with Sue. He would apologise for his actions and leave her a couple of weeks to cool down before he had another crack at her. It was quite amazing how little wives told their husbands. James had been in this situation before. It could be managed with a little smooth talking and gallant behaviour. The reality was he knew Sue fancied him and so he knew she would keep her stupid mouth shut. He was beginning to get annoyed with her hot-cold tactics – one moment she wanted to go for a drink with him or nip into a quiet spot, the next she would freeze him out – silly bitch!

Richard had heard Lauren shout that James had arrived. This could be fun, he thought to himself and it could be a great deal more fun if he was going to successfully drop Sue Parker in it. Richard planned to accidentally mention to Dave Parker that James and Sue were late-night drinking in a quiet little snug in a certain Wicklow hotel. Yes, he thought wickedly, there was definitely room to do a serious amount of damage. He could get James tanked up again and encourage him to have another shot at Sue.

Dave Parker had other plans, however. Sue had told him everything and he was bloody well going to take control of the situation. He marched straight out to the hall of Innishambles and discreetly but firmly took James by the arm.

"A word in your ear, Dr Harrington," he said, his voice cold and hard and not open to negotiation.

James had no choice as he was guided back out of the drawing-room and backed into a corner of the hall.

"Dave, hello," James tried.

"Don't even go there, Doctor," he spat out the word 'doctor'. Then he lowered his voice to the level of a whisper. "I know about the passes you've been making at my wife. She has told me everything."

"What are you talking about?"

"Act ignorant and I swear I'll have you killed."

"Dave, I assure you –"

"Shut the fuck up! Do you hear me? Just shut the fuck up! Now listen – for a change."

James became deathly pale and closed his mouth.

"Do you know the pain involved in a broken limb, Doctor?"

James nodded.

"You've mended a few in your day, I dare say."

James nodded mutely.

Dave Parker spoke again. "You used painkillers?"

The doctor nodded again, stuck to the spot.

"If you ever come anywhere near Sue again, I swear I'll have both your legs broken – slowly." Dave's face was only inches away from James's. "My friends don't carry painkillers, James. They're not very nice people, James. Don't think I'm joking, James. In the dead of night, I'll have both your legs broken. You'll rue the day you cross me."

James was terrified. He knew that Dave spoke the

truth. He just nodded but he felt a definite trickle in his trousers. Christ, he had peed in his pants!

"Do you understand me?" Dave asked menacingly.

James just nodded. He could feel the undiluted aggression that oozed out of Dave Parker's pores. He had never experienced anything like this before. His life was really being threatened. It was the worst experience he had ever had.

"Are you perfectly sure you understand?"

James nodded again.

"Fine, now get the fuck out of this house! And don't come near my wife again – ever again, *capiche*?"

James nodded yet again.

"Good." Dave Parker turned on his heel and walked back into the drawing-room and his wife.

When he saw Dave re-entering the drawing-room, Richard knew by the look on his face that something serious had gone down. He was too serene, too confident-looking. He went in search of James who was still standing frozen to the spot with his back pressed up against the wall.

"Hey, are you OK? You look like you've seen a ghost."

"If I have, it was my own," said James, daring to speak at last. "He threatened to kill me, Richard."

"Who? Dave Parker?"

"Yes, he threatened to kill me!"

"Shit!"

"Yeah, I think I'd better go. Look, he even spilled his bloody beer on me," he said, explaining away the damage to his chinos. He walked towards the study.

"Hey, don't go! We'll get you a change of clothes although I'm not sure what we'll find here. It's a house full of women! But hell, this isn't his house. Feck him!"

"No, really, Richard, I don't feel too welcome or too comfortable."

"What you and I need is another night on the tiles, James," Richard offered. They stopped and stood in the relative privacy of the study door.

"Damn sure and a million miles away from Sue Parker too. Next time we'll do it in Dublin." James managed a weak smile.

"Yeah, you can crash in my house, unless you get lucky of course!" Richard offered.

James laughed, although he was still shaking. "Wasn't too impressed with your bird last time. You'll have to do better if we're going to swap again."

Richard laughed too. "OK, but remember I'm older than you – I'll take any pussy I can get!"

They walked into the study together.

"I think Lauren left my coat in here," said James. He grabbed his jacket from an armchair.

"Jesus, I hope she's out of earshot now," Richard said, looking around him as he walked James to the front door.

But Lauren was not 'out of earshot'. She was well out of view but comfortably within earshot. She had heard every damn word of their horrible conversation. She was literally frozen with shock and horror. When she heard them coming and heard talk of Dave Parker threatening to kill James, she quickly, instinctively, hid under the desk in the study. Now, as she sat there and shivered she realised there was a good chance she was going to be ill. Her father had said the most unbelievable things. Her own father – she scrambled to her feet and ran to the toilet.

"Saskia," Barney shouted across the kitchen. The noise level had risen several octaves. "It's Nicolas Flattery on the phone. Do you want to call him back or take it in the study?"

"I'll take it in the study."

Richard was back in time to see Saskia go. So that relationship wasn't as 'over' as the girls had said it was.

"Nicolas, how good to hear from you!" Saskia was pleased that he had phoned. Obviously they were going to stay close, even if they weren't a couple any more.

"Just what the hell were you playing at?" he thundered.

"What?"

"The bloody refuge. It's all over *LA This Morning*."

"I don't know what you're talking about, Nicolas."

"*LA This Morning* is like *the* TV show that anybody who's anybody watches over here. The main feature on it this morning was that I'm in financial trouble and I'm selling up my refuge in Ireland."

"Oh."

"Oh? Shit, Saskia, you'll have to do better than that. How the hell did it get out? Why didn't you do a nice quiet sale for six million like you did on your own house? Instead, you've totally humiliated me."

"It's not a humiliation to be selling a very expensive refuge that you were subsidising, Nicolas."

"Jeez, Sas, you don't understand anything, do you? It doesn't look good. Over here you always have to look like you're on top of everything and that you're loaded."

"Well, you're not loaded," Saskia snapped.

"I'm not that bloody broke. *LA This Morning* made me out to be penniless."

"Well, if you're not penniless, Nicolas, why am I bankrolling your refuge? I put thousands into your bloody account over the last couple of weeks."

"Saskia, what you do with your money is your business."

"There's gratitude!"

"Ah, for Gawd's sake, Saskia! Get real!"

"No, you get bloody real! For your information, Kelly got a news crew to do a story on the plight of the refuge to see if she could find another sponsor. I think it was a terrific idea. She's a real doer, that girl."

"What?" Nicolas thundered down the phone. "And you sanctioned that? Christ, Saskia, what were you thinking? I know what this is about. You're pissed because I broke up with you. Isn't that why? You're trying to get back at me!"

"OK, now you're just being childish." Saskia was beginning to lose her patience. "That's simply not true."

"Yes, it is. You want to go out with a big Hollywood star and you're angry because I'm moving on."

"Nicolas, were you always this full of crap or is it a function of moving back to the thin air of LA?"

Nicolas was on a roll however. "I know what you're up to. You're trying to discredit me over here."

Saskia could feel herself getting very angry. "Do you know what, Nicolas? Sell your own bloody house. Get the hell out of my life!" She hung up in fury. Damn him anyway, she fumed as she looked at the phone.

"Kelly!"

Saskia heard Barney, Tiffany and Lauren call Kelly's name in unison. She hurried to the hall.

"Where have you been?" Barney asked as he went to hug his fiancée but she pushed him away.

"I went to The Hitching Post. I had to be alone for a while," Kelly scowled.

Just then Richard and Edwina arrived too.

"What's the matter, pet?" Saskia asked when she saw Kelly's miserable face.

"Cancel the party. The engagement's off. I'm not pregnant."

CHAPTER 25

It was one of those times when everything goes quiet at the exact same moment for no particular reason. Kelly had not shouted. In fact she barely spoke over a whisper, but everything else was quiet and everybody heard her clearly.

"What?" Tiffany and Lauren ran to their sister's side and Saskia instinctively grabbed her stomach.

"How can that be?" Tiffany asked, confused.

"Dr Harrington said it's an absolute certainty. He even did three tests on me. I didn't believe the first two."

"Where's he gone? He was here a few minutes ago." Tiffany looked around, looking for validation of Kelly's story.

"He had to go," Lauren offered coolly.

"But did you tell him that you did a home pregnancy test and it was positive?" Saskia asked.

"Yes, of course I did," Kelly snapped impatiently. "He said I must have got it wrong."

"Kelly," Barney approached her, "I think we have to talk."

"What's there to talk about?" Kelly burst out crying again.

"Tiffany, Lauren, come with me. The Condons need minding. They're in the kitchen." Saskia called her other daughters away and glanced at Edwina and Richard, signalling them to leave Barney and Kelly alone.

Gently, Barney took his girlfriend's hand and guided her into the privacy of the study. As she cried and cried he held her in his arms and let the sobs drench his new shirt.

"Jesus, I'm such an idiot, Barney. I've mucked you around yet again. I'm so sorry. I didn't mean to lie. I swear I thought I was pregnant."

"Hey, it's OK. Really, I mean it. We can have a baby another time."

Kelly looked at Barney.

"But Barney, we were breaking up. We only got back together *because* of the pregnancy. I can't hold you to a promise you made because you thought I was going to have your baby."

"Kelly, if anything it's the other way around. We broke up because I thought you wanted to live life a little. I thought you were too young to settle down. If you still want to settle down with me, God knows I want you." He looked a little panicky. "You on the other hand might want your freedom now that you've discovered that you're not going to be a mummy."

"Oh, Barney, I don't know what I want any more. I'm so bloody confused. All I do know is that I was very happy for the last week. I was excited at the idea of a baby, *our* baby, coming and I was looking forward to you and me living together. Now the refuge is going, the baby is gone." She started to cry again. "And I can't very well hold you to a proposal you made in the understanding that I was pregnant!"

Barney tightened his arms around Kelly's body.

"Kelly, I love you as much now as I did this morning, probably more, because I love you more and more each day. If you're not pregnant, so what? We'll just have to put some more work into it!"

Kelly looked at him and laughed. "Do you really mean it? Do you still want to marry me?"

"Yes, of course!"

"OK then, I'll still marry you even though I'm not pregnant!" Kelly threw her arms around her boyfriend. "I love you, Barney!" She hugged him tightly.

"Phew," he squeezed her back.

The party had an odd feeling of suspended animation. The conversation was polite but there was a definite edge to the atmosphere until Barney and Kelly came out of the study, arm in arm and smiling broadly.

"Well?" Lauren asked, although it was pretty obvious just by looking at them. "Do we have an engagement to celebrate or not?"

Kelly looked at Barney and then around the kitchen at the expectant faces.

"We do!" she smiled.

Cheering exploded and the stereo was turned up loud again. Saskia was the first at their side. With an arm around each of them she squeezed.

"I'm so happy for the two of you. Long life and happiness to you both."

Richard followed behind. As he hugged Kelly, he

slipped an envelope into Barney's hand. "You're my special girl, Kelly. Never forget that. Barney is a very lucky man to have got you and believe me there's absolutely no rush with that baby. I'm in no particular hurry to be a granddad!" They all laughed good-naturedly as the Condons came to pay their respects.

"I gather you thought you were up the pole," Arthur Condon smiled merrily, "and now you're not. How very Irish!" He laughed heartily. Only his wife sensed that he had said the wrong thing.

"Please excuse my husband – he's an old fool," Camilla apologised as she handed Barney and Kelly a small box. "Happy engagement,"she said politely and pulled her husband away.

Tiffany grabbed Lauren's arm and whispered urgently. "So where exactly do you think Max bloody Condon is now?"

Lauren's mind was still reeling, having heard her father and that bastard, James Harrington, talking. She wasn't even thinking about the Condon boys.

"I don't know where he is – not that you should care. Remember you have one job to do today and that is to ignore him. Leave the rest to Francesca." Lauren stormed off.

"What the hell has got into you?" Tiffany asked her sister's back but she didn't get an answer.

Richard walked up behind Saskia so she didn't see him coming.

"Having a good time?" he whispered into her ear from behind. It was an intimate gesture that startled her.

"Oh, I didn't know you were there."

"Sorry, did I give you a fright?"

"No, no, well, yes, actually."

"Saskia, you look exquisite tonight. I hope I'm not overstepping the mark when I tell you you look utterly beautiful."

Saskia's hand rushed to her hair. She had really meant to get it done that day but there just hadn't been time.

"Oh, Richard, it's kind of you to say that, but really I'm still trying to figure out how Kelly got it so wrong."

"It would have never happened in our day!" He winked at her.

"It bloody well did happen in our day!"

"No, what I mean is, we wouldn't have got the results mixed up – you know, thinking you were pregnant when you weren't." There was no doubt, Richard still had that old black magic. He was pure charm through and through. She felt a familiar glow when she was near him. He had an ability to make her feel like she was the centre of the universe, by focusing all his attention on her –

But then something in her mind jarred.

"What did you just say?"

"I was saying how beautiful you are!"

"No, no, after that."

"Oh, it would never have happened to us."

"And after that?"

"Jesus, Saskia, I don't know. What's wrong?"

But Saskia had remembered what he said, something about getting the results mixed up. God, was it possible? When did Kelly do her pregnancy test? She had to talk to her eldest.

"Excuse me, Richard, I have to do something."

"Wait, before you go. Do you remember we touched

on the subject of when I could meet Robin? Officially, I mean. You know I want to meet her as her father."

"Oh, yes," Saskia's mind was on the possibility of carrying another baby, not on her three-year-old baby. "Tonight is not a good time, Richard."

"Well, I'm collecting Tiffany on Monday for college. What about then? The house will be quiet."

"Fine," Saskia replied as she walked away.

She left him standing alone.

Damn her, Richard fumed silently. Saskia was proving very difficult to seduce. Then he spotted Lauren staring at him.

"Hi, honey, how are you? Having a good party?"

She looked at him with a glare of pure venom and then turned and walked away.

"Jesus, women!" Richard sighed and went off in search of another drink.

"Tiffany! There you are." Max grinned like a game-show host. "I was wondering, when were you last in Puerto Banus? I go there quite a bit you know. In fact, I once sailed a boat called the *Tiffany* into Puerto Banus."

Tiffany felt her face flush. She didn't trust herself to talk and so she busied herself loading the dishwasher.

"Oh, I can't remember," she eventually managed.

"Well, hell, was it this summer or last summer or the one before that?" he asked, sounding a little exasperated.

She stopped loading for a minute and looked at him. Remember what Francesca said: cool, cool, cool. She heaved a great big sigh. "I really don't remember – look, what's your name again?"

"Max!"

"Yeah, Max. It was about three years ago I think, maybe four. It doesn't matter really because I don't forget faces and I'm pretty sure I've never seen you before."

He laughed merrily. "Gawd, I can never remember a face!" he confessed.

With piercing clarity, Tiffany remembered his casual chats with all those beautiful people in the port and he subsequently had to confess that he didn't have a clue who any of them were. Tiffany desperately wanted to remind him but somehow she found the inner strength not to. Francesca's tutoring had not been in vain. She sighed again as if totally bored with the conversation.

"Yes, well, why don't you go and enjoy yourself. I'm a little busy here, Matt."

"Max, my name is Max."

"OK. Max, go and enjoy yourself. Whatever – Jeez."

Tiffany noticed that he actually looked crestfallen. The god that was Maximilian Condon actually looked beaten. He raised his hands in resignation and loped off to the drawing-room to find his twin and a drink. It was only then that Tiffany spotted Francesca standing in the door frame to the scullery.

Francesca began to clap.

"Go, girl! Round one to Tiffany Dalton."

"My God, were you there all the time?"

Francesca nodded. "Just in case you needed a little help but you didn't. You stood on your own two feet."

Tiff began to giggle. "It's bloody hard work."

"It'll be worth it, I promise you. Revenge is a dish best served cold and speaking of things best served cold, where's the champagne stashed? Any more punch and I'll have forgotten my own name!"

Tiffany laughed at her friend. "I think you'll find some chilled Bolly in the scullery kitchen."

Francesca grinned. "Music to my ears, Tiff, and don't worry about that old sod. We'll teach Max Condon to mess with a Dalton woman!"

Camilla Condon was getting restless. She had come to the party but really there weren't many neighbours to meet. The nice older couple from next door, the Taylors, had gone home already. They even took a very excited Robin home with them for a special treat. The Parkers had disappeared some time ago, Dave Parker being particularly protective of his slightly squiffy wife. The rest of the party revellers were too young.

"Arthur, we really must go now," she pleaded with her husband yet again. Arthur, however, didn't want to go.

"I like this fella, Richard Dalton. We're having a good chat. You go on without me."

"Are you staying locally tonight?" Richard asked, concentrating very hard in order to speak clearly. The punch was considerably stronger than he had realised.

"Yesh, we've checked into the B&B in the village. That way the boys can stay out as long as they want." Arthur chuckled and elbowed Richard.

"As long as they stay away from my girls," Richard said, attempting to pour himself another glass.

"All right, then," Camilla continued indignantly. "I'm going now. You and the boys can make your own way when you feel like it."

Arthur slapped his wife's small neat behind. "All

right, old girl! We'll follow you later. Mind how you go, now!" He waved her off as Saskia, ever the hostess, escorted her to the front door.

"Are you sure you're comfortable walking home alone, Camilla?"

"I don't have much choice," the older woman sniffed.

"What about your boys? I'm sure one of them could walk you home and return to the party later." Saskia went into the drawing-room and found the twins.

"Would one of you mind walking your mother back to the B&B? She's a little nervous alone on the country roads."

"Sure, no problem," Seb smiled. He watched Lauren as he left the room. She didn't even notice him leaving. "What the heck," he sighed as he took his mother's arm. "I think I've had enough of this party anyway."

Max followed him out, "Actually, Bro, so have I. If you want to stay, I'll walk Ma home."

"Christ, Max, this isn't like us. Is it something we ate?" The boys laughed amiably together as they glided out of Innishambles.

"These Irish women are a lot of work," Max grumbled as he took his mother's other arm.

Richard and Arthur settled down into the sofa in the kitchen together.

"So, I hear you're planning to develop the lands around Innishambles," Richard said.

Arthur laughed, good-naturedly. "Nothing is a secret for long in these parts."

"Well, it is a small village. Don't worry. I don't even live here any more. I won't tell anybody." Richard saluted. "Scout's honour!"

"But you are Saskia's ex-husband?"

"Yes, but as you can see it was an amicable divorce and the house is hers now. She can do whatever she wants with it."

Arthur looked like he was concentrating, trying to weigh up the situation.

"Well, you can't really stop me so why not?" he concluded, obviously deciding to tell Richard his plans. "I'm going to tear down Innishambles and then build a complex similar to the one in Ballymore Glen, only considerably larger – about fifty houses I should think."

Richard felt himself sober up very quickly. He did his best not to look shocked. "I thought you'd like this old house!"

"Eh, I do. She's a beautiful old house but unfortunately she's smack bang in the middle of the land so she'll have to go. Shame really but that's progress for you."

"Arthur, I hate to be the one to break this to you but Innishambles has a preservation order on it."

"Nothing to stop me lifting the roof and when the house is sufficiently damaged thanks to the gloriously wet Irish weather, I'll be able to tear her down."

Richard forced a smile. "Absolutely," he lied. "So why are you in such a rush to move in if you're really planning to pull Innishambles down?"

"I'm not in a rush to move in. I'm in a rush to get Saskia out. Do you have any idea how long it will take to destroy this house? I figure if I can get the roof off by the end of September, I'll have the winter months to do most of the damage. In the meantime I'll apply for the planning permission for the rest of the houses that I'm developing. We can start building those and, by the time they're finished, it will be time to tear down Innishambles!"

Richard winced at the idea. He would have to warn Saskia.

"Clever man, cheers!"Richard toasted his newest enemy.

"Cheers, old chum!" Arthur toasted him back.

Kelly and Barney had escaped to the sanctuary of the old playroom. So far, the party revellers hadn't discovered it.

"Here you are," said Saskia, joining them after Camilla was safely dispatched.

Kelly sighed.

"Are you all right, pet?" Saskia stroked her eldest child's hair.

"How the hell does a pregnancy test give you a wrong result? I know you both think I'm losing it but I swear it was a positive result. Even the girls will vouch for that."

"Is it possible that you could have miscarried since you did the test?" Saskia suggested.

Kelly sighed. "Dr Harrington mentioned that too. No, I haven't had anything like a period or a miscarriage. Nothing!" She threw her hands in the air.

"Did you leave the pregnancy test-stick in the sun or something that might have affected it?" Barney asked, trying to be helpful.

"What?" Kelly looked at Barney impatiently. "You think sunbathing can get you pregnant, Barney?"

"That's not what I meant and you know it. I was just wondering if the pregnancy stick could have been tampered with in some way."

"No, it wasn't even out of my sight –" Then she stopped.

"Wait a minute, it *was* out of my sight. Robin was messing with it! Hey, could she have done something to it?"

Saskia's stomach tightened. "What do you mean Robin was messing with it?"

"Well, I did the test but you and Robin came back from your walk early. I did it the day after my twenty-first party. In fact it was the day I actually turned twenty-one. Do you remember going out for a walk with Robin, Mum? But then you had to come home quickly because the weather was so bad."

Saskia's stomach tightened even further. "Go on," she urged her daughter.

"Well, I did the test and then shoved it in the bin to hide it from you." She looked at her mother sheepishly. "Sorry."

"It's OK. Go on." Saskia felt the panic rising.

"Well, then you went out for the pizzas and we rushed up to get the pregnancy-test kit back. Anyway, it was gone. Robin had seen me putting it in the bin and taken it out and you'll never guess, she put it in your bedside locker. Imagine if you came home and found that there!" Kelly laughed. "Hey, maybe one of your perfumes fell on the test stick and affected the result. Don't they use urine in some perfumes?"

"God, none of the ones I use, I hope." Saskia tried to hide her rapidly growing sense of panic.

"Well, there has to be some sort of logical explanation," Kelly said, sounding very exasperated.

"I'm sure there is," Saskia agreed, now almost certain that she had the explanation in *her* stomach.

* * *

Much later that night, Dave Parker sat alone in his study

and stewed in his own anger and self-loathing. Sue had been particularly buoyant by the time they got home. The kids were happy to fall into bed, it was so late, and Sue was more than happy to seduce Dave. He was relieved to have some temporary distraction. She was enthusiastic enough for both of them. Despite his best attempts, however, Dave was really just going through the motions. His real problem was with his emotions. How could he live with Richard's son under his roof? Why hadn't Sue told him once she discovered that their son had a blood type incompatible with both of his parents? Was it possible that she hadn't twigged? This question kept haunting him. Was there any way that Sue could be an innocent in all of this? Too many questions and not enough answers. Then as if by some masochistic tendency, Dave was inevitably drawn back to his own actions. How could he even think about condemning his beautiful wife for her *possible* wrongdoings when he knew full well what was a certainty: he had been in bed with his secretary less than a week ago? What kind of morally depraved animal was he? Could he not keep faithful to his own wife – the woman he loved above all else? What kind of pathetic piece of shit did that make him? Dave hated himself. He wanted to hate Sue but he couldn't. He didn't have any – or, at least, enough proof. Maybe he was just going mad or hitting a mid-life crisis – yes, that was it, he was going through his mid-life crisis. In a panic, the reality of his situation hit him. He couldn't tell his wife and he couldn't not tell her. To tell her might finish his marriage and not to tell her would mean his marriage was a sham. One thing was certain; he couldn't go on like this. It was going to drive him mad.

361

CHAPTER 26

Saskia awoke feeling absolutely miserable. It took a few moments for her to remember why. That was it, she was pregnant. She had to be. Reluctantly, she hauled herself out of bed and into her en suite, where she rooted around for the spare pregnancy-test stick. Wilma, who was still exhausted from all the excitement of the party the night before, was keeping her company. The little dog sat comfortably on Sas's bed and watched her mistress get more and more agitated.

"Where did I leave that second bloody pregnancy tester, Wilma?" she asked her little dog as she rummaged. "Little did I know when I accidentally bought a twin packet that I would need both test sticks! Ah, hell, I must have thrown it out. God knows, I never thought I would need it!"

"Mum, who are you talking to?" Tiffany appeared at her door.

Saskia jumped guiltily. "Oh, good morning, darling. I was talking to Wilma actually. Nothing strange in that. How are you this morning? How is the house?"

"It's OK – the house is more or less back to normal." Tiffany smiled at her mother and then jumped onto Saskia's bed like a child. Wilma snapped at her competition. "Oh, sorry, Wilma, I didn't see you there!"

Tiffany scooped up the little dog and was rewarded with a lick for her apology.

"You seem very chirpy," Saskia commented.

"Oh, Mum, I've never been better. I think I've just met the man I'm going to marry!"

"*What*? Tiffany, you're only eighteen!"

"I know. That doesn't matter. Look at Kelly and Barney. She started to go out with him when she was eighteen!"

Saskia instinctively backed off. "You have a point there. So who is this Mr Wonderful?"

"His name is Maximilian Condon. His parents are buying this house. To be honest, I met him a few years ago. You'll never guess where! In Puerto Banus. Anyway, he doesn't remember meeting me there so I'm pretending that I don't remember him either. In fact, I'm desperately busy pretending that he bores me at the moment!"

"Whyever are you doing that?"

"To get his attention, of course," Tiffany explained patiently. Her eyes were huge and bright with excitement. She couldn't contain her grin. Saskia saw quite clearly that her daughter was under the bewitching spell of love. "Oh, that old chestnut – treat 'em mean and keep 'em keen."

"That's the one," Tiffany laughed. "Do you think it will work? Will I get him up the aisle?"

"Slow down there, Juliet. Don't forget that you're heading up to college on Monday. You don't want to lose

363

your head over this Romeo totally. Hey, how old is he?"

Tiffany looked a little sheepish. "Well, actually, he's a little younger than me. He's only just turned seventeen so he'll be doing his Leaving Cert this year."

"Where are those boys going to school?"

Tiffany thought about this for a moment. "You know, I don't know. To be honest we didn't talk much just yet. I was too busy pretending to be uninterested! It was Lauren who told me he was seventeen."

"Gosh, it's a difficult time to change countries, isn't it? As for their schooling, they won't be familiar with the Irish Leaving Cert syllabus."

"You're right, Mum. I know! I can help him." Tiffany giggled.

"That would be a very nice thing to do. Just don't let him interfere with your studies, OK?"

"OK."

"What were you saying about the house? Have you been tidying again, Tiffany?"

"I couldn't sleep."

"How much have you done?"

"Everything."

"The entire house? All by yourself?"

"Yep! It wasn't too bad. We did a lot of it last night."

"Tiffany, you're a treasure. Where are your sisters?"

"Robin, as you know, is still over in Cathy's, Lauren is only getting up now and Kelly is in Barney's house – surprise, surprise."

"Where would I be without you, Tiffany?"

"Up to your neck in beer-bottles and punch-glasses! Come on downstairs. I'll put the kettle on."

As Tiffany danced out of the room, it only served to

remind Saskia of how old she herself was. Her second daughter talking about marriage and here she was looking for a pregnancy tester. This was ridiculous. She was well past her motherhood years and rapidly heading towards her grandmotherhood years! Feeling utterly miserable, she wrapped her dressing-gown around her body and dragged herself down the stairs after her daughter. Unconsciously her mind wandered back to Richard. There was another reason to be miserable. He had got drunk with Arthur Condon. Edwina had eventually dragged him home to Dublin. He hadn't even said goodbye to her.

In the kitchen, Tiffany continued to prattle on merrily, "Dad was in great form, wasn't he?"

Lauren scowled at the mere mention of his name.

Saskia was only half-listening. Her mind was on the missing pregnancy-test kit. "Yes, Dad and Edwina," she answered absently.

"Hey," Tiffany giggled, "what do you think about Kelly? No baby!"

"No baby," Saskia whispered to herself as she inadvertently touched her stomach. Then she looked at her girls.

"I have to go out," she announced, suddenly all business. "Will you collect Robin from Cathy's house?"

"What's suddenly got into you, Mum?" Lauren asked. "You're acting very strangely."

Saskia didn't have time to invent explanations. "Look, I just have to go out, to do something. Will you please collect Robin?"

"Yes, of course," Tiffany answered her mother. "Where are you going?"

But Saskia was running back up the stairs to change. She realised that she had to find out once and for all whether or not she was pregnant. She didn't want to explain to her girls that she would have to go into Wicklow to a chemist to get another bloody pregnancy-test kit. She didn't want to have to explain that she thought she was pregnant at her age. She didn't want any of these hassles. She just wanted a peaceful and quiet life, the way things used to be years ago, when Richard – no. She wouldn't let herself think about those times.

Driving into Wicklow, Saskia's mind raced. Kelly was getting married to a man who was just about to lose his job. Tiffany was falling in love with a boy younger than her and it was definitely going to affect her studies in a bad way. Lauren and Robin? Thank God, they seemed to be on an even keel at the moment. No such luck for her own life however. Bad enough that she was having startling daydreams about her ex-husband, it now looked like she might be pregnant by a man who was no longer in her life. And as if all of that wasn't enough, she had chosen now to sell her house and she was due to move this day next week. Saskia thought that she might cry. She shut her eyes tightly to stop the tears and nearly crashed the car.

"Drive carefully," she admonished herself. "For your sake and the bab–" No, she wouldn't say it in case she tempted fate.

Safely in Wicklow town, Saskia rushed into the chemist and bought the first packet she saw. Then she ran into the hotel next door and into the ladies'.

She ripped the box open in the little toilet cubicle and peed on the single stick. As she waited for the result she passed the time by shoving the box and the plastic wrapper into the sanitary disposal box next to her. Saskia looked at the stick. Still no result. Then she realised to her dismay that she had thrown out the instructions. They were absolutely irretrievable in the bin. "Typical," she muttered to herself as she sat on the loo. She didn't panic however because, in truth, she knew how the damn test stick worked. A line in one of the windows meant she wasn't pregnant. A line in both meant she was. Simple as that. There was no way she would be able to sit still for three minutes, however, so she decided to get out of the loo. She retrieved her coat from the floor where she had thrown it. As she was about to shove the stick in her bag, she glanced at the windows again. They both had a pink line. "Jesus," she squealed as she flopped back onto the toilet seat. "That wasn't three minutes!"

She stared, unblinking, at it. The lines were faint but there were definitely two of them. As she watched them, the lines became clearer and more distinct. There was absolutely no doubt this result was positive. Saskia, at the age of forty-two, was pregnant again.

* * *

Jayne Mullins was in a wonderful mood. When she woke on Saturday morning she stretched luxuriantly in bed and stroked her stomach. Wouldn't it be the most amazing thing if she managed to get pregnant by Raymond, she thought wickedly. Jasmine, Edward and Francis were a hell of a handful at times but it would mean that she and Raymond were joined together for ever if she did get pregnant by him. Last night had been so unexpected.

Jayne had been pinning her hopes on their next date. It

never occurred to her that it could have happened as easily
as it did. The kids were in good form because it was only
a week to the house move and they were very excited about
trying out their new pool. Raymond had shown them
where Ballymore was on the map. He had also informed
them that they wouldn't have to return to their old schools.
They would be going to new schools in Wicklow but
because it hadn't been sorted out completely yet, they were
going to have an extra week's holidays. That meant more
to the children than the actual house move. As the children
were packed off to bed, Jayne had suggested a glass of
wine to unwind with. Raymond however, pulled out a
bottle of Moet, which he had in his fridge in the study.

"It's a special occasion," he smiled.

"Why?" Jayne asked.

"We are into our last week in this house. This day next
week, we move!"

"Well, that's true, Raymond," Jayne laughed, "but
usually people have the bubbles *after* the move, not before."

"We can have more then," Raymond smiled.

"Hey, I'm not going to stop you!" she laughed as she
got two champagne glasses and settled down on the same
sofa as him. They weren't sitting right beside each other,
but they were close.

As he refilled their glasses, Raymond started to speak
hesitantly.

"Jayne, I can't thank you enough for all the help
you've been to me over these last few years."

"Hey, Raymond, it's OK. Don't get all sentimental
now. It's my job. Remember?"

"Well, that's just it. I was wondering if perhaps it had
become more than a job?" He looked at her shyly.

"What are you saying?"

"Well, I could be wrong, but I get the feeling that you and I have been getting a little closer than the man of the house and a nanny should be lately."

"Raymond, I have never done anything to –" She began to defend herself.

"No, it's not a bad thing," Raymond interrupted her. He poured them each another glass and gulped most of his own down in one go. "I don't know how to say what I'm trying to say, Jayne. You're so young and beautiful and I'm so old, for God's sake."

Jayne stroked his cheek gently. "No, you're not. You're not old. You're a gorgeous man, Raymond."

"Do you think so?" he asked shyly.

"I think you're the most wonderful man I've ever known, Raymond." Pumped with courage from the champagne, Jayne decided that it was make or break time. Raymond really didn't have a clue. She stretched over the gap between them and kissed him on the lips.

When she stopped Raymond just looked at her helplessly. His eyes scanned her face, looking for something. It was obvious to Jayne that she was going to have to take the initiative. Gently she took his champagne flute from him and placed it on the floor next to hers. Then she stood up and, taking him by the hand, pulled him onto his feet. Next she reached up and kissed him again. This time he responded. He wrapped his arms around her thin body and hugged her as he kissed her deeply.

Jayne only broke away for long enough to take him to her bedroom. He followed her like an obedient child. Safely in her room, she locked the door and returned to his arms. This time his kisses were stronger and more demanding. She knew that he wanted her. He was aroused and God knows she was. She had wanted Raymond so much for so long, she thought, she might come just at the thought of him. It wouldn't be the first time.

He fumbled with her clothes, trying to pull up her shirt. Jayne decided that he was definitely a little out of practice. She pulled off her blouse and unclipped her bra in two quick actions. Raymond looked at her and laughed. "God, you're good at that!"

"What about you?" she asked as she decided to continue pulling off her clothes. She dropped her jeans and pants and pulled them off with her socks all together.

"Christ, I'm not as fast as you anyway," he chuckled as he sat on the side of the bed and began to peel off. It was only as he did this that Jayne realised he was in fact considerably older in manner than the young guys she had slept with. He undressed like an old man! Slowly he balanced an ankle on his knee and pulled off a sock. Then the other foot. At this rate it would be morning before she got him inside her. Jesus, at least now she knew why Edward, Raymond's eight-year-old, was so slow getting dressed in the mornings.

Jayne began to help him get undressed. The same way she helped Edward sometimes. When they were both naked, she jumped on top of him. Hungrily she kissed him. She was so wet! She couldn't believe that at last she was with Raymond.

Gently, he stroked her body. It was soft and smooth and willing. Unable to contain herself any longer, Jayne began to mount Raymond's deliciously large penis. That was something she hadn't known about him.

"Now I see why they say you're the 'biggest man in the beef business!'" Jayne laughed as she feasted her eyes upon his manhood and guided it into her. She arched her spine in the ecstasy of the moment and threw her head back.

Raymond lay back on the bed and watched her.

He felt almost like a third party. The evening had taken a surprising turn. This was all like a dream, however. He thought he could wake up any minute and realise he was alone in his own bed. Jayne's body began to move up and down on his. He could see and feel her getting more aroused.

"Jesus, this is glorious, Raymond," she purred. It didn't even sound like her voice. "Oh, fuck – you're gorgeous," she murmured as she moved harder against him. It still didn't sound like her. She began to dig her nails into his shoulders. "What about you? Are you going to come with me?"

Raymond had a massive hard-on, but he didn't feel like coming.

Her body went taut as she whimpered and clung onto his shoulders, squeezing his body with her thighs.

"Oh yes! Raymond!" she cried and then Raymond realised why she sounded so odd. It wasn't Caroline. It would never be Caroline again.

He wrapped his arms around Jayne's slim shoulders and gently began to cry.

After a few minutes, Jayne stirred. She went to kiss him on the cheek as she dismounted his body, but she tasted the salt.

"What's wrong?"

He smiled through his tears. "Usually it's the girl who's meant to cry isn't it?"

"Why are you sad?" Jayne asked.

"You're the first lady I've been with since Caro."

"Oh, Raymond," she kissed him and wiped his tears. "I know you loved Caroline, but you have to live life again. She would want it this way."

Raymond looked at Jayne. "Yes, perhaps you're right."

Within minutes Jayne was snoring softly. Raymond waited until her breathing was slow and steady. Then he slipped out of her bed and gathered his clothes in the dark. He was terrified that the children might hear him. Ever so slowly, he quietly unlocked the bedroom door. He hadn't realised that she had locked it. Perhaps she was right – what if one of the children walked in? Then again, he realised sadly, it was the first time since his children had been born that he had locked them out of his life. It was certainly something Caroline would never have dreamt of doing. Feeling even more miserable, he tiptoed back towards his bedroom, clutching his belongings. He felt appallingly guilty as he sneaked along his own landing. How could something that felt so wrong be right? To his immense relief, he was not discovered creeping naked through his own house.

Later, as he lay in his own bed, safely wrapped up in his paisley pyjamas, he thought about the situation. Being in bed with Jayne was about as much fun as having a tooth pulled. She was way too 'wham, purr, thank you, sir,' for him. He realised he didn't really fancy her.

The thing about Caroline was that Raymond had fancied her like crazy. His late wife wasn't the most beautiful woman in the world but she was full of fun and mischief. Her eyes danced and she was always smiling. These were the things that Raymond found irresistible. When

Raymond and Caroline had sex together, they had pillow-fights, they had Jacuzzis together. Jasmine, his daughter, had been conceived in a lift in Mauritius.

He just wasn't in love with Jayne. But it was now also abundantly clear that she liked him – a lot.

After his conversation with his daughter, he had given the matter considerable thought. Perhaps he should just *make* himself like her for the sake of the kids. They had had sex now – surely that had consummated their relationship. After a brief courtship, he would propose and they could get married and the children would have a mother whom they already loved. He knew that his kids loved Jayne and she loved them. Everybody would be happy. It was the obvious solution. It had to be.

CHAPTER 27

Dave Parker liked to be in the office by six o'clock on Monday morning, so when Sue returned from bringing India to school, she was slightly surprised to find him working in his study at home. Their eldest child had been particularly difficult because she was utterly fed up that the school year had begun again.

"Everybody has to go to school," Sue had explained as she dressed the highly uncooperative six-year-old.

"You and Daddy don't go," the young girl scowled.

"No," Sue tried to remain patient, "but we did when we were your age."

"Well, it's just not fair!" India would not be appeased. She refused her breakfast as a mark of protest and clung to her mother's leg when they got to her new classroom. As a result, Sue was fairly jaded and fed up by the time she returned home from the school run. She yawned and wondered could she sneak up to her room for a short lie-down without DJ or Guy discovering she was back in the house. They were happily engrossed in a painting party with Lisa.

Dave, however, heard the front door open and came out to greet his wife.

"Sue, hi. How are you?"

"Oh, I assumed you were gone to the office. I didn't even notice your car."

"It's around the side of the house. Is yours running OK?"

"Yes," she replied a little sheepishly. "Its little cross-country exercise last Friday doesn't seem to have done it the slightest bit of harm. Sorry about that."

Dave looked at his wife and smiled weakly. "Sue, I wonder could you come into the study? There's something I need to discuss with you."

"Sure." Sue walked in and took a seat, comfortable in the knowledge that nothing serious was wrong. He had given her all the reassurance that she needed on Friday at the side of the road and they had made the most wonderful love later that night, after Kelly's party. At least she *thought* it was wonderful. She didn't remember that much about it!

"What is it, Dave?"

He fell into the seat next to her. "Sue, firstly I have to make sure that you know how much I love you. You do know that I love you more than anything else on this earth or beyond. You do know that, don't you?"

Sue laughed and took his hands in hers. "Yes, darling, I know that. Is that what you wanted to tell me?"

He looked at the ground. "No, there's more."

She tried to see his face to understand his tone. It was difficult to read.

"What's up, Dave?"

"Do you remember our one solemn promise?"

"No secrets." Sue repeated their private mantra, feeling a slight churning sensation in the pit of her stomach.

"Sue, there's something I have to tell you and it's going to hurt. I'm only telling you because I love you so much and we have no secrets."

The churning moved up a gear. "Now you're making me nervous, Dave. What are you trying to say?"

"Do you remember last weekend when Guy had his crash and you couldn't contact me?"

"Of course."

"Well, do you remember that you were fairly steamed up with me for being so uncontactable?"

"Dave, you have to understand –"

"Hush, no, you had every right to be fed up. It's just that, well, I'm afraid I got very drunk after it and I ended up getting . . ."

"What are you trying to say, Dave?"

"Well, I'm afraid I got a little too close to Penny."

"How close?"

"We were both pissed, Sue."

"How close, Dave?"

"I ended up in her hotel room – but we didn't have sex!"

Sue shot to her feet. "Well, I'm bloody glad to hear it!" She crossed the room to the window. "Did you kiss?" she asked, her voice disturbingly level and cold.

"Yes."

"Did it go much further?"

"A little, but then I sobered up." Dave's voice was shaking. "I thought I was with you, but then I realised it was her. We were drunk!"

"And that's meant to excuse it," she spat.

"Jesus, Sue, I'm so sorry. I swear we stopped before I went too far. Penny knows I love you. She didn't know what she was doing either," he exaggerated slightly.

"What were you wearing during this 'encounter'?" she asked. Her voice still deadly calm.

"What?"

"You heard me. What exactly were you wearing?"

"Nothing."

"And Penny?"

"Nothing," Dave answered honestly. "But we didn't have sex – I swear to you. It stopped there."

"I think I would like to be alone for a while," Sue said.

"What do you mean?"

"Get out."

"Of the room?"

She swung around. *"Of the bloody house!"* she screamed at him. "Last Friday night you did God knows what with your secretary. Get out of my sight!"

"We didn't have sex!" Dave rushed over to where she was standing. He tried to take her in his arms but she pushed him away.

"Will you stop saying that!" she screamed at him.

"Sue, it would have been a lot easier *not* to tell you. I had to tell you because we always said we would be honest with each other. I love you more than life itself. I'm so sorry that this happened. It will never happen again, I swear."

"Damn sure it won't," Sue thundered. "Now, get out."

He had had no idea how this conversation was going to go but he knew that he couldn't *not* tell her. He just couldn't. It was eating him up. As he looked at her now, at her blind rage and wild fury, he began to get cross.

"How can you just stand there and be so judgemental?" he stammered.

"I beg your pardon?" She snapped her head around to look at him.

"You – you heard me. How can you stand there and rage at me when we both know the truth about Guy and you still haven't confronted me about it?"

"What exactly are you talking about, Dave?" Her voice had reached a new level of calm. One he had never heard before.

He had not planned on bringing up the Guy-blood thing – it had just come out. Now in seriously uncharted waters, however, he regretted it. Unable to meet her eyes, he studied the floor. "You told me you were A positive, I told you I was A positive. James Harrington told me that Guy was O negative and that meant one of us or at least one of 'his parents' had to be O negative." As he spoke, his conviction grew. "Who is O negative, Sue? Do you know anybody who is O negative? Is Richard Dalton O neg, Sue?" There, he had said it. He had voiced his biggest fear. The room suddenly went very cold and what was the briefest of seconds felt like hours dragging by.

"Is that what you thought, Dave?" Sue spoke barely above a whisper. "Did you think Richard Dalton is Guy's father?" There was no venom and no fury in her voice now – just a great distance. She laughed but there was only misery in her tone. "And you talk about trust," she scoffed.

Dave looked at her and realised in that second that he had made a huge mistake – probably the biggest mistake of his life. He turned and left the room and the house.

* * *

It was nine a.m. when Richard's car pulled up outside Innishambles.

"Daddy," Tiffany ran out and threw her arms around him. "You remembered!"

"Of course I remembered. My God, I know I was fairly well oiled but how could I forget something as important as this?" He smiled down indulgently at his daughter.

Saskia stood at the door of Innishambles as the dogs swept past her feet, out to greet their old master.

Richard slapped Dudley and Dexter on the ribcages, "Hello, boys, how are you?"

"Welcome," Saskia smiled at her ex-husband. "Do you have time for a cup of coffee? Or are you eager to get back on the road?"

Richard looked at Saskia. She looked tired. "I'd love a coffee if it's OK with you."

She nodded and walked back into the house. She was angry with herself for being so ridiculously happy that her bloody ex-husband could afford her the time for a simple cup of coffee,

"I'm really sorry I got so pissed the other night," he said as quickly as he could, once in the familiar kitchen.

"Oh, isn't that what parties are for?" Saskia replied lightly, anxious to hide her disappointment.

"No, it isn't. I didn't even get to say goodbye. Sorry," he said again.

"It's OK. Really." Saskia smiled at him.

"Have you ever noticed, I always seem to be apologising to you these days?" He laughed nervously.

"Guilt complex," Saskia said before she realised what she was saying. "Oh, God, I didn't mean –" she began to get flustered.

"Hey, relax," he laughed. "You're probably right." Another nervous laugh. "Actually, Sas – em, there's something I need to discuss with you."

Here it comes, she thought. He's found another woman. She could feel the panic rising. "What is it?"

"You were a little distracted the other night but do you remember that we talked about introducing me to Robin – properly, I mean."

Saskia had completely forgotten. There was so much going on in her life. Robin walked into the kitchen.

"Am I going to school yet?"

"In about half an hour," Saskia told her impatient little girl. Then she turned to Richard. "Robin starts Montessori today. Don't you, pet?

"Wow, you're a big girl now!" He tried to sound impressed. He wasn't really good with small children. He was much better when they were a little older and more easily charmed.

The child looked at Richard. She didn't know exactly who he was but he had been around the house a few times recently.

"Is Tiffany going to Dublin now?" she asked.

Saskia turned to her three-year-old and crouched down to her level.

"Yes, she is, darling. Do you know who she's going to live with?"

"Daddy," Robin answered easily.

Richard and Saskia looked at each other in shock.

"Yes, that's right." Saskia wrapped her arms around Robin. "How did you know that?"

"Tiffany said so," Robin replied. The child looked at Richard. "Are you Daddy?" Saskia was reminded yet again how much a three-year-old can take in just by being in the same room as adults when they're talking. She vowed to keep adults' conversations out of her baby's earshot in the future.

Richard got down on his hunkers too. "Yes, Robin, I'm your daddy. I'm Tiffany's daddy too."

Robin looked very suspicious. She glanced at her mother for reassurance. Saskia nodded gently and smiled at the child.

"You're my daddy too?" she asked incredulously. "I didn't know I had a daddy." She laughed as if 'a daddy' was a fashion accessory.

"Well, you do, and I'm him!" Richard said good-naturedly, delighted at how smoothly this was going.

"Do you want to give him a little hug?" Saskia asked hopefully. "Now that you know he's your daddy?"

Robin thought about this for a moment and then she shook her head, breaking out of her mother's embrace.

"No, thanks!" She ran to the door of the kitchen, off to find Tiffany again. "I prefer Nicolas," she said and was gone.

The mood changed utterly. Both adults stood up coolly.

"Well, it couldn't have gone totally smoothly," Saskia tried to explain.

"No, no. I think, all things considered, that went quite well. It will take time."

"Yes," Saskia agreed without conviction. She knew that in reality Nicolas was the male figure in Robin's life. Well, he had been to date. Now that relationship was over. God, what a mess, she thought manically.

"How do you think she knew I was Daddy," Richard asked perplexed.

"You know kids – they pick up on a lot more than we realise. I guess she's been listening to conversations around the house over the last few days and she heard that Tiffany was going to be living with you."

She busied herself making the long-promised coffee.

"There's something else I have to tell you about, Saskia." Richard's tone was serious. "It's about Innishambles."

"What about it?"

"The Condons plan to tear it down."

"They can't – it's a listed building."

"I know. I told Arthur Condon that. He's going to take the roof off and let the building fall into ruin. Then, when it's in bits, he'll be able to tear it down."

Saskia paled in shock. "Oh, no! This is all my fault!"

"Have you signed the contracts yet?"

"Yes. He signed them first and then I signed them. It's a done deal. We're moving out this Saturday."

"What's it Mum always says about Saturday moves?"

"Saturday's flitting makes for short sitting," Saskia replied automatically. She remembered the first time Edwina had said that to her. It was after her return from hospital when Robin was a tiny baby. That was just before Saskia's life turned totally upside down – just around the time that she had discovered that Richard had had an affair with their au pair – and all the rest! Saskia shivered at the memory. How could she possibly still have feelings for this man?

Richard brought her back to reality. "Then there's nothing to be done. We can't stop him."

Saskia began to cry. "I've messed everything up. Poor old Innishambles!"

This time Richard did put his arms around Saskia. She let him hug her as she cried gently.

"It's all right. Something will happen. It will be OK. You'll see."

"You're being very understanding considering I'm selling off your old home," Saskia sniffed.

"You were only doing what you thought was right for you and the girls. I'm hardly in a position to judge!" He laughed, making her laugh too.

"We're a right pair," Saskia laughed.

"I wish we were," Richard replied.

"What?"

"A pair," he said.

Saskia's body tensed instantly and so Richard let her go.

"Now, where's that coffee you promised me?" he asked as he walked to the window. "Wow, I'd forgotten how spectacular the view is from here. Hey, is it OK if I go out to say hello to Polly and Mooner?"

"Of course," Saskia said. Her back was to Richard. She didn't dare look him in the eye.

As he walked out the back door to greet the horses, Saskia's mind raced. Now she knew that it definitely wasn't her imagination. He had said that he wished they were "a pair". After all she had done to him. Damn it, she had destroyed him financially. She had ruined his business reputation in a most public fashion. It would have utterly destroyed a weaker man and yet he still wanted to get back with her. How strange life was! If only it was Richard's baby she was carrying and not Nicolas's. That's it, she thought. I'm going to ring Nicolas tonight. I have to.

* * *

The atmosphere in Rathdeen Refuge was dreadful. It was almost as if the animals knew that it was to close. Barney had spayed a beautiful bitch first thing and now he wondered if he was even going to be able to find her a new home at all. Perhaps the kindest thing would have been to put her to sleep. He was utterly miserable. Kelly was no better. She was working twice as hard as she had done in the previous weeks because she felt dreadfully guilty about having slacked off over the last month in the belief that she was pregnant.

She scrubbed herself clean and joined Barney in the post-op room.

"Jesus, have you finished mucking out the stables already?" he asked, surprised to see her.

"Yep, now that I'm not being fragile with myself, I can move twice as fast."

Barney turned to his girlfriend and embraced her. "You were very weak for some reason. When do you get the blood-test results back from Dr Harrington? OK, you weren't pregnant but you were very weak for the last few weeks."

"I'll ring him this afternoon and find out. His suggestion was that I was just low in iron. Hardly reason enough to take to my bed the way I did!".

"Don't be so hard on yourself. I'm sorry that you're not pregnant but maybe it's for the best now that the refuge is to close."

Kelly looked nervous. "But, Barney, we haven't been using protection for ages. Once we thought I was pregnant, we stopped using condoms. Why didn't I get pregnant after that?"

Barney kissed her softly. "Yeah, that did occur to me

too. Listen, Kelly, it sometimes takes ages to get pregnant. I'm sure we'll have no problems, trust me. Look how fertile your mother is, for God's sake! She had produced four beautiful fillies!"

"That's not me though, is it?"

"Actually, it is. When it comes to babies and baby-making, just like horses, you look at the mother's mother."

Kelly knew from his tone that he was half-joking and half in earnest. She gently elbowed him in the ribcage.

"Please don't worry about making a baby. When the time is right, we'll have one. Just you wait and see," he reassured her.

"Hey, have you called K9 yet?" Kelly asked, cheering up somewhat.

"No, I don't know what to say to them."

"Why don't I handle them?" Kelly asked, her eyes sparkling at the challenge.

"That's a great idea, Miss Businesswoman-of-the-Year. I've got to check on Daisy's baby!"

Daisy was the refuge's resident donkey who was in the family way.

"Is that a hand-up-the-bum job?" Kelly teased.

"I'm afraid so," Barney winced.

She burst out laughing at his discomfort. "Who would want to be a vet?"

The little brown and white dog lying on the post-op table next to them began to moan.

"Another spay job?" Kelly asked, gently stroking the dog.

"Yep, only I really don't know what we're going to do with her. She has such a lovely temperament. She deserves a good home."

Kelly bent over and kissed the little dog as she began to come out of her sedation. "Barney, I think we should call this one Hope."

"OK," he agreed. "Just don't get too attached to her. She can't stay!"

"I hear you," Kelly nodded. Then she addressed the dog again. "Now I'm going to have a chat with K9 dog foods and we'll find you the finest home in Ireland!" Her voice was firm with resolve. "I know I can milk them for a couple of hundred grand!"

* * *

By the time Dave got to his office in Dublin, he secretly hoped that Sue would have called. In reality, however, he knew that there was very little chance that she would have. He had never seen her look so hurt or so distant from him. How was he going to undo the damage he had done this time? Which bloody damage did he start with? There was no way he was going to be able to work but his Dublin office was like a refuge to him. At least he would be able to think there.

"Hi, Dave!" Penny was at her desk.

"Oh, hi Penny. Any calls?"

She rose and followed him into his office. "Here's the list. To be honest, there's nothing major there." She paused for an instant and hovered over his desk as he sat down. "Dave, can we talk?"

"Yeah, sure. Are you OK?"

"Well, no, actually, I'm not."

Dave felt panic rising for the second time that morning. This was all he bloody well needed.

"Penny, talk to me. Is it about eh –"

She looked at him and smiled. As he looked at her now, it seemed to him that she had aged somehow in the last week. She looked a lot more womanly than she used to – certainly not nineteen!

"Dave, I'm afraid I have to hand in my notice."

"What?"

"Look, Egypt was a little crazy but it has definitely changed the relationship between us. You're a nice guy, but I think I need a fresh start, somewhere else."

He looked at her again. "You look different, Penny. What is it?"

She studied her boss for a moment. "I've grown up – copped on. Call it what you will. I've learnt a lot in the last week, Dave, and I have to say that I don't think I really respect you as much as I used to. To be honest I had you up on a pedestal as this terrific boss and wonderful father and husband, but you're not, are you? You're just like all the rest – a poor old sod, trying to make a crust."

Dave stared at her in shock. "Now, just hang on there one minute, Penny –"

"No, Dave. I won't. I've just decided actually. I'm leaving right now."

"You can't just walk out on me like that. Can you at least finish out the month so I have the chance of getting somebody new?"

"Your problem, Dave. Not mine."

Dave had a brainwave. "What about Sean?"

"I've decided to leave him too. I'm moving to London. God knows I've enough saved. Poor little innocent Penny! I've been saving for my wedding for the last three years.

Well, I'm going to move to London, buy myself an entirely new wardrobe and set myself up in a gorgeous little flat in Chelsea or Knightsbridge."

Dave couldn't believe that this was his PA – good old uncomplicated, highly predictable Penny – talking. She had always been clever and efficient, but woman of the world – not.

"Don't worry about my reference, Dave. I've written it for you. It's wonderful. Needless to say if anyone does phone to check up on it, you will speak of me in glowing terms."

The hidden threat in her voice was not lost on him. The only way she was going to stay quiet about their Egyptian experience was if he did as she asked. He might have told his wife about it but he certainly didn't want it getting out in his business circles. He knew he was beaten.

"Bon voyage, Penny."

"Goodbye, Dave."

"Good luck," he added, realising he meant it.

"Thank you," she walked to the door but stopped before she walked out. "Dave, have you told Sue about us?"

"Yes."

"I'm not sure that that was a good idea."

"You may be right there. It might cost me my marriage yet."

"I don't think so."

"Why not?"

"She phoned half an hour ago. She's on her way."

CHAPTER 28

Tiffany was as giddy as a schoolgirl by the time she arrived at Edwina's house in Dublin.

"Gran, hi, I'm here," she laughed lightly.

"Really, girl, when are you going to stop stating the obvious?" Edwina asked her granddaughter.

"And enough luggage for a lifetime," Richard grumbled as he passed through the hall with the first two large cases. "I thought I brought all your belongings up last Friday."

"What do you have so much luggage for?" Edwina asked.

"Now, Mum! Do you remember our little conversation?" Richard glared at his mother. She visibly cowered. Richard had told her to put up and shut up. She was to be extremely nice to Tiffany and no complaints of any sort. Edwina was now well and truly scared of her son. He had never hit her but what he was able to do with words! He had an ability to cut her down in a single comment. Edwina knew that her son was a bully but he was all she had.

389

Tiffany, however, saw her grandmother shrink away from Richard.

"What has Daddy been saying to you, Gran? You're not to take any flack from him now, do you hear me?"

Despite herself, Edwina smiled at Tiffany, grateful for an ally. "Come into the kitchen and have some tea. Leave that heavy work to your father. I want to hear all about your college plans."

"Oh, you've organised a full meal for us, Gran!" Tiffany gushed as they entered the kitchen.

"Well, I'll try to keep you fed," Edwina chortled. Tiffany realised that her grandmother was really making an effort to welcome her into the house. Edwina continued, "Now, first things first. Did you have a good time at your going-to-college party last Friday night?"

Tiffany's eyes sparkled with excitement. "Well, actually, it's funny you should mention it. Did you see the rather stunning young man I was talking to?"

"He was a little difficult to miss – a very attractive young man," Edwina smiled.

Tiffany sat at the table and glanced around to make sure Richard was well out of earshot.

"Gran, he's my new boyfriend. Isn't he gorgeous? His name is Max Condon. His parents are the ones who are buying Innishambles."

Edwina began to serve the lunch. "Is he starting college this year too?"

"No, he's only doing his Leaving Cert. Can you believe I'm dating a younger man?" Tiffany giggled.

"Where will he be going to school?"

"He doesn't know yet."

"But surely the school term starts this week?"

"Well, his family have only just moved here. They're not moving into Innishambles until next week. I don't think he's that bothered, to be honest."

Edwina looked shocked. "Surely he has to get stuck in for his Leaving Cert year?"

"Gran, he may be extremely cute but I don't think academia is his strong point!"

"In this day and age? Is he mad? What's to become of him?"

Tiffany felt the judgmental, condescending Edwina rushing back.

"To each his own," she defended her boyfriend although, secretly, it did rather surprise her that he could be so relaxed about the whole affair.

"So he and you are boyfriend and girlfriend?"

Again Tiffany felt uncomfortable. "Well, not in so many words. It's not actually that official yet. You see, I'm playing this game. It's all about being really hard to get and then the boy wants you."

"So he's not actually your boyfriend at all?" Edwina cut in.

"Well, he will be, very soon."

"How many times have I told you not to count your chickens before they've hatched?" The old woman sighed impatiently as she shook her head.

Richard arrived back into the kitchen. "That's everything in your room. All ten bags! God, Tiffany, you know how to pack!"

"Thanks and thanks to both of you for letting me stay here. I know you did it for years, Dad, but I would hate to have to commute every day. It's too far for that."

"You get used to it but, I have to be honest, the traffic

wasn't nearly as heavy in the old days." Richard took a bottle of champagne from the fridge. "Now don't expect this every lunch-time but considering you've just moved to Dublin for college we thought we should have a little celebration." Richard smiled as he showed her the bottle of Moet.

The cork popped and Edwina rushed to put a champagne glass under the frothy flow.

"Now this is a nice way to pass a Monday lunch-time!" smiled Tiffany as her grandmother handed her the first glass.

Richard filled two more glasses and then sat down at the table with the ladies. He raised his glass to toast his daughter.

"To new beginnings," he smiled at her.

"To new beginnings," Tiffany and Edwina echoed as they joined in his toast and then tasted the cool sparkling liquid.

The three dug into big plates of tagliatelli.

"Do you want to go in to Trinity this afternoon?" Richard asked.

"Well, today or tomorrow, I don't really mind," Tiffany said as she ate hungrily.

"I'm going into town this afternoon so I could give you a lift if you like."

"What are you doing in town? In fact, while we're on the subject, Dad, would you tell me what line of business you're in now?"

Richard smirked at her. "Ah you know, a little bit of this, a little bit of that."

Tiffany looked at him warily.

"Nothing illegal!" he added. "Jesus, you Dalton women

are all so suspicious." He glanced from his daughter to his mother.

The two women looked at each other and nodded in agreement. Tiffany lifted her glass towards her grandmother.

"Cheers," they said together.

"OK," he raised his hands in defeat and then he wiped his mouth with a napkin. "I manage property portfolios."

Tiffany got interested. "Do you mean where people own a lot of different properties and you make sure they're all rented out and in good working order and stuff."

"And stuff," Richard agreed as he broke off a large piece of garlic bread. "That's exactly what I mean." He wasn't going to explain to his daughter that the portfolios that he managed were in fact all his own!

"OK." She seemed satisfied with that.

"Now, do you want that lift or not?"

"Yes, please," Tiffany decided. "Trinity, here I come!" She raised her glass again and this time Richard and Edwina clinked with her.

* * *

After Dave Parker left the house, Sue ran to her bedroom and collapsed onto her bed in floods of tears. In a funny kind of way she didn't actually want him to leave the house. Now that he was gone, she felt desperately alone. She obviously had sounded like she meant it when she said, "Get out." As she lay there her greatest emotion was of shock. On reflection it was a bit shitty of her to accuse him of not trusting her. In fairness he knew about her past with Richard Dalton. Why shouldn't he jump to the same conclusion as she did, even if it was the wrong one?

Sue had let her fears about Guy's blood type wash over her as soon as she discovered that they were unfounded. It never occurred to her that Dave was under the same misapprehension – that he still thought it was necessary for one of the parents to be O negative. "Damn James Harrington, damn him to hell!" she shouted, glad to have somebody else to direct her anger at. Slowly her tears subsided. She began to wonder about her husband. If he genuinely thought that Richard Dalton was Guy's father since the accident, it meant he had been stewing for over a week now! It certainly explained why he had been so distant since Egypt. It would also explain – the truth dawned on her – why he got drunk in Luxor! She had been so flippant on the phone from the hospital. God, she remembered now: he had asked her, pushed her even to come clean and tell the truth. For a conversation she couldn't have recalled a few minutes after she had it, she could remember every word of it now – every nuance. When she asked him, he had replied, *I'm A positive . . . Of course I'm sure. I'm a regular blood donor . . .Why? . . . What were you wondering, Sue? . . . Honey, is something wrong? . . . What do you want? . . . Blood?* . . . As she recalled their talk now it was so blindingly obvious. Of course he knew and she had just treated him like a fool. It was quite clear on reflection that James had told him one of the parents had to be O negative. Dave knew from that moment on that she was lying to him. Her husband, her best friend – the one she swore she would keep "no secrets" from was the wronged party here.

But what about Dave and Penny? If Dave had issues he wanted to discuss with his wife, he should have just come out and said it. Getting drunk and shagging his secretary was hardly the solution. *"How could he? The bastard!"* she howled at an empty room. She let her mind race through the possibilities. Had he and Penny enjoyed each other? Then she remembered that Dave had said that they didn't actually have sex. Instinctively she knew he had been telling the truth about that. So what had they done? Her mind was tormented. Was Penny wild and reckless? She probably was. Sue knew that she herself was shy and demure in the bedroom. Penny was probably the exact opposite. That's why Dave was so attracted to her. As she sat on her bed, clutching her knees close to her chest and rocking, Sue caught sight of the earrings resting on her dressing-table. They were her present from Egypt. She jumped from the bed and grabbed them. Without considering the consequences, she hurtled them through the air with as much force as she could muster. One of the rather large Alexandrite stones made contact with her full-length mirror, causing it to crack loudly.

"That's all I need," she wailed. "Seven years bad luck!" She sat back down on her bed and looked at the damage she had caused to the mirror. Thankfully Lisa had not heard the breaking glass. She was downstairs keeping the younger children occupied.

"Oh, Jesus," Sue whispered to herself as she looked at the mirror. It had been a present from Dave for their first wedding anniversary. The rich mahogany surround was beautifully French-polished and the mirror stood on its original Victorian stand.

"This is so you can see how beautiful you are," he had said to her when he gave it to her. "Happy first anniversary, Sue. I love you!"

She remembered it like it was yesterday. What am I

doing, she thought to herself. On the night of Guy's accident, she herself nearly ended up in a very compromising position with James Harrington. Subsequently she did end up in trouble with him and when she told Dave, how did he react? With love and understanding. And of course, a few years ago, when he found out that she had *accidentally* had sex with Richard Dalton, how did he react? With love and understanding. He has one near-miss and how does she respond? Like a spoilt bitch.

She stood up and looked at her reflection in her badly cracked antique mirror. She looked jagged and distorted.

"Why are you being such a bitch, Sue Parker?" she asked herself.

Falling back down on to the bed, she answered, "It's obviously because I am a bitch!" She had never felt more wretched. There was just so much pain and mistrust to work through. Maybe there was too much. Maybe she and Dave weren't going to make it through. The truth is there was too much damage done when she and Richard Dalton had sex and even though it was years ago now, it was quite clear that there was a big hole in the Parker marriage as a result. And what if . . . she could barely think it. What if Guy really was Richard's baby? The possibility had always lingered in her mind. How could she condemn her husband for such fears and doubts when she had the same ones? James had said that it was a one thousand to one chance for two A positive adults to produce an O negative child. She still clung to that slight possibility.

She sat and stewed in her own misery for some time. Could she forgive Dave for his foreign philandering? Could he forgive her if Guy was not his son? Thankfully, he had already forgiven her for her original mistake with Richard and he had forgiven her for her near miss with James Harrington. Then it occurred to her: Dave was a hell of a lot more forgiving than her it seemed. Damn this! She would forgive him for his one indiscretion and she would fight to save her marriage – she wasn't going to give up without a bloody good fight. Glancing at her watch, she was surprised to see that Dave had been gone almost an hour. "Time flies when you're having a crisis," she said as she tip toed through the minefield of broken glass on her bedroom floor. She walked into her clean bright en suite and turned on her cold tap. She splashed cold water on her face and looked at her reflection. "Go and get your husband and bring him home!" she told herself with as much conviction as she could muster.

Sue went down to Lisa and her sons and told her nanny that she would have to collect India from school – she had business to attend to in Dublin. She fixed herself a strong coffee and then she went to her room to prepare herself and to make one very important phone call . . .

When she got down to the repair work, even Sue was quite surprised at how bad she looked. Her eyes seemed to have sunk deep into her head and her skin was stretched tightly across her face. There were dark rings under her eyes and her lips were thin and pale.

"To work," she announced as she began to expertly conceal the damage of her histrionics. Sue started by gently massaging her face and neck with her luxuriant Lancôme moisturiser. After secondary school, her father had packed her off to finishing school for a year. The one thing she took seriously from the entire year was her beauty care class. Madame Blanc, her teacher had always insisted that the girls buy the very best cosmetics. "How can you expect to look magnificent unless you are wearing magnificent make up?" the lady would ask daily. Then she would continue as she catwalked up and down the classroom, "you buy cheap and nasty, you look?"

"Cheap and nasty," the young ladies would reply.

Sue picked her little bottle of Photogenic, Ultra Confort, light-reflecting make-up, "I'm relying on you!" she said to it, as she began to cover her blotchy, multi-toned skin.

An hour later, Sue emerged from her room, looking like a lady who lunched. Her Gucci dress was one she had bought recently and had not yet had the nerve to wear. The neck was cut very low and a matching slit up the front of the skirt was cut alarmingly high. She looked utterly gorgeous and highly provocative. The gold fabric shimmered slightly as she moved. She had been delighted to see that *Vogue's* predictions of shoulder-pads making a comeback were in fact accurate. In her Gucci, her shoulders looked square and her breasts full. She forced herself to walk tall. Every stride gave a glimpse of the long thin legs that she usually kept under wraps – well, not today. It had occurred to Sue that before facing Dave, she would have to face Penny Shorthall. That girl was so fired!

"My God, Sue, you look amazing," Lisa gushed when she saw her boss descend from the bedroom. "And your figure!"

Usually Sue Parker's taste was a little more refined and a lot more conservative. She went for understated and chic. Today she was sassy and confident.

"Thank you, Lisa. I'm going out for a while now. I'll be home by five."

"Take your time, Sue. I have nothing planned for tonight," Lisa sighed.

Sue looked at her nanny. She was such a pretty and friendly girl. How come she hadn't met her mister right? Then again, perhaps she was lucky. Relationships were so bloody complicated.

"I'll bring back pizzas! How about that?" Sue smiled.

"OK." Lisa laughed good-naturedly. "Have a nice afternoon."

Sue couldn't bring herself to answer.

* * *

With Tiffany gone to Dublin, Kelly in the refuge and Lauren back to school at last, Saskia and Robin were alone in Innishambles for most of the afternoons. That morning, Robin had started Montessori and she had loved it. Saskia had planned on having a quiet and companionable afternoon with her youngest. She wanted Robin to settle into Montessori slowly and comfortably. That was why the little girl had only spent an hour there on her first morning – nothing too ambitious, the teacher had suggested.

Saskia collected her at eleven thirty. She smiled indulgently at her daughter and then they headed for home.

"I miss my big sisters," Robin sighed as soon as she got into the car.

"So do I, pet, but Lauren will be home from big school later."

A new bus route had been opened between Wicklow and the village of Rathdeen. It went straight through

Ballymore village, which meant that Lauren could now get the bus home. It saved Saskia an ocean of time.

"And Kelly," Robin continued.

"Yes, sweetheart. Your eldest sister will be home after she has finished in the manor."

"And Tiff."

"No, Robin. Do you remember we discussed this? Tiffany will live with Daddy in Dublin during the week now because she's in college."

The child scowled. "I want Tiffany," she whined, "and Daddy."

"What?" Saskia was sure she had misheard.

"I want Daddy," she looked at her mother hopefully, "here."

"But, Robin, Daddy has never lived here, not in your lifetime anyway. Whyever would you want him here all of a sudden?"

"All the girls in my class have a Mummy and a Daddy in their house," Robin explained simply.

Saskia thought her heart would break. Her first day in Montessori, one bloody hour and already she had figured out that she was a little different.

"Your daddy loves you very much, Robin. It's just that we live apart. Tiffany lives with Daddy in Dublin and Robin lives with Mummy in Innishambles." As she said it, she realised that even that would change in the near future. The house move would be another trauma for the poor little mite.

"I don't want that daddy," Robin said impatiently. "I want Nicolas. He's my proper daddy."

Saskia was stunned. Robin had never called Nicolas 'Daddy', not in all the time they had been together.

As Robin played in the back of the car with her colouring book and ate more crayons than she actually coloured with, Saskia worried yet again about the house move. She was now pretty sure that the decisions she had made so hastily were because she was full of pregnancy hormones, but what could she do about it now? Everything was legally binding and more or less irreversible. Saskia realised what she really needed was somebody to talk it out with. She was embarrassed at how much she had relied on Cathy Taylor recently. Poor Cathy seemed to be minding Robin more than Saskia was and she had been a tower of strength the day Kelly arrived up to her house and announced that she was marrying Barney. No, she couldn't lay more grief on Cathy.

"Sue Parker," she said to Robin. "We haven't had a good chat in ages. She'll be able to advise me!"

"Hooray," Robin agreed. "Let's go to the Parkers' house."

Saskia decided not to phone. That was making too big a deal out of it. She was in the car already – why not just head over for a quick chat and perhaps an energising cup of coffee? She could also check to see if the humungous bunch of flowers that she had sent Guy and Sue had arrived yet. It was a sort of apology/get-well-soon bunch of roses. Unfortunately for Saskia, Sue was just saying goodbye to her boys and Lisa as the Dalton women arrived.

"Sas, I'm so sorry but I'm heading up to Dublin right now," Sue said as she got into her car. "I'd love a good chat with you soon though. Is everything OK?"

"Oh, yes, it's nothing too major. I'm just beginning to worry – have I made the right decision about moving into Ballymore Glen?"

"God, Sas, if I had the choice, I'd be in there in a flash, honestly. Now, I'm sorry, I really have to fly."

Felling somewhat mollified, Saskia nodded and waved. "That makes me feel better. Thanks, bye." They waved Sue off as she drove out the driveway.

"Gosh, she was in a hurry, wasn't she?" Saskia smiled at Lisa.

"Yep, I don't know what got into her. I've barely seen her all morning."

Saskia sighed, "She's probably off for a girlie lunch or, knowing her, a hot date with her husband! That woman has a terrific life."

Lisa agreed and then she asked, "When are you moving into Ballymore Glen?"

"We're actually moving in next Saturday. You must come up and have a look around the place next weekend. I can't believe that it's that soon! God, what am I doing wandering around the countryside? I should be at home panicking!"

Lisa laughed. "If there's anything I can do to help, just call. Perhaps I could mind Robin for you on Saturday. Moving house with a small child can't be easy."

"Thanks, I might just take you up on that," Saskia replied as she thought about the even smaller life in her stomach. She made a silent promise to herself that she would definitely phone Nicolas that very evening.

* * *

"Knock, knock," Sue put her head around her husband's office door meekly.

Dave jumped to his feet.

"Sue, hi! Sorry there was nobody to greet you or guide you in. Er, Penny's gone."

"Where has she gone?"

"London, I think. In view of my utter stupidity, she doesn't want to work for me any more."

"Hey, it takes two to tango!" Sue could feel his discomfort.

Dave looked at his wife. "Jesus, Sue, I really am so sorry. It was a really stupid thing to do. I know it's no excuse but I was totally pissed and caught up in the atmosphere. As soon as I realised what I was doing, I got the hell out of there."

Sue wanted to cross the room. She wanted to embrace him but she couldn't.

"Dave, do you think that Richard is Guy's natural father?"

He looked at her. "James Harrington said that one of us had to be O negative if Guy was O neg. The reality is we are both A Positive. It certainly doesn't look too good."

"James was wrong."

"What?"

"Usually, one of the parents should be O neg but it's not an absolute. I've gone through the whole thing with a specialist in the last half hour on the phone."

"My God."

"Yes, James was generalising. He doesn't know our – my history."

"Oh Sue, that's in the past!"

This time she did cross the room. He rose to greet her but she took a seat across from his desk.

"You've been very good about my stupidity in the past but the truth is we have to work it out, Dave. It is blindingly obvious that we can't just ignore it."

403

"Sue –"

"Let me just tell you what this expert said. I got his number from my obstetrician. He said that they're still making up new blood groups all the time. It's by no means black and white and it's very complicated. Yes, what James said is usually the case but not always. It is possible, admittedly not probable, but it is possible for two A positive parents to produce an O negative child."

Dave watched her. She was finding this line of talk very difficult.

Sue continued as she studied the floor. "The only way to prove beyond any doubt who Guy's father is – is to do a DNA test."

"Jesus, Sue, we don't have to go that far, do we?"

"Well, I think we do –" Now she was crying.

Dave was out of his seat in a flash and over by her. He hugged her tightly. "No, this is madness, sheer madness. I know Guy is mine. I can feel it in my bones. I haven't had the slightest shadow of doubt about it since the day he was born. It was just that bloody James Harrington that set my mind in a tailspin and even then that was because I was so far away. Sue," he took her tear-stained face in his hands, "I adore you and our three children. Please can we just start again? I'm so sorry about Penny. I'm such a fool."

"Shh," she said, "I'm the fool. I know you made a mistake and that you didn't mean it. I'm only sorry that I didn't forgive you quicker."

"You are?"

"Dave, you and I are doing our best. I know that you love me as much as I love you. OK, now we've both fucked up once."

It was a shock to hear her use such harsh language. Usually Sue abhorred strong language.

"Let's just call it quits," she suggested.

"Oh, yes please," Dave said as he took his beloved wife into his arms.

They hugged each other tightly.

"I do think we need a little counselling too," she said. "What do you think?"

"If it's what will make you happy, I'll do it," he agreed.

"I think I might come with you on your future business trips too," she said with a little laugh.

"That would be wonderful," Dave agreed. Then he looked into his wife's eyes. "Now can we go home?"

"Yes," she smiled at him. "Together."

CHAPTER 29

Innishambles was incredibly quiet on Monday evening. Kelly was down at Peartree Cottage with Barney, and Robin was asleep in bed. Lauren was watching the television alone.

"I miss Tiffany," she said to her mother when Saskia walked into the room.

"Yes, she's usually so full of chat. It does seem very quiet without her."

"Who will I fight with over the remote control now?" Lauren moaned.

"Oh, come on. It's not that bad. You can watch what you want now."

"I know, but it's no fun if I just *get* what I want without having to fight for it," Lauren argued.

"I heartily disagree with that principle," Saskia said.

"What principle?"

"What you just said: that it's only worth something if it takes a lot of effort to get it."

"Did I say that?" Lauren asked, looking perplexed.

"More or less," Saskia laughed.

"Oh. I guess I agree with it. It's much more fun watching *Sex in the City* if I know Tiffany wants to watch *The Business Show* on Sky TV at the same time."

"You're not alone," Saskia continued. "Did you know that it has been proven that people will stay on the phone longer, in a phone box, if a queue has formed outside?"

"Now how the hell did they figure that one out?"

"I'm not sure," Saskia admitted.

"I guess I just miss Tiffany," Lauren sighed.

"So do I, pet."

"Poor little Robin! We'll all have moved out before she's grown up!" Lauren said innocently. "She'll have no one to fight with for the remote control."

Saskia's eyes flashed as she looked at her daughter for any hidden meaning. Was it possible that Lauren had guessed that Saskia was pregnant? Her daughters were very perceptive.

Lauren's eyes were fixed on the television however. There was no hidden message or question.

Saskia felt the knot in her stomach returning but it wasn't pregnancy nausea. It was the dread of phoning Nicolas. She had to do it. This baby was his. He obviously had a right to know. It was just so messy. They had broken up. Their relationship was over but now she was carrying his baby. They would be tied together forever. She forced herself to get up. It was late now which meant it was morning time in LA. This was the only time they could talk.

The last time she had spoken to Nicolas, they had had a thundering row. Saskia winced at the memory. The last two times they had spoken, she had ended up hanging up on him! It was definitely her turn to apologise.

"I'm just going into the study for a while," she said. "Are you OK here?"

"Mmm," was all she got by way of reply as her daughter got involved in yet another American soap. Saskia was comfortable that there was small chance of her daughter walking in on her conversation.

As she left Lauren, she entertained the possibility of getting back with Nicolas. If they were going to have a baby together maybe it was a sign. Could she move to the States? Was it really such a wild idea? Kelly was setting up her own life with Barney. Tiffany was living in Dublin now, more or less. There was just Lauren and Robin to consider. Lauren even said she liked the idea of moving to the States. All that sun! She resolved to keep her mind open. Nicolas was working again. Perhaps they could rekindle what they had at the beginning of their relationship. Then she thought about Richard. It would be good to get away from him. They were becoming too close and he was saying the most outrageous things. Did he really want to get back with her? He certainly wouldn't, once he discovered she was pregnant again. Richard had been furious when he heard that Robin was on the way. He was well and truly finished with being the father of babies.

Nicolas? Now that was a different matter. They had been together for the last couple of years. Their break could have been just a small glitch. Saskia began to seriously think about living in the States. LA would certainly be different from Ballymore! She dialled Nicolas's number.

"Hi!" a young girl giggled. There was loud music blaring in the background.

"Oh, hello. May I speak to Nicolas please?" Saskia asked, slightly surprised to hear a young woman answering the phone and what the hell was the loud music for? It was morning time in LA.

"What? I can't hear you! The stereo's too loud. Who's this?" the girl asked with a strong LA twang.

"I'm his – his –" God, what was she? "I'm his ex," she replied hotly. He was having a bloody party. It had to be! And it was still in full swing from the night before.

"Hang on." The girl dropped the receiver and went in search of Nicolas.

He sounded harassed when he took the phone call.

"Hello?" his voice sounded different somehow.

Saskia took a deep breath, "Nicolas, you're obviously having a party so now isn't a good time. Can you call me back later?"

"What for?" he asked blankly.

He wasn't going to make this easy for her.

"Actually I was just phoning to apologise. But now can't be the right time, can it?" The music was so loud Saskia could barely hear him. "Have you been partying all night?" She tried not to sound reproachful. So much for being broke.

Nicolas was obviously quite distracted.

"I'm cool. Why did you say you were phoning again?" He sounded very chilled out.

"There's something I need to tell you." This conversation was not going as she had hoped. "Can you phone me back later? When you've had some rest."

"Jeez, babe – why so heavy?"

Some girl grabbed phone. "He's mine now," she laughed. "Go away!"

Nicolas grabbed the phone back. "Ignore her. She's stoned. Look, do you want to come over?"

What the hell was he on? Saskia wondered furiously. He had to be drunk. "How the hell can I come over, Nicolas? Call me back when you sober up!" She was about to hang up again when she remembered that that was exactly what she had done the previous two times. Not this time. She would remain polite and composed.

He heaved a big sigh and then continued, "Babe, whatever you have to say – just say it. Let it out!"

Why was he talking so strangely, she wondered. Saskia took a deep breath. "Look, Nicolas, there's no easy way to break this to you so I'll just come out with it straight. I'm pregnant."

"*You're what?*"

"I'm pregnant."

Somebody turned the music up. Tears began to sting her eyes and she wiped them away angrily. It was so much easier for men. There he was partying and here she was, literally carrying the baby.

"Oh shit. It's just that you and I have broken up. I guess you'll have to abort," he sighed.

"*What?*" she couldn't believe her ears. "I want to be quite clear about this, Nicolas. There have been so many mix-ups around here lately. Are you asking me to have an abortion?"

"Yeah, Jeez. It's not such a big deal, is it? I mean we have broken up."

"So you keep reminding me," Saskia cut in.

"Look, babe, I was of the understanding that you and I had really finished, you know. It was over." He paused hesitantly. "I was going to phone you. It's just been so crazy here." The background noise in his apartment was deafening. "You see, I'm, eh, I'm engaged to be married."

"You're *what?*"

"Well –" his discomfort was audible. "That woman you were talking to – Mandy – we're engaged to be married. That was what I wanted to tell you."

"And this is his engagement party!" the girl next to him shouted into the phone.

Saskia lost all ambitions of remaining civil on the phone. "Screw you! Nicolas, you can sell your own bloody house and this time I really mean it. I want nothing more to do with the refuge or you for that matter! I never want to speak to you again!" She slammed down the phone.

Saskia sat in the study for some time letting her situation sink in. She didn't know whether to laugh or to cry and so she did a little of both. Nicolas – getting married! He had sounded so weird on the phone. It was obviously after a night of drinking. And as for the girl! She couldn't have been more than mid-twenties. She sounded very young and silly. She never would have thought Nicolas would go for someone like that. God, what was she going to tell Robin? Nicolas really was an old fool. He even said Mandy was stoned. He was going to marry somebody who did drugs. What a difference a month made! Then it twigged. Nicolas must have been stoned too. It would certainly explain why he sounded so different and why he kept saying stupid words like, 'chill' and 'babe'. Saskia just couldn't believe it of him. Heck, if he was so easily swayed, she was bloody well better off without him. It certainly was not an ideal situation but she was a big girl and she had handled bleaker times. Invariably her mind wandered back to Richard. Damn

411

that man, she just couldn't stop thinking about him, it seemed. Well that was utterly useless now. He wouldn't be impressed when he heard she was pregnant again. Jesus, why did she have to be so fertile?

"Mum, here you are! I was calling you."

"Kelly!" Saskia looked up and quickly wiped her eyes. "Welcome home. How's Barney?"

"Oh, he's OK. He's just a bit down about the refuge. He's going over figures and they make for depressing reading."

"I'm so sorry, Kelly."

"Hey, it's not your fault! Life's full of ups and downs. What I really want to do is to open a kennels and a pooch parlour. I'm trying to convince Barney to let me do it from Peartree Cottage." She looked at her mother. "Mum, are you OK? Are you crying?"

Saskia looked at her first-born.

"Yes, I suppose I am crying. I'm so proud of you, Kelly. You have an innate ability to rally in the face of all adversity. I admire you."

"Mum," Kelly looked bashful, "if I'm determined to succeed, it's only because you have always preached to us that we can do anything we set our minds to."

"Yes, but that fire in your spirit, that tenacity. I think that's a gift from your father's genes."

"Oh, I'm not so sure. You're pretty tenacious yourself, Mum. Why are you suddenly so maudlin?"

Saskia ignored the question. "Kelly, I'm sorry."

"What are you apologising for now?"

"I'm sorry for not being more supportive when you thought you were pregnant and that Barney wanted an abortion. Did you feel dreadfully alone and scared?"

"Well, it was pretty freaky but you were there for me."

"Not enough."

"Yes, you were. You were totally cool about me living here with the baby and you didn't give me grief – well, not too much anyway!" She laughed at her mother. "What's all this about, Mum?"

Saskia looked at Kelly. She was standing, staring at her mother – her big brown eyes even wider with concern. Kelly was the double of her father, so much so it startled Saskia sometimes. She knew she would have to tell her girls sooner or later and so she took a deep breath and told her eldest, "I'm pregnant and Nicolas wants an abortion."

"Oh, Jesus!"

"I think somehow our pregnancy-test sticks got mixed up. It's a hell of a coincidence but I did a pregnancy test the morning after your twenty-first too. I only realised what happened when you went through the story the other night."

"Robin ran away with my test stick," Kelly said. "Or that's what I thought. Then she got it back from your bedside locker."

"Ah, that would have been *my* test stick. I left it there when I did the test. Robin greeted me in the hall with what must have been your pregnancy-test stick and when I saw the negative result I was delighted. Then I carefully shoved it down into the bottom of the bin in the kitchen so no prying hands could get at it."

Kelly added, "She saw me put my test stick in the bin in the family bathroom. When I went back to bed she must have wandered in and taken it out to give to you."

Saskia winced. "That makes sense. She kept saying

413

'Kelly's' to me and I just thought she was ranting. I completely ignored her."

Kelly dropped into the sofa in the study. "So I was never really pregnant."

"It would appear not." Saskia looked at her daughter tenderly. "Does that upset you?"

"It shouldn't, but it does a little."

"I'm sorry I was so short with you up in Cathy Taylor's house too," Saskia said deciding to come clean about everything.

"Hey, you got a shock. Speaking of shocks, I can't believe you're having another baby. How are you?" Kelly looked at her mother.

"Well, I'm a good bit older than you to be carrying on like this, but what can I do about it now?"

"And bloody Nicolas wants an abortion – the shit!" Then Kelly thought of something. "Forgive me for asking, but after my own experiences – are you absolutely sure that Nicolas wants an abortion. Did he actually say that?"

"Oh, there was no misunderstanding, darling," Saskia laughed bitterly. "In fact, because of your crossed wires with Barney I was quite specific. I made him repeat it. I asked him outright if he was saying he wanted an abortion. He said it was the only solution." Tears trickled down Saskia's cheeks and then she added, "Nicolas is engaged."

"*What*?"

"Yes, he's engaged to somebody called *Mandy*," she said putting on an American accent.

"Christ, he didn't hang about, did he?"

"Mandy is probably the casting director on the show he's in."

"Oh, yeah? Is he sleeping his way to the top?"

Saskia started to laugh a little. "Come on. I think I could do with a hot chocolate."

"Sod that," Kelly snorted. "It's time for champagne. We're going to have another baby in the house. This is a time for celebration. OK, you're the one who's going to be carrying it, not me, but Mum, we're going to have a *new baby* in the house. He or she will be a playmate for Robin!" Kelly began to get animated. "A baby is always good news, Mum. Let's have some champagne."

"Oh, seeing as you put it like that," Saskia laughed.

Kelly went to investigate what champagnes they had in the scullery fridge. She returned with Lauren and a nicely chilled bottle.

"Seeing as you've told me, you're going to have to tell this one as well." She elbowed her younger sister affectionately. "I even have the perfect champagne."

"What is it?" Saskia asked, enjoying her daughters' company and feeling considerably better than she had done for some time.

Kelly held the label up to face her mother. "It's Mumm, of course!"

CHAPTER 30

Like every other situation in Maximilian Condon's life, he didn't take this one too seriously. Admittedly, no woman had ever ignored him as successfully as Tiffany Dalton. In fact, on reflection no woman had ever ignored him! Max always enjoyed life. He couldn't remember a time when he hadn't. His platinum blonde hair and his casual air attracted people to him like bees to honey. It wasn't just women – it was everybody. People loved to be around Max and his brother Seb. They had discovered at an early age that they could really do anything they wished. The twins were never properly punished by their chain of governesses and nannies and, at the tender age of thirteen, Max began to enjoy a much more *fulfilling* tutoring from his then nanny.

She was sent away in disgrace when Arthur found Max's face buried deep between her ample breasts one evening. The real disgrace, as far as Max's father was concerned, was that he himself was hoping for that particular position. After that, the boys grew up quickly.

For some reason they seemed immune to the trials and tribulations of ordinary folk.

They fell into modelling jobs during their summer holidays. Another year they got jobs as escorts in a national beauty pageant. One of the organisers literally stopped them in the street and offered them the jobs and a huge salary just to accompany beautiful girls around London. Then of course there was the year that Annabel Foxthorp's father asked them to take the *Tiffany*, a beautiful forty-foot sailing boat from Cowes to Sardinia.

It was that particular memory that jarred in Max's memory that Monday night. Suddenly he remembered meeting a very pretty Irish girl that summer – and her name was Tiffany too! Ordinarily he wouldn't remember such details but her name was the same as the boat. Could it possibly be the same Tiffany? Surely she would have remembered? Damn it, everybody remembered Maximilian Condon. Even he remembered the night. They had a particularly nice meal in Antonio's restaurant in the port and then they had a bloody good shag on the beach. Admittedly she didn't want to be walked home the following morning – that was a little odd too. Max had to find out whether or not it was the same girl. He had Francesca's number. She had given it to him at the party and so he had no qualms phoning her for Tiffany Dalton's number. Francesca gave him the number for Innishambles but Tiffany wasn't there. Lauren Dalton gave him her sister's new number in Dublin.

Before Maximilian managed to get through to Tiffany, however, she had already received a panic call from Lauren and, straight after that, she got a call from Francesca.

"I just rang Innishambles looking for you. I'm sorry – I hadn't realised you had moved already," she said breathlessly. "Lauren just gave me your new number but the good news is that she gave it to Max too. He's going to phone you, Tiff."

Tiffany laughed at Lauren and Francesca's excitement. "Well, he can only phone me if you two get off the bloody phone!"

"Oh, yeah, sorry. Now remember! Treat him mean and keep him keen."

"I remember."

"OK, well good luck then!" Francesca almost hung up. "Oh and Tiffany?"

"Yes?"

"Phone me back to tell me what happens!"

"OK."

When she put the receiver down, the phone began to ring instantly. Tiffany sat there and watched it ring. Edwina rushed out.

"Well, are you going to answer it?" she asked indignantly.

"Oh, yes, Gran. I just have to let him stew a little."

"Really," the old woman grumbled and shuffled back into her front room.

"Hello," Tiffany answered.

"Hi, could I speak to Tiffany, please," Max asked comfortably.

"Speaking."

"Tiff, hi. It's Max Condon."

"Who?"

"Max – we're buying your house, remember? Well, your house in Wicklow that is – not the one you're in at the moment."

"Oh, Max. Yes, hello."

"Hi," he repeated. Silence. She waited.

Then he spoke again. "Look, this is a strange question, but did we meet in Puerto Banus three years ago?"

She held her breath and counted to five as slowly as she could. He had remembered! Then, as trained by Francesca, she exhaled slowly and acted as uninterested as she could. "You've already asked me this, Max, and the answer is still the same. I don't remember you."

"I was on a boat called *The Tiffany* and one night I met a girl called Tiffany. It just seems like a hell of a coincidence," he ventured.

She thought her heart would stop. This treating `em mean really worked! Tiffany pretended to sound bored. "Look, Max, I'm sorry but I really have no idea what you're talking about. I don't know how else to say it. Was there anything else?"

"Er, yeah. Could I see you again?"

This time Tiffany was quite sure that her heart had completely stopped. She let out a pained sigh. "I start college tomorrow. I don't know when I can fit you in."

"You could show me around your college tomorrow then," he suggested a little more brightly.

"I suppose."

"Come on, I'm really good fun! I promise!"

She knew it was all too true.

"OK, I guess, but you're not to get in the way. All right?"

"I give you my word, precious," he purred.

* * *

As planned, Tiffany was waiting for him outside Trinity

College when his bus pulled up. He waved at her and half the women within a forty-foot radius glanced in his direction. Max had a slight swank when he walked which he appeared oblivious to. Tiffany teased him about it. She said he permanently walked like he was on a catwalk which, amazingly, he took as a compliment.

"Hello, delicious," he called to her from a distance.

Tiffany squirmed. Why couldn't he call her by her name? As she felt his long thin arms wrap themselves around her waist and squeeze her hungrily, however, she gave way to feeling like the luckiest girl on campus. Max brought his lips down on hers and kissed her passionately. It felt like the most natural thing to do in the world. She didn't have the willpower to stop him. He took his time and moved his tongue around in her mouth. He slipped his hand down inside her trousers and under her pants. She shrieked and broke away in a fit of giggles.

"Max, you're incorrigible. Look, it's broad daylight and we're in the middle of Dublin." Tiffany had completely lost her cool calm composure. She was going to have to get it back and fast. Baby steps, she said to herself desperately.

"Dublin, Spain, wherever!" he replied languidly as he draped his arm over her shoulder. Then he whispered into her ear. His voice was husky. "And anyway, it's nowhere I haven't been before!" At the same time, his eyes scanned his surroundings.

Mean, mean, mean, Tiffany thought manically. She pushed him away.

"Look, Max. I don't know what you're talking about but I assure you I have no memory of ever meeting you in Spain. You must be mistaken."

He ignored this put-down. "Come on, delicious, show me your new college. Trinity, isn't it?"

"Yes, Max, it's called Trinity. I was in here yesterday and I met some other Economics freshmen. I've arranged to meet them for a drink soon. How does that sound?"

"Freshmen?"

"Yes, they're first-years too, like me."

"OK, whatever. Drink sounds good!" he said with a wicked grin.

"Well, actually it was just for a coffee kind of drink," Tiffany added, slightly embarrassed. "This is freshman week," she explained as they entered the chaos of the courtyard together. The mood was positively carnival as different societies shouted and catcalled trying to attract new members.

The sun shone brightly and it was getting hotter.

They wandered through the throngs for a while and then collapsed onto the steps for a rest. Max lay down to enjoy the sun properly. He used Tiffany's lap as a pillow and closed his eyes so he could face the sun and tan himself comfortably. Her conversations with Saskia and Edwina had got Tiffany thinking.

"Max?"

"Mmm?" He sounded like he was in the middle of a very pleasant daydream and she was interrupting him.

"I was just wondering – have you decided what you're going to do after school?"

"No," he replied as if it didn't really matter.

"But what are you going to do with your life?" Tiffany asked in surprise.

"Something will come up. It always does."

"Don't you want to go to college?"

"I'm here now, aren't I?"

"No, I mean wouldn't you like to attend classes?"

"I'm sure I could go to a few if I wanted to. Do they check your ID into every lecture?"

"That's not what I mean. Wouldn't you like a degree?" Tiffany was getting impatient.

Max opened one eye and used his hand to shelter himself from the glare of the sun. He looked at Tiffany. "No, delicious. I have no desire to go to college. In truth, I have no desire to sit my – what do you call the Irish equivalent of the A levels?"

"Your Leaving Cert."

"Yes, that's it. I have no desire to sit that either."

"But what will you *do*?" Tiffany asked, frustration evident in her voice. Life without some sort of formal education was incomprehensible to Tiffany. She was a worrier and somebody who liked to have life mapped out. It was becoming clear that Max was not! He sat up, obviously discarding any aspirations he had of falling asleep.

"Sail, ski, ride – who knows. Hey, I could become a gigolo – you know, one of those escort boys who accompany rich women around the world."

"You mean a prostitute," Tiffany snapped.

"Oh Gawd, no, something a little more fun." He wrapped his arm around Tiffany's waist again and whispered into her ear. "Speaking of fun. Is there anywhere you and I can get a little privacy?"

"It's time to meet my friends for a drink," Tiffany said, pushing him away.

"OK, delicious," Max smiled. "Perhaps later?"

Tiffany didn't think so but said nothing.

* * *

"Seb, fancy meeting you here! What are you doing in the roaring metropolis of Wicklow?" Lauren asked her soon-to-be-neighbour when she bumped into him.

"Oh, hi, Lauren! Mum took me down to see the school here. Max and I are due to start next bloody Monday."

"Welcome to the club," Lauren moaned, suddenly feeling very self-conscious in her Mount Eden school uniform. "We started back yesterday. Where's Max?"

Sebastian shrugged. "Damned if I know. He was meant to be coming down with us to meet the school principal but he just went out. We're in a rented house in Dublin and he just walked out the front door. He didn't even tell *me* where he was going."

Lauren wondered if her elder sister, Tiffany, might have a better idea but said nothing. "When are you moving into Innishambles?"

"I don't know. When are you moving out?"

"Next Saturday. I'll miss the old place."

"Don't worry, Lauren – if you miss your bedroom too much, you can always come back and visit." He raised one perfectly sculptured eyebrow.

"Relax, Seb. I'll get over it!"

"Well, you know the offer is always there," he said through one of his utterly adorable lopsided grins.

"*Sebastian*!" Camilla Condon called him from her old Volvo.

"Well, see you soon," he said and ran off to join his mother.

"Who was that?" Camilla asked, thinking that possibly she recognised the young girl.

"Lauren Dalton – she lives in Innishambles," Seb told his mother.

Camilla suddenly remembered. What a mess this situation was developing into. It was only the previous night that Arthur Condon had come clean about his plans for that exquisite house. Camilla was furious.

"Why did we go and look at it if you had no intention of living there in the first place?" she cried.

"Well, in the beginning I was looking for a home. You know that, old girl! I was just very surprised at the price of houses over here – they're so damnably expensive! Then I got to thinking, we could do the same thing as that chap did in Ballymore Glen."

"We don't know anything about property development," Camilla argued.

"What's there to know?"

"I can't believe you're going to damage that beautiful old house, Arthur!"

"Can't be helped, old girl, casualties of war and all that!"

"But couldn't you build around the house?"

"Doesn't make sense. Best way is to start with a clean sheet, a blank canvas."

"Six million seems like an awful lot of money if we're going to pull that beautiful old house down."

"It's the land, old girl, that's what we paid the money for," he added impatiently. "Look, Camilla, leave the business side of things to me. You need to sort out some schooling for the boys. That's your job."

"Well, now I don't know where to send them to school. Should it be Wicklow or Dublin? Where *are* we going to live while you're doing all this developing, Arthur?"

"Simple. We're in this rented house now. We'll just stay here for the foreseeable future." Then he thought about it some more. "Actually, perhaps we should move to Ballymore when the development gets underway – just to keep an eye on those confounded builders. We can rent somewhere down there, I'm sure."

"Arthur, you really haven't thought this through, have you? Are you suggesting that the boys change schools in the middle of their academic year? This is their final year. They'll have to settle down and study."

"When have they ever settled, Camilla, old girl?"

That was as far as the conversation had gone. Camilla felt utterly disillusioned and lost. She had been terrified at the idea of moving to Ireland in the first place but at least when she saw Innishambles, she thought she had found a house she could call home and now it looked like Arthur had only bought it so he could destroy it. What was to become of her and her wayward sons? Camilla hadn't even packed up their house in Surrey yet. The family were living out of suitcases, which didn't bother her husband or her boys at all. They just took each day as it came. She wasn't like that. She needed plans and agendas. She couldn't figure out when she was even going to get the chance to return to England to pack up and move properly now.

Arthur was to meet with somebody from Wicklow County Council that afternoon. Perhaps he would have a clearer picture of the situation by the time she got home. Then at least she could make a final decision on where the boys should go to school. With Seb in the passenger seat beside her, she headed out of Wicklow onto the road for Dublin, hopeful that the news at home would be good.

* * *

Tiffany climbed onto the bus that would take her from
Trinity to Edwina's house with a heavy heart. She had had
a catastrophic afternoon.

Maximilian Condon was the love of her life. He was
utterly gorgeous to look at and she envied his casual
attitude towards life but trying to get him to mix with
her new college friends had been a disaster. When they
walked into The Ref, most of the female students turned
to give him the once-over. In fact, so did some of the male
students! It gave Tiffany a great sense of pride when he
draped his arm over her shoulders proprietorially. Max
was her boyfriend and they could all shove off, he was
spoken for.

Unfortunately it was downhill from there. Her friends
were already seated and they were deep in conversation
about 'England's xenophobia towards the Euro,' as Bill
put it.

Tiffany was embarrassed for Max who was as English
as the queen.

"It's not xenophobia, Bill," Tiffany argued. "Is it, Max?"

Max laughed, obviously bored with the conversation.
"I don't even know what xenophobia means. Now, who's
for a real drink?" The little group looked at him in mild
surprise. Nobody wanted a drink so he went to get one for
himself.

"Where did you get him, Tiff?" Bill teased. Then he
began to mimic Max's Etonian accent: *"I'm not very bright,
but I'm dead cute!"*

"Stop that, Bill," Sandra snapped at her classmate.
"He seems very nice, Tiffany." She gestured at Bill.
"Ignore him! Just because Max isn't another bloody
economist! He does seem lovely."

"Thanks," Tiffany smiled weakly, but she was mortified. She realised that her relationship with Max would have to be a strictly off-campus affair.

Her freshmen friends tried to include him in the conversation, but Max didn't seem to want to get involved. He continued to give all his attention to Tiffany, gently stroking her back and nibbling her ear. She pushed him away gently at first, like she would do with Robin, her baby sister. Eventually however she turned to him and snapped, "Look, would you bloody give over for a while. Jesus, is sex all you think about?"

For the second time in twenty minutes her little troop of friends were stunned into silence as they looked on at this domestic that was getting interesting. Max looked at her and nodded wickedly. Even she cracked up laughing when she saw his little-boy-butter-wouldn't-melt-in-his-mouth face.

"I think we'd better be going," she sighed eventually. She dearly wanted to talk with her new friends but it just wasn't possible when Max was with her. Max kissed all the girls goodbye and Tiffany was sure that Bill, for all his teasing earlier, flashed a jealous look towards Max as each woman gave him her undivided attention.

"That was good fun," Max said just before he caught his bus. "When can I see you again?"

"Gosh, Max, it's going to be a little crazy over the next few days. I have to find all my lecture halls and tutorials," Tiffany explained.

"Well, what about the weekend? Are you going home? Damn it, Tiff, all work and no play –"

"Tell you what, I'm going down to Ballymore on Saturday morning. You know we're moving house and obviously I'm going home to help. Would you like to help too?"

It wasn't exactly what Max had in mind but it was pretty obvious that he wasn't wearing the pants in this relationship. Not yet anyway, he thought playfully. "Sure, no prob, delicious." He wrapped his arms tightly around her waist again and began to kiss her passionately.

"Somebody get those two a room!" Bill was passing by the bus stop just outside Trinity.

"Yes, please," Max winked at Bill mischievously in agreement. He was utterly unembarrassable, unlike Tiffany. She was mortified. She pulled away. "Now tell me, Tiffany Dalton, once and for all. Was it you that I met in Puerto Banus the summer I was sailing *The Tiffany* from Cowes to Italy?"

"Really, Max, I don't know what you're talking about." Then she changed the subject. "OK, if you're going to help us move house, I'll see you here, say around nine o'clock in the morning on Saturday. We can go down together on the bus."

"Ouch, that's early, but if it makes you happy, delicious!" Max mounted his bus and blew her a kiss from his seat. Christ, why does he have to call me that? She cringed to herself as she smiled weakly and walked away even before his bus had pulled off.

Bill's taunts rang in her head: *"I'm not very bright, but I'm dead cute!"*

Miserably she fell into her own seat on her bus for Clontarf. If she was dating the man of her dreams, why wasn't she happier?

* * *

"Look, Mister. We've been through this twenty times already. It isn't gonna change."

"Yes, but that's just plain preposterous," Arthur Condon fumed. "I mean, how the blazes did Ballymore Glen get built and I can't do this?"

The Wicklow planning authority man was really beginning to lose his patience. It was well past closing time in his office, but this guy just wouldn't leave.

"It's very simple. That land was zoned for development, residential development. Your site is zoned agricultural. It's for grazing animals." He added caustically, "Usually developers check out how a site is zoned *before* they buy it."

"Well, how do I get my land rezoned?" Arthur Condon asked as the true nature of his dilemma began to sink in.

The clerk sighed. "Look, I'll go through it one more time. First you have to put an ad in the paper to notify the public of your intentions. During this time they can object. Then you need to put a proposal in to the next County Council meeting. They will have to take a vote to change the County Development Plan. It all takes time."

"I don't have that much bloody time," Arthur stammered.

The clerk was examining Arthur's files again. "I don't hold much hope for you," he said.

"Why not?" Arthur asked. He could feel his temperature rising.

"That house, it's a listed building." The clerk pointed to Innishambles on the map.

"That's my problem." Arthur was beginning to feel physically sick.

"Yes, and under Irish law it's your responsibility that

it's kept in good condition. If anything happened to that house, there's no way you'd get your land rezoned." The tone left Arthur in no doubt; they weren't going to fall for the old 'roof fell off' story.

"This is a very complex and drawn-out issue –" the clerk stopped talking when he saw the expression on Arthur Condon's face. "Hey, are you all right? You don't look too good."

Arthur Condon fell back onto the ground clasping his chest. He knew what was happening. He was having another heart attack.

"My wife," he stammered as the clerk rushed around from his side of the counter. "Get my wife, please!"

"Somebody call an ambulance! This guy's having a heart attack!"

"No," Arthur argued, the pain in his chest getting sharper. "Please, get my wife!" Then he lost consciousness.

* * *

Max got home first, just ahead of the others so he was the one who answered the phone and got the news about his father.

Seb and Max set out for the hospital with Camilla Condon within minutes of their return from Wicklow. She was in floods of tears. A woman not usually given to emotion, this current display shocked the twins more than their father's heart attack did.

"It's all my fault," she kept repeating.

"That's not true, Ma," Seb said. "You know Pa has a dodgy ticker. If he cut down on the whiskey a little perhaps, or if he cut out those bloody huge cigars he might be a little healthier!"

"Damn it, the man has to live," Max argued. "What point is there in living if you never take a drop or enjoy a good cigar? He'll be fine, Mum. Just you wait and see."

Camilla, however, wasn't convinced. This was his second heart attack. Arthur regularly drove her utterly batty, but she loved him to distraction and couldn't bear the idea of living without him.

He was, as expected, in intensive care. The family were permitted to go in for a few minutes only. Arthur could barely talk; he just nodded at them and closed his eyes gently again. The twins and Camilla were ushered out of the room soon after.

"He's had a mild heart attack, Mrs Condon, but he is still very weak," the ICU nurse explained.

"I must speak with the consultant," Camilla said, sounding a good deal stronger than she actually felt.

"You're in luck. Here he is now," the nurse smiled.

"Hello, I'm Mr McMillan. You must be Arthur's wife and sons." His smile was warm and open as he guided the three of them to seats just outside the ICU unit.

"Is my husband going to be all right?" Camilla asked urgently.

"Well, so far, the prognosis is good." Mr McMillan spoke softly and calmly. "He has stabilised but he is in a very weakened condition. Mrs Condon, we'd like to do an angiogram on your husband. That way we'll know what caused the heart attack."

There was a collective sigh from the Condons.

Max explained their reaction. "We've been through this before, a few years ago."

"This isn't your father's first heart attack?" Mr McMillan looked a little more concerned.

Camilla spoke up. "He had one a few years ago in England and after it he had an angiogram and an angioplasty. I can get his heart specialist in Epsom to phone you if you like."

"Yes, please. That would be most helpful. Well, if I can speak with Arthur's doctor in the UK tomorrow morning, we'll pencil the angiogram in for tomorrow afternoon. Have you spoken to him?"

Camilla shook her head sadly. "He seemed too weak to talk."

"Perhaps if you boys stay out here," Mr McMillan looked at the twins, "I think he should be able to talk to you, Mrs Condon."

"I don't want to put him under any undue pressure," she said, unsure of the situation.

"Come with me," the doctor smiled. "I'm sure we can get a few words out of him!" What Mr McMillan didn't add was that he didn't want Arthur Condon to die in the night without having said goodbye to his wife.

"Arthur," the doctor gently whispered, "I have your wife here. Will you just say hello?"

Arthur opened his eyes again and the loud beep-beep of the heart monitor sped up alarmingly.

"Oh God, is he OK?" Camilla asked urgently when she heard the intrusive noise from the machines.

Mr McMillan bent over the bed. "Just relax," he said to Arthur. "If you have anything to say, say it. If not, rest."

Arthur Condon looked at his wife as he had never looked at her before. "I love you, old girl," he whispered.

The tears began to flood down her cheeks. "I love you too. You old fool!"

His voice was hoarse. "I'm afraid I've made rather a mess of our pension plan, old girl."

"Shh, that doesn't matter now. All that matters is that you get better." Camilla knew that Arthur had collapsed in the County Wicklow planning office so she had deduced that his meeting hadn't gone too well.

"I'm afraid that we'll have to sell Innishambles, probably at a considerable loss too," he mumbled.

"Don't worry about that now," Camilla urged. "Please rest. We'll sort all of that out at some time in the future."

Mr McMillan returned. "Now you won't stop talking," he whispered good-naturedly. "OK, I think that's enough for tonight, Arthur. Camilla can come back in the morning."

Camilla bent over and kissed her husband on the cheek. The skin seemed softer than it had been. His cheeks had hollowed. He was deathly pale. It felt like he had aged by twenty years.

"See you tomorrow, old girl." He tried to wink at her, but his eyes closed and they wouldn't open for him again. He was too too tired.

CHAPTER 31

Raymond Saunders woke up in a cold sweat again. This was becoming a regular occurrence for him. It was a dream he had been having since Caroline died, but over the last couple of weeks it had taken a nasty turn. He was dreaming about his late wife. They were young again and very much in love. Invariably the dream evolved into their wedding day and he could clearly see her walking up the aisle towards him. When he lifted the veil, however, it was his nanny, Jayne Mullins, under the white lace. Every time the dream turned into a nightmare and it was always the same. Jayne would start to laugh. It sounded like a wild witch's cackle. In his nightmare she had no teeth or the few she had were coal-black. He would turn around and scream for Caroline but she had changed into a ghost-like figure again and she was being sucked down the aisle by some irresistible force. He would try to run after her but his feet were stuck like glue to the tiled church floor. He could see her getting pulled away from him but he was never able to reach her. Then he would wake up sweating and panting.

"That sounds like it was a good dream!" a muffled voice from beside him whispered.

Raymond jumped. "Jesus, Jayne! I didn't realise you were here."

"Relax, the children are still sound asleep. I checked on them a few minutes ago," she lied. She had been giving the matter some thought of late and if Raymond Saunders had decided to sleep with her on a regular basis, he could damn well live with the consequences. Jayne sat up in the bed and kissed him on the cheek. "You know, we're going to have to tell them sooner or later."

"What would you have me tell them?"

"Well," Jayne thought about this for a moment, "we could say that you and I have become a good deal closer and while I'm not taking the place of their mother, we have become boyfriend and girlfriend."

Raymond tensed at the mere mention of Caroline. He had been having great difficulty with his plans to marry Jayne. She was a nice girl but the fact that he didn't love her was just too overwhelming to ignore.

"I'm not sure that they're ready for that kind of change just yet." He smiled weakly at Jayne.

"*They're* not ready or *you're* not ready," Jayne snapped as she threw her legs over the side of the bed. "Really, Raymond, you're sending me very mixed signals here. What exactly do you want?" Jayne lost the run of herself. She was always so good at controlling her damn temper around him, but not this morning.

She picked up the vase of white lilies that she had so carefully arranged some days before and hurtled them across the room in frustration.

"Hey, Jayne, what's got into you? Calm down."

"Calm down? Calm down? Is that all you can say? How can I relax when I have no idea what you have in mind, Raymond? One minute you're very happy to be very *friendly* with me and the next this abstract bullshit. You're blaming the children. You're hiding behind them because you don't want to move on. It's time, Raymond. It's time to move on." She picked up his clothes that lay on the sofa next to where she stood and threw them at him. "Move up and on!" she shouted.

She grabbed her dressing-gown and pulled it on, wrapping it around her naked body angrily. She had secretly planned to wake Raymond up with a gentle seduction. Those ideas were long gone now. As she flounced out the door the three Saunders children were running in.

"What happened?" Jasmine asked breathlessly. "We heard a big bang." Then she saw the flowers strewn on the floor in a puddle of water. "Oh dear, what's going on?"

"It was simply a little accident," Jayne answered lightly, and then she continued, "I was just waking up your father." She turned to Raymond again, her voice a few degrees cooler than when she talked to the children. "This is your wake-up call."

With schizophrenic ease she turned and smiled warmly at the children. In a friendly and excited tone she informed them, "It's house-moving day!"

Raymond looked at her in wonder. Was this even the same woman who had just screamed like a banshee at him? She was smiling at the children happily as if she hadn't a care in the world. He had to hand it to her, she was a bloody good actress. He tried to suppress his feelings of mistrust. Wasn't that a talent all women had?

He even remembered Caroline being capable of showing him one face and the children another. Didn't all women do whatever it took to protect their children? Raymond just didn't know.

* * *

Saskia had been sound asleep and then in one sudden movement she was sitting bolt upright in the bed, her eyes wide open.

"Oh God, we're moving house today!" she squealed.

She jumped out of bed and ran into the shower. As she lathered up, she looked at her tummy. There was no sign of a swelling or growing baby. That was a little odd for Saskia because usually the first sign that she was pregnant was the growing tummy. She began to rub her stomach in circular movements, making a lovely soapy design.

"Hello, Junior," she said to her belly. Sharing her news with her girls the previous night had somehow made the whole thing much more real. It was the first time she had spoken out loud to it. It felt good. Damn Nicolas Flattery. Well, it didn't matter anyway, Saskia decided. She was a woman of independent means and a damn good mother. She would bring up this baby herself and sod him!

Kelly and Lauren had already got Robin her breakfast.

"What's got into you two this morning?" Saskia asked her elder daughters suspiciously.

"Good morning, Mum," Kelly smiled. "We thought you could do with a rest."

"Yeah," Lauren laughed. "Kelly's been getting away with murder for the last few weeks because we all thought she was pregnant. It's time she began to pull her weight again!"

"How do you feel today?" Kelly asked her mother.

"Actually, I feel a lot better having told you two. I'm full of energy and raring to go!"

"Well, do take it easy. Today is going to be a tough day physically."

"What are you talking about, pet? The furniture removal men will do all the difficult stuff."

"Perhaps, but it will still be a crazy day – just mind yourself! Let me and Lauren do the tough stuff."

"Is Tiffany coming down to help today or has she sodded off to Dublin indefinitely?" Lauren asked.

"No, she's coming down with Max Condon. He's going to help out too," Saskia said.

"So they're an item now?" Kelly laughed.

"Yep, a match made in heaven. Or should I say a match made in Innishambles!" Lauren grinned.

"What are you talking about?" Kelly asked her younger sister.

"Oh, nothing. It's just a bit funny them getting together, what with her being the one moving out of Innishambles and him being the one to move in."

"Ah, about that," Saskia coughed nervously. "There's a chance that they won't be moving in."

"*What*?" the girls chorused.

"Well, your father heard, now it's not definite by any means –" Saskia stuttered.

"Mummy," Kelly spoke sternly, "spit it out!"

"Well, they want to develop the land around Innishambles. That may involve destroying the house."

"No way!" Lauren shouted. "They can't do that. This is a listed building."

"Who knows?" Saskia winced. "Look, it's not even

definite. Your father just heard rumours. We'll have to wait and see."

"How could anyone destroy this beautiful old house?" Kelly cried.

"I was born into this house. We should never have decided to sell it," Lauren snapped. "Shit, shit shit!"

"Shit, shit, shit," Robin imitated her sister.

"How many times have I said that the language in this house has to be cleaned up, on account of little ears?" Saskia gestured towards Robin as she glared at Lauren.

"Sorry," came the reply, then, "Do you want me to take Robin over to Cathy's house now?"

"Oh, Lauren, that would be very helpful. I'm not even dressed yet and the removal men will be here in about half an hour!"

"No problem," Lauren sighed. She knew that she couldn't take out her anger on her mother. Now that she knew about Nicolas being broke it put a whole new spin on the mother's actions. It wasn't Saskia's fault if she had to sell Innishambles. Lauren made a concerted effort to act positive. "Come on, little sis." She picked Robin up in her arms. "You lucky little devil, you're getting out of all the work. Oh, to be three again!"

Saskia downed her breakfast of a single slice of toast and a black coffee in one minute flat and then she shot back upstairs to throw on a pair of leggings and an old jumper.

"No point in getting all dolled up if I'm going to be up to my neck in dust and dirt all day," she sighed.

"Hi, Mum, I'm home," Tiffany yelled up the stairs as she and Max walked in the front door.

"And just in time too," Kelly shouted from the study, where she was packing personal files into a big box.

After introducing Max to Kelly, Tiffany went off in search of her mother.

"You look gorgeous," Tiffany laughed sarcastically when she saw her mother. "Where did you find those old things?" She nodded at Saskia's leggings.

"Hey, I'm dressed for work – unlike you, madam." Sas eyed up Tiffany's new clothes. "Where did they come from?"

Tiffany looked embarrassed. "Daddy gave me some money for clothes during the week. He said it was only because I was starting college and it was luck money."

"Well, that was very kind of him." Sas felt a stab of envy. It was obvious that Tiffany and her dad were getting very close. "How is Edwina?"

Tiffany's face clouded. "She's still a silly old cow!"

This made her mother feel better and she laughed. "Tiffany, you shouldn't speak about your grandmother like that!"

"Why not? You do!"

"That's beside the point." She winked at her daughter. "Now, we have a huge amount of work to do. Let's get started. I'm not sure how all our stuff is going to fit into Number 5, Ballymore Glen."

"Don't worry, Mum, we'll fit! In fact I think your timing is very good. Kelly is almost out of your hair and I'm in college for all of the academic year. You'll only have Lauren and Robin at home. There'll be plenty of room. Speaking of my younger sisters, where are they?"

"Lauren is dropping Robin over to Cathy Taylor's house for the day. Cathy is so much help – I don't know where I'd be without her." Saskia looked at her daughter and summoned all her inner strength. Out of all her children Tiffany would be the one to disapprove of her pregnancy. She would not be impressed with Saskia's apparently active and rather careless sex life.

"Tiffany, there is something I have to discuss with you –" Saskia braced herself but her daughter cut in.

"Oh, Mummy, there's something I have to discuss with you too. Max's dad, Arthur Condon, had a heart attack."

"What? Is he OK?"

"Max says that he will be. It happened last Tuesday. He's had an angiogram and they found one large block, so they gave him the angioplasty the day before yesterday. If everything goes well, he'll be taken out of Intensive Care today."

"Why the hell didn't you tell me on the phone? We've talked practically every day, for God's sake!" Saskia's tone was harsher than she intended.

"Sorry, I thought I would wait until I saw you face to face. I just thought it would be better to be told in person rather than over the phone."

"Well, you were wrong. You should have told me as soon as it happened. Damn it, you're talking about the man who has bought this house."

"There's more."

"What is it?"

"I'm afraid he had his heart attack in Wicklow County Council. They were telling him that there was little or no hope of getting this land converted from agricultural to development, and as for Innishambles, if anything happened to it –"

"Enough!" Saskia snapped. "You know what? It's not my problem. He has paid for the place. There's no backing out now and, what's more, I've paid for Ballymore Glen so we're moving and that's all there is to it!"

"God, Mum, you sound so mercenary!" Tiffany scolded. "You know, you're talking about a man who was at a party in our house just over a week ago!"

Saskia sighed. "I'm sorry if I sound a bit harsh. I guess I'm under a little pressure. I do hope he's going to be OK for his sake and his family's."

With that the doorbell rang. Dudley, Dexter, Woody and Wilma were fit to burst with excitement, there was so much commotion around the house.

"Mum, the furniture-removal men are here," Kelly yelled up the stairs. "They're going to start on the kitchen. Max has very kindly offered to help me take Polly and Mooner and the dogs over to the refuge. We'll be back in half an hour. OK?"

"That's fine, Kelly! Tell the men I'll be down in five minutes!" Saskia yelled from her room as she finished getting dressed. "See you later!"

"That was fast," Tiffany sniffed.

"What was?" her mother asked.

"Max has teamed up with my gorgeous older sister!"

"He's only helping out, Tiff. Don't start feeling jealous – men can sense that. It scares them!" She looked at her daughter's anxious eyes and then burst out laughing. "Oh, Tiffany, come here and give me a big hug. How was your first week at college and tell me more about you and Max Condon."

"Oh, Mum, he's lovely. He's so attentive and everybody loves him – everybody except my economics friends."

"Oh?"

"Well, he is lovely but Max doesn't have much ambition. He's a little – how can I put it? – *relaxed* about his future, if you know what I mean. But it's funny when we walk down the street you should see the looks we get. Everybody thinks he's a ride."

"You know, being a 'ride', as you so eloquently put it, isn't the be-all of everything," Saskia said.

"Yeah, I wish he had a little more ambition, but he doesn't. Anyway this week was a little crazy because of his dad."

"Are you sure he's going to be OK?"

"The doctors think so, but he's still very weak."

"Missus," a hard and husky accent spoke to them from outside Saskia's bedroom door.

"Oh, yes, er, hello," she jumped up to get to her door. When she swung it open, a huge man in blue jeans and an old Iron Maiden T-shirt greeted her.

"Hello," she smiled at him. "Welcome to Innishambles."

"Howaya?" he smiled back, revealing a broad bright smile and dancing eyes. "I'm Harry." He stuck out his hand.

"You're the man I spoke to on the phone – Harry as in *Harry's Removals.*"

His chest swelled with pride, happy that she had made the connection.

"That's me. We're millin' away in the kitchen now." His Wicklow accent was thick and friendly. "We were just wondering, is the fridge coming or going?"

Saskia felt an energy rush as she went downstairs and walked into her old kitchen with Harry. All of her kitchen furniture was gone and loaded up into the back of Harry's van already.

"The fridge stays, Harry. It definitely stays – right here."

* * *

"Welcome to the neighbourhood! I'm Bob Bolton, damn glad to meet you!" Bob Bolton thrust his hand and a tin of Budweiser out towards Raymond Saunders.

"Hi, Bob, I'm Raymond Saunders." He took the beer. "Cheers."

"We live in Number 1, just arrived the day before yesterday. I figure you guys have just moved in today?"

Raymond laughed. "Just moved in? The furniture hasn't even arrived yet. We loaded everything up in Dublin and saw the truck off. Then we did one last lap around the house to check we hadn't forgotten anything. Anyway, it had a good half hour lead on us and we've still managed to beat it here."

"Hell, you haven't got any furniture? Why don't y'all come to me and Cindy for a barbeque this evening?"

"Ah, Bob, that's very kind of you but –"

"Hey, no buts. The only butts I like come in girl jeans!" He winked at Raymond. "We'll see you guys around seven. Bring the kids!" Bob walked down the driveway again as if the matter had been resolved perfectly.

"Eh, thanks," Raymond shouted after him. He realised that to argue would be futile and, anyway, they had no food so the timing was excellent. They would also get a chance to meet some of their new neighbours. "See you around seven."

"Who was that?" Jayne came up behind Raymond. All signs of the fiery temper of that morning were gone.

"Bob Bolton. He lives in Number 1. We've been invited

down to his place for a barbeque this evening at seven o clock."

"Wow, that's very kind of him. But where will we get a baby-sitter at this short notice?"

Raymond swung around to look at her. "It's with the kids, Jayne. You hardly think that I would leave them alone on the first day in a new house?"

"Sorry," Jayne sniffed.

Raymond was now sure of it. Their relationship was changing. It was clearly deteriorating since they had become intimate.

* * *

"Here we are!" Saskia turned the key in the front door of number 5 and she let Kelly, Tiffany, Lauren and Max walk in before her.

"It is lovely," Kelly enthused.

"It's so bright," Lauren admitted. "And these carpets! How the hell are we going to keep cream-coloured carpets clean with four dogs?"

Tiffany was first to reach the kitchen. "I love this place. The Aga is huge! And so clean!"

Saskia heaved a sigh of relief as she listened to her girls chattering from different rooms in the house. Max was a little more laid back – he just wandered around, smiling occasionally, and then walked out the back of the house to have a cigarette. The girls sounded very upbeat and positive. Maybe, just maybe, she had been right to downsize from Innishambles to this.

Harry arrived just behind them. He let out a low whistle.

"Nice gaf," he said appreciatively. "OK, lads, let's ship the gear in."

Then the havoc commenced. Saskia had not realised how much furniture she had. The dining-room was considerably smaller than her old one and so her huge dining-table was dismantled and left in bits lying on the floor. The massive loungers from her Innishambles drawing-room dwarfed her new room, but the biggest heartbreak for her was her kitchen sofa. This was a fixture she had had since she got married. Some people might have thought it strange to keep a sofa in the kitchen but for Saskia it was 'a must'. It was where she had held and nursed all her babies. It was where the children made up beds when they were sick. It was where Saskia and Richard had often downed a bottle of wine or three together and it wasn't going to fit in her new state-of-the-art traditional kitchen. It wasn't going to fit in her new life. She was gutted.

"Where will I put it so?" Harry asked, oblivious to her sadness.

"I don't know," Saskia replied helplessly. "Where will it fit?"

"It's gonna have to be the garage until you get a little sorted out, Missus," Harry suggested.

"No! I can't do that. There has to be somewhere in the house to put it," Saskia said, panicking.

"Well," Harry rubbed his chin speculatively, "you could put it in the hall, but it would look a little out of place. It's kinda of knackered, if you don't mind me saying, and the hall is gorgeous and new and all."

"The hall it is!" Saskia said, relieved that it could at least be kept in the house. "Anywhere but the garage!"

Bob Bolton pushed the front door open and smiled at Saskia.

"Hi there, I'm Bob Bolton, damn glad to meet you. Me and Cindy live in Number 1!"

"Oh, hi, Bob. I'm Saskia Dalton."

"Hi, Saskia. Say, would you guys like to come to a barbeque in my place tonight around seven o'clock? The Saunders are coming too." He smiled broadly. "It's a kind of a get-to-know-your-neighbours thing!"

"Gosh, that's very nice of you, Bob, but I have a big family."

He dismissed that with a wave of his huge hand. "Cindy comes from a family of fourteen. Bring them all. I have enough food to feed the state of Texas!"

"Oh, OK then."

"Great, see you around seven?"

"Around seven," Saskia nodded and he was gone.

CHAPTER 32

It was a warm, balmy evening, the kind that made you feel good to be alive, Saskia reflected.

Kelly seemed to pick up on her thoughts.

"Mum, you know this place really is absolutely gorgeous." She smiled over at her mother. They had both called it a day and were enjoying aperitifs out on the large, sun-drenched patio to the rear of their new house in Ballymore Glen. Tiffany and Lauren were still changing.

Saskia looked at Kelly. "It is lovely here, but do you prefer it to Innishambles?"

"That's a tough call. It's so nice having an ultra-modern kitchen and a totally reliable cooker and fridge."

"Come on, the old Aga up in Innishambles may have been a little neurotic but the fridge never gave up," Saskia argued.

Kelly laughed. "No, it was just so bloody loud. Don't you remember it hummed all the time?"

Saskia played with a strand of her hair as she sat in the fading heat of the setting sun. "It's funny," she sighed, "I miss that hum."

Kelly slapped her forehead in despair. Max came out to join them.

"Max, thank you so much for all your help this afternoon," said Saskia. "You really were an asset."

"No problem, Saskia. I do have a favour to ask, however."

"Sure, what is it?"

"Would it be OK if I stayed here tonight – on a sofa or something? It's just that if I stay for the barbeque, I won't have any way of getting back to Dublin."

Saskia looked concerned for a brief moment but then she smiled at the young man. "You won't try to take advantage of my daughter, will you?"

"Scout's honour!" He gave her one of his innocent smiles as he raised three fingers to his eye in a scout's salute.

"OK, you're on the sofa in the front reception hall, where I can check up on you any minute of the night."

Tiffany and Lauren were upstairs enjoying the huge mirror and terrific lighting in their new family bathroom. Tiffany's good humour was positively tangible to Lauren. She looked at her older sister.

"So, you and Max are an item then?"

"Yes, at last," she glanced sideways at Lauren as she applied her mascara and managed a quick wink, "and I have you to thank for it, little sis."

"Well, you really did it yourself. It's actually amazing how easy it was in the end, isn't it?"

"Hey, it wasn't that easy. I put a lot of charm, wit and personality into snagging that man!" She giggled. "And to be honest I'm still doing what Francesca said. You know, treating him mean and staying cool."

"Well, by the look on his face today I think you can warm up a little, so to speak," Lauren said.

"How do you know?"

"God, Tiffany, he can't take his eyes off you. He follows you around the place like a love-sick puppy."

"Really?"

"Can't you see it?"

Tiffany laughed, "I'm too busy being cool and ignoring him."

Lauren gently elbowed her sister. "Relax the chill factor. You have him. He's putty in your hands now, Tiffany."

"Yeah, and as thick as putty too," she mumbled under her breath.

"What did you just say?"

"Nothing."

"Yes, you did say something. I heard you!" Lauren pushed her sister gently but Tiffany was an expert at changing the subject when she wanted to.

"Well, actually I was thinking about Dad. You know he really has changed, Lauren. You were right. Do you remember the other day you were saying you'd like to see Mum and Dad back together? Well I think you might be right."

Lauren stopped brushing her hair. Memories of the conversation she had overheard between James Harrington and her father came rushing back. "No, I wasn't. Mum and Dad should never get back together again. *You* were right. He is still a shit."

"How can you say that? Lauren, you were the one that had copped onto Nicolas's and Mum's split long before the rest of us and you're the one clued in enough to see that there's a chance of Mum and Dad patching things up," Tiffany argued.

Lauren swung around on her sister. "Look, I was wrong, very wrong. Dad is still the same old slime that he always was. I think I would be happy if I never saw him again."

"What is going on here?" Saskia stood at the bathroom door and stared at her two girls. They looked as guilty as sin.

"Lauren, what's wrong? Why are you so furious with your father? Has he done something to you?"

Lauren was horrified that her mum had overheard her outburst.

"Would you both just leave me alone!" she screamed as she rushed out the door past Saskia.

"Do you have any idea what that was about?" Sas looked at Tiff.

"Search me."

Saskia nodded, knowing that Tiffany was telling the truth. "OK, she'll tell us when she's ready." A brief smile touched her lips but inside she vowed to get to the bottom of her daughter's outburst. Saskia would not be taken for a fool again, not by Richard Dalton or any man.

Finally Tiffany and Lauren arrived down to the others. Nobody made any reference to the incident upstairs. Max let out a low soft whistle, "Wow, you girls look fantastic!"

Tiffany's skin was still quite brown from a summer helping out in the refuge and she wore a light slip dress. It was cerise pink with shots of purple going through it. The strappy sandals were the same colour pink.

"My God, do you get vertigo in those?" Kelly asked when she saw the shoes.

Tiffany giggled nervously.

"More new clothes?" Saskia asked. Tiffany nodded guiltily.

"Yeah, suddenly I think I want to go to college just so Dad can buy me a new wardrobe of clothes," Lauren snorted.

Then the doorbell rang.

"I'll get it," Kelly jumped to her feet, knowing it was going to be Barney.

"Hi, honey. How was your day?" He gave her a kiss and a hug.

"Fine. Amazingly, we did survive without you," she laughed. "Max, Tiffany's new boyfriend, helped us out, but Harry and his mates did most of the heavy work." She gave him another kiss and then added, "But I did miss you!"

"I'm sorry. I had to go to Carlow but at least now I can tell you why."

"Why?" Kelly looked suspicious. She had been utterly fed up with Barney when he announced that he had to go back to his old hometown on the day of the house move.

"This is why!" Flamboyantly, Barney pulled out a small box from his trouser pocket. It was covered in a faded navy velvet material and, even to Kelly's untrained eye, it was a small jewellery box.

"What's this?" she asked shyly.

Barney still held it lovingly. "Well, as you know my mum died when I was very young, but I vaguely remember being told that she had left me her engagement ring. Naturally, aged five, I didn't give it much thought. In fact I only remembered when Lauren teased me about how I was going to afford to buy you a ring now that the refuge is closing."

He handed the box to Kelly.

"Anyway, I went back to Mary Stephenson, the lady who owns the jewellery shop in Carlow, the one that Mum used to frequent. The shop is as old as the hills and to be honest so is she now. In fact, I was half-expecting her to be dead and buried at this stage. Anyway, she remembered me clearly. She said I hadn't changed a bit which isn't very flattering, considering I haven't seen her in over twenty years!" Barney's eyes were bright with excitement. "I swear, Kelly, it was like a time warp! I asked her did she have anything belonging to my mother in storage. Jesus, it was amazing! She just nodded and smiled and told me that she knew I'd be back for it one day or another. She went off to the back storeroom and came back with this!"

Kelly had been listening to his story and holding the box securely. Now she looked down at the little lid and gingerly opened it, terrified that she could somehow damage the contents. Inside she saw the most exquisite antique diamond solitaire.

"Ohmigod, Barney, this is beautiful!" It twinkled at her magnificently.

Barney took the box back from her and yanked out the ring. He dropped down on one knee at the front door of number 5, Ballymore Glen and proposed – again.

"Kelly Dalton, will you do me the great honour of being my wife?"

He slipped the large stone onto her long thin finger and it fitted perfectly. Kelly was laughing but tears of happiness rolled down her face.

"Yes, Barney, yes, yes, yes I will marry you."

He got up from his knee and bear-hugged her. "It's

yours, Mrs Armstrong." He smiled at her, admiring her bejewelled hand. "Happy engagement!"

They went in to the others and everybody ooed and ahhed at Kelly's newest acquisition.

"Hey, you could flog that and get another few months for the refuge!" Lauren suggested.

"No way, that was my mother's and her mother's before that. It doesn't leave the family," Barney explained as they all headed down the lane to number one, Ballymore Glen. It was time for Bob Bolton's barbeque.

It was still warm and fairly bright when they were strolling down the road. The smell of barbequed meat began to waft towards them as they approached the Bolton's house.

Lisa Keyes was walking up to them.

"Hi folks," she smiled. Then she handed Saskia a bottle wrapped in gold paper. "This is just a small house-warmer," she explained. It was obviously a bottle of champagne.

"Oh, Lisa. How thoughtful of you, thank you!" Saskia gave the girl a tight hug.

"Look, we're just popping into the Boltons' house here for something to eat. Why don't you stick your head in to say hello?"

"Gosh, I don't want to intrude." Lisa looked uncertain.

"Well, if it looks like it's going to be a crashing bore, you can make your excuses," Saskia reasoned.

"Well, I guess it would be nice to meet some new neighbours. I'm trying to meet some new kids so I can invite them to Guy's birthday. He doesn't know many children yet. That reminds me, can Robin come? She's his best friend."

"I'm sure Robin would love to come!" Saskia smiled. "She's in Cathy Taylor's house this evening. She's staying there for the night because number five is still a little upside down." She rang the Boltons' doorbell.

Bob Bolton walked around the house from the side.

"Welcome, everybody!" He beamed. He was wearing a chef's hat and a plastic apron that said *'Texans Barbeque Bigger'* and he was holding yet another tin of Bud. "Come this way, don't stand on ceremony. Come on," he laughed. "The beef's this way!"

Introductions were done and Bob would not hear of Lisa leaving.

"Heck, if you mind the Parker kids, you're practically a resident in Ballymore!" Bob had already met Dave Parker (in O'Reilly's pub). It was rapidly becoming clear that Bob already knew most of the village of Ballymore! He had actually tried to convince Dave to bring his family to the barbeque but the Parkers were having some quiet, family time. Bob beamed at his guests. "OK, who's for a beer? Barney, as of now, you're officially in charge of the bar – gotit?"

"Gotit!" Barney mimicked him good-naturedly.

Cindy arrived after everybody had got their drinks and was settled comfortably. Saskia, who hadn't met her before, couldn't believe that anybody could be so thin and still have the capacity to walk.

"My God, that woman is skin and bone," she whispered to Kelly.

"Yeah, Lauren warned me. She must eat nothing! Let's watch her," Kelly giggled mischievously.

The drink began to flow and the food mountains began to stack up. Bob, true to his word, cooked about twenty steaks and the same amount of burgers. The doorbell rang again.

"That'll be the Saunders," Bob guessed correctly.

Raymond arrived in, looking not dissimilar to Pierce Brosnan in a pair of cream chinos and a cream jumper. He was thin and tall and his dark brown hair was cut short, exaggerating his high cheekbones and slightly sad eyes.

Max, who had been helping Barney out quite proficiently at the bar, was the first to notice his dinner companion. Jayne wore a tight aquamarine dress. It was obvious that she was wearing nothing underneath.

"Hello," he sidled up beside her, "and what can I get you?"

Jayne, who mistook him for bar staff, gave him a cold stare. "Double gin and tonic and make it fast!"

Jasmine, Edward and Francis arrived in behind their dad and Jayne. They were a little shy but when they saw the food they lost all timidity and lunged at it with great gusto.

"You'll have to excuse my kids," Raymond smiled. "They've been swimming all day and naturally enough now they're starving. I'm afraid we have no food in the house yet so, outside of a few sweets, this is the first thing they've eaten since we got here."

"Heck, we have too much food. You must take loads home with you," Cindy gushed. Saskia noticed to her dismay that Cindy was eating with the same amount of enthusiasm as the children.

"Have you noticed?" she whispered to her eldest daughter. "Cindy does eat. How does she stay so thin?"

"We'll get her secret out of her later!" Kelly smirked.

"Has your furniture arrived yet, Raymond?" Bob asked.

"Yep, just about!" Raymond replied as he took a welcome gulp of cold beer.

Jayne piped up. "It will take us ages to sort it all out, however. Won't it, pet?" She stroked Raymond's forearm but he pulled it away, affording her only the briefest of grins.

Jayne was getting a little impatient. She waited long enough. Now the gloves were off. She had given him all the grieving time and space he needed. She had waited. He was the one who had started into this relationship and he could bloody well accept its responsibilities too. They were lovers – she wasn't going to become his mistress – no way. If he wanted the candy, he could pay the price. Now in Ballymore, Jayne was going to make sure that everyone knew she was a hell of a lot more than his nanny!

* * *

Tiffany Dalton felt happier than she had in years. She knew that she looked wonderful. It was a glorious summer night. Her college friends seemed fantastic and she was getting on terrifically well with her dad regardless of Lauren's delusional misgivings.

She had moved away from the barbeque area just to enjoy the sights and the sounds of the late summer air. The Boltons' swimming-pool looked divine. It was definitely the biggest in the complex. The patio lights danced on the water's surface and the underwater lights made it look bluer than the Caribbean.

"Hello, delicious!" Max came up behind her. "It is rather gorgeous here, isn't it?"

"This is heaven, Max," Tiffany agreed.

"Say, fancy a midnight skinny-dip?" He grinned at her.

Tiffany's head was light from the champagne. (Lisa's

house-warmer present to Saskia had quickly been converted into a house-warmer for the Boltons!) She felt totally relaxed and the night was certainly made for romance so she was open to the possibility.

"How could we go for a swim?" she asked. "Everybody is watching."

Still standing behind her, Max began to hug her and nibble at her ear, "I couldn't help overhearing that Raymond Saunders has a swimming-pool too. We could christen that one for him while he's down here. What do you think?"

"I think you're a brat," she laughed, "but an adorable one!"

Max took her hand and gently walked her around the side of the Bolton's house. Nobody even noticed their departure.

"My God, what if we're caught?" Tiffany giggled nervously as they approached the pool of number six.

"How could we possibly get caught? Everybody is down in Boltons' having a '*damn good time*'." He tried and failed miserably to copy Bob's Texan accent. "Now let me see what you have on under this exquisite dress." He began to pull it up and over Tiffany's head. When he had taken it off, she stood in front of him, wearing only a thong. She looked shy and uncertain of herself. Tiffany had already privately decided that she wanted to be with Max and what Lauren said only convinced her even more. He was crazy about her and she was crazy about him. It was the right thing to do.

"I didn't think you were wearing a bra," he laughed. "You are quite perfect, delicious!" Then he whipped off his own clothes in a flash. Utterly comfortable in his own nakedness he grabbed her hand and pulled her into the pool with him.

"OK, let's have some equine love!" He laughed as he splashed her.

"What?" She didn't understand.

Max dived deep under the water and swam towards her.

He grabbed her feet with his hands.

"Max," she squealed.

He moved his hands up to her knees.

"Max," she giggled.

He grabbed the two cheeks of her bottom with his two hands.

"Oh, yes, Max," she groaned

He popped his head up and out of the water, still holding her bum,

"You know, delicious, you have the most adorable body." As he said it, he coaxed her thong off with his feet.

"You're not so bad yourself."

"I have a little something for you," he said as he kissed her mouth and face.

Tiffany loved the feeling of the warm water on her body. She had never swum naked before and the freedom was a real turn-on.

"We're all slippery!" she giggled.

"Sure," he purred as his hands began to work on her body, "haven't you heard the expression – slippery when wet?"

"Oh, I didn't realise that this was what they were talking about!"

"Well, seeing as we're on the *slippery* subject – can I slip this in?" he asked as he kissed her. Tiffany could feel the hard penis he was referring to. It pressed up against her groin, anxiously looking for somewhere more comfortable.

Tiffany giggled again, utterly enjoying the sensation.

"'K," she said through kisses and, in one fluid movement, Max pushed his manhood up and inside her.

He groaned loudly. "God, you feel good! You're such a tight little bitch," he teased.

Gently he pulled her legs up and wrapped them around his own body.

"I like this water thing – you can carry me," Tiffany smiled as he moved inside her.

"Yes, it does allow for ease of access," he murmured.

Tiffany felt a cold shiver go down her spine. It was obvious that Max had done the swimming-pool-love-scene before.

"I think I'm going to come, delicious. Are you ready?"

Why did he have to call her that all the bloody time? she thought, irritated. She would have it out with him later.

"Yes, yes," she lied – she no more felt like coming!

"Ahhh," Max made some guttural sound that indicated to Tiffany that he had well and truly come.

Oh well, she thought, I can't expect him to be gorgeous and a wonderful lover. This made her giggle to herself.

"What are you laughing at?" Max asked as they were climbing out of the pool.

"Oh, nothing," she smiled.

Thankfully the Saunders children had thrown their towels on the ground next to the pool earlier that day so Tiffany and Max were able to dry off with them.

Then Tiffany remembered, "Hey, when we were jumping into the pool, you said something about 'equine love'. What were you talking about?"

He looked at her, slightly confused. "Equine love? You know, bonking in the pool!"

"Max," she looked at him patiently, "equine is horses. Aquatic is water. This would be aquatic love."

He gave her one of his lopsided grins. "Oh, OK."

As she pulled her slip-dress over her head, she looked at her boyfriend with a slight resignation. Yes, he looked like a Greek god, but the *Brain of Britain* he wasn't.

Back at the barbeque, Lisa Keyes had been racking her brains as to why she knew Jayne Mullins' face. Then finally it clicked. She was standing next to Barney and Kelly when her memory kicked in.

"At last, I remember. It was Montessori school," she said aloud.

Barney and Kelly looked at Lisa.

"What do you remember?" Kelly asked, still fiddling with her new engagement ring.

Lisa walked up to Jayne.

"Now I know you," she said rather aggressively. "You're not Jayne Mullins, you're Jayne Griffin. It's the hair that threw me. You used to be a brunette."

Jayne's face turned white with horror. "I don't know you. I don't know what you're talking about."

"Yes, you do. We started Montessori training together in Limerick. Back then your name was Jayne Mullins but you got married to the guy who ran the school, Mr Griffin, and you quit school."

Raymond looked at Jayne in raw shock. "Jayne, what is she talking about?"

461

"I have no idea. I've never seen this girl in my life before," Jayne spluttered.

"Well, she certainly seems to know you! At a guess I'd say you're both of an age," Raymond said coolly. Jayne was too flustered for it to be lies.

"Yes, it's all clear as day now," Lisa continued. "There was hell to pay at the time because Mr Griffin was engaged to be married. You nearly destroyed the girl *he* was engaged to. My God, you're Raymond Saunders' nanny now? You never even qualified! You just took off to get married!" And then Lisa remembered why. "Jayne Griffin! You were pregnant."

Raymond glared at her. "Is this true, Jayne?"

Bob Bolton, who had gone into the house to get more beer, came back out. "Is everything OK?" he asked Lauren who was standing next to the door watching the situation develop.

"Well, Bob, it appears that Raymond's rather affectionate nanny, in other words, his girlfriend, is married. She may even have a kid!"

Then Lauren started to whisper, "I wouldn't mind but she was only saying to Kelly and me about ten minutes ago that she and Raymond were getting married themselves soon."

"And she's married already? What's the big deal? Cindy was married when I first met her."

"Ah, but you're in Ballymore now, Bob!" Lauren winked at him as she lightened his load by one Budweiser.

Jayne had been vehemently denying Lisa's claims and pleading with Raymond to take her home when the doorbell started to shrill incessantly.

"Gawd, somebody's in a hurry to be let in," Cindy drawled as she minced her way through the house to the front door.

Cathy Taylor rushed past her as soon as Cindy opened the door.

"Where's Saskia?" the old woman asked breathlessly.

"Out the back," Cindy said as she pointed the way. "Hey, are you OK?" But Cathy was gone off in search of Sas.

"I just met Tiffany in the lane," Cathy gasped breathlessly. "She told me you were here. It's Robin! Saskia! She's gone!"

Saskia jumped to her feet.

"What do you mean 'she's gone'? Where is she gone? What's happened?" Saskia looked at her watch: it was one o'clock in the morning.

"It was about half an hour ago. I was just going to bed and I stuck my head in, to check on her. Her bed was empty. Saskia, I've searched my house high and low – inside and out but when there was no sign of her I thought I'd better get over to you to see if she came back to your new house. I haven't been up to number five yet, I met Tiffany coming down the lane and she told me you were in here." Briefly Cathy nodded at Cindy Bolton.

Saskia couldn't take it in. "My God, Cathy, what could have got into her? She loves your house and she's never done anything like this before!"

"I put her to bed at eight o'clock and she was happy and sleepy. She was asleep ten minutes later. I know because I checked."

"Christ, where do we start?" Saskia couldn't seem to

function, such was her shock and horror. "This has to be a mistake – did you check under the bed?" She began to wring her hands – something she always did when she didn't know where to begin with a problem. She was heading for a massive panic attack when thankfully Barney took control. Max and Tiffany had arrived back on Cathy Taylor's heels. Barney spoke.

"OK. Everybody, calm down. Let's figure this out in an orderly way."

He turned his attention to Cathy. He put his hands on her shoulders and looked straight into her eyes. "So, you're certain that she's not in or around your house and you haven't yet checked anywhere else. Is that correct, Cathy?"

"Yes, Barney, I searched high and low in my little cottage. It's not too big as you know but she's not there. Frank is still up there in case she does come back but I thought it better to get to Saskia as quickly as possible. Plus I hoped she might have made her way back to you." Cathy's voice was trembling. "*A grà*, I'm so so sorry. I don't know how this could have happened. She seemed so happy. I'm to blame –"

Barney cut her off. "Nobody is to blame, Cathy. You're like a grandmother to that child. Now don't get upset – I need straight thinkers! Sas, did she know that you were house-moving today?"

"Well, yes, of course. I had explained all of it to her but she's only just turned three, Barney. She's too small to fully comprehend."

"That's what I'm worried about. We have to split up. Saskia and Lauren, you head over to Innishambles. Maybe she went there. Max and Tiffany, if you guys can go up to number five – she might try to make her way home. Cathy, you should go back to your house in case she turns up there again."

"Well, don't forget Frank is still up there. God love him, he's praying as we speak for her safe return."

Saskia began to cry. "My baby, where's my baby?"

"Lauren, take your mum. Do you still have keys for Innishambles?"

Saskia nodded. "They're at home – I mean in number five – up the road."

"Fine, go home and get them and then head up to Innishambles. Cathy, if Frank has your house covered, perhaps you could go up to the refuge. She could go there. Who knows?"

"Can I help?" Lisa asked.

Barney shrugged. "Start looking everywhere."

"What are we going to do?" Kelly asked her fiancé.

"I need to get Owl, you need to get Polly. On horseback we'll cover more land."

"But Polly and Mooner are both up in the refuge now. It would be faster to take both of them out rather than you heading back to Peartree Cottage," Kelly argued, "and we could bring Cathy up there at the same time."

"Good thinking," Barney agreed. "Smart girl!" he whispered.

Raymond stepped forward. "Can I do anything?" he asked sombrely.

Barney looked at the man. "Have you drunk much?"

"I'm sober," he said.

"Fine, get in your car and drive around the neighbourhood. Every little helps."

Raymond turned to Jayne. "Can you please take the children home and put them to bed?"

"Raymond, about what that girl said –" Jayne stuttered but he put his hand up to stop her.

"Not now. We'll talk in the morning." He turned on his heel and walked away from her.

CHAPTER 33

"OK, this is all just some bad dream and I'm going to wake up in a moment," Saskia cried as she turned the key in the front door of Innishambles. "God, I said goodbye to this house forever just a few hours ago. It just shows you. Nothing in life is a certainty." She was babbling, but Lauren let her. It was probably good for her.

Saskia ran into the house. It was dark and it smelt different already. It was empty of furniture and so her voice rang through the still air. "*Robin!*" she cried out. Then she turned to Lauren. "You try upstairs, and I'll go around the downstairs and out the back."

The young girl took the stairs two at a time and bounded into Robin's room. Nothing. Without the benefit of furniture, the room looked much larger but much more lonely. "Robin?" Lauren whispered. Saskia was out the back around the stables and through her dear old walled garden. "Robin?" she called. "Robin, where are you, sweetheart?" but there was no response.

"She's not here, is she?" Lauren asked her mother when they met up again.

"I don't think so. Oh, Lauren, she's so small. Where could she be? It's the middle of the night. You don't think she's been kidnapped, do you?"

Suddenly Lauren thought of her father. "Shit, Mum, you don't think that it was Dad, by any chance?"

Saskia swung around. "Never! Your father may be a lot of things but a kidnapper is not one of them."

Lauren nodded in agreement. Then Saskia continued, "But he is her father. He has a right to know."

Instantly Lauren regretted mentioning him. "Mum, it's a Saturday night. God knows where he is! Let's tell him about it when it's all over." In truth, she was terrified of where her father really might be and wanted to protect her mother from even more pain.

"He'll go crazy with worry," Saskia fretted. She looked at her watch, "My God, it's two o'clock in the morning. Where can she be, Lauren? I have to phone Richard."

"OK, let me phone Dad," Lauren suggested, knowing that her father would probably be chatting up some floozy at this time of night. The least she could do was to keep her mother away from that!

"Thanks, pet, the more help we have the better."

Lauren went into the study in order to get out of her mother's earshot. The room was empty of furniture and paintings. It looked very lonely. The only item remaining was the phone, which sat on the floor. Reluctantly she dialled the digits of her father's mobile phone. It almost rang out but just as Lauren was about to give up it was answered – by a girl.

"Hello." She could hardly be heard over the loud music in the background. Richard, or at least Richard's phone was in a nightclub.

"Hello," Lauren said. "Can I speak to Richard Dalton, please? He's the owner of this phone."

The girl on the other end of the phone line laughed, "Oooo!" she said in mock fear. "Here, honey, this must be your phone."

Lauren could hear their conversation mixed with the background music.

"Where did you get that?" Richard was laughing. "Are you rooting through my clothes, Sunshine? Relax, there'll be plenty of time for that later!" He took the phone and spoke. "Hello, Richard here, who's phoning me at this hour of the morning?"

"Dad, it's Lauren. Are you drunk?"

"Lauren! What a question! Mind you, it is two o'clock on a Saturday night so if I was a tiny bit under the influence, would it be so awful?" He laughed, "And anyway, why in God's name are you ringing me at this hour?"

"Dad, it's Robin. She's gone." Her tone was cold with hostility; her father was as much of a wild boy as ever.

"Gone? Gone where? Whersh your mother?"

This time she sighed. There was no point in trying to talk to him. He was slurring his words and quite obviously fairly well on.

"I'm in Innishambles with Mum. Robin was meant to be spending the night with Cathy Taylor but she just disappeared out of her bed. Look, forget it, Dad. You're obviously pissed. Call me when you sober up tomorrow. We'll find her. Go back to your partying." Lauren hung up in disgust and went in search of her mother.

"Well, what did he say?" Saskia asked hopefully. She really wanted his support right now.

469

"I'm afraid that Dad is over the limit so he can't drive, Mum. We're on our own." Lauren didn't have the courage to meet her mother's gaze and so she studied her shoes.

"Lauren?"

"Come on, let's keep looking."

"Honey, first look at me. What's wrong?"

She burst out crying. "Oh, Mum, I'm sorry! I was really hoping that you and Dad were going to get back together again but now I realise he's as much of a bastard as he ever was!"

Saskia was startled. "What are you talking about? What did he just say? Did he just do something to hurt you?"

"No, it wasn't just now. It was at Kelly's party. I overheard him and James Harrington. They were talking and laughing about shagging and swapping girls and –" she fell into her mother's arms, "it was awful!"

Saskia felt the hairs on the back of her neck stand up. The absolute bastard! How could she have possibly thought that he was capable of change? Once a shit, always a shit. Richard had stooped even lower, however. To ruin Saskia's own life was one thing but to be so careless as to talk about his exploits within earshot of his teenage daughter – so help me I'll kill him, she thought furiously.

Barney opened up the Refuge and tore around the clinic, the tack room, the hay barn and the kennels. He checked everywhere inside and out calling Robin's name. Kelly saddled up her two horses. Even though it had been well locked up, Cathy went around the large manor checking every room and switching on all the lights in the hope that Robin might see them and find her way to the house.

Kelly gave her two horses a sugar lump each. "Well, Polly and Mooner, have I got some work for you! You're going out and you're going to have the ride of your lives tonight. We have to cover every inch of Innishambles, the refuge land and the Taylors' place as quickly as possible."

Barney rushed into the stables.

"Any luck?" Kelly asked hopefully.

Barney shook his head. "No, she's definitely not in the house or in the refuge. I didn't think she would be, to be honest. It was very well locked up. Cathy can keep an eye on this place while we're out."

They mounted the two big horses and galloped off into the darkness. The animals snorted with excitement. Cathy watched them from an upstairs window in the manor. My God, she thought in horror, those huge horses are going too fast. If they stumble upon her without seeing her, they'll trample her to death. She banged on the window but Kelly and Barney were out of earshot.

Tiffany was pacing the floor of number five.

"I don't want to stay here. I wish there was some more we could do!" The four dogs, who had been collected from the refuge earlier, walked up and down with her.

"I'm sure I could find a way to amuse you if you like." Max tried to embrace her.

"Shag off! Is sex all you ever think of?"

He looked at her wickedly. "Yep," he grinned. "And anyway you weren't complaining earlier, delicious!"

Finally she exploded. *"Will you stop calling me that?"*

"What?" He looked wounded.

"Delicious! I'm not delicious. I'm Tiffany. Got it? My name is Tiffany, not 'Delicious'."

"OK, OK," he grumbled from under his platinum-blond fringe. "Christ, there's no need to get so sketchy!" He stretched luxuriantly and took out his box of Marlborough Lights.

"Tetchy, Max. The word is tetchy not sketchy. Sketchy is something you do with a pencil and paper. Tetchy is what you get when somebody is pissing you off no end." She glared at him. "And please don't light up in here."

"Christ, delicious, I know you're upset about your little sister but don't worry. She'll come home. This is a safe neighbourhood. Just relax a little, would you?"

Tiffany sighed and looked at Max. He was probably right. She was just uptight because there she was bonking in some neighbour's pool and her baby sister had disappeared into the night.

She stroked Max's exquisitely sculptured jawline. It wasn't his fault if he was a little confused by English vocabulary!

"I'm sorry. You're right. Go on. Have your cigarette outside. I'll search this house from top to toe again."

He grinned at her. "That's more like it." He kissed her deeply. "Any chance of a quick shag before I light up?"

"Get out!"

Lisa Keyes scoured the entire main street of Ballymore but there was no sign of little Robin. Raymond Saunders flashed his car lights as he drove towards her. He pulled the car over to her and zapped down his electric window.

"Any luck?" he asked.

"I'm afraid not. What about you?"

"Well, I'm not really sure where I'm going. That's the problem."

"Hey, I've covered all I can on foot. Why don't I guide you? I know the local countryside really well."

"That would be terrific," he said as he reached over to open his passenger door.

Lisa ran around the front of the car and hopped in. She was fit and nimble. Then she turned to look at Raymond. "Thanks," she smiled. Raymond caught his breath. She was so similar to his late wife in looks, it was incredible.

Lisa saw the shadow cross his face. "Is something wrong?"

"No, no, not at all," Raymond lied as he turned his attention to the night road and started up the ignition.

"Good, because you look like you've just seen a ghost! OK, let's try the Rathdeen road first."

And they drove off into the night.

* * *

When the front door of Innishambles opened, Saskia hoped against hope that it would be Robin.

"Nicolas! What the hell are you doing here?"

His tall broad shoulders almost filled the door frame. He was wearing a light brown linen suit that was badly crumpled. The white linen shirt underneath highlighted his newly acquired sun tan. He was browner than she expected him to be and his hair had lightened up in the Californian sun. It had grown long again. Damn, he looked bloody good.

"I came as soon as I heard." He dropped the canvas holdall he had been carrying.

"How the hell could you have heard? You live in LA! And anyway, we don't need your help here. We can manage perfectly well on our own."

He tried to approach her but she backed away. "Saskia, I've literally just got back from the States. I've been travelling for almost twenty-four hours now – thanks to bloody plane delays and missed connections! Anyway, I arrived up to the manor five minutes ago."

That explained the crumpled suit and the unshaved look, she thought. He continued, "That's where I met Cathy. I thought the house would be locked up and in darkness but it was lit up like a Christmas tree. Every light is on. Saskia, she's just told me what happened – about Robin."

"Yes, well, you can get on the next plane back to your beautiful America and bloody LA. We can manage very well without you here, thank you very much," but she had begun to cry.

"Saskia," he tried again, "I love you. I've never stopped loving you. We've had the most almighty cock-up in communications –"

As he spoke the sound of a helicopter could be heard overhead.

"Did somebody call the army?" Lauren asked as she ran back in to her mother. "Nicolas! What are *you* doing here?"

"Hi, Lauren! I've just flown in from the States, via London, Gatwick actually." Nicolas looked skywards even though they were indoors. "Hey, that's pretty neat!"

"What is?"

"The first thing I did when Cathy told me that Robin was missing was to phone Kevin Cantwell. He's the guy who rebuilt the manor for me. Do you remember him, Lauren?"

She shot Nicolas a look, but it was obvious he knew her past.

"Naw, it's the son you'd know better if I'm not mistaken! Anyway, I phoned him and hauled him out of his bed. He bought a Colibre chopper a few months ago so he's very kindly agreed to cover the area from the air. The really neat thing is that he has a huge searchlight on the nose of that bird so he can do some serious searching!"

Saskia looked at her ex-boyfriend and nodded gratefully. "Nicolas, thank you. This is all my fault."

"This is not your fault, Sas. Don't you remember? You once told me that Kelly took off when she was about three years old too?"

"My God, that's right. I had forgotten. She was cross with me because I wouldn't let her have a pony."

Nicolas laughed. "That's right. I'm sure Robin is just hiding under a bed somewhere. It's probably just the house move that freaked her out. If she's going to turn up anywhere, it's here, in Innishambles."

"Oh Nicolas, I should never have sold it. I'm such a fool." Saskia began to sob again.

"Hey, you did what you thought was right and Gawd knows that I didn't help ringing from the States telling you that I had run out of money. I'm afraid it's still true but I could have presented it in a better light. Please, please, forgive me, Saskia."

She looked at him with cold eyes. "Does your fiancée know that you're here?"

"Sas, I don't have a fiancée! I never had. I have to explain your phone conversation last Monday –" but he was interrupted.

Kelly came bounding in the front door of Innishambles. "We have her!" she cried as Barney walked in a pace behind, carrying a small shivering bundle.

"Robin!" Saskia and Nicolas descended upon her.

"Where did you go?" Saskia asked, trying to keep her voice light.

"She was down at the river," Kelly explained. She and Barney stared at Nicolas for an instant. Where the hell had he appeared from? They had the sense to say nothing, however. Kelly continued, "That helicopter was flying along the River More and shining a spotlight on the banks. We would never have found her without him."

Robin, however, only had eyes for Nicolas. "Daddy!" she squealed with delight. "You're home!"

Saskia felt the panic rise in her stomach. Is that why she ran away? She took her youngest in her arms. "Oh, Robin what got into you?"

Suddenly the three-year-old looked like she might cry so Saskia rapidly changed tack. "It's OK, honey. We're not mad at you. We were just so worried. What did you think you were doing?"

"Well," Robin looked around her. Saskia, Nicolas, Kelly, Barney and Lauren were staring at her. She liked an audience. "Well, I knew that we were moving house and I just remembered that I hadn't said goodbye to the fish in the river," she explained simply.

"I think she must have fallen asleep beside the river bank," Kelly added. "She was sitting up and crying when we got to her. I reckon the chopper would have woken her."

Barney thought of the others. "I think I should go and tell everybody else the good news."

"I can phone Tiff in Ballymore Glen and Cathy in the manor and Frank Taylor in his house from here," Lauren volunteered.

"Thanks," Barney smiled beginning to relax for the first time in an hour. "Kelly and I will track down Lisa and Raymond Saunders on horseback."

"Thanks so much, Barney." Saskia hugged her future son-in-law.

"No problem," he smiled and headed back out the door, winking at his fiancée as he did so. She came over to give him a kiss and a hug. They walked out to the front door of Innishambles together. "See you in Peartree later?" he whispered.

Kelly hesitated. "I need to see if Mum is OK first. Jesus, when did Nicolas bloody Flattery get back? I thought that shit was out of our lives."

Barney wasn't convinced. "Perhaps. But remember you once thought that *this* shit was out of your life too?" He pointed at himself.

She grinned and nodded. "You have a point. Just let me check if Mum is OK and then I'll follow you over."

"Tell you what. I'll come to collect you at number five. That way I can make sure all the Dalton women are OK."

Kelly's heart swelled with pride. Her fiancé was a wonderful man!

Robin looked at Saskia and Nicolas together. "I'm sorry, Mummy. I'm sorry, Daddy," she said in her sweet little voice. Kelly thought her heart would break when she saw the three of them together. Saskia had told Kelly all about introducing Robin to Richard and telling her that he was her 'Daddy', but it was quite obvious that the three-year-old considered Nicolas her real father. Robin had an arm around Saskia's neck and the other around Nicolas. Whether she wanted to or not, Saskia was locked into a family embrace with her ex-boyfriend and her daughter. As Kelly watched them she wondered if perhaps her mother should give it another go. It certainly looked like Nicolas wanted to, the way he had wrapped his arm around her tightly.

Lauren walked back into the room. "I've phoned everybody. They all send their love."

"Lauren," Kelly said, "would you help me take Polly back to the refuge? I don't want to have to walk home alone after I leave her there."

Lauren was about to object, anxious to be near her baby sister, but then she caught Kelly's eye and understood. It was time to leave Nicolas and Saskia alone with Robin.

"Is it OK if I go with Kelly, Mum?" Lauren asked.

"Yes, yes of course," Saskia replied absently. Her attention was on Robin whom she was holding and gently rocking.

Quite suddenly there was only Nicolas, Saskia and Robin in the big old empty house. He looked around the place.

"Gawd, this place sure looks sad without the furniture, doesn't it?"

"We'll really miss it," Saskia sighed. "Although, I'm not sure what's going to happen to it now. The man who bought it has had a heart attack. I'm not sure that he's in a position to develop it as he originally planned."

"Develop it?" Nicolas looked horrified as he held Robin in his arms.

"Yes, Arthur Condon – Tiffany is going out with his son Max – Arthur planned to tear down Innishambles and build something like Ballymore Glen but I doubt that will happen now that he's had a heart attack. It was a crazy idea in the first place. Innishambles has a preservation order on it."

"And with good reason. It's beautiful, far too beautiful to tear down." Nicolas looked around.

"Perhaps, but money talks," Saskia said, her voice becoming cool again.

"Saskia, *we* have to talk," Nicolas ventured. Then he noticed Saskia wince as she tried to tighten her hold of Robin. The three-year-old was beginning to fall asleep again and she was obviously too heavy for Saskia to hold indefinitely.

"Here, please let me carry her. I've really missed her."

Saskia let him take Robin in his arms. The little girl's eyes were heavy.

Nicolas continued as he paced the floor, "Seriously, Sas, we have to talk – please."

"I think we did quite enough of that the other day," Saskia said as she walked over to the window and gazed out into the darkness. "I don't even know why you came back. Where's Mandy?"

"I don't know and I don't care," Nicolas said but his voice was light with mirth.

"Jesus, that was fast, Nicolas."

"No, it wasn't. I only met Mandy for the first time yesterday morning."

"What?" Saskia was confused.

Nicolas continued pacing the floor as he held Robin. "I got home from a few days in New York yesterday and I was greeted by my son Nick Junior and his new girlfriend – Mandy."

Saskia stared at Nicolas as the vague possibility of a

massive miscommunication began to form in her mind.

Nicolas was smiling lovingly at her. "Saskia, I think you had a rather colourful fight with *my son* last Monday. Would that be possible, do you think?"

"No, that couldn't be! I'm sure it was you I was talking to!" Saskia stammered.

"Saskia, I was in New York last Monday. Nick and his fiancée were living in my apartment when I was away. I gather it's slightly nicer than Nick Junior's room on campus. Anyway they were staying there – which I liked for security reasons – when you rang. Mandy answered and she told Nick that his ex was on the phone. Nick thought you were his ex-girlfriend until you said something about selling his house for him. Nick doesn't even own a car, not to mention a house!"

Saskia sat down on the floor because there was no furniture to sit on and her legs certainly wouldn't support her. Could she have made such a stupid mistake?

"But that's not possible," she stammered without conviction. Then she remembered that Nicolas had sounded a little strange and he had used odd jargon like 'chill' and 'babe'. "But, how did that happen?" She tried to make sense of the situation. "Surely Nick or I should have twigged."

"Well, that's the one thing I was furious about. He eventually came clean with me about throwing the party. Sas, they were all stoned. I don't think that Nick would have noticed who you were if you were standing in front of him! It was Mandy who teased him the next day about his ex phoning him. I don't think he even remembered his conversation with you until she reminded him! That's when he began to think about it with some modicum of logic."

"I can't believe I could have made such a stupid mistake! Although you two do sound slightly alike, being father and son and from the same continent. But it's amazing that he could have thought me an American with my soft Irish lilt."

Nicolas laughed. "Saskia, you know Nicolas! He thinks linguistics is a sexual position! And, after all, *you* thought *he* was me!"

"I guess I was a little distracted. I rang your number and asked to speak to you. When Nicolas came to the phone, I just assumed it was you. The music was so loud but you did sound quite unlike yourself."

When Kelly had asked her if it was it possible that there had been some misunderstanding, Saskia had been positively short with her. She privately thought Kelly and Barney had been eejits to have a misunderstanding over such an important conversation and now it looked like she had been equally moronic! Maybe it was genetic, she reflected as Nicolas continued to talk.

"When I got home, Nick Junior asked me if I was selling the manor." He looked a little sheepish. "I hadn't told him just how bad things had got financially. Anyway, when I told him everything, he told me about his weird conversation. I convinced him to phone his ex and she said that she certainly had not phoned him. That's when I realised that it was you who had called." Nicolas stopped and looked at Saskia. Robin was fast asleep in his arms but he didn't dare put her down and so he whispered. "Saskia, are you carrying my child?"

She looked at him as her eyes spilled over with tears and her lower lip wobbled of its own accord. All she could manage was a gentle nod.

"Oh, Gawd," Nicolas's eyes glassed up too. "This was more than I could ever have dreamt of. You're carrying my baby?"

She nodded again and rose to her feet, trying to hug him around Robin.

"Get off," the three-year-old grumbled in a semi-slumber, making the two adults laugh through their tears.

* * *

Raymond Saunders was the next to arrive up to Innishambles.

"I just wanted to see if anybody wanted a lift home," he offered.

Saskia rubbed away her tears. It was turning out to be an extremely emotional night.

"Raymond, this is Nicolas Flattery. Nicolas, this is Raymond Saunders. He's one of our new neighbours in Ballymore Glen."

They shook hands. Then it was decided that Raymond could take Saskia and Robin back to number five where Robin would be put to bed under the watchful eye of her mother. Nicolas needed to have a word with Kevin Cantrell who had just brought down his chopper in the front paddock of Innishambles.

"Is it usually this hectic around here?" Raymond asked as he started up his car to chauffeur the two Dalton women home.

"Always," Saskia yawned, "always."

* * *

Tiffany and Max had opened another bottle of champagne to celebrate Robin's safe return and Saskia happily took a glass as soon as she had Robin safely tucked up and sound asleep in her bed.

Kelly was the next to get home.

"I thought Lauren was with you," Saskia said, still a little hyper.

"She was until she and Connor Cantwell rediscovered each other. He was in the chopper with his dad. I think they're rekindling that old flame!"

"Where's Barney?" Saskia continued. "Has he tracked down Lisa Keyes yet? "

"Yes, Mum. In fact Raymond and Lisa had teamed up." Kelly smiled. "And Barney is dropping Cathy back to her house."

"Thank goodness. So everybody is safe and sound," Saskia said.

Then Kelly began to whisper. "Mum, what about you? Nicolas?" She raised her hands in the air inquisitively.

Saskia sighed and shook her head. "You wouldn't believe it if I told you. Suffice it to say we're back on talking terms and I was wrong about *Mandy*!" She still said it with the blonde bimbo voice. Both women started to laugh.

"Phew! If you don't mind me saying so, Mum, if you're carrying his child, it might be a good idea to give him a good hearing," Kelly suggested gently.

Saskia looked at her eldest and smiled. "When did you get so old and wise?"

Kelly changed the subject. "Barney is outside. I think we'll just slip away. We don't want to get into any more partying. I just wanted to check in with you. Do you mind if I stay in Peartree Cottage tonight?"

Saskia looked at her eldest. She was a young woman

now and very much in love. "Go on," she smiled, "and for God's sake make a date for that wedding of yours. Preferably sooner rather than later!" She laughed as she patted her own stomach.

"Thanks, Mum, you're the best!"

As she went out the front door, Nicolas walked in. Kelly looked at him aggressively. "If you hurt my mother, I'll kill you."

He looked at her in amazement. "Kelly, I assure you, I love your mother very much. I will never hurt her."

"Fine, well, just see that you don't!" and she was gone.

He went into the kitchen to meet Saskia.

"This place looks great," he said brightly.

"You are joking?" Saskia looked at him uncertainly.

"Well, OK, it does need a bit of settling in but it will be fine in a while."

Saskia looked at him for a moment and then burst out laughing. "Thanks for trying to sound positive! The truth is I have far too much furniture. We'll have to lose most of it."

Max sauntered into the kitchen and saw Nicolas for the first time.

"Oh, hi! We're just looking for another bottle of shampoo." He smiled confidently.

"Why?" Nicolas asked, confused.

Saskia laughed again. She had cheered up considerably. "Nicolas, this is Maximilian Condon. Max, this is Nicolas – er, a friend of mine. Nicolas, when Max says 'shampoo' he's actually talking about champagne." Then she turned to Max, "I think you've had quite enough booze for one evening, Max. How about turning on the kettle?"

He groaned good-naturedly and left the room again.

"That's a good-looking guy," Nicolas started.

"Yes, he is. I certainly hope he doesn't hurt Tiffany."

Nicolas turned to look at Saskia. "Speaking of hurting, honey, we have to talk."

Saskia looked deep into his eyes. They were pools of concern and very definitely full of sincerity. She remembered something she had once heard, that the eyes are the mirrors of the soul. If that were true, in his soul Nicolas was utterly sincere and quite obviously still in love with her.

"This is all so sudden," she started uncertainly, "and you were very hurtful about the publicity we got for the manor. We were only trying to get it out of the financial mess it was in!"

He crossed the room to close the kitchen door and then came back to her and took her by the hand. Gently her guided her to the only two chairs in the kitchen that weren't covered in boxes and bags of stuff. He sat down and so did she. "I am so so sorry about that. I was hurt and embarrassed. I way overreacted."

She nodded and shrugged.

"OK, now can I explain a few things?" he asked.

She nodded again, grateful that she didn't have to talk.

"Firstly, you must know how much I love you. That has never changed, Saskia. You have to understand that when I went to America I was very defeated when I realised that I couldn't sell my book. I felt like a failure. I hadn't just failed myself, however; I felt that I had failed you too. It was way easier to stay in the States. Then I got this job offer and everything sort of fell into place. It became much easier to stay there than to come back here to you – empty-handed and with all those debts." He winced, then looked at Saskia and kept talking. "I was miserable without you, Sas. That's the truth, but I thought you were better off without me. You've only known me as a success, I didn't think it would be fair to come back with nothing to offer you, but all that's changed now. You're having my baby! Jeez, I'll do anything to stay with you. I'll work in a chipper, I'll shovel shit, I'll do anything. I love you. If you can just accept me for what I am, we can get through this. I swear I'll do what it takes –"

Saskia was crying – again! "Oh, Nicolas, how did I ever give you such an impression! I was never with you because of your money. I was with you because I loved you for what you were, not what you were worth."

"But I'm worth nothing now. Worse – I have negative equity!" He laughed miserably.

"I don't care, you old fool. We're not exactly in the poor house, Nicolas. But what about your work? Your new acting role?"

"I quit."

"What?"

"I quit. As soon as I realised that you were carrying my baby, I knew that I had to be with you no matter what. I know that may not be the most politically correct thing to say but it is the truth. The baby has helped me realise that you're all that matters to me, really. I'll never leave you again, not ever." He looked at her hopefully and then continued nervously, "That is, if you'll have me back."

Her smile broadened and her eyes began to sparkle again. "Come here, Nicolas," she laughed as she stood to give him a big bear hug.

"Gawd, I missed you," he said as he rose and hugged her tightly.

"I missed you too," she replied honestly, "but you will have to give me time to think this through, Nicolas. You can't just swan in and take up where you left off. Will you give me time? Will you give me space?"

He kissed her on the forehead. "Do I have to?" he asked with a mock moan.

Saskia's voice was becoming stronger however. "Oh yes. I have to think about *me* and what I need. I also have to think about my girls. My God, Robin ran away from home tonight! I need to give her a stable environment and plenty of *constant* love." She stressed the word constant, leaving Nicolas in no doubt that he was still not totally forgiven for going AWOL. She pushed him away from her gently.

"What about our baby?" he asked.

"Our baby is going nowhere just at the moment," she smiled as she patted her stomach. "I'm not sending you away, Nicolas. I'm just asking for a little thinking time. OK?"

"I guess," he said glumly. It was quite clear that he had absolutely no choice. He had never heard her sound so strong.

Saskia had never felt so strong. It was exhilarating.

CHAPTER 34

Sunday morning dawned with a pale blue sky and the promise of another lovely day. It was almost mid-morning when Jayne danced into the kitchen like Mary Poppins. She had been asleep in her own bed by the time Raymond got home the previous night which was a good thing. He needed time to think. This morning, thankfully, the children were in the pool already so they didn't witness his hostility.

"Is it true?" Raymond asked, his voice ice-cold. It was clear that he was in no mood for games.

"If you're talking about that ridiculous incident last night, no, of course it isn't." Jayne sat down at the table with him. "I don't know who that girl was. I've never seen her in my life before."

"Jayne, I already know that you studied to be a nanny in Limerick. I'm going to have the story checked out either way, so the best thing you can do now is to tell me the truth."

"You bastard," she spat. "If you trusted me, you wouldn't check out some crazy story from a complete stranger!"

"No, Jayne, I wouldn't. So I guess the conclusion we're drawing here must be that I don't trust you."

"You fucking bastard! You've trusted me in your bed for the last month! After all I've done for you –"

"Is it true, Jayne?" Raymond repeated. "Are you married?" He kept his voice calm and under control.

"What if it is? What difference would that make?"

"Oh, I think it would make quite a difference."

"I was a kid, I didn't know what I was doing. He was a pathetic wimp and a stupid fool. He had no idea how to run that bloody school."

"Is that why you hit him?"

"What the hell are you talking about now, Raymond?"

"Lisa Keyes and I had a very good chat late last night, after you and the kids had gone to bed."

"How dare you talk about me behind my back? What did she say?"

"She said that the baby never materialised. Did you lose it or was it just a figment of your rather active imagination?" He waited for a reaction from her but she just sat looking at him, wide-eyed and mute with anger. "And there were some pretty strong rumours that you hit him. Is that true, Jayne?"

"He was such a fool, Raymond. You have no idea. I could have run that college and made it fly. It could have been something –" her eyes glazed over at the memory.

"Were you violent with him, Jayne?"

"No! Not violent, but he did need a good wake-up call. I had to shake him into reality, the old idiot – although sometimes he would just get me so mad –"

Raymond saw that she spoke through clenched teeth and he noted her hands were in tight fists. In a flash he remembered the lilies incident the morning before. This girl was definitely capable of violence.

Jayne talked manically. "That school could have opened other branches in other counties. Can you imagine what the demand for good nannies is, Raymond?"

"Were you pregnant with his child?"

"No!" She snapped back to real time. "Don't be so naïve! I would never have been stupid enough to get caught, unless I wanted to, that is."

Raymond sighed. "I think you should pack your bags, Jayne."

"Why? I'm not going anywhere."

"Yes, you are. You're leaving this house. You're unstable, Jayne – you need help."

"Dream on, Raymond. I've been working for you for the last four years. We've been sleeping together for the last few weeks. You can't just throw me out. I'll get you for unlawful dismissal, sexual harassment, abuse – you name it!"

Raymond looked at her. It was clear that he had never known her really. Christ, he was lucky that nothing had ever happened to the kids while they were in her care.

"What do you want?" he asked simply.

"I want to be your wife."

He tried to sound reasonable. "Jayne, you're already married."

"One hundred thousand euro then."

"What?"

"Give me one hundred thousand euro and you'll never see me again."

It was suddenly quite clear that Jayne had already thought this through. Raymond reckoned that she had known instantly last night. Lisa Keyes had blown her cover. It was all over for her.

"Where will you go?" Raymond asked.

"I've always fancied The States."

"What about your husband?"

"Sod him."

"One hundred thousand euro and I'll never see you again? You promise."

"I promise," she smiled angelically.

Raymond took out his wallet and wrote the cheque there and then.

She took it from him and studied it for a minute.

"If this bounces," she warned menacingly.

"It won't bounce," he said.

"Fine, I think I'd better go and pack!" She smiled as if they were the best of friends and were going on a holiday together. "Actually, it won't take that long because I still haven't unpacked my stuff since we moved in yesterday." Raymond watched her leave the room and then gently reached inside his breast pocket to switch off the small tape recorder he was wearing. He regularly did it in business meetings and so he was used to the small, tricky piece of equipment. He had recorded their entire conversation – as a little insurance, just in case she did decide to return at some time in the future. He got the feeling however that she would never be back.

The phone shrilled loudly beside him.

"Raymond, darling, is that you? I'm so glad I've tracked you down." It was Cassandra Booth-Everest.

"Hi, Cassy," he smiled into the phone. "We've moved house but I kept the same number so it wasn't that difficult, was it?"

"Oh, it's just so much work trying to organise social evenings. One must have compatible people. You know how it is. Anyway, Georgie and I are having a light fork supper on the first Friday in October for a few friends. We were wondering if you would come along?"

"I'm not sure if I can, Cassy. I'm afraid I don't have a nanny any more. I don't know if I can get a baby-sitter."

"Dash it all, Raymond, bring the children! Your little angels can play with my little darlings. You know, you really have become a hermit. You can even bring a date if that makes it easier for you."

"Well, if you put it like that, Cassy, the kids and I would love to come."

"Smashing! Oh God, you're not bringing that upstart! The nanny-with-notions that I met in Dali's, Jennifer someoneorother, are you?"

"No, Cassandra. That was Jayne," he corrected her gently. "She's very much out of our lives." As he said it, he heard the front door close. Jayne wasn't even going to say goodbye to the kids. The bitch.

"No, but I might bring along a young lady friend called Lisa."

Raymond smiled. He felt like a great weight had been lifted from his shoulders. And as for Lisa Keyes – maybe, just maybe.

* * *

Because it was Sunday morning, Dave Parker let Sue sleep in. He got up when DJ started his habitual five a.m. chants. He plodded into his youngest son's room and smiled at the little monster.

"When are you going to give us a sleep in, DJ?" he asked as he stretched and yawned.

"Milk," DJ demanded impatiently.

Halfway through their second Teletubbies video and their third bottle of milk, Guy joined them.

"Where's Mummy?" he asked, after the novelty of bear-hugging his father had worn off.

"Mummy is having a sleep in, this morning. I thought it would be nice if we let her have a big rest. What do you think?" Dave asked the highly unconvinced boys.

"I want Mummy," DJ whined.

"So do I," agreed Guy.

"Mummy's here!" Sue walked into the playroom. She was wrapped up snugly in her snow-white brushed-cotton dressing-gown.

"Hey, I wanted you to have a sleep in, Sue." Dave sounded deflated.

"I did! My God, it's almost nine o'clock. I don't remember the last time I slept in that late. Thank you, Dave." She looked at him lovingly.

He rose from the sofa where he had been cuddling his two sons and crossed the room to his wife. He kissed her on the lips and smiled at her.

"God, I love you, Sue."

"Phew!" She smiled. "Because I love you too!"

"I'd do anything for you."

"You're doing more than enough, Dave. I really am so sorry that I was so slow to forgive you last week, after all you've done for me –" Her voice got shaky.

"Slow? You practically forgave my utter stupidity right away. Well, within a few hours anyway." He squeezed her playfully.

"Thank God it's all over now," she said into his broad strong shoulder as she embraced him again.

"I was thinking –" Dave paused.

She sensed his change of mood. "What is it?" She pulled away suspiciously.

"Well, do you want to move into Ballymore Glen?"

"Oh, Dave!" Sue's eyes filled with excitement. "But I thought that they were too expensive?"

"Hell, we can afford it. I don't know why I'm throwing all the money we make back into the business. After what we've been through, I think we need to enjoy life a little more – live a little."

She threw her arms around her husband. "You're the best husband a woman could ever have."

"I'd settle for being the best husband *you* could ever have."

"That too!" She hugged him tightly.

"That's settled then. Will you ring Bingham auctioneers first thing tomorrow or will I?"

"Oh, I think I can manage that!" she said, laughing.

Dave continued, "I was also thinking –" he stopped again.

"What is it now?" she laughed.

"Let's get away. Just you and me. Lisa can mind the kids for a week or ten days. I want to take you off to some desert island and have my wicked way with you."

"OK!"

"Where would you like to go, Sue?"

"As long as I'm with you, I really don't mind. It could be Mullingar or the Maldives."

Dave burst out laughing. "Well, nothing against Mullingar – I mean, it's a very friendly place – we even have a shop there – but I was rather thinking of somewhere a little further away. How about Mauritius?"

Sue stared at her husband, unable to hide her excitement. "I don't even know where Mauritius is."

"Well then, Mrs Parker, I think we'd better get a map!"

* * *

Richard Dalton woke with a feeling of impending doom. He didn't know why – he couldn't quite focus. He was woefully hung over again. Edwina knocked gently on his bedroom door. She knew how angrily he could react if he was in a foul mood. That said, she couldn't believe how he could sleep this long, especially after the phone call she had just received from Saskia Dalton.

"Richard, are you awake yet?" She peeped around his door.

"Mmmm," he groaned.

"Richard, Saskia has just phoned. She wanted me to tell you that you're not to worry. They found Robin. She's not lost any more."

There was no reaction from Richard for a moment. Then suddenly he was wide-awake.

"Robin! Jesus. That was it! What did you just say, Mum? Is she OK?"

Edwina sighed. Her son really was useless. "Yes, Richard, the crisis is over. Robin has been found. Evidently Nicolas Flattery organised a chopper-search or something and they found her early this morning. Saskia just thought you should know. She also asked that you might call her back when you're available to talk."

Richard blinked at his mother, trying to push the

pounding hangover away. "You must have that wrong, Mum. Nicolas Flattery is in LA."

"No, no. I'm quite sure that Saskia said that it was Nicolas who organised the chopper-search." She turned to go. "Anyway, call her as soon as you can. I'm going out for a walk, Richard. I need some fresh air." Her tone was very definitely disapproving. "You might consider opening your window for a while too. It smells like a brewery in there." Then she left him.

Richard lay back on his bed. A bloody chopper-search, that was sharp. He should have thought of that himself. He had been too pissed by the time Lauren phoned him. It wasn't his fault that he was in no fit state to help. Why didn't she bloody well phone him earlier? He felt even worse as he thought about the rest of the night. He must have been really pissed. He didn't want to think about it but, involuntarily, his mind went back to the point when he took that tart back to her place.

"Don't worry," she had said. "It happens to all guys at some stage in their lives."

"It's never bloody happened to me," Richard growled, willing his dick to do its job and stand to attention.

"It's probably just the booze," she said, trying to cheer him up.

"It's not the bloody booze," he snapped.

Then she lost her patience. "Well, if it's not the whiskey, it must just be that you're getting old, honey." She smiled at him coldly as she handed him his clothes. "Not much point in you hanging around if all you're going to do is *hang around*."

"Bitch," he grabbed his gear from her and dressed as fast as he could. Then he stormed out of her Rathgar apartment with a lethal concoction of fury and shame churning up in his stomach. Thinking about it now, he cringed. Of course, he reasoned, it was the whole Robin thing. Subconsciously he had been worried about his youngest daughter. That was it. This whole Saskia project was really taking it out of him. The sooner he got her back and he got his domestic life sorted out, the better.

He took a hot shower and then turned it sharply to the freezing setting. It served its purpose. He was wide-awake and alert in an instant. He shaved and dressed. Critically, he studied himself in the mirror. Not too bad for a guy who had only got a few hours' sleep.

Within half an hour, he was on the road to Ballymore. He didn't bother to phone – he had to see Saskia face to face. Too much effort had gone into this particular project to fail now, he fumed. It had all been going so well. Tiffany was living with him. He was once again welcome under Saskia's roof. He had been dropping subtle hints and she had not rejected them out of hand. Richard knew that he had to get rid of Nicolas bloody Flattery again. What the fuck was the Yank doing back in town?

As he drove out of Dublin city, he decided that the time had come to tell Saskia everything. It was time to come clean. Well, as clean as he ever would be with her. If this didn't get her back, nothing would.

* * *

Kelly lay in bed in Peartree Cottage admiring her beautiful solitaire diamond engagement ring.

"I take it this means that you like it," Barney smiled at her as he walked in with the breakfast tray.

"Oh, Barney, it's absolutely beautiful."

"Well then, let's cut to the chase and pick a date."

"We need to pick a venue first. You know hotels are booked up for years in advance these days."

Barney looked at Kelly. "Why does it have to be a hotel? Why can't we have it somewhere a little more intimate and more personal? Like here?"

"Here?" she laughed. "We wouldn't fit many people in. Would we?"

"How many do you want?"

Kelly thought about this. "I really don't know. It would have been lovely to have a wedding ceremony in Innishambles or in the manor but I guess that isn't really a runner any more, is it?"

Barney shook his head in agreement. "After the big engagement party, I'd be really happy with a small family affair."

"Actually, Barney, I'd like a small intimate wedding too." But still her mind was playing with the notion of getting married in Rathdeen Manor. It really would make an amazing venue for a small wedding . . .

"Terrific." He kissed her on the nose. "Well, how about we get married in Ballymore church and then we have a small party here afterwards, on say, December the thirty-first?"

"You want to get married on December the thirty-first?" Kelly gushed. She became very excited. "Barney, that's less than four months away! Ohmigod – there's so much to organise!"

"Well, what do you say? Will you marry me on New Year's Eve?"

"Yes, yes, yes." She covered his face with kisses. "I will!"

* * *

In number 5, Ballymore Glen, Max had been driving Tiffany crazy all morning. He came out with the dumbest things and he was absolutely no help unpacking. The girls were trying to get Lauren's room finished and settled.

In utter exasperation, Tiffany finally suggested, "Why don't you take the dogs for a walk?"

"Yeah, that's a good idea. I want to explore Innishambles anyway. I mean, we are going to be living there." Tiffany caught Lauren's eye as Max walked out.

"Doesn't he know what his father intends to do with Innishambles yet?" Lauren asked in disbelief.

"God love him, Sis. Max is usually the last to find anything out!"

"Wow, you don't sound like a woman in love," Lauren laughed as she unwrapped some of her belongings. "What happened to the blond-haired blue-eyed god you were so deeply devoted to? If I remember correctly, he was 'far too good for us mere mortals'."

Tiffany laughed good-naturedly and threw a cuddly toy at Lauren. "I think I have well and truly fallen out of love!"

"I don't believe this! You were mad about that guy. What's changed?"

Tiffany sighed and sat on the edge of the tea chest that she was unpacking. "You know, I think I was in love with an idea of what I thought he was like. Not the real Maximilian Condon. Does that make sense?"

"Yes, of course it does. This reminds me of when you had your crush on Barney."

"Feck off! I was a kid then. This is different."

"I'm sorry, go on."

"Well, Max is a lovely guy, but let's face it, he's a bit of a himbo – you know, a male bimbo."

"So he's too thick for you basically?" Lauren giggled.

"Yes, in a word."

"Are you going to break it off with him?"

"Yes, when we get back up to Dublin, tonight."

Lauren looked at the sister squarely. "Are you absolutely sure about this?"

Tiffany thought about it. "Yes, I am. Really I am."

"Wow, so that old expression really is true!"

"What expression?"

"Be careful what you wish for, because it might come true!"

Tiffany thought about this for a moment. "You know, you're absolutely right. I wanted Max more than anything in the world and now that I have him, I want rid of him." She laughed. "It'll teach me to be more selective in what I pine after in the future!"

"Well, good for you," Lauren smiled. "I always thought you were too smart for him, anyway."

* * *

James Harrington didn't really want to go to Ballymore. Damn it all, it was Sunday but Saskia Dalton was an old patient of his and she was very persuasive. She had explained that Robin had been missing for a few hours and, although the child had slept well, Saskia just wanted a professional to give her the all-clear.

James gave Robin a complete checking over and the little girl was fine.

"But no more running away, young lady!" He spoke sternly but his eyes were friendly.

"Thank you for coming on such short notice." Saskia looked at James. "I just had to be sure. You understand."

"Absolutely. Robin will be fine. I think she probably got a bit of a scare too. Hopefully she won't try it again. That said, I would take the precaution of locking the house every night – just to keep her in!"

"There is one other thing," Saskia looked at the floor.

"What is it?" James asked as they walked together to the front door of number five. Saskia glanced around to ensure that neither Max Condon nor Robin could hear her. She had told Tiffany privately the evening before.

"Well, I appear to be pregnant again! I'm only telling you as my GP, you understand."

"Should I say congratulations?"

"Oh, yes. I'm very happy about it," she replied defensively.

"Great," James smiled broadly. "Have you seen your obstetrician yet?"

"No, I'll make an appointment soon."

James remembered that Richard Dalton had told him that he and his wife were in the process of getting back together again. That conversation had taken place very late at night and both James and Richard had been pretty smashed when they were discussing it but obviously the reunion had taken place!

"Congratulations, Saskia. Pass on my best wishes to Richard."

She looked at him blankly. Then she realised. James simply assumed that it was Richard's baby. She was too embarrassed to clarify the situation with him.

"Obviously it wasn't planned," she blurted, "but now that it's happened – well, we'll be fine!"

"That's the spirit, Saskia. If you have decided that you don't want any more babies after this, though, we should consider alternative methods of birth control."

Richard's had a vasectomy, Saskia thought instantly. Equally quickly she pushed the thought out from her mind. She wasn't in a relationship with Richard!

"Saskia, are you OK? You suddenly look quite pale."

"Oh, sorry. Hormones," she waved her hand in the air as if trying to dispel them. "Don't worry, I'm absolutely fine."

"Well, I'll be off now," James took his jacket and left Ballymore Glen to the waves of Saskia and little Robin.

As he cruised down the plush driveway of Ballymore Glen, he got his first opportunity to admire the huge private mansions. He let out a low whistle and almost knocked over the young lady who was attempting to cross the laneway.

He pulled his car over and got out.

"Hey, are you OK?" he said to the rather attractive blonde. "You practically walked out in front of me!"

"No, I'm bloody well not OK," she sniffed. "I've just lost my job, through no fault of my own. I did my best and he didn't even give me a reason and now I have no idea where I'm going or even how I'm going to get there."

Jayne Mullins afforded James one of her best butter-wouldn't-melt-in-her-mouth smiles. He was smitten.

"Hop in. I'll give you a lift." He grinned wolfishly at her.

As he reached the magnificent gates of Ballymore Glen, Richard Dalton was just arriving.

They waved and slowed their cars down to greet each other.

"Fancy meeting you here," James laughed.

"Hi, James, what the hell are you doing here on a Sunday morning?"

"I was just checking Robin over after last night's little walkabout."

"Jesus, yeah, is she OK?"

"She'll be fine, Richard. How are you?"

"Don't start! You missed a good night." Richard laughed as he threw his eyes to heaven.

"Enjoy them while you still can," James laughed, thinking about the new baby.

Richard assumed it was a reference to the fact that he was getting too old for the field. "Couldn't agree more," Richard laughed, winking at James's female companion. "Eat, drink and be merry, for tomorrow we marry!"

Jayne Mullins liked the sound of that! "So, what's your surname, James?" she asked as they drove off.

"Harrington," he glanced over at her and smiled as he took in her long well-shaped legs and trim figure. He began to accelerate.

"Harrington? That's a nice name," Jayne smiled indulgently as she tried out Jayne Harrington in her mind. Yes, she thought: Jayne Harrington sounded nice.

CHAPTER 35

Saskia was exhausted by lunch-time Sunday. When the doorbell rang, she hoped that Lauren or Tiffany would answer it. Robin seemed to be absolutely fine after her midnight adventures, but it had put years on Saskia. Her three-year-old was jumping on the bed as she tried to make it.

That's where I'd like to be, she thought fondly, only *in* it, not *on* it! Then she yelled from the bedroom, "Is anyone going to get the door?" As always, it was Tiffany who answered her mother's call for help.

"Daddy!" she beamed at Richard. "Hi, welcome to Ballymore Glen. Wait till you see this house! It's amazing!"

"Hi, gorgeous!" Richard hugged his daughter. "Do you want to come up to Dublin with me later or do you want to wait until tomorrow morning?"

Tiffany thought about this for a moment. "My friend, Max, is still here since last night. Could he have a lift too?"

Richard raised a paternal eyebrow.

"It's OK. He slept on the sofa. Mummy chaperoned us. Anyway we didn't get much sleep yesterday. I suppose you heard about Robin?"

"Yes, that's why I'm here. I wanted to see if she and your mum are OK."

"Dad, that was kind! I'll just go and get Mum."

Saskia had already heard her ex-husband's deep voice however. As soon as she realised that it was him she rushed into her en suite and slapped on a quick layer of foundation. She tried to steady her hand as she applied her eyeliner and mascara. "What am I like?" she giggled to herself and Robin who was watching studiously. "He's my ex!"

"Can I have some?" Robin asked, eyeing up the basket where Saskia kept all her lipsticks in a heap.

Tiffany arrived up into her mother's new bedroom. "Mummy, Dad's here. He wanted be sure that you and Robin were OK after last night's scare." She tickled her little sister.

"Thank you," Sas smiled, realising that there was no way she was going to be able to stall him long enough to change into something more presentable. As she walked onto the upstairs landing, however, Saskia saw Lauren stomp from the bathroom into her bedroom.

"I'm not here if he's looking for me," Lauren whispered savagely.

Sas felt it like a blow to the stomach. How could she be so forgiving? Richard was still the same playboy he had been and he was so bloody careless at Kelly's party that Lauren overheard an entire conversation, the content of which she should never have been exposed to. Her resolve became firmer as she winked at Lauren.

"Don't worry, pet. I'll sort your father out."

"Richard, we weren't expecting you." She looked at him coolly.

"Hi, Sas. I was so worried after last night's phone call from Lauren that I came as quickly as I could. Sorry I didn't phone first."

She overtly looked at her watch. It was almost one o clock. Hardly the crack of dawn. He ignored her gesture.

"How is Robin? Is she OK? Do you have any idea why she did it?"

They walked into the kitchen and Saskia sat down. "Look, Richard, I don't know why she ran away. She said that she wanted to say goodbye to the fish. Maybe that's all there is to it."

"That's bloody ridiculous," Richard laughed.

"No, it's not. You may remember that Kelly ran away when she was three years old too?"

"Did she? I don't remember," Richard shrugged indifferently.

Saskia couldn't help comparing his lack of interest with Nicolas's genuine concern. "She often went down to the river with Nicolas. They do regular walks down there together and she loves the river."

"I see." He backed off slightly. Robin wandered into the kitchen and regarded Richard warily. She had *borrowed* some of Saskia's pearly pink lipstick.

"Hi, gorgeous," Richard smiled at the three-year-old. "How are you? You remember me? Daddy."

"You're not my daddy. Nicolas is my daddy!" Robin shouted at him and rushed over to the safety of her mother's leg.

"This may not be the best time, Richard." Saskia looked at him angrily. "She got very little sleep and she still isn't used to the new house."

Richard looked around and decided that it was safer to change the focus of attention. "How do you like it here? Are you settling in?"

"We'll manage just fine, thanks." The coldness in her voice was tangible.

"Look, Sas. I'm really sorry that I didn't get down sooner. The truth is I was out with a bunch of lads last night and I was well over the limit by the time Lauren phoned me."

"It's none of my business where you were last night, Richard, but while we're on the subject can I ask you to keep your current exploits to yourself?"

Richard guffawed. "What exploits? I'm bloody celibate these days."

"Don't lie to me again, Richard. Lauren heard your entire conversation with James Harrington at Kelly's party last week. She's still very upset about it," Saskia snapped.

Richard was silenced for a moment. "Oh, God, I'm so sorry. Where is she? I can explain. That was all bullshit."

"Richard!" Saskia glanced at Robin. "Language," she mouthed at him.

"Rubbish," he corrected himself. "It was all male bravado. It was all lies, I swear."

His face was the picture of sincerity but then again that was his forte. Richard could look at you solemnly and tell you day was night, Saskia reminded herself.

"Well, whether or not it was rubbish is really academic. What you do in your own time is your business, but what you expose the girls to is very much my business. Lauren needs a role model, not a playboy, as a father figure." Again, her mind's eye flashed to Nicolas.

"Where is she? Let me explain to her."

"She's not here." Sas knew that Lauren didn't want to see him.

"Yes, she is. She's upstairs,"Robin announced, delighted to clarify the situation.

Saskia crouched down to her daughter's level and spoke to her. "Will you go and watch some cartoons, please, honey?" Robin ran off, delighted to be let watch daytime television.

"If she doesn't want to see me, I understand," Richard lied, "but please tell her that I love her and I'm so sorry she heard that entire bogus conversation."

"I'll pass all of that on," Saskia replied crisply. Inside though, she was longing to believe that he was not out playing the field again. "Do you want a coffee?"

Richard beamed. "I'd love to stay to lunch, if I'm invited."

She smiled at him; despite her best efforts she was warming to his presence. Damn it, he was her husband of some twenty years and the father of her children. It was just too big to ignore.

The back door of the house swung open and the four dogs rushed in, followed by the tall and languid figure of Maximilian Condon.

"Hi," he smiled at Richard. "This house is always so full of people. It's like Victoria station!"

"You must be Max," Richard shook his hand. "Were you taking the dogs for a walk? Very thoughtful of you."

"Yeah, Tiffany won't let me smoke in the house," he

explained. "Still, the walk probably undid the damage the cigarette did to my lungs."

"I hear that your father had a heart attack. I hope he's going to be OK."

"Thanks. They say he'll be fine. He'll be out of hospital in a few more weeks."

"Which hospital is he in?"

"I think it's called Vincent's Private."

"Oh, well, tell him we're all rooting for him. OK?"

Saskia thought how genuinely nice Richard could be. He was such an amicable man when he wanted to be.

Lunch was a very pleasant affair. Lauren was the only difficulty: she refused to come out of her room. Kelly and Barney popped in for a while. Tiffany and Max went for another walk after lunch because poor Max was aching for a cigarette and they took Robin with them to give Saskia and Richard a little peace. True to his word, Nicolas did not come near the house. Nor did he phone. Saskia had asked for space and that was what he was giving her.

Richard poured another glass of red wine for his ex-wife. She was in great form now, thankfully.

"Saskia, I need to talk to you."

"What is it?"

"Sas, honey, I don't think it's any secret to you that I really miss you desperately."

"Oh, Richard, don't go there," she said without conviction.

"Yes, I will go there." He pulled his chair over to hers. "I have to go there. Saskia, in case it's not painfully obvious I'll tell you – I'm still hopelessly in love with you.

I never stopped loving you and all I want is for us to get back together again, to be a family."

She looked at him in silence.

"Look, I know that I screwed up big-time. I know I did a huge amount of stupid stuff, but I've been in the doghouse for almost three years now. Haven't I suffered enough?" He could see that she was listening to him. Her mind was open to the possibility. That was a good start.

He took her hand. "Saskia, the girls need their father. I need them too and God knows that I need you."

She could feel herself getting emotional again. Jesus, she thought desperately, all I ever do these days is cry!

"Oh, Richard. I don't know. Seeing you is so good. I want to believe you but how can I?"

"Please, if you just give me one more chance I'll prove to you that I'm worth it." It was time to move in for the kill, he decided. "And there's something else I have to tell you."

"What is it now?"

"I'm the developer behind Ballymore Glen."

"What?"

"It's me! I'm the developer behind Ballymore Glen."

Saskia pulled her hand back from him. "How can that be?" Her mind was spinning. "What are you talking about? You didn't have that kind of money."

"Well, to be honest, I've been very lucky. I took a punt and it paid off."

She looked around her kitchen. She had bought Ballymore Glen from her ex-husband! Damn it, this was more lies!

He didn't sense her change of mood. "I bought the original site relatively cheaply. Strictly between you and me, it only cost me five hundred thousand euro for the twenty-five acres."

"Christ, that seems cheap!"

"Yes, well, don't forget that was three years ago, before the massive hike in prices and of course it was before the land had planning permission."

"But where did you even get five hundred grand?"

"Oh, you of little faith," Richard teased Saskia, but his eyes sparkled.

"Mum let me use her house as security."

"Wow!"

"Yes, I owe her big-time. I couldn't have done it without that first leg up. After that, obviously the land appreciated considerably when it was rezoned and then the value of the land went through the roof as the entire property market in Ireland has done and so I've cleared quite a little fortune. I can't take credit for that. I just got lucky. I guess you could say that I was in the right place at the right time!"

Saskia gazed at him. "Are you telling me that you single-handedly developed that entire site – I mean all these houses – all of Ballymore Glen?"

"Well, obviously I subcontracted the actual building to a construction company, but yes, I am the sole proprietor of the company that owns the land and now the houses. Mind you, I owe the banks a fair whack, but I'm paying that off pretty smartly now that the houses are being sold."

Saskia seemed to sink down even deeper into the seat. "I don't believe it. I bought a bloody house off my ex-husband without even knowing it. What kind of fool am I? You're a bloody multi-millionaire and here I am downsizing with the girls." She burst out crying.

"Hey, hey, hey," he jumped up from his seat and wrapped her in his arms. "I know we're not married any more, but we still share the same family. Why do you think I'm here discussing all of this with you? I've done this, I've made this money for us, for you and me and the girls."

Saskia was sobbing but she didn't care. "This is all so confusing, Richard. Why couldn't it have worked out? Why couldn't we just have stayed a happy family? If you just –"

He cut her off. "There's no such thing as *The Brady Bunch* in real life, Sas." Then he laughed and sat back down next to her.

Saskia looked at him in surprise and then she began to laugh too.

"That's more like it, honey. Here, blow!" He put his hanky to her nose as if she were a child and made her blow. She did.

When she was slightly composed again, he pulled his chair even closer to hers and took both her hands in his.

"Look, it's a little bold of me telling you about my new-found wealth before I ask you the next question, but I wanted to cloud your judgement. I wanted to influence your decision. Here it is, Saskia."

He took a deep breath as he studied the floor. Then he looked straight at her. "Can we give it another go? You and me, I mean?"

"Oh God."

"Sas, we could work. Really we could. Don't you remember the first twenty years? They were great. I know we could rekindle that," he ploughed on. "I've been in therapy for the last two years. I could explain why I went so off the rails. It wouldn't excuse it but there are reasons – low self-esteem, chronic insecurity – I could go on. I will if it would influence your decision."

"Stop!" Saskia cried as the reality of her situation sank in. "Richard, we can't. You don't understand. The last time it was you, now it's me. We can never get back together. I do love you. I don't think I ever stopped loving you, but we can't get back together again."

Richard looked at her, utterly perplexed. Damn it, he had a momentum going – he almost had her. What the hell was wrong with her now? He wouldn't let go of her hands.

"It's Nicolas. You're still together, aren't you?"

"Yes, no, yes – oh, Richard. I'm bloody pregnant and it's Nicolas's child."

"*You're what?*"

Saskia began to cry again. This time it was Richard who pulled away.

He stood up and crossed the room to the kitchen window. He gazed out on the new lawn of number five. All his efforts, all his bloody work and now this. Fuck Nicolas Flattery!

"Could you have an abortion?" Richard asked quietly.

Saskia took a gasp. "How could you even suggest such a thing? You of all people! Look at the children I've produced! They're magnificent. I could never kill a child that I'm carrying."

"I need some air," Richard snapped and stormed out the back door.

Saskia heaved a deep and melancholic sigh. It was quite obvious that a new baby, somebody else's baby, was not part of Richard's bold bright future. The sound of a mobile phone intruded into her silence. The tone was not familiar. It had to be Richard's. Slowly Saskia dragged herself up onto her feet. They ached after the exercise of the day before. Moving house was not easy. She followed the sound of the persistent ringing into her hall. There, draped casually over her banister rail, was Richard's jacket. It looked good there. It felt good to have it there. The phone was obviously in the pocket. She reached the coat just as the phone cut off. Saskia picked up the jacket and hugged it. Richard Dalton, her ex-husband, wanted her back. He still loved her – desperately. Not enough to take on another man's baby, though. Sas buried her face in his jacket and inhaled deeply. It smelt like he did. The aftershave was sporty and vibrant, like him. It was so familiar. After all these years, Richard had not changed his aftershave. She loved it. She loved him. The phone began to ring again. It made her jump. She found it in the pocket and clicked the phone into life.

"Hello," she said.

"Hello, is Richard there?" a young girl asked.

"Yes, he is. Whom shall I say is calling?" Saskia felt that familiar sense of foreboding and misery return to the pit of her stomach.

"Tell him it's Marie, from last night," the girl giggled.

That was all that Saskia needed to hear. She cut the line and walked back into the kitchen. Richard was just returning from outside. He saw her with his jacket and phone and looked at her for some explanation.

"I think you'd better put this on and leave." She gave him his jacket and phone.

"What's up?"

"One of the *lads* from last night just called you." She

looked for his reaction. "Marie?" She stared at him and waited. Guilt flooded his face as the phone began to ring again.

"Saskia, I can explain," he started.

"Get out, Richard."

"No, wait!" He switched the phone off to stop it ringing.

"I just don't get it, Richard. Why did you even want to come back if you're still playing the field?"

"You're my wife. You have my kids. We *should* be together. Look, would you think about having this baby and then letting Nicolas take it back to LA?"

"What's your shrink's name?" She locked eyes with him again.

"What?"

"Say it fast, Richard. What's his name?"

Richards's eyes scanned the room, looking for inspiration but it was no good. Saskia knew what he was up to.

"Murphy," he spluttered unconvincingly.

"You were never a good liar when you were put on the spot, Richard. Oh, yes, very smooth with the charm and the stories you had prepared earlier but you were always lousy at spontaneous lying. So you're still a lying cheating bastard." Her look was one of pure venom. "Get out, Richard!"

"Saskia, what about the money? I can give you anything you want, if you'll just come back."

"Yeah, and turn a blind eye to your wild nights and compulsive lying. I don't think so."

"Saskia, this is crazy. I love you. You love me – you even said so."

"Yes, and it's true, God help me. But just because I

515

love you doesn't mean you're good for me. I used to love cigarettes too and I've managed to live happily without them for the last twenty years. I guess I'm just going to have to get used to living without you too. Out, Richard." She was pushing him towards the door.

"I'll buy you Innishambles back!" he offered.

"Get out, Richard."

"I'll give you anything you want," he tried again, "money, holidays, diamonds!"

"Out!" she shouted over his protests as she shut the door in his face. He looked at the closed door. Bitch, he thought. You haven't heard the last of me.

"I'm meant to give Tiffany and Max a lift back to Dublin," he yelled.

"They can catch the bus!" Saskia shouted through the door.

"You're my wife and I will get you back!" he yelled but there was no response. She had obviously walked away.

Lauren tiptoed down the stairs and followed her mother into the kitchen. She had heard the commotion.

"Is everything OK, Mum?

"It is now, pet." She hugged her daughter.

Lauren noticed that Woody and Wilma and even Dudley and Dexter were hovering near Saskia protectively. It wasn't that long ago that the two larger dogs would always stay by Richard's side through thick and thin.

"Did you and Dad have a fight?"

"More of a clearing the air, I think," she said with resignation.

"I'm so glad you saw through his lies, Mum."

"I'm sorry that you had to witness that." Saskia looked at her daughter.

"I'm kind of glad. To be honest, up until recently I had been hoping that you and Dad were getting back together. Naturally that all changed when I overheard that terrible conversation –" Lauren looked like she might burst out crying. It was very unlike her.

"Oh, sweetheart! Your dad loves you and your sisters so much. He's just a natural playboy and that's why I could never take him back. I don't doubt his love for you guys and I do believe in a strange way that he loves me too – but not in the way I need to be loved."

"Go, girl!" Lauren laughed. "In the way you *deserve* to be loved!"

They smiled at each other and hugged some more. Then Lauren continued. "So that brings us round full circle to the man who loves you more than anything else in the world. He loves you even more than his acting career." She stopped and looked at her mother expectantly.

"Let's deal with one man at a time," Sas laughed.

"OK, I'm just so glad that you realised what a shit Dad is."

"I was just in the right place at the right time, Lauren," she explained, repeating what Richard had said earlier. "The right place at the right time!"

CHAPTER 36

Upon their return, Tiffany was utterly fed up to hear that Richard had already returned to Dublin.

"But he promised," she whined.

Lauren gave her the inside story on Richard and Saskia's fight, however, and then Tiffany mellowed considerably. She stopped making a fuss and got her stuff for college together quietly. Max, as always, was more of a hindrance than a help. Luckily, there wasn't actually that much stuff left because most of her possessions were now in Edwina's house.

Maximilian acted like a true gent when it was time to go. He kissed Saskia's hand and thanked her for her exquisite hospitality.

"It's not exactly *The Ritz*, Max. I'm afraid we're still a little topsy-turvy here, but it will all come right in the end – of that I have no doubt."

"Nor do I, Sas." He beamed down from his considerable height over her and for the first time Saskia saw how lethally effective his charm was. She dearly hoped that he would not hurt Tiffany.

"Before you go, could you give me your mum's phone

number, Max? There's a small matter that I want to discuss with her."

"Sure." Not even the tiniest flash of curiosity crossed his face but the Dalton girls had their ears pricked.

"Mum, why do you want her phone number?" Lauren asked in a loud whisper.

Saskia was ready for their attack however. "Not that it's any of your business, I just want to offer my support following Arthur's heart attack." The girls accepted this, Saskia noted with relief.

When they pulled into Bus Aras, in Dublin, Tiffany knew that the moment had come. She had listened to Max's inane drivel all the way from Wicklow town and she was fit to explode. On more than one occasion her mind had wandered back to her freshman friend, Bill. Now there was a smart boy and cute to boot. Of course he wasn't as drop-dead gorgeous as the one and only Maximilian Condon, but his mind! Now that was a turn-on.

"What? You're breaking up with me? You can't do that!"

"I'm sorry, Max." Tiffany tried to do it softly. "You're a really nice guy – it's just that we're very different people. I'm about to embark on my college life and you have a totally different agenda."

"But what about last night in the pool? What about Puerto Banus? Don't you like being with me?"

She ignored the reference to Spain. "Fun, but not exactly grounds for a long and fulfilling relationship, Max." She looked at his genuinely crestfallen face. "Look, I'm sure we can still be friends –"

"Pu-lease! Don't use that line on me. Do you know how many times I've used that one on girls in the past?"

"Well, Max, perhaps what goes around comes around. What do you think?"

This stung him. "Is this because I had sex with some of your friends? You know – Francesca Murray and that other little one in Ballymore Glen the day we went to view them. What was her name?"

Tiffany felt her blood beginning to heat up again.

"That was Stephanie," she reminded him. This guy had simply no idea of the damage he could do. "You know," she said, doing her best to control her temper. "If this is the first time you have been blown out and you don't like it, you might consider treating women a little better, Max."

"Ah, I didn't think of that," he replied honestly.

"No, I didn't think so." She gently patted him on the cheek. "There's no denying it, you're very cute, Max. You're just a little thick. She mimicked his accent, "Sorry, old boy!"

Quite suddenly he seemed to perk up. "OK, delicious. How about a goodbye shag first? In the back of the bus." His eyes sparkled with mischief.

Tiffany looked at him and laughed. "Goodbye, Max." She reached up and kissed him lightly on the cheek. Then she turned and walked away.

"Tiffany!" he called after her. "Will you at least tell me? Was that you on the beach in Puerto Banus?"

She stopped and turned around to look at him. "I can safely tell you with absolute honesty, Max, that the girl you slept with on the beach in Spain and I are totally different women." She smiled, turned on her heel and walked out of Bus Aras.

Max would have watched her go if a foxy little redhead

hadn't walked in the revolving door just as Tiffany was walking out.

* * *

Saskia woke quite suddenly on Monday morning. She knew exactly what she had to do; she just wasn't sure that she could pull it off. She got Lauren out to her school bus and Robin off to Montessori in a flurry of cornflakes and fuss.

"Mum, you're particularly hyper today. What's on your mind?" Lauren asked.

That girl never misses a trick, Saskia thought with a mixture of frustration and admiration.

She tried to dismiss her daughter. "It's all in your mind, Lauren!"

With the girls gone the house became very quiet. Saskia sat down with a strong cup of black coffee. As she studied the dark pool in her mug, she thought about the precious bundle she was carrying in her stomach and rushed to change it for a frothy milky cup of decaffeinated coffee.

With only Woody and Wilma for company, she sat in the welcome silence and gathered her thoughts. Dudley and Dexter were getting used to their new station at the front door of number five! Saskia looked around her brand-new state-of-the-art traditional kitchen and smiled. It really was beautiful. The woodwork was a light brown and the worktops a glorious dark grey, almost black granite. The AGA shone like a new penny. There was no doubt: Ballymore Glen was a fine home. It just wasn't *her* home.

Saskia phoned Bingham Auctioneers.

"Oscar, I've decided I want to put number five back on the market," she explained in a simple matter-of-fact voice.

"You can't be serious," Oscar spluttered. "Haven't you just moved in?"

"Yes, I have. Lock, stock and two smoking barrels! We've totally moved in and we've sold Innishambles, as you well know. That means that this is my principal place of residence and so the one good thing is that I won't get done for any Capital Gains Tax when you sell this for me for – shall we say two and a half million?"

"Ah, Sas, I think that's a bit rich!"

"Do you? How many houses are left in this little development?" Saskia's tone was quite cool.

"Well, actually, I've just sold the last one. Number three is gone to the Parker family. You probably know them –"

"Sue and Dave? Yes, I do. I had heard that she was very interested. That is indeed good news because that means you have no more houses in this development for sale. If they're all gone, I'm quite sure that you'll get somebody for this one."

"But, Saskia, it will be a second-hand sale which means they'll get done for stamp duty. I really think you're aiming a little high at two and a half million euro. I mean, damn it, Rathdeen Manor has only a value of four million on it."

"What?"

"Er, yes. I was meant to phone you about this but things have been a little hectic."

"Well, Nicolas Flattery is home himself now so he can deal directly with you. That said, Oscar, could you please

phone him this morning with that valuation? He will be
sad to hear it's so low."

"With hindsight, Saskia, I think Innishambles did
particularly well. You're a very lucky woman."

He was trying to lighten the mood but Saskia wouldn't
let him. She really felt that he had been underhand in the
way he had let her buy a house from her ex-husband.

"Perhaps, but not as lucky as Richard Dalton by all
accounts," she said.

"Richard? Oh, yes. Quite the businessman he is," Oscar
coughed.

Saskia sighed. There just wasn't any point in being
cross with Oscar Bingham. He was just another of Richard's
little pawns. Well, two could play that game, she decided
resolutely.

"Never mind, Oscar. If anyone can get two and a half
million for this house, it's you. Just do your best. OK?"

"Absolutely!" he agreed, warming to her encouragement
and relieved to hear her more friendly tone.

As she rang off, Saskia let it sink in about the manor.
Four million euro! That was two million less than
Innishambles. The Manor had a pool and a tennis court.
This property game was absolutely insane!

* * *

When the weather was good, Dublin was one of the nicest
cities in the world, Saskia decided as she turned her car
into the car park of the Burlington Hotel. She found a
parking space easily. Surely that's a good omen, she
thought. In truth she was nervous as hell but she was
damned if she was going to show it. Ninety-eight per cent of
people in negotiations think they're in the weaker position,

she reminded herself. If I believe I can – then I can. It's that simple.

"I know I can," she said resolutely as her eyes scanned the hotel lobby. Then she saw Camilla Condon sitting alone and looking almost regal. Saskia waved and walked over to her.

The older woman looked incredibly composed. To look at her, one certainly wouldn't think that her husband was lying in an intensive care unit. Camilla rose to greet Saskia.

"Please sit. It's good to see you." Saskia smiled warmly. Quickly a member of the Burlington staff joined them.

"Can I get you something, Camilla?" Saskia offered as she put in a request for a glass of sparkling water.

"Thank you, no. I have some Earl Grey tea here. That is an elegant sufficiency," she said and gestured to her silver tray.

Saskia looked at her and, much to her amazement, she didn't feel threatened. Camilla Condon really was from another era. She remembered something she had heard Richard say to the girls however: never underestimate your enemy – it can be fatal.

She snapped back to the matter in hand.

"Thank you for agreeing to meet me so soon," she started.

"Well, I would have met you this morning, only as you know I was with Arthur."

"I do hope he's getting stronger. How is he?" Saskia asked, genuinely concerned.

"You didn't hear then. I'm afraid that my husband has had a little set-back. I think you should know that it was in no small way connected to a visit by your ex-husband last night."

"*What?*"

"You didn't know, did you?" Camilla asked.

"No. I have no idea what you're talking about."

"Last night, Richard visited Arthur and they began to talk about selling Innishambles. I don't know the entire conversation because Arthur is still very weak but they had an argument. Richard offered him two million for Innishambles and the conversation got quite heated."

"The bastard!" Saskia sank into her chair. Were there no lengths he wouldn't go to? Then, coming out of her private thoughts, she looked at Camilla. "Oh, God, I had no idea. I'm so sorry. I feel obliged to apologise to you even though I'm sure you're aware that Richard and I are divorced."

"A prudent decision," Camilla said crisply as she sipped her Earl Grey. Then she continued, "But you did say on the phone this morning that you wanted to meet about the possibility of buying Innishambles back."

Saskia nodded. "That's right. Firstly I have to say I am truly sorry about Richard's behaviour. I think what he did was appalling – visiting Arthur in hospital." Then she paused and took a deep breath. "OK, I can better his offer but not by much. I offer you three and a half million for Innishambles." Saskia froze and waited for a reaction.

Camilla stared at Sas. "Six million. That's what we paid you for it. I'll sell it back to you right now for the same amount if you want."

Saskia shook her head. "Camilla, I'm afraid we won't be able to do business after all. You see, I don't have six million euro. All I can afford is three and a half million. That will be almost four with the stamp duty and legal fees and that's all I have left in the world. I do appreciate that you paid more but I think I have to say with respect that Oscar bought it under the misguided notion that he could develop the land. If it did have development potential it would certainly be worth more, but it doesn't."

"Four million," Camilla tried.

"I don't have it. Sorry. In fact, the manor is on the market with that price-tag and it has a pool and a tennis court. It's a much better buy." Saskia rose to go. "Sorry to have wasted your time, Camilla. Truly I am."

"Wait!" Camilla spoke in almost a shriek. Her regal supremacy left her as she slumped down into the chair. "I'm tired, Saskia. I'm tired and I want to go home to Epsom with my husband and my boys."

Saskia sat back down and listened.

"We don't fit in here. It was a mistake to come. The boys are totally unsettled. They'll never even pass their finals at this rate and this bloody house is now hanging around our necks. I'm scared it'll kill Arthur."

"I understand, but how can I help?" Saskia raised her hands in query.

"How much do you have of the six million we gave you?"

"Only four, if that."

Camilla glanced at her sideways. "You go through it fairly fast, don't you?"

The two women were interrupted by the shrill of Saskia's phone.

"I'm sorry," Saskia smiled at Camilla. "I'll turn it off."

"No, don't switch it off on account of me. Really, take your call."

Saskia nodded gratefully and answered her phone.

She didn't like to ignore it when Cathy was minding Robin especially since her youngest had run away.

"Hello."

"Saskia Dalton, it looks like your good fortune is still holding!" It was Oscar Bingham. "I had one party interested in Ballymore Glen who wouldn't get off the fence. He was very upset yesterday when I told him that the entire complex had been sold out so I decided to put in a call to him this morning, following our little chat." His voice was so ebullient, Saskia couldn't help but get excited.

"What happened, Oscar?"

"I've sold number five for your asking price – two and a half million. And you'll never guess who's bought it – Chris De Burgh!"

The flood of emotions was almost overwhelming for Saskia. The first was relief, enormous relief. "Thank you, Oscar. Thank you so much. I'll sign all the necessary documents with my solicitor as soon as is physically possible." After she had hung up she looked at Camilla Condon. She squared her shoulders. "It would appear that I have more income at my disposal than I had originally anticipated, Camilla. I can buy Innishambles back from you for six million euro. That's what I sold it to you for – that's what I can buy it back for."

To Saskia's utter amazement, Camilla began to lose her composure. She started to shake slightly. "You had me over a barrel, Saskia. I would have parted with it for considerably less."

"Perhaps, but I believe there's more to doing business than the profit. I would rather be poorer and able to live with my own conscience than rich and with the burden of guilt. Life is too short. Well? Does that mean I have bought Innishambles back? I'll give you what you gave me."

Camilla began to smile. "Tell you what, I'll sell it to you for five and a half million!"

Saskia looked suitably surprised, "You're talking yourself out of money?"

"What I'd really love is for both of us to be happy with this deal," Camilla explained. "I would certainly be over the moon with five and a half million euro. I can live with a loss of five hundred thousand euro for Arthur's utter stupidity. The old boot needs to learn a lesson or he could do it again!"

"In that case, you have a deal!" Saskia thrust out her hand to shake Camilla's. "Five and a half million euro!"

"Mrs Dalton," Camilla smiled as she took and shook Saskia's hand, "Innishambles is yours – again."

* * *

Barry McCourt, Saskia's lawyer, laughed when he got her call.

"Saskia, you're some woman for one woman! You've made half a million on Ballymore Glen and half a million on Innishambles. I don't suppose you'd consider going into property speculation and pension-fund management as a full-time career? You're infinitely better than most in the trade."

Saskia laughed and for the first time acknowledged her success. "I guess you're right, Barry. Only I have to tell you, it was luck for the most part."

Barry returned to business. "Is the Condons' solicitor going to contact me or do you want me to chase him?"

"Oh, I don't think you'll have to chase him. He'll be in touch in the next day or two."

"Well, congrats on your tidy profit. Are you going to invest in Spain? Like you've been talking about?"

"No, Barry. Spain can wait because there's been a change of plan. I have bigger fish to fry!" She laughed, giving nothing away.

* * *

Despite her fantastic luck in getting Innishambles back, the week dragged by for Saskia. She spent her mornings alone because both Lauren and Robin were in school. This was her time to do a lot of thinking about her life and where it was going. When she was truly honest with herself, she had to admit that since Richard had returned to their lives, she had been having some secret fantasies about reuniting with him. Now the part of her that still genuinely cared for him – perhaps even *loved* him – howled and cried at the pain of losing him yet again. In her darker moments she questioned herself and her sanity for letting him go if she still wanted him so much but she would not permit herself to dwell on that. He was poison and she knew that she could never go near him again. It was imperative that she always remember that but then again she had managed to forget it and almost forgive him in the space of three short years! She decided to sit down and write herself a letter reminding herself of all the dreadful things he had done. As she wrote, her resolution strengthened. The ink mixed with the tears she cried as she wrote. They were tears for the pain that he had caused her and her girls. Then she made a solemn promise to herself. Richard Dalton was well and truly out of her life forever. When it was finished, Saskia was exhausted. The emotional strain was enormous. She took the letter and put it in her bedside locker. Any time she felt weak or in any way positive about Richard Dalton, she would read that letter, she promised herself.

Next it was time to think about Nicolas Flattery! Being a woman was hard work, Saskia decided. Nicolas was a considerably more complex issue. Did she love him? She really didn't know. Did he love her? Saskia felt pretty sure that he didn't know either. He had been reasonably content to stay in the States and end their relationship before he heard about the baby. On reflection, she had been content to let him go – but then again that was when she thought that she was possibly getting back with her ex-husband. It was all so confusing. Saskia was delighted to get an interruption in the form of Declan, the postman. He had also been their postman in Innishambles and so there had been no problem about losing post in the house move.

"Only one today, Mrs Dalton," he beamed at her.

Declan always seemed to be in such good form. It was a pleasure to talk to him, Saskia reflected.

"I hope it's good news," he said as he handed over the handwritten letter.

"I could do with some," she answered taking the letter and instantly recognising the handwriting. It was from Nicolas.

She fell onto her old sofa that stood so incongruously in her hall and ripped it open.

My darling Saskia,
   I have done as you asked. I have given you the space you

530

requested. Every day that passes, however, my anguish grows. I miss you. I so desperately want to hold you and kiss you and love all the misunderstanding away. I was such a fool to leave you to go to the States. It was a huge mistake on my part. My one fear is that I'm making another one now – leaving you alone at this time. I want to be with you more than anything else in the world but I made you a promise and I respect you too much to break it. If I can't come to you, please come to me – when you're ready – only please be ready now.

I love you more than life itself.

Nicolas

"Yoo-hoo, is anybody here?" Cathy Taylor walked in the back door of number 5, Ballymore Glen.

"I'm in the hall," Saskia called from the sofa.

"I just popped around to see how you are and to ask you if I could take Robin to play for the afternoon!" came Cathy's voice as she came through to the hall.

The fact that Cathy knew Nicolas had written and posted a letter to Saskia the day before was no mere coincidence. In truth, Cathy had sat him down and made him write the letter. Left to his own devices, the poor old fool would have pined indefinitely! She stopped suddenly when she walked into the hall and saw the tears flowing down Saskia's face unchecked.

"My heavens, *a grà*! Whatever is the matter?" Her strong Wicklow accent was soft and warm.

"Oh, Cathy, I got a letter from Nicolas. He says he loves me and he misses me and he wants me to come to him!"

"Ah!" Cathy sat down on the sofa beside Saskia. "And how do you feel, *a grà*?"

"I don't know. I don't know anything any more!" She cried some more as Cathy hugged her maternally.

"Of course you don't. Isn't it full of hormones you are? If you can decide between eggs and toast in the morning, isn't that something?"

Saskia looked at Cathy and couldn't help laughing. "But what will I do?"

The old woman let out a long sigh. "You know," she said, "I make it my business *not* to give advice. I think the best thing to do is to just listen and wait for them that have the problems to figure it out themselves." She looked at Saskia. "But this time, I'll make an exception seeing as you're pregnant and not capable of making any class of a decision!" She studied the floor for a moment in contemplative silence. Then she drew in a deep breath and looked at Saskia, eye to eye. "*A grá*, go to him," she said.

Sas didn't say anything. She just looked at Cathy's soft old face. The wrinkles were too many to count but her face was warm and so friendly and just at the moment it was full of concern.

"He loves you. I see him every day and he's wasting away without you. You don't want that on your conscience on top of everything, do you?" She laughed and continued. "If ever I saw a man in love, it's him. He has enough love for the both of you to be honest. But in time I think you'll come to love him back the way you used to."

"Did I love him, really love him? I don't remember any more." Saskia looked exhausted.

"I've known you for close on twenty years now, *a grá*, and I have never seen you as happy as you were in these last three years with Nicolas Flattery – nor any of your girls for that matter. He is a good man and he loves you more than anything, Sas."

Saskia began to get excited. "Should I go? Will I?"

"Yes. Now."

"Oh, I can't go now! I have to collect Robin from Montessori in about twenty minutes."

"I'll do that. Go. Now, Saskia."

CHAPTER 37

When Kelly phoned and said that she wanted a family meeting, Saskia's first reaction was panic.

"Kelly, you couldn't pick a worse time. I'm packing up Ballymore Glen today. Harry is coming to collect all our belongings tomorrow!"

"Ah, *Harry's Removals* strikes again! Well, at least I'm glad to see that he's coming on a Friday and not a Saturday! Remember what I said to you when you moved into Number 5?"

"My God, I had forgotten that. We moved in on a Saturday, didn't we?"

"Looks like Gran was right – Saturday's flitting really does make for short sitting!" Kelly laughed. "You certainly didn't last long in Ballymore Glen!"

"Don't tell her or she'll never let us forget it," Saskia sighed. "Look, what do you want a family meeting about? It's not you and Barney, is it?"

"God, no. We're fine. I would like to discuss it with everybody together though. Where's Nicolas?"

"He's helping me here, of course." Then suddenly,

Saskia had a thought. "Oh, Kelly, please tell me it's not your health. Did you have those tests done to find out why you were so tired? You know, when we all thought you were pregnant?"

"Relax, Mum. Yes, I had those tests – mind you, not with bloody James Harrington. I went to the new guy in Wicklow and he said that I was rudely healthy. Everything came back clear. I was just a little iron deficient. He put me on a course of iron tablets."

"Thank God for that. So you want to meet. When?"

"Well, I've phoned Tiff and she says that she can be home on Saturday. If you and Lauren and Nicolas are free, we have a date."

"Well, I guess we could all meet up on Saturday morning – in the manor if you like. Of course Robin will be running around but that won't be a problem, will it?"

"No. In fact, I would kind of like her to be there. This will affect her too."

"Kelly, at least give me a hint as to what all of this is about."

"No," Kelly was firm but she was laughing. "All I will say is that I think you'll like it – so don't start fretting. OK?"

"OK."

* * *

By Saturday morning Saskia was fretting. Nicolas tried to soothe her.

"She said it was something good. You have to trust her," he tried to reason as he walked around his kitchen and prepared brunch.

Lauren, who had a particularly late night, was not

happy with her mother's wake-up call. "Well, she could at least have arranged for an evening meeting. That way we could have got some bloody sleep!"

Saskia was temporarily distracted, "So, Lauren, you and Connor Cantwell seem to be getting on pretty well again," she teased.

Lauren caught her mother's eye and smirked. "It certainly looks like it!"

"Why did you break up in the first place?" Nicolas asked as he put an egg on the pan.

"Well," now Lauren was beaming, "he had made me promise to phone him after the summer if I still wanted to go out with him. Do you remember that he went to the States on work experience?"

"Yes," Saskia said.

"Well, I did phone him once last September but his brother said that he was out on a date and so I hung up and never tried again."

"Well, the little –" Saskia started but Lauren jumped to her boyfriend's defence.

"Mum, he wasn't on a date at all! That was just his brother acting the gobshite! Not only was Connor not on a date but he never even knew that I rang so he thought I had forgotten all about him."

"He could have phoned you," Nicolas suggested gently as he lined the sausages up on the grill.

"Connor is a little shy. He always was. In fact – this is so sweet," Lauren, continued positively animated, "he told me last night that he simply assumed 'a cracker' like me would have been snapped up before he had time to get back from the States!"

They all laughed.

"Is that what he called you? A cracker?" asked Saskia.

"Yep."

"Well, you are a cracker, Lauren. I'm glad he appreciates you!" Saskia crossed the kitchen and hugged her daughter.

Tiffany arrived in from Dublin just as the food was ready.

"Hello, everybody," she threw her bags down and went to hug her mother. "Hello, baby!" She patted her mother's tummy. Then she hugged her youngest sister. "Hi, Robin – God, I miss you in Dublin!"

"I miss you too," Robin agreed.

"Where's Kelly and what's all this about?" Tiffany asked.

Nicolas, who had started setting the table answered. "She hasn't arrived yet. How are you? Did I hear that you broke up with Max Condon last weekend?"

"Afraid so," but she was smiling.

"You look very happy for somebody who has just broken up with the love of their life, Tiff," Lauren teased.

"I'm my own woman, little sis. I don't need a man to make me happy!" She tossed her head back in mock indignation.

But Lauren was not so easily convinced. "So, have you told Bill that you're single again?"

Tiffany looked at her sister and crumpled into laughter.

"Who's Bill?" Saskia and Nicolas asked at the same time.

"Hello, the house," Barney Armstrong walked in the back door of Rathdeen Manor with his little dog yapping at his heals. "We brought Nina with us, I hope you don't mind." Behind him trotted another little dog with all the confidence of a thoroughbred – which she definitely wasn't!

"And who is that?" Saskia laughed at the indignant little dog. Barney scooped up the second little animal. "This is our newest acquisition and Nina's new best friend. Her name is Hope."

Woody and Wilma were delighted to see their old friend and equally thrilled to make a new acquaintance. Even Dudley and Dexter came over for a sniff and a bark.

Then Kelly walked in with a smile on as wide as the Grand Canyon.

"At last," Lauren announced. "What's all the mystery, Kellser?"

"Yeah," Tiffany agreed as she scooped up her little sister, "why are we having a family meeting?"

Kelly presented a long cardboard tube to her family. "This is why," she explained.

"What's this?" Saskia asked as Kelly handed her the tube.

"Open it up."

Saskia did as she was told but Kelly was too excited. She cleared away Nicolas's beautifully set table and rolled out the large white sheets of paper on the table.

"I didn't want to tell you what I was working on until I had approval but if you'll all support me and Barney, we think we can turn Rathdeen Manor around!"

"What?" the family chorused.

Kelly turned to Nicolas. "Nicolas, I know that this was your dream and the manor is your home, but if you'll let me have my head here – I really believe that we can do it."

Nicolas looked into Kelly's eyes. "Kelly, I always knew you were made of strong stuff. Believe me, if there is anything you can do to save the manor, you have my blessing. As it is, at the moment, I'm going to lose everything – so if you can save it, I'll be forever in your debt." He kissed her gently on the forehead.

Saskia looked at her eldest. "Kelly, darling, no disrespect but do you have any idea how much this will cost to run and sustain?"

"Oh yes, Mum. I've taken the advice of three different businessmen! All of whom I trust!"

"Who?"

Kelly beamed. "Raymond Saunders, David Parker and Bob Bolton."

"*Damn glad to meet you,*" Tiffany and Lauren chorused.

"They each helped me with ideas and accounts and they're all in agreement that it could work."

"How?" Saskia was still not convinced.

"Well, there is one very bitter pill that we'll have to swallow."

"What's that?" Tiffany asked.

Kelly looked at Barney and he looked at Nicolas. "I'm afraid we'll have to close the refuge. That's the one single reason that the place is financially haemorrhaging so badly."

Everybody looked at Nicolas Flattery for a reaction.

He looked at Saskia and then at her four daughters and finally at Barney. "Hey, it was a dream! It worked for three years. Kelly, it was going to have to close anyway. At least this way you've saved the house and the land. It's what I would call damage limitation." He managed a smile.

Kelly crossed the room and hugged him. "Believe me, if there was any way to keep it going, I would have."

"I believe you." He hugged her back.

Then Lauren interrupted them. "Whatever happened to K9 pet foods? Weren't they going to give you loads of money?"

"I've been talking to them. You see, they want to sponsor the refuge but, if we close the refuge, there'll be nothing for them to sponsor."

"Hell, that does seem like a terrible waste!" said Nicolas.

Kelly hesitated for a second as if trying to decide whether or not to mention something. "OK, now this is seriously for the back-boiler but Dave Parker was telling me that there is a possibility that we could get what's known as 'charity status' for a refuge. If we did, there could be tax write-off opportunities for large companies."

"What do you mean?" Lauren asked.

"Companies like K9 could give us donations out of money they were going to have to pay in tax anyway, so effectively it doesn't cost them anything. Dave reckons that's why K9 were so enthusiastic to donate," Kelly explained.

Saskia marvelled at how Kelly was slipping so comfortably into the business world.

"Well, I don't really want to talk about that today because there's no guarantee that we'll get charity status. We need to concentrate on the manor first."

"So how the hell are you going to save the manor?" Tiffany asked. Kelly returned to the table. "Well, we've been talking about it for long enough. I needed to talk to some serious business heads about it too but Dave, Raymond and Bob all think it's a runner. Barney and I want to open the manor to guests! We want to make it into one of those Hidden Ireland type houses. Just think of it, we can supply riding and fishing facilities. God, this place even has a pool and a tennis court! Most of the old houses don't have those kinds of luxuries!"

Saskia wasn't convinced. "Have you done the sums?"

"Yes, that's why I talked to Dave and Raymond. Do you know that some of the Hidden Ireland houses charge up to two hundred euro a night! And that's before dinner."

Lauren scoffed. "Don't tell me you're planning on cooking, Kelly. You can't boil water!"

"No, that's what I need you guys for!" She looked at her sisters. "It's going to be very lean for the first season. We'll need all of you to work for free next summer. What do you say?"

The kitchen went very quiet.

"Well, don't all shout at once," Kelly laughed and the others joined in.

"I'll cook," Tiffany agreed.

"I guess I'm on cleaning duty then," Lauren grumbled but she was smiling broadly. "To be honest, I had been giving out to Tiffany that I didn't know what I wanted to do after school and recently I've been thinking about getting into the tourism industry. Why not start at home?"

"What can I do?" Robin asked from the comfort of Saskia's lap.

"You can help me with the babies," Saskia said softly.

"What?" Everyone turned to her.

"More than one?" Kelly asked, aghast.

"It certainly looks that way," Saskia smiled sheepishly. "I was with Dr Maguinness during the week and he did an ultrasound on me. It's very early days but he says there's two of them in there."

Lauren slapped her brow. "My God, double trouble!"

"Great," Kelly laughed. "That'll be even more help to muck out the stables in a few years' time!"

Then Barney got involved.

"Well, if you ladies can run the manor, Kelly is going to do what she's always wanted to do. She's going to open a kennelling facility and a pooch parlour. I really think that will make a tidy fortune."

"And what are you going to do, Barney?" Saskia asked softly.

"I'll run a private practice out of the state-of-the-art veterinary clinic that Nicolas built for the refuge."

Kelly continued. "It will be run as a private limited company. Dave Parker is working out the details right now – articles of association and all that business stuff – for me."

"I could have done that," Tiffany sniffed.

"You can help me keep the books in order, Tiff," Kelly smiled.

"I hate to pour rain on your parade, Kelly, but who will do the breakfasts? I'll help out, of course, as soon as the babies are a little older but I will be rather busy for a few months at least," Saskia said.

"It's OK, Mum. I knew you were going to be a little preoccupied although I didn't realise you were going to be quite that busy! Twins? My God! But Barney and I have planned everything out without your help for at least the next twelve months. Cathy Taylor has jumped at the chance. I told her she would have shares in the company and she was thrilled! She said that she was never a shareholder before and if all she has to do is breakfasts for it, it's cheap at the price!" Everyone laughed as Kelly tried to mimic Cathy's lovely soft brogue.

"Well, it certainly looks like you've thought of everything," Saskia replied. She looked at her eldest daughter, the one who had transformed into such a beautiful, strong woman over the last few months. Saskia could feel herself swell with pride. She must be doing something right to have produced such an amazing young lady. "You know something? You're wonderful. I say – go for it!"

"And the rest of you?" Kelly looked at her sisters and Nicolas. "This will only work if you're all behind me one hundred and ten per cent!"

"I'm with you," Tiffany agreed.

"Let's do it!" Lauren nodded.

"Me too," Robin beamed.

Saskia laughed. "Believe in your own ability, Kelly. Believe in –"

The girls all chorused with her, knowing what she was going to say. *"The power of a woman!"*

Then Kelly looked at Nicolas. He smiled at her and hugged her again. "Thank you," was all he said. Then he shook himself before he was overcome with emotion. "Now, who's for a fry?" he asked expansively.

* * *

The following week, Robin could hardly contain herself such was her excitement. She had never been invited to a birthday party before. She was well used to parties in her own house, but to have to get dressed up and go out to another person's house! Surely this was the height of maturity! Kelly and Barney brought her down to the Parkers' house because Saskia and Nicolas were spending some quality time alone. Guy Parker thought he was the most important little man in Ballymore. It was his third birthday party and 'everyone' in Ballymore was coming. The Saunders children had agreed to come even though Guy was "only a baby". The lure of the bouncy castle and a resident magician however was enough to attract them.

Lisa Keyes was rushing around making sure that every little person had something to eat, while Sue Parker was looking after the grown-ups.

"Can I get you a drink?" she asked Raymond Saunders.

"It's a little early for me," he smiled. "How about a coffee? I can help if you like."

"If you feel like mucking in, could you please lend Lisa a hand? She's being jumped on in the bouncy castle! Your kids are suffocating her – I think they like her."

"She does seem very nice," Raymond smiled.

"She's a terrific nanny. We would be lost without her," Sue agreed. "Raymond, I heard your nanny left your home recently. If we can help you out at all, just let me know."

"Thanks."

Then Sue's expression changed. "Mind you – you're not to get any notions of stealing *our* nanny!" She laughed lightly.

"God, no," Raymond said. He wasn't thinking about stealing Lisa but he was definitely wondering about dinner with her. She was the most tantalising cocktail of prettiness and fun – very reminiscent of –

"Raymond," Dave Parker slapped his new friend on the back, "how are you?"

"Good thanks. Hey, your wife was just telling me

about your house purchase. That's good news. When are you moving into Ballymore Glen?"

Dave groaned but he smiled. "Two weeks today. We are looking forward to it. It's just the move that's a hassle. Can I get you a drink?"

"Not just yet, thanks. I'm going to save your nanny. She's being killed by my kids." He laughed and was gone.

Dave followed his wife into the kitchen.

"And what about you, honey? Are you having a good time?"

She slipped into his arms. "Oh, yes. I'm very happy. What about you?"

"Fine," he smiled. "I'm just happy to be with you."

"Am I interrupting anything?" Kelly asked as she came in. "Sorry, I need a refill of orange squash."

"Relax, Kelly. Here, there's some in the fridge." Sue gave another jug to her guest and then she added, "You know, you're very good baby-sitting Robin like this for your mum. How is Sas?"

"She's really good. In fact, I'd say she's positively blooming. You did hear that it's twins, didn't you?"

"Yes. Can you believe it? She'll have her work cut out for her, won't she?"

"Well, the thing I'm most happy about is that she and Nicolas are back together. They are so good for each other."

"Robin seems to love him too," Dave added.

"Absolutely," Kelly agreed. "It's funny but just a few weeks ago, Mum was trying to introduce Robin to Dad so she would know her natural father and it went really badly. In fact, it was a total fiasco. Robin kept fighting with them and saying that Nicolas was her real dad." She shrugged and continued, "And now I know what Robin was talking about. You should have seen the three of them together the night Robin ran away – Mum and Nicolas and Robin. He was holding her and hugging Sas. If ever there was a family unit, it's the three of them. Robin was right – Nicolas *is* her dad." She smiled. "I think I've finally convinced Mum to forget about trying to introduce Dad to Robin. Nicolas is her proper father in every sense of the word and she's better off for it." She looked at Sue and Dave. "Have you heard about Dad?"

"What has he done now?" Sue asked.

"He's gone! Shot through here! He's in Tenerife. He says that he's following a business lead but I think he's fed up that Nicolas and Mum have moved in together."

"I'm sorry, Kelly."

"Yeah, he's some piece of work. But I have Barney. I just thank God that Mum has Nicolas." She smiled. "Hey, I'm going on. The kids will be wondering where the orange juice is!"

The Parkers embraced in silence as Kelly left them. They were both thinking the same thing.

"You know you are his natural father, don't you?"

"Yes," Dave agreed. "I can feel it in every fibre of my body. No matter what our blood types say I am and I always will be Guy's dad. I believe that."

Sue looked at her husband and kissed him on the nose. "Thank God for that!" Then she moved out of his embrace, "But just in case you wanted a little more proof, I got it!"

"What are you talking about?"

"I don't want you to *believe*, I want you to *know*!"

Dave watched Sue take an envelope out of a drawer. "What's that?" he asked but he already knew.

"It's an early birthday present!"

"Sue, my birthday is in December."

"Open it and read it."

He did as he was told. He scanned the page, "Blah, blah, true parentage, one hundred per cent – I don't believe you did this!"

"I had to – for the sake of both our sanities. I know that you were happy to believe that Guy is your son but I needed more. I wanted to be absolutely certain – one hundred per cent – and now we are."

Dave continued to scan the letter, too excited to start at the top and read it coherently. "University of Iowa?"

"Yep, I got them on the Internet. It's a *True Parentage* service they offer! All I needed was a clip of your hair and a clip of Guy's. I cut a bit off your head a few weeks ago when you were asleep," she giggled. "Then I sent them off in the post and they did the rest. Dave, your DNAs match! There is no doubt. You are Guy's father."

Dave didn't know what to say, so he said nothing. He hugged his wife tightly. The relief was unbelievable. All the pain and insecurity washed away. The lack of trust vanished like a vapour and the deep profound gratitude in having such an amazing wife overwhelmed him.

"I never doubted it," he whispered into her hair. Although they both knew it was a lie, she was glad to hear him say it.

So what if they re-wrote a little piece of history for the sake of their marriage. "Nor did I, darling." She hugged him tightly. "Nor did I!"

EPILOGUE

December thirty-first dawned with a clear blue sky. A fine layer of ice covered the ground and the air was clean and crisp. The morning had been pure bedlam with the three elder Dalton girls fighting over the showers as usual.

"Surely I should get some extra privileges, considering I'm the bride today," Kelly yelled to the house at large. But her tone was good-humoured and her sisters just laughed at her. Robin had been in her flower-girl outfit since seven a.m. Her dress was the palest pink and tiny flowers were sewn into the hemline. The tiara, however, was her crowning glory. Robin was quite sure that this was in fact her day and not Kelly's.

Nicolas, who had moved into Innishambles with the Dalton girls when they eventually moved back into their home, was wandering around the house in his big white towelling bathrobe. He had already brought all the Dalton girls their breakfast in bed and now it was Saskia's turn. Her tummy had a lovely round bump at this stage and the last scan had confirmed she was carrying twin boys!

"I've told you before – we were reliably informed that Robin was a boy and she turned out to be a girl," Saskia warned Nicolas.

"Hey, I would love two little girls," he laughed. "Women are so much nicer to be around!"

As he placed Saskia's breakfast tray on her bed, Robin came bounding into the room.

"The hairdresser has arrived," she told her mother.

"Well, then, I really must get up. Gosh, everything seems so peaceful I can't believe that we're hosting a party for one hundred in a matter of hours!"

"You haven't heard the pandemonium on the landing!" Nicolas laughed.

"The girls are fighting over the bathroom!" said Robin.

"But don't worry about the wedding party, Saskia. We'll let the professionals take care of that," said Nicolas.

"Thank God for caterers! Although I'll never believe Kelly again when she says that she wants a 'small' party." Saskia laughed as she got out of bed. "I'm so happy that it's in the manor and not here though. It will be nice to come back here to Innishambles and leave that noise and mess for somebody else to worry about." She took a triangle of toast from the tray on her bed and bit into it. Nicolas had made it just as she liked it, dripping with real Irish butter and smothered in homemade marmalade. Then she padded over to her bedroom window and gazed out on the frost-covered land. Kelly had obviously let Polly and Mooner out for a morning romp already. They were cantering the length of the ice-covered field, snorting out great white plumes of warm air from their vast lungs.

"I'm so happy to be back in Innishambles. I love this

place," she sighed as she finished her toast and licked her fingers. "It's home."

Nicolas came up behind her and wrapped his arms around her and her large belly. "You love Innishambles and I love you." He kissed the top of her head. "If you're happy, I'm happy."

"And to think I nearly lost it."

"But you didn't. In fact, you made a nice profit! Speaking of which, have you made a decision on how you're going to invest the rest of your new-found wealth?"

"Yes, I have," Saskia said. "I'm going back to my original plan. I'll buy a few apartments in Dublin and rent them out. The income stream I get from them can pay for the children's education."

"Wow, you really do have it all thought out!" Nicolas was impressed.

"Well, I don't want to leave myself exposed ever again."

"You know I'll never leave you again."

"I do believe you. It was really the father of those children I was thinking about, to be honest. He's a loose cannon and I don't want to ever have to turn to him again."

Nicolas was lost in thought for just a moment and then he made a decision.

"Look, Saskia, there's something I wanted to tell you when Kelly and Barney had gone on their honeymoon but perhaps I should tell you now."

She looked at him suspiciously. "What is it?"

"Well, it's just that I thought you might need some cheering up when they left. The last few weeks have been so crazy."

"Nicolas?"

"Brad Steinway called last Monday?"

"And?"

"I've got a book deal!"

"What? And you didn't tell me?"

"I was waiting for the right time!"

"With who? For how much?"

"Well, it's still just an offer, you see. I haven't signed anything yet."

"How much?"

"It's a three-book deal."

"For how much, in God's name?"

"A million."

"Euro?"

"Pounds sterling!"

Saskia threw her arms around him. "I knew you'd do it! I just knew it. You only needed a lucky break." The strength of her bear hug amazed him bearing in mind that she was pregnant.

"Easy," he laughed. "Mind our babies! Now, Sas, we really can't say anything until Brad has met with the publishers and gone over the fine print. We certainly can't say anything until I've signed the contract. OK?"

"OK, OK, OK," she covered his face with kisses. "Hey," she laughed, "we're both millionaires now – at the same time!"

"Not just yet," he said, erring on the side of caution as usual. "And remember I've been a millionaire before. It can slip through your hands very easily unless you keep your head screwed on the right way!"

Saskia sighed but she was still obviously thrilled with his news.

"Now what about the rest of your breakfast?" he asked.

"Oh, Nicolas, I'm too excited to eat any more, especially after your news – and of course this is Kelly's morning!" Then she looked out the window to check the weather. It was a glorious bright blue sky. There was the single white line of a jet plane far far above.

Nicolas stood behind her and hugged her. "You should see Kelly! She's positively walking on air!"

Saskia sighed. "It's been lovely having her here for the last few nights. Wouldn't it be lovely if she and Barney lived here instead of Peartree Cottage?"

"Ah, so she hasn't told you yet?" Nicolas shifted slightly.

Saskia turned around to him, "Told me what?"

"Kelly and Barney plan to move into the manor."

"What? When? Why? I thought they wanted to rent all the rooms out to make more money out of the place."

"Yes, well, they've figured out a way to make even more money. They're renting Peartree Cottage out to Lisa Keyes."

"Why?"

"She's going to open a kiddies' playschool there. Peartree Montessori, I think she's calling it."

Saskia smiled. "And I bet I know who her business partner is too! Mr Raymond Saunders – they're a match made in heaven, those two."

Nicolas continued, "So that's why Barney and Kelly are moving into the manor." He hugged Saskia tightly. "Anyway I like it when there's just the three of us in Innishambles – you, me and little Robin."

"Well, that will be five of us very soon!" Saskia studied her stomach. Nicolas laughed.

"I just thank God that Barney and Kelly got their planning permission to convert the manor into a guest house," Saskia went on.

"It's just like you always say, Sas. Everything is working out perfectly!"

"Yes," Saskia agreed. "It's a huge relief. Instead of *costing* a fortune, the manor will soon be *making* a fortune! I'm so proud of Kelly. And Dave and Raymond have been a huge help."

"Indeed they have," Nicolas agreed, "and don't forget Bob Bolton! Everyone in the family being a shareholder is a great idea too."

Saskia turned around to face Nicolas. "As long as you remember that you're just a sleeping partner!"

"MmmMMMmmm," he grinned at the connotation and kissed her on the lips, "and don't you forget it! I can ask to have a look at the books any time I want, although my main interest is really in the bottom line!" He squeezed her bum.

"Nicolas, not now!" She gestured with her eyes towards Robin who was happily eating Saskia's deserted breakfast.

"Robin, honey, can you go and tell the hairdresser that Mummy will be along in five minutes – I'm just going to have a quick shower first."

Delighted to be able to help, the three-year-old hopped off the bed and scooted off on her new mission. Nicolas crossed the room and locked the door to the master bedroom.

"What exactly did you have in mind, Mr Flattery?" Saskia giggled.

"Well, I'm going to help you get sudsy, of course. With

that beautiful round tummy, I just know that there are parts of you that you can't possibly reach any more!"

* * *

The main street of Ballymore was absolutely deserted. The entire village had turned up at the church to see Kelly Dalton get married. Nicolas looked at the beautiful lady he had the great honour of walking up the aisle. Richard had been a pedigree bastard. He had still not forgiven Sas for rejecting him and his recently recovered wealth. He had not returned from Tenerife to walk his first-born up the aisle. Kelly said she understood but Saskia knew she was only saying that.

"How do you feel?" Nicolas asked Kelly tenderly.

"Fine! A little nervous, but fine." She beamed up at him. Nicolas gave her a reassuring hug. Kelly Dalton was absolutely gorgeous. Her big brown eyes sparkled with love and excitement this morning. Her long dark curls were clipped up, like a southern belle. She wore an ivory-white silk dress with very little detail. "That's so Kelly," Saskia had explained. "Simple and effortlessly beautiful." The corset-type top pulled in her already impossibly thin waist and the dress spread out like an old-fashioned ball gown. The long narrow sleeves finished in a point accentuating her tiny wrists and hands. The neckline was cut low but even with the Wonderbra, Kelly didn't have a very large bust. Bust or not, she looked absolutely gorgeous!

They heard the organ start up.

"Ready?" he asked.

"Ready as I'll ever be!" She took a deep breath and fell into step with Nicolas.

Robin, who had been waiting as patiently as a three-year-old could, marched up the aisle as soon as she saw them approach.

The December sun hung low in the sky and thus an unexpected perk of the day was that the normally dark little church in Ballymore village flooded with streams of bright blue light as they filtered through the stained-glass windows. The effect was definitely magical. Kelly thought she was floating instead of walking.

The first pew she passed at the back of the church held Harold and Maureen O'Reilly, from O'Reilly's shop. They were grinning at her like a pair of Cheshire cats. Maureen was nodding approval. Doubtless she would take credit for matchmaking the pair in the future. Next she walked past Michael and Bridget Molloy. Michael who owned The Hitching Post had been so nice to her the evening she arrived in without any money. She had been in a right state having just discovered that she wasn't in fact pregnant. She had gone straight there after her appointment with Dr Harrington. James had been so offhand and impatient with her that afternoon – although now she knew why. Sue Parker had recently told Kelly and Saskia the whole story about his unwanted advances towards her. They had been talking about him because he was in the local paper following his marriage to that dodgy nanny, Jayne Mullins. Good riddance to both of them!

Kelly continued to float up the isle. Next she passed by the Condon family. She was surprised when Saskia suggested inviting them and even more surprised when they accepted. Camilla and Saskia had in fact become firm friends. The boys looked utterly gorgeous as always.

Kelly was delighted to hear from Tiffany that, meeting Maximilian at the pre-wedding party the night before in The Hitching Post, she had felt absolutely nothing for him. That was definitely over! Arthur Condon looked considerably better too. He had given up the booze completely and he had also given up property speculation. Their savings were safely tucked up in that infamous British institution – Lloyds. Time would tell, Kelly thought.

Next she walked past the Parker family, all of them. There was India, Guy and little DJ, being positively angelic for once. Dave and Sue stood together arm in arm. As usual, Sue looked absolutely stunning. She wore a fantastically broad-brimmed deep scarlet hat. It hid her eyes and accentuated her exquisite jawline. She had told Saskia and Kelly recently that she had decided to start working. She wanted to open an haute couture section in some of the larger Parker stores. Everyone agreed that it was a terrific idea.

Raymond Saunders beamed at Kelly with Jasmine his daughter by his side. Edward and Francis stood next to them but Kelly noticed with great amusement that Edward wasn't looking at her at all. He was far too interested in the dress! Lisa Keyes stood a little distance from Raymond, not that it made any difference. Everybody knew that they had become 'an item'.

Bob and Cindy were in the next pew. She still looked ridiculously skinny but Kelly could clearly see the beginnings of a little swell on her tummy. Bob was so proud he announced it when she was only four weeks pregnant but nobody minded. The population of Ballymore was going to explode over the next twelve months!

Then Kelly glided past her friends. Some of the gang were beginning to cry already – eejits! Francesca Murray wore a stunning shocking-pink mini-dress; she had already told Kelly that she intended to seduce the twins simultaneously at the wedding party.

"I've never done it with twins!" she giggled.

"Have you no shame?" Kelly had laughed at her.

"Hey, life is for living!" Francesca defended herself. Stephanie Butler and Patricia Dillon who were old classmates of Kelly's stood with Oscar Bingham, their boss. He had somehow managed to inveigle an invitation for himself. Kelly didn't mind. He had, after all, managed to get Saskia two and a half million euro for Ballymore Glen.

Then she came to the front pew of the small church. Barney stood and stared in wonder at his wife-to-be.

"You're gorgeous!" he whispered. He himself looked like a little boy on Christmas morning. She smiled back at him lovingly and then she looked over to her sisters. Father Shannon gave her all the time she needed. He did not want to rush this precious experience.

Tiffany and Lauren stood protectively on either side of their mother. Behind Tiffany was her new beau, Bill from her economics class in Trinity. Next to Bill was Connor Cantwell. He and Lauren had been inseparable since they got back together.

Edwina Dalton stood next to Bill and Connor. Kelly hadn't really wanted to invite her but Tiffany, who now lived with just her grandmother, had insisted. She said that Edwina had nobody since Richard disappeared and in all honesty she had mellowed considerably. Despite the girls' strong protests, Saskia had invited Edwina down for Christmas and convinced her to stay for the time between then and the wedding. Edwina had been the perfect houseguest and while not quite the 'doting granny', she was definitely trying her best to be nice to everybody. It was a pleasant change.

The Dalton girls were smiling proudly at their older sister. Tiffany winked and crossed her fingers at Kelly. Lauren mouthed the words, "Go, girl!" at her.

She turned to Nicolas, "Thank you for walking me up the aisle."

"Thank you for letting me." He beamed down at her.

"Sure you might do it to Mum one of these days," Kelly winked at him.

"Maybe, if she'll let me!" Nicolas winked back as he gave her hand to Barney. Kelly kissed her fiancé on the cheek and then she glanced over to where her mother stood. Saskia was looking at her first-born. The woman's eyes said it all. Kelly read the emotions as they danced across her mother's face. She saw pride, wonder, admiration and hope. She saw a little fear and an ocean of love.

Nicolas came to Saskia's side just as she was about to start crying – again! Tiffany, ever considerate, moved over so he could stand next to her mother.

"Are you OK, Sas?" he asked when he saw her face.

"Yes," she sniffed. "I'm fine. I just have so many hopes for Kelly. I think my heart could burst."

Nicolas put his arm around her shoulders and squeezed gently. "You know she's going to be absolutely fine. She has Barney and he's a made man now!"

Saskia looked up at Nicolas, not quite understanding what he meant. Barney was a good vet but he wasn't exactly a multi-millionaire yet.

Nicolas explained in a low whisper. "A man may achieve great things with his life or he may achieve nothing."

Father Shannon coughed to get his congregation to quiet down, so Nicolas cut his little speech short. He smiled down at Saskia and kissed her forehead. "Barney is lucky because he has Kelly and what makes or breaks a man is simple: it's *The Woman He Loves*.

The End